Readers have fallen  the Cornish

Betty Walker lives in Cornwall with her large family, where she enjoys gardening and coastal walks. She loves discovering curious historical facts, and devotes much time to investigating her family tree. She also writes bestselling contemporary thrillers as Jane Holland.

Courage for the Cornish Girls is the third novel in Betty Walker's heart-warming series.

The Cornish Girls series:

Wartime with the Cornish Girls
Christmas with the Cornish Girls

BETTY WALKER

Courage for the Cornish Girls

avon.

Published by AVON
A division of HarperCollins*Publishers* Ltd
1 London Bridge Street
London SE1 9GF

www.harpercollins.co.uk

HarperCollins*Publishers*
1st Floor, Watermarque Building, Ringsend Road
Dublin 4, Ireland

A Paperback Original 2022
1

First published in Great Britain by HarperCollins*Publishers* 2022

ISBN: 978-0-008-52514-9

Typeset in Minion Pro by Palimpsest Book Production Limited,
Falkirk, Stirlingshire

Printed and Bound in the UK using 100% Renewable Electricity
at CPI Group (UK) Ltd

Courage for the Cornish Girls

CHAPTER ONE

Penzance, West Cornwall, April 1942

Demelza Minear gritted her teeth, holding on tight until the van left the bumpy ups-and-downs of the sheep field track and began heading into Penzance along the main road. Then she exclaimed, 'Goodness, Tristan, I swear every tooth in my head is coming loose! This is ridiculous. Can you and Father not lay a proper road from the farm to the gate so we aren't jolted to bits every time we go into town?'

Her younger brother grinned, twisting the big steering wheel with one desultory hand as he smoothed down his springy ginger hair with the other.

'C'mon, sis, don't waste your time on daydreams.' Tristan overtook a bicyclist on a sharp bend and earned a horn blast from an oncoming car, barely glancing at the irate driver as they coasted down the narrow hill road into town. 'Since when has Father ever cared about our comfort? *If the tractor and the postman can manage that track, so can we,*' he added, mimicking their father's slow, grating voice.

'I'm not sure Mr Franks has any teeth left to lose,' Demelza muttered, thinking of the elderly gentleman who'd taken over postal deliveries for their area since the rest of the postal service had signed up to do their bit.

Something in her tone made Tristan glance at her sideways, frowning. 'What's up? You're not still fretting about that row with Father?'

'Not fretting so much as fuming. But I suppose you'll be on *his* side,' she replied, nettled, 'just like Aunt Sarah.'

Her brother meant well, but he was still only nineteen years old, four years younger than Demelza, and already enjoyed far more freedom than she did, always consulted on farm business, while knowing far less about the economics of farming than Demelza did.

'No doubt you think women should be kept in their place too,' she continued, 'not allowed out on their own. Especially not to the pub or the picture house, where they might be lured into sin by any number of wicked temptations.'

Tristan laughed. 'Now you're just being silly, Dem. If women weren't allowed to go to the pub or the pictures, where on earth would I take them on a date?'

Reluctantly, she laughed too. But in truth, the situation wasn't funny. 'Honestly though, Tris, he's driving me mad.' She twisted her hands in her lap, staring at the sparkling blue expanse of sea that lay before them as they descended into Penzance. It was only a short ride from the farm into town but took a good half an hour on foot. 'I love Cornwall. I don't want to leave. But perhaps I need to get away. Find out what my life would be like without someone constantly telling me how to live it.'

'You can't mean it.' Her brother sounded shaken. 'Leave Cornwall? And the farm? But where would you go? How would you get by?'

'Girls my age are leaving home and taking jobs all the time, aren't they? I could try London or the Home Counties.'

Demelza shrugged, though after saying it out loud, she felt incredibly daring. She'd only ever planned her escape in secret before, beginning after the Pathé news reels at the Penzance Cinema showed girls her own age in head-scarves and uniforms, laughing as they worked together in factories upcountry, living away from their families and earning their own money. She relished the thought of so much freedom, having hoped since childhood for a more exciting and adventurous life, even if her longings were still vague and unformed. 'Daydreams,' her father had often said, dismissing her attempts to talk to him about her future. And perhaps they were.

Trapped on the family sheep farm day after day, working like a drudge in the kitchen or doing the laundry, escape did seem like an impossible dream. Would she ever drum up the courage to leave for real?

'For the war effort, I mean,' she added, in case he hadn't understood.

'You want to take a job in a factory?'

'Maybe. Why not?'

'Do you really need to ask?' Tristan sounded stunned. 'We couldn't possibly manage the farm without you. Father's not getting any younger, and I'm already taking on most of the lambing and shearing for him. And you know Aunt Sarah's not fully recovered from her stroke yet, and the doctor said she might never get back to normal.

3

If you weren't there, who would cook and clean the place, and look after the chickens? Who would add up the accounts and deal with the bank?'

She merely shrugged, not seeing any point in causing an argument between them by explaining how unhappy she was at the farm. It wasn't the workload so much as the boredom she felt. Though it was true she had even less time to herself these days; doing the farm accounts had once been Aunt Sarah's job, but since the stroke she found them too difficult, so Demelza had agreed to take over the arduous task. But her brother was probably right; escape was nothing but a dream. She was wasting her time even contemplating it.

They were in the centre of Penzance now. Tristan swore and braked, coming to a halt behind a van that had stopped to deliver vegetables to one of the shops on Market Jew Street and was now snarling up traffic on this busy Saturday afternoon.

Demelza turned her head, staring up at shoppers on the footpath built above the road. She felt stricken inside, even though all she'd done was voice a mad desire to escape, and even then, only to her brother, who she knew would never tell their father.

She recognised many of the passers-by, having lived her whole life in Penzance, and nodded at a few of the women who stood queuing with their ration books outside the butcher's shop, their hair set in neat rolls under head-scarves, wicker baskets over their arms. Not for the first time, she wished her ginger hair could be made to set in soft, pretty, feminine rolls like theirs. But it was too like her brother's; springy and impossible to manage.

She looked down at her hands, wishing she'd never raised the subject of leaving Cornwall. She felt awkward now, and maybe Tristan was right. Maybe it was selfish to want to abandon the farm and work in a factory instead, knowing she'd be leaving her family in the lurch. Besides, with the war still raging, farm produce was desperately needed, perhaps more so than ever before. Agricultural work was protected; she had not been sent to work elsewhere because of that, and nor had Tristan.

But her father kept such a tight rein over her existence it made life intolerable. Sometimes he even refused to let Demelza leave the house if he deemed her clothing 'unsuitable'. It was ridiculous. She was twenty-three years old, for goodness' sake, not thirteen; she shouldn't allow herself to be ordered about by her father like this.

'Look, do you want me to drop you off to do your shopping now, or will you wait until I've spoken to Mr Ellis up at the veterinary surgery?' her brother asked.

Tristan's mission in town was to collect eye drops for a newborn lamb with pink eye, and Demelza had used the excuse of needing a new colander to escape the house. A good excuse, given their old one had lost both its handles and was battered beyond repair.

'I'll wait,' she told him, her mind still worrying at her problem.

Having cleared the parked delivery van, they crawled through slow traffic along the seafront, everyone stuck behind a large, rumbling, mud-flecked tractor taking up most of the road.

It was a sunny April day, and being a weekend, there were plenty of people on the beach, defying government policy on public safety by sunbathing in deckchairs, building sandcastles, and wading ankle-deep in the shallows. A few hardy types were even swimming in the milky blue sea, a dazzle of sunlight on the water.

There had been a dull, heavy droning somewhere over the sea for some minutes, the familiar sound of an aeroplane coming their way. As the droning grew louder and more insistent, the siblings both instinctively glanced out to sea. Demelza stiffened, sitting up straight in her seat at the sight of tilted metal wings against a perfect blue sky, still too far away to be clearly visible.

'Is that one of ours?' she whispered.

Tristan was staring at the aeroplane too. 'Not sure.' He braked, squinting up into the sky. 'But I don't think so.'

All around them, other people were looking out to sea and pointing; one woman walking her dog called out, 'Run!' and then everyone on foot started scrambling for shelter as the noise of the plane's engines intensified.

The air-raid siren went off, its eerie wail rising into the warm Saturday afternoon with heart-pounding familiarity.

'Tris,' Demelza whispered, staring into the sky. 'We need to get off the sea front.'

'Agreed.'

A few drivers ahead of them had already wrenched their cars around, turning and driving away in a haphazard fashion. Tristan also attempted to turn their van, but it was chaos by then, the road blocked in both directions.

'Damn it, I can't move an inch.' He turned off the engine in frustration and reached for the door handle, glancing round at her. 'Come on, we'll have to ditch the car and run for it. We're sitting ducks, right out here in the open.'

But it was too late.

The aeroplane could be seen clearly now and the Luftwaffe markings denoted the plane as belonging to the enemy. Demelza couldn't take her eyes off its sinister metallic body.

The pilot banked to the left as it approached the land. Demelza started to breathe more easily, believing that everything would be fine, that he was turning inland. But at the last minute, the pilot corrected his course, swung right and flew straight across the foreshore. The terrifying sound of gunfire filled the air as he peppered the beach and seafront with a hail of bullets, and everything inside her seemed to freeze like ice.

'Get down!' Tristan yelled and they both ducked low in their seats, instinctively covering their heads, though of course if one of those bullets hit the van, there would be no protection.

Bullets spat and whined overhead, the noise hellish, like something out of the matinee films they showed at the cinema.

For a few awful seconds, Demelza truly believed they were both about to die. She thought fleetingly of her father; what he would say when he learned of their deaths and how he would cope with the farm on his own. Abruptly, terror gave way to a hot streak of rage. She was too young to die, she thought with furious impotence, wishing she could jump out and scream up at the enemy pilot. She hadn't done anything with her life yet. And now it was about to be snuffed out by someone she'd never even met?

Somehow though, the crazy zigzag of vehicles along the sea front escaped being hit, as though the pilot's line of fire had been confined to the beach all along. The plane's engines changed note, and with a burst of wild relief Demelza realised he must be heading back out to sea.

The danger was over.

Somewhat belatedly, the bay's anti-aircraft guns finally spluttered into action, firing noisy shells as they countered the attack.

But the pilot had already soared away over the millpond-still sea and was a mere speck in the distance by the time Demelza finally dared to sit up and peer out of the van window again.

Tristan swore under his breath. Normally, she would have told him off for bad language, but this didn't seem the time. Besides, she felt rather like swearing herself.

'Those poor people on the beach.' She fumbled for the door handle and jumped out of the van, though her legs were shaking and her heart was still hammering fit to burst. 'I hope nobody was hurt.'

'Dem, where on earth are you going?' Tristan sounded astonished.

'I have to check … there could be casualties.' Breathless, Demelza set off at a run for the beach front, shouting over her shoulder, 'Don't worry about me, Tris. Just go to the vet's and come back for me later.'

She dashed along the sea front and onto the beach below. It was immediately obvious that a few beachgoers had been hit by the aeroplane's strafing fire. People were running, looking panicked, some of them shouting for help.

Other passers-by like herself had already gone to offer assistance to those nearest the seafront. An elderly gentleman was being supported back to his deckchair, and another man appeared to have fallen onto the pebbles, perhaps shot. Several people were clustered about him, making it hard to see what was going on.

But it was a small, unattended group down at the water's edge that caught Demelza's eye. A large woman in a flowery dress was kneeling over what looked like a body on the shingle, with two young, dark-haired boys in shorts looking on, pale figures armed with buckets and spades. A girl with dark braids was waving a handkerchief frantically, calling up and down the beach, 'Help! Help us, please!'

As Demelza instinctively ran their way, she noted that someone else was doing the same from the opposite end of the beach. A young woman in flats and a yellow sun-dress, her long blonde hair swept up and neatly clipped into position, was splashing recklessly through the shallows. She was shouting something that Demelza couldn't catch, the words carried away by the constant roar of the tide.

Drawing closer, Demelza could see a man lay unmoving in the foaming surf, a frightening bloom of red staining his white shirt just below his chest. A young collie dog was running to-and-fro around the man's body, barking wildly, up to its belly in sea water. That the fallen man was the dog's master was immediately clear to Demelza; they had two collies on the farm for herding the sheep, both deeply loyal to her father, slinking by his side wherever he went, their upturned gazes fixed to his face.

What she didn't know was whether the poor man was wounded or dead, and she checked her headlong pace, steeling herself for the worst. Ever since she'd walked in as a child to find her mother's body, she'd had a morbid fear of death. But she was determined to overcome it. The country was at war, for goodness' sake, she told herself fiercely. This was no time to be a coward.

CHAPTER TWO

Blow the Germans, Lily Fisher thought crossly. She hadn't enjoyed a proper day off work in months, and had thought a few days with her family in Porthcurno would be just the trick for her jaded spirits. If only Gran hadn't persuaded them all to take a day trip to Penzance today, she could have been sitting peacefully in the back garden at home, sunbathing or reading a magazine, lazy pastimes she had almost forgotten existed since starting work as a nurse.

Before the war, she'd never have imagined life as an eighteen-year-old could be this intense and exhausting. There was always some kind of emergency in the St. Ives convalescent home where she worked, and even when it was quiet and she was off duty, her body ached from the constant hard labour and her mind was numb with all the terrible things she'd seen. But at home with her family, it was easier to pretend that horrible other world didn't exist, that they weren't at war with Germany and she wasn't a nurse who spent her days and nights caring for wounded servicemen. Not that she begrudged doing her duty for

King and country. But some days it did take an awful toll on the mind and spirit…

They'd been having such a lovely day out in Penzance too, she and Gran, Aunty Violet, and her younger sister Alice.

Having travelled in on the first bus from tiny Porthcurno, they'd spent the first hour in Penzance looking around all the quaint little shops but not buying anything – even though Gran had saved up her ration coupons in the hopes of finding some nice material to make a few summer dresses for Alice – and then decided to eat their picnic lunch early on the beach.

After walking barefoot along the water's edge and skimming stones out into the sea, they'd eventually found a nice little spot by some rocks. It was sheltered from the breeze but had a majestic view across the bay towards St. Michael's Mount – a small, conical hill that rose out of the sea on the far side of the bay, covered in trees and fascinating buildings and topped with a medieval-looking castle.

'St. Michael's Mount is like something out of a fairy tale, isn't it?' Lily had accepted a bloater paste sandwich from Gran with a grateful smile, even though it tasted a bit too fishy for her liking. 'With knights and princesses and wicked witches in towers.'

'Must be difficult getting to and from the mainland,' Alice replied rather indistinctly, through a mouthful of bread. Lily's little sister was surprisingly practical and level-headed for a girl just turned seventeen, despite being a complete bookworm who rarely ever had her head out of a library book. 'I mean, for shopping and going to the dentist. Do you think they always wait for the tide to go out, so the causeway is uncovered, or do they just jump in a boat and row for it?'

Gran handed her a boiled egg. "Ere, don't talk with your mouth full, Alice. I know you've gone back to school to help with the little ones, but that don't mean you have to behave like a kid yourself. What would your mum say if she could see you now?'

Their mum had died in the Blitz, leaving both Lily and Alice orphans in their grandmother's care. Gran had done her best for them, of course. But she was too busy running a café back home in Dagenham, to the east of London, to keep her eye on them every day. So, the onerous task of keeping them in line had fallen to poor, hardworking Aunty Violet.

These days, Violet was as much a mother to them as their own mum had been. Lily suspected Alice didn't always appreciate how much Vi had done for her sister's kids, bringing them out of harm's way to sleepy Cornwall and skivvying as a cleaner to keep bread on the table, all out of the goodness of her heart. But Alice was barely older than the kids she was now helping to teach at the big school in Penzance; she'd understand the world better once she was older and had taken a few knocks.

Lily couldn't remember being as fresh-faced and inno-cent as Alice at her age. But then she'd had a rude awakening at seventeen, assaulted by her great-uncle on his Cornish farm before Violet had hurriedly taken them all to the tiny village of Porthcurno instead.

Ignoring her grandmother's complaints, Alice continued. 'I wonder if anyone really lives on the Mount, or if all those buildings are abandoned.' She bit into the egg, her gaze fixed on the faraway castle. 'Might be a fun place to explore.'

'We ain't going to St. Michael's Mount today, with or

without a boat,' Aunty Vi told her firmly and turned to Lily. 'When do you have to go back to work, love?'

'Day after tomorrow,' Lily said, happy at the thought of spending another whole day at home with her loved ones.

Lily had been granted four days' official leave from her work at the Symmonds Hall Convalescent Home for Wounded Servicemen, which overlooked the Atlantic Ocean at windy St. Ives, further along the Cornish coast. She'd been feeling a bit down over the winter and had unluckily managed to catch the flu, after which Matron had insisted she take a break before resuming her duties.

'I don't like to see nurses dragging themselves around the wards as though they're in worse shape than the patients,' Matron had told her sternly. 'Go home for a few days, Nurse Fisher, and get some rest. Then come back smiling.'

Lily hadn't thought it would be possible to cheer up. Not after the long, hard winter they'd endured with the war still raging overseas and seriously wounded men coming in every week, taking up all the available beds, some unfortunately not making it…

But the sun had been shining every day since she'd left St. Ives, and today's picnic on the beach at Penzance had been gloriously peaceful. Until, that is, some blasted German pilot flew out of the blue sky towards them and begun indiscriminately spraying walkers and sunbathers with bullets.

Luckily, it was still early enough in the year for there not to be many people swimming. Because that was where the bulk of the bullets had landed, pinging and plopping into the shallow waters as people ran screaming for cover further up the beach. The few swimmers out in the bay had wisely dived under the water, no doubt hoping to escape notice.

14

Then the enemy plane had banked steeply and flown away after only one run at the beach, thank goodness.

Perhaps the pilot had been frightened off by the anti-aircraft guns, now firing across the sea in its wake. Or maybe he'd deliberately been trying to avoid killing too many people, Lily thought. Maybe the Germans had their orders too but didn't like them any better than the British soldiers did. Killing people was not a very nice thing to do, whoever was doing it. Especially innocent women and children playing on a Cornish beach on a sunny spring day.

At the first sound of gunfire, Alice, Aunty Violet and Gran had abandoned the picnic food and all of their possessions, dashing to the nearest large rocks for shelter. Lily, hard on their heels, had heard a scream of anguish, and glanced back to see a man in shirt sleeves fall backwards into the surf, presumably hit by a stray bullet.

She hadn't even paused to think.

'You lot stay safe, you hear me? Jerry's gone now but he might come back for another run.' Lily tossed the last of her bloater sandwich at Alice, who'd eagerly tried to catch it. Waste not, want not. 'I need to check if that man's still alive.'

'Lily Fisher, you get back here right now,' Aunty Vi began hotly, but the rest of her words were lost in the roar of the tide as Lily ran along the water's edge towards the fallen man, now surrounded by what she guessed must be his wife and family.

Reaching the terrified little group at the same time as the tall blonde girl, Demelza bent over with one hand clamped to her side, having run so fast across the large beach that she had a stitch.

'Can … I … help?' she asked through gulped breaths.

Looking round at once, the large woman in the flowery dress gasped. 'Oh, thank goodness. I didn't think anyone would come. Yes, please help, I don't know what to do.'

The other young woman paid no attention to the foaming water, splashing through the shallows and soaking her shoes and the hem of her knee-length yellow dress without any outward sign of concern.

'Been shot, has he? Right, let's get him out of the water first.'

The young blonde had spoken crisply and with a strong London accent. Stooping, she lifted the man by his shoulders, seeming unperturbed when his head lolled backwards in an alarming fashion.

Casting Demelza an assessing look, she asked, 'Can you grab his legs? We need to get him further up the beach, away from the water.' She paused, waiting until Demelza was in position. 'That's it. One, two … lift.'

Together, they hoisted the wounded man out of the surf and carried him slowly to a drier spot a few hundred yards away; there was a largish patch of gritty sand among the pebbles so he could lie flat there.

The large woman in the flowery dress followed, clucking anxiously the whole time, and occasionally holding her side as though in pain. 'Oh, please be careful,' she said breathlessly. 'Should you be moving him at all? Won't it make things worse? Perhaps we ought to have waited for a doctor.'

The girl and two young boys trailed after them too, looking worried and despondent.

Demelza and the other young woman settled the man

down as gently as they could. The red stain on his shirt looked awful; Demelza couldn't take her eyes off it.

She had seen plenty of dead animals in her time – living on a farm, you could hardly avoid it – but only one dead human. Anguished, she pushed that old memory away and concentrated on the wounded man.

Wounded, she stressed to herself. Not dead. Or not yet, anyway.

'Don't you worry, I'm sure someone will have told the hospital what's happened by now,' the blonde was telling the woman in a soothing way, though Demelza noticed how keenly her gaze kept scouring the sea front as though hoping to see an ambulance approaching. 'What's your husband's name?'

The other woman glared. 'He's not my husband,' she snapped, her face flushed. 'He's my brother, and his name's Jeremy Lister.'

'I see.' Bending over the unconscious man, the blonde looked round at the woman oddly. 'Are you Miss Lister, then?'

'Of course not. How dare you? I'm Mrs Maynard.' The woman's lip quivered, and her voice almost broke. 'Mrs Emily Maynard.'

'Try not to fret, Mrs Maynard. It won't do your brother any good if you get upset, will it? And it could be bad for the baby.'

It was only at that moment that Demelza realised what had been staring her in the face all that time. No wonder the woman in the flowery dress had taken such quick offence at the suggestion she was single. Mrs Maynard was not 'large'. She was *pregnant*. Her arms and legs were, in fact, quite dainty. But her belly was enormous, rounding under her dress with unmistakeable prominence. And she was rubbing her belly now, looking really quite upset.

But something else struck Demelza as strange.

None of the children were crying, sniffing, panicking or showing any of the natural emotions they ought to be feeling at the sight of their family member having been shot. They were merely looking on in silence, their faces glum.

Gingerly, the blonde pulled Mr Lister's shirt free from his waistband to peer at the wound beneath, and the man stirred, groaning.

'Oh, what are you doing now?' the pregnant woman cried, slapping at her hand. 'Leave my brother alone. You're hurting him.'

'No need to get your knickers in a twist, love. I know what I'm doing.' The blonde continued to study the man's wound without even looking up at her. 'I'm a trained nurse.'

Demelza looked at her with fresh respect.

It made sense now; no wonder this young woman had spoken so calmly and authoritatively, showing no fear or distress. Because she'd seen it all before, possibly hundreds of times.

A trained nurse.

Once again, Demelza wished she knew what to do with her life. Perhaps she too could get some training and make herself useful in the war effort…

'Is there anything I can do to help?' she repeated. 'Anything at all? I hate just standing about like this.'

The blonde looked up at her in surprise. But before she could reply, the man on the ground opened his eyes and gave a strangled cry, beginning to struggle.

CHAPTER THREE

Lily was glad that the man had regained consciousness – that was always a good sign – though he was clearly alarmed to find them all staring down at him as he thrashed about, struggling to get up and no doubt in awful pain.

'Back in the land of the living, Mr Lister? That's marvellous. Now listen, I won't lie to you. You've been shot.' The man gave another despairing cry, but she continued in the calm voice she used with all of her patients, however badly they were hurt. 'And I need you to stop moving and lie perfectly still, or you'll only make things worse.'

To her relief, he stopped trying to get up, his bulging eyes fixed on her face.

'How ... how bad is it?' he asked hoarsely.

'There ain't nothing for you to worry about, Mr Lister,' she lied, knowing it was better not to be *too* truthful with a badly wounded man. 'As soon as the ambulance arrives, you'll be taken to hospital and the doctors will soon patch you up. Come tomorrow or maybe the next day, you'll be right as rain.'

She glanced up at the young Cornish woman who'd asked so earnestly if she could help.

'Could I borrow that scarf of yours?' she asked, and then added apologetically, 'I'm afraid it'll get ruined.'

'That doesn't matter,' the young woman said without blinking, and dragged off the thin blue scarf she'd been wearing. 'Here.'

'Thanks, love.' Lily bundled it up into a makeshift dressing pad and pressed it hard into the man's wound. He cried out again, jerking in pain. 'Sorry. But we need to stop the bleeding.' She instructed his sister to keep the dressing in place, holding it down firmly. 'Don't worry about hurting him. He'll thank you for it later.'

'This young lady's a nurse, Jeremy, and she says you're going to be all right,' his sister told him tearfully, valiantly holding the blood-stained scarf in place over his stomach. 'I'm with you, dear. Best do what she says and try not to move.'

'I'm Demelza,' the young woman said, crouching down to look at Mr Lister.

'Lily,' she responded with a quick smile. 'Look, I'm sure he'll be fine,' she said to reassure her, though that wasn't true. He was losing a great deal of blood.

'Of course he will,' Demelza agreed blandly, but locked gazes with Lily above his body.

She knows I'm lying, Lily thought.

'Miss? I fink I can hear a bell,' the young girl with the hanky announced, pointing up into the town, and indeed Lily could hear it now too. From her accent, she wasn't a local either. 'Is that the ambulance, d'you reckon?'

'I expect so, yes.' Lily stood, rubbing the sand and blood

off her hands as best she could. It was hard not to show her relief as the tinkling bell of the ambulance grew louder, for she had been worried they might lose him before he could reach the hospital. She glanced down at the groaning man, trying for some light humour. At the convalescent home, making jokes sometimes helped patients through a difficult situation. 'You hear that, Mr Lister? Your carriage awaits, milord.'

'Eh?' He seemed confused now, his eyes clouding over. Lily began to be seriously worried for him.

She was more used to patients who'd already been patched up in a field hospital before being sent to the home for long-term recovery, and could only hope she'd done her best for the poor man by compressing the wound while they waited for help. She wasn't used to dealing with serious injuries like this, and even though her training had covered the basics of frontline nursing, reading about it in a manual was no substitute for hands-on experience.

Lily gave the young girl with the hanky an encouraging smile. 'Is that an East London accent?'

'Close enough, Miss,' the older of the two boys chirped before the girl could answer, also in the same breezy accent that reminded her of home. 'We're from Barking. Got sent down 'ere on account of all the bleedin' bombs.'

'Is that so?'

'We ain't cowards though,' he added hurriedly. 'We never minded them German bombs. Only my ma said we had to come. So 'ere we are. Mrs Maynard and Mr Lister took us in at their place, though it's been a shockin' squeeze. They've only got the one spare room, see? Packed in like sardines, we are.'

'I can imagine,' Lily said, grinning.

She could do more than imagine, of course. It sounded only too familiar to her as she'd spent her first year in Cornwall sharing a bedroom with her sister and aunt, and knew what it felt like to be displaced and homeless. Still, these kids were putting on a brave face, just as she and Alice had done when they first arrived off the train in Cornwall.

'I'm Eustace Tomkin,' the dark-haired boy continued, and jerked a thumb at his brother, 'and this here's Little Timothy – we call him that because our ma says he's shorter than what he ought to be – and that's our big sister Janice with the hanky there.'

'Hello, Eustace, Little Timothy, Janice. Nice to meet you.' Lily's smile had widened while he was speaking and she stuck out a hand. 'I grew up in the same area myself. Like you, we only came down here when the bombing got too much for us. My family's from Dagenham.'

'Oh, our aunt and uncle live over in Dagenham. It's a long bus ride but we went there for Christmas once. Lovely plum pudding, my aunt does.' The boy shook her hand, pumping it up and down enthusiastically. 'Nice to meet you too, Lily.'

'Nurse,' Lily corrected him with a laugh, shaking hands with the other two as well. 'You can call me Nurse Fisher.'

The ambulance had stopped on the sea front. Lily took a few steps up the beach and waved her hands in the air, shouting, 'Oi, over here! We need a stretcher.'

But it was no use.

The ambulance men were too preoccupied to hear her, busy talking to the portly gentleman who'd collapsed in the deckchair, though he didn't seem that poorly if he was able to sit up and talk. He certainly hadn't been shot.

'Bother.'

Frustrated, she looked around for the other young woman. Demelza, she'd said her name was. A proper Cornish name, as her friend Sister Rose would say, the senior nurse in charge of the convalescent home back in St. Ives.

Demelza was still standing guard over the wounded man, hands clasped together under her large bosom. Dressed like a Land Girl in green knitwear and muddied brown trousers, she was a short, heavy-set girl with an open, trusting face and long-lashed green eyes, her hair a riot of ginger curls that Lily suspected no amount of straightening with a hot tong would ever correct, bright strands almost alight in the spring sunshine.

Lily instinctively liked her.

'Demelza,' she said with a quick smile, hurrying back to them, 'I don't suppose you'd mind nipping up to tell those lads we need a stretcher down here? This chap needs to be seen by a doctor, and urgently. There's a hospital in Penzance, isn't there?'

'Oh, yes,' Demelza told her, the young woman already striding away on her mission as though glad to be of use at last. 'I'll be right back.'

With a mixture of scolding and cajoling, Demelza rapidly persuaded the first ambulance man she met to bring a stretcher down onto the beach.

But as she hurried back to the ambulance with him, explaining breathlessly about the wounded man as she went, the second ambulance man caught up with them.

23

'Bernard? Where are you going?' The man wasn't a Cornishman, though she couldn't place his accent; his voice was deep and lazy, almost a drawl. 'I'm thinking we should take Mr Porter up to the hospital, just in case. He says he's fine now, but you never know with these old gents. What do you say?'

When Demelza turned, ready to remonstrate with him too, she took a startled step backwards, confronted by a big bear of a man with wild fair hair, just a trifle too long to be entirely respectable, and eyes as starkly blue as the Cornish skies above them.

Goodness, she thought, trying not to stare. His looks and stature reminded her of drawings of Viking warriors in the history books she'd read at school.

Her first thought was that she was glad he wasn't wielding a battle axe or broadsword, though just looking at him in his ambulance uniform was impressive enough.

Her second thought, rather more nagging, was that he wasn't in a military uniform.

But perhaps he had some health problem that wasn't visible, meaning he couldn't be a soldier. Because every other man she knew who was able to fight and wasn't in a protected profession for the war effort had done his bit for King and country and joined up. And she knew being an ambulance driver wasn't a protected profession, unlike farming.

Yes, she was sure that must be it. Because if she had ever seen a born warrior, this man was it. Gosh, she thought more sympathetically, poor thing, he must be absolutely chafing at the bit, not able to fight for his country.

'Can't,' the silver-haired man said shortly. 'We need to

take a stretcher down there.' He pointed out the group on the beach where she'd left Lily tending to Jeremy Lister. 'Man's been shot.'

'*Shot*?' The other ambulance man's eyebrows rose steeply in shock or disbelief. 'Says who?'

'Says me,' Demelza burst out, her voice high and indignant. Flustered, she took a deep breath as the ambulance man's attention turned more fully towards her; that intense blue gaze moving up and down her in a way she wasn't sure she liked. She tugged at her heavy-knit jumper, suddenly self-conscious. 'It's true. His name's Mr Lister, and he was hit when that German plane shot up the beach. The nurse is worried he may die.'

'I'll get the stretcher,' Bernard said, and disappeared into the back of the ambulance.

The other man's gaze was arrested, fixed on her face. 'Wait, there's a nurse with him? Where did she come from?'

'She was just there … I don't know why.' Demelza shrugged, feeling almost wild with panic at this delay. 'Look, that's not important. She asked me to tell you to fetch a stretcher down to him right away. There's no time to lose.'

To her relief, he nodded, his expression deadly serious now. 'No need to worry, Miss,' he told her, and there was something in his voice that made her feel completely safe, almost as though everything in the world was going to be all right, even though she knew that wasn't even remotely true. Not while they were still at war with Germany. 'Bernard and me, we'll get him to hospital, double-quick.'

'Thank you,' she said huskily.

'Got it,' Bernard called, jumping out of the ambulance with the bulky stretcher tucked under his arm.

25

'Let's go.' The other man gestured down the beach, nodding at her to go first. 'After you, Miss.'

They ran down the beach as fast as they could. But by the time they returned to the small group, it was clear that something had changed while Demelza had been gone, and for the worse. The two boys were huddled together, finally looking anxious, and Janice was reluctantly holding Mrs Maynard's hand. The pregnant woman was still kneeling but was now holding her rounded belly with a look of acute suffering, puffing and panting as though she'd been running about.

Lily, mopping Mr Lister's brow with Janice's handkerchief and talking to him in a low voice, looked up as Demelza came running back to them. 'Thank goodness.'

She stood to direct the two ambulance men on how to handle the hurt man, giving them a quick account of his condition, and then turned back to Demelza.

'Listen, Mrs Maynard is having pains,' Lily told her quietly. 'She says she's due in less than a month. I can't be sure, but it's possible she's going into labour. With the shock of the attack, and all that.' She leant a little closer and whispered, 'She's a widow. Husband killed in action only a few weeks ago. I think this was the last straw.'

Demelza nodded, her heart wrung. A young widow, about to give birth, and with her brother seriously wounded too.

'What do you need me to do?' she said, drawing herself up.

'Someone has to look after these kids. She says they arrived from London last week, and she only agreed to take them because her brother wanted to help out with the war effort. He's got a lung condition, wasn't allowed to join up. But he's likely to be in hospital for some time, if he even makes it, and she won't be up to minding three evacuees on her own. Not when she's just had a baby.' Lily looked at her directly. 'Will you take them to the Penzance Evacuation Placement Office? See if they can be found somewhere more permanent to live?'

If he even makes it…

It was too dreadful.

But look after three kids?

'I don't know much about children,' she admitted. 'Or where to find the Placement Office. Especially on a Saturday. What if I get stuck with them all weekend?'

'I'm sure that won't happen,' Lily said persuasively. 'There's bound to be an emergency place available for them somewhere in Penzance—'

She stopped short as the pregnant woman shrieked, her eyes rolling, and then gave a blood-curdling groan as her brother was borne carefully away on the stretcher by the ambulance men. Poor woman, Demelza thought; she must be afraid she might never see him again.

'Of course, I'll do whatever I can if there's nobody else,' Demelza said hurriedly, not wanting to seem churlish.

'Thank you, that's the spirit.' Lily went to help the pregnant woman to her feet. 'Can you walk, Mrs Maynard? You probably need to go to hospital too.'

'Must I?' Mrs Maynard gave her an unhappy look, saying between panting breaths, 'I want to give birth at home … like my mother did.'

'Trust me, you can never be too careful when a baby

comes early. Besides, you may find just turning up at the hospital is enough to calm things down. And you'll be able to check on your brother too.'

'Oh, very well.' Mrs Maynard grimaced at another pain. 'I think … we need to hurry.'

Lily began to support her up the beach, only pausing to flash a quick grin back at Demelza and the three watching children. 'Good luck!'

The two men were almost back at the ambulance with Mr Lister on the stretcher, the big man leading the way. She watched him curiously as they negotiated the narrow steps up off the beach, once again wondering what his story was, and why he had become an ambulance man, a job usually reserved for older gentlemen or those with health issues that meant they couldn't reasonably be expected to march and fight. Well, she would never know, would she? It was unlikely she would ever see him again.

Biting her lip, Demelza turned to find all three children in a row, looking up at her hopefully, their eyes full of expectation.

It was rather intimidating.

She straightened, trying to appear confident and in control, though in truth she had never felt less sure of herself. What on earth would Tristan say when he discovered she'd saddled herself with three homeless evacuees? Or her father, if she failed to find them a new home and had to turn up at the farm with them in tow? She blanched, imagining her father's fury. It didn't bear thinking about.

'All right, gather your buckets and spades, and put your shoes back on; we'd better get going.' Demelza watched as the kids scrambled to obey. 'Where's that collie dog gone?'

'Some bloke took him. Eustace said. 'Friend of Mr Lister's.'

'Oh, right.' Demelza hesitated. 'I ... I don't suppose any of you know where this Placement Office is?'

Lily helped Mrs Maynard up to the sea front, only to see the ambulance carrying Jeremy Lister pull away at a slow, lurching pace. Thankfully, there was an ornate Victorian bench a short distance away for her flushed, puffing patient to sit on, and within maybe half an hour, another ambulance, even more battered than the first, had arrived to take its place.

The driver, a portly man in his fifties, leant out of his window to study Lily and Mrs Maynard with surprise. 'Morning, Miss. We got word another ambulance was needed.'

'That's right,' she said, and helped her patient to stand.

'Jerries, was it? These pilots get bolder and bolder with every day that passes,' the ambulance driver said, and scanned the beach as though half-expecting to see heaps of blood-stained bodies. 'Nobody else shot, then?' He sounded almost disappointed.

'No, but this lady needs your immediate assistance,' Lily said tartly.

His gaze came back to her face, uncertain, and then shifted slowly to Mrs Maynard. 'Funny turn, is it?' he said in a patronising voice, and both men chuckled. 'No need for an ambulance for that, Miss. I daresay she'll be all right after a nice cup of tea.'

'No, she won't,' Lily said without preamble. 'The baby's on its way.'

He sat bolt upright then, with a quick glance at his companion. 'Oh, well, in that case…'

The two men scrambled out and came to help a moaning Mrs Maynard up into the back of the vehicle.

'So, this one's our only casualty?' the driver asked, a good deal more politely than before.

'As far as I know. I think we were all very lucky. Or else the pilot's heart wasn't in it.' Briefly, Lily explained what she'd seen of the attack, and how the terrible shock of seeing her brother shot seemed to have precipitated the onset of labour in Mrs Maynard. 'I'd better come with you and speak to the doctor.'

The other ambulance man, a younger man with a limp, took this with a sceptical expression, rubbing his stubbly chin and saying drily, 'Right you are, Miss.'

'I'm a trained nurse,' she explained, a slight snap in her voice, 'and I've already delivered one baby in my time. Mark my words, this woman needs to be admitted straight-away.'

Lily was secretly pleased when the two men jumped to attention at this revelation, the younger one even straight-ening his uniform and gazing at her with new respect. While they saw to Mrs Maynard's comfort, Lily turned and stood looking across the now empty beach, unsure whether she should accompany them to the local hospital or just walk away in search of her family.

Worry crept into her heart. She had no idea where her own family had gone. No doubt they would have emerged from hiding once the pilot had gone, collected their picnic and hats and coats, and trailed up to the sea front to wait for her. But she couldn't see them anywhere. It was a bother; she didn't want to get into the ambulance with the pregnant woman until she'd informed her family where she was going; after all, labour could take hours. But at the same time, there was no time to waste.

Perhaps it would be enough to hand her patient over to a local midwife or doctor, if one was available at the hospital. She knew how short-staffed these rural hospitals were, with most practitioners having signed up or been posted to one of the bigger cities.

The ambulance men had secured the patient. 'Right, you coming with us then, Miss? There's room for one more.'

'I think so, yes.' She was just climbing up inside when she heard her aunt's voice.

'Lily?'

She turned at once and was pleased to find Aunty Violet, Alice and Gran in front of her, sand on their clothes and clutching their belongings in a rather forlorn fashion.

'Thank goodness you found me,' Lily told them with a quick, apologetic smile. 'Look, I need to go with this lady to the hospital. She's nearly nine months gone and about to pop, bless her. I might be ages, so you'd better head home without me.' She saw Gran open her mouth to protest, and added, 'I'll catch the last bus home. If I'm too late for supper, just stick my plate on the range to keep warm.'

Gran shook her head but didn't try to stop her. She knew how much Lily loved being a nurse and helping people. 'Go on with you, love.'

'Wait, who was them kids we saw you with down on the beach?' Alice demanded, her face alive with curiosity.

'Oh,' Lily said, grinning, 'fellow evacuees.'

'You don't say?' Aunty Vi was staring.

'They've only recently arrived from Barking,' Lily explained briefly, aware of the ambulance man waiting impatiently. 'I'll tell you all about it later. But it looks like they'll need somewhere new to live after this, poor things.'

A moan of pain from inside the ambulance made Lily give them a hurried wave and duck inside.

'See you soon,' she called out airily, and was just in time to see Alice pull a face when the ambulance man closed the door behind her.

CHAPTER FOUR

'Bloomin' Germans! They certainly know how to spoil a grand day out.' Exasperated, Violet's mum stared up the hill into the centre of Penzance with a deeply furrowed brow. 'I was just starting to enjoy meself too.'

Violet Hopkins smiled at her mother sympathetically. 'I know how you feel, Mum. These Jerries, they're so selfish … never thinking of anyone but themselves.' She gave a wink, trying to lift their spirits with her little joke, but it seemed nobody was listening; her mother didn't even smile, and her niece, Alice, was in a world of her own, as usual.

'Well,' Violet went on, trying for patriotic enthusiasm instead, 'at least our Lily got a chance to show off her skills, eh? I thought it were smashing, the way she didn't even stop to think, just ran off to help that poor man who got shot.'

Her mother gave a wan smile at last. 'She's a regular guardian angel is Lily,' Sheila agreed, but gave a heavy sigh, restless as ever. 'What shall we do, then? It's too early to head back to the bus stop. And I don't fancy blowing any more money on a cream tea.'

Mum was looking a bit worn these days, Violet thought, covertly watching her. Though perhaps that was only to be expected, what with the war dragging on forever; Violet herself had felt a bit down in the dumps recently, unsure if the world would ever return to normal. Besides, Mum's arthritis had started playing up since she'd moved down to join them in Cornwall. Their first winter in Porthcurno had been damp and misty, living by the sea, and Mum had taken to complaining about her 'old bones'.

Still, it wasn't all bad. They weren't being bombed nightly anymore, and they all had far more colour in their cheeks compared to the grey pallor of their Dagenham days.

Some days Violet missed the busy hum of living so close to London. Porthcurno was such a small place, little more than a rural village that had only sprawled into a makeshift town with the arrival of troops and personnel to man the listening station there. But there was no denying that life in Dagenham had been unhealthy for them all, the streets wreathed in smog from home fires and factory chimneys even before war broke out, their only taste of fresh air a quick gander around the local park on Sunday afternoons.

Here in Cornwall, there was more fresh air than anything else, Violet thought wryly, except maybe green fields.

One thing she didn't miss though was the constant fear of enemy bombers overhead. That German pilot strafing the beach with his machine guns just now had given her such a fright, despite the brave face she'd put on in front of young Alice. She kept having a recurring nightmare about being caught out when the air-raid siren went off, unable to outrun a falling bomb. In her dreams she always ended up buried in rubble, like her late sister, Betsy, who'd been killed in an air raid back in Dagenham. With their father Ernst missing in action overseas, Betsy's two daughters had been left to their gran and Aunty Violet's care, and though Violet had fretted about the responsibility at first, she wouldn't be without her dearest girls now.

Lily was all grown-up these days, of course; now that she was working as a nurse in St. Ives, they barely ever saw her. But Violet was convinced that Alice still needed a helping hand, even though she'd sprouted so tall this year, she towered over her grandmother. It was hard to tell the girl anything though; she knew her own mind.

Despite George Cotterill having personally recommended her for a job at the school in Penzance, helping to teach the younger children to read and write, Alice seemed bored in her new post. She often spoke with enthusiasm of the old days when they'd mopped out the secret underground tunnels at Eastern House together, a light in her face, as though pining for that drudgery.

Frankly, Violet couldn't understand her youngest niece's restlessness. After cleaning duties at the listening post, landing a teaching job was impressive indeed, even if it was only down to all the young male teachers having enlisted, leaving vacancies in schools up and down the country.

The silly girl ought to be counting her blessings, not chafing to leave already. Violet blamed it on all the spy and adventure novels she was forever reading.

'Perhaps we could walk back up to the haberdashers,' Violet suggested, having earlier spotted her mother drooling over some pretty material at the back of the dusty little shop. 'They had some fancy ribbon that would do nicely for Alice's hair. She ought to look posh for her new job, don't you think, Mum?'

Her mum shrugged but didn't dismiss the idea. 'Better than wandering about with nuffin to do, I s'pose. And I could use a new card of darning cotton; our old one's nearly finished.' She dropped her handbag onto the crook of her arm and glanced round at her youngest grand-daughter. 'What do you think, Alice, love? Would you prefer pink or yellow ribbons in your hair?'

Alice was rummaging in one of the bags she was carrying, which had contained their picnic lunch. 'Hmm, Gran?' She looked up vaguely, a thick lock of dishevelled fair hair hanging down over one eye, like a moorland pony. 'I hate ribbons, they make me look like a twelve-year-old. Though I wouldn't say no to visiting the book shop again. I know we can't afford to buy anything, but I still like to read the titles and see what stories they have. I'm making a list in my head of all the books I'll buy once the war's over, you see,' she added dreamily.

Violet's mum laughed and shook her head. 'Proper little bookworm, you are. Well, maybe, if there's enough time.'

They began to walk back up into the town centre, moving in the general direction of the haberdashers, but before they'd even reached the main street, Violet sighed. 'Hang on a tick, would you?' Sick of her worn-out shoes rubbing against her heel, she stopped and leant against a wall to remove them, one by one, and shake them out. 'I love the beach, don't get me wrong, but it would be much better without all this blasted sand.'

'Me too,' Alice said, munching on the remnants of their picnic lunch. She held up a squashy triangle of bloater paste sandwich with a doleful expression. 'I dropped this when Lily threw it to me; I swear there's more sand than wich in it now.' She crammed the last of it into her mouth and shrugged. 'Not too bad though,' she finished.

As they continued walking, heading for Market Jew Street, Violet stopped in surprise.

''Ere, ain't that them kids from the beach again? The ones with the man Lily was helping,' she asked Alice in an undertone, nodding towards three young children waiting outside a tall red-brick building across the road.

'The evacuees, you mean? I think so.' Alice studied them thoughtfully. 'I wonder what they're doing.'

The children looked dispirited, which was hardly a surprise given what they'd just witnessed. The younger boy was snivelling and wiping his nose on the sleeve of his grey cardigan; the older boy was kicking a stone repeatedly against the wall of the building, his hands in the pockets of his short trousers; and the girl with dark, braided hair was standing in a miserable huddle, arms folded, staring gloomily at nothing as though wishing herself a million miles away.

Nobody appeared to be with them.

'Poor little souls,' Violet muttered. 'Lily says they're from back in Essex like us.' Her heart hurt at the sight of the little boy crying his eyes out; he looked barely ten years old. It wasn't right to leave them standing on the street like that. Not after the shock they'd had. 'I'm going to ask them if everything's all right.'

She ignored her mum's grumbling and crossed the road to speak to the kids.

'Hello there,' she said with a sympathetic smile, 'My niece Lily's the girl who helped that gentleman down on the beach. The one who was shot.' She paused, worried in case she'd misunderstood what Lily had told them before getting into the ambulance. It had all happened in such a hurry. 'He … wasn't your dad, was he?'

The older boy had stopped kicking his stone and turned to stare to her. 'No. We was staying with 'im and his sister, Mrs Maynard. We're evacuees,' he explained, and raised his chin defiantly. 'Only, Mr Lister can't look after us now, can he? They've taken 'im to the hospital and it don't look good. Nor his sister can't, neither. She's having a baby, and she won't want us big kids around once she's got her own little nipper to look after.'

Violet suppressed a grin at his worldly-wise air. 'Our Lily said you three have come down from Barking. Is that right?'

'Can't deny it,' he said, with a sniff. 'Who are you, then?'

'Miss Violet Hopkins.' Violet looked him up and down. 'And what's your name? How old are you?'

'I'm Eustace, and I'm eleven. That's snivelling Timothy. He's nine.' The younger boy threw him a resentful glance, but his brother paid no attention. 'Janice's the eldest; she's fourteen.' He pulled a disparaging face. 'But she's a girl, so that don't mean she's in charge or nuffin.'

'All right, so who *is* in charge?' Violet looked up and down the street, more than a little concerned for their welfare. Back in their own town, no doubt they'd be perfectly able to fend for themselves out on the streets. But this was a new place to these kids; she doubted they even knew which end was up yet. 'Is nobody with you?'

Eustace nodded to the red-brick building behind him. 'Some interfering woman and her brother are in there, talking to the evacuees' officer. Trying to find us a new gaff.' He was clearly unimpressed. 'They told us to wait out here. Bloomin' ages ago.'

Violet studied the building. The large sign above the door said 'Fire Guard Station', but below it, in smaller lettering, she read 'Evacuation Placement Office, First Floor'.

'*Lady*, you mean,' she said, correcting his speech automatically, as she would have done Alice once. 'Not woman.'

'Yeah, right,' Eustace said, and went back to kicking his stone.

Her mum and Alice had joined them by now.

'Hello,' her mum said more cheerily, her experienced eye soon alighting on young Timothy, still red-eyed and sniffing. 'Who's this lot, then?'

Violet introduced the three children and explained their situation, and where they'd come from. 'I expect the lady who's looking after them will be down soon,' she added in a low voice to her mother. 'But shall we wait to make sure the kids don't come to any harm on their own? That older boy looks a bit of a tearaway. I wouldn't put anything past him.' She glanced up at the cloudless blue skies above Penzance. 'Besides, you never know, that German pilot might be back for more blood.'

Her mum shivered. 'Oh, don't.' But she nodded. 'Yes, let's wait with them. Best idea you've had all day.' She whipped out a clean hanky and presented it to Timothy with a winning smile. 'There you go, lad. You can keep that. Better than dirtying your sleeve.'

'Fanks.' Timothy buried his face in the huge white hanky and blew his nose.

'Oh, Timmy, not so loud! Sounds like a bloomin' trumpet,' his sister complained, clapping her hands over her ears.

Violet grinned. 'Janice. You're fourteen? You'll be finishing school this summer, then? You look older.' A compliment never hurts, she thought, though she noticed the girl barely glanced in her direction. She gestured towards Alice, thinking perhaps the age gap was the problem. 'This is my niece, Alice. She's seventeen and helps out at the local school here in Penzance. Not so far off your own age.'

The two girls looked at each other with wary suspicion.

At that moment, they heard someone coming down the stairs inside the red-brick building, and a moment later a young woman with a bright mass of ginger curls emerged into the sunshine, followed by a young man who was so obviously her brother, Violet almost laughed, looking from one unruly mop of hair to the other.

'Hello,' she said impulsively, and held out her hand to the young couple. 'I'm Violet Hopkins.' She explained again that Lily, who'd helped on the beach, was her niece, and introduced Alice and her mother Sheila too. 'I've just been chatting to your young charges here. Such a terrible shame about the people who've been looking after them. I hope the gentleman – Mr Lister, was it? – wasn't too badly wounded.'

The young woman shook her hand. 'Yes, me too. That poor man. My heart goes out to him, and to his sister. I'm Demelza, by the way. Demelza Minear.' She nodded to the young man behind her, who leant forward with a grave smile to shake Violet's hand. 'This is my brother, Tristan.'

'What lovely names,' Alice burst out, staring at them both with sudden interest. 'Like something out of a medieval poem.'

Demelza's eyes widened. 'A medieval... Sorry?'

'Give over, pet, they don't want to hear about none of

your funny books,' Sheila said, a touch impatiently, before turning her attention back to Demelza and Tristan. 'Sorry about that. I'm her gran. Her head's up in the clouds, that one. Did you manage to sort somewhere new to stay for these young whippersnappers?'

'I'm afraid not.' Demelza gave the three evacuees an apologetic look. 'We explained the problem to the placement officer. We were lucky to find him in the office on a Saturday, but even so, he couldn't give us any good news. Apparently, everyone on their list has already taken their full allowance of evacuees.' She bit her lip. 'There might be a few places available in Marazion, just along the bay. But not for another week or so, when the officer has been able to visit a few homes and make enquiries. And it would mean splitting them up.'

'Splitting us up?' Eustace looked outraged. His arm came around his younger brother's shoulder in a protective gesture. 'Not bloody likely.'

'Language,' Sheila said sharply. 'That's a bad word and there's ladies present. You apologise right now, my lad.'

Eustace bridled a moment, but then his gaze fell before the stern look in her eyes. 'Sorry,' he muttered.

Violet was watching the young Cornish woman. 'So, what will happen to them? They can hardly go back to an empty house.'

'I don't mind an empty house,' Janice said.

'Yeah,' Eustace agreed. 'We often did for ourselves back in Barking. We can make sandwiches. Or boil an egg.'

'We don't have any eggs,' Janice pointed out scathingly.

'Well, we'll find summat to eat,' Eustace insisted, his face stubborn. 'We don't need grown-ups.'

41

Demelza glanced at Tristan, and then said, a slight blush on her face, 'Actually, you'll be coming home with us until things are settled. To our farm. It's not far, just a mile outside town. We'll make sure you're all right.'

'A farm?' Timothy's little face had lit up.

'I still don't know what Dad's going to say,' Demelza's brother said, looking uneasy, shaking his head.

'Bit of an ogre, is he?' Eustace demanded.

'Hey, none of that cheekiness,' Violet's mum told the boy, and tutted under her breath. 'Didn't your mother never teach you any manners?'

'Our mum's dead,' Janice shot back.

'And our grandma too,' Timothy added in his high-pitched voice. 'And we don't know where our dad is. He went off when we was little, and Mum said good riddance.'

Eustace nodded to this tale of woe. 'We got took into care. Only then they sent us down here.'

'Oh dear.' Sheila looked at Violet, her face puckering with ready tears. 'Poor little mites.'

Violet knew she was thinking of her own daughter, Betsy, lost in the Blitz. And she too felt instant sympathy for these children. But she was worried. From personal experience, she knew how awful it was to be housed with people who didn't really want you there.

Her gaze sought Tristan's a little shyly. 'Excuse me, I don't want to interfere, but did you mean your dad won't like it if you take this lot home with you?' She looked at Demelza too, including her in that question. 'It's none of my business, but … it might be better to ask him first, don't you think?'

Tristan glanced at his sister, saying, 'She's right, Demmy. It would be awful if Dad said no when we'd already got there. And you know what he's like when he's made his mind up. There'll be no budging him.'

'But they haven't got anywhere else to go,' Demelza pointed out, sounding tearful now.

Sheila took a deep breath. 'Oh yes, they have.' When Violet stared at her mother, she pulled a face. 'I'm not leaving three innocent children to go hungry in some empty house. Not when we've plenty of room at ours now Lily's gone.'

'Well, if you're sure…' Demelza blinked. 'That would certainly be better than my father blowing his top when we turn up with unwanted visitors in tow. But where do you live?'

Violet felt like she was going mad. Take three kids home with them on the bus? And without even asking Mr Cotterill if they could? Their employer had leased them the cottage they lived in, which belonged to Eastern House where Violet worked, now a government communications and listening post. George Cotterill was a good-natured man and was now married to their lovely friend Hazel, but even he had his limits. She only hoped he wouldn't throw them out.

'Porthcurno,' she said shortly, and wasn't surprised when Demelza looked at her in surprise. 'Yes, I know. It's miles away.'

'But it's more fun than Penzance,' her mum said hurriedly, smiling at the children. 'There's loads of soldiers, for starters. And long walks in the countryside. There's a nice little village schoolroom for the young 'uns too. Though Janice would have to take the bus into Penzance for big school.' She winked at the girl. 'You can sit with Alice on the bus; she's just started work at the school here as a teaching assistant.'

'And general dogsbody,' Alice put in drily.

With a wistful expression, Demelza turned to study the three young children. 'Well, I suppose that does sound better than them coming to us. But you'll have to speak to the placement officer and give him your name and address. There are ration books to take into account too, you see. And their things will need to be collected from Mr Lister's house. Janice has a spare key.'

'I'll go up and see the officer straightaway,' Sheila said eagerly, and bustled inside the building.

It was clear to Violet that her mother had the bit between her teeth on this one, and no amount of persuasion would deter her. Mum had been noticeably bored and restless lately, missing her busy café in Dagenham; no doubt looking after three high-spirited children would be just the boost she needed.

Violet could think of better things to do with her time than run around after a lively bunch of evacuees. But there was no point sticking her oar in. Not once Mum's mind was made up.

'How do you feel about moving to Porthcurno, kids?' Demelza asked, almost as though hoping they might rebel and beg to go home with her instead.

Silently, Janice sucked a plump, dark braid into her mouth and glared into the distance, obviously unimpressed with this new development.

Eustace picked up the stone he'd been kicking and pocketed it, a grin on his face.

'I like long bus rides,' Timothy announced, and blew his nose again.

CHAPTER FIVE

Demelza had not known what to do with the three evacuees once Lily had left her alone with them. She badly wanted to help, but had no real experience with children, and couldn't fathom what they were thinking from their fierce, mobile expressions that changed from minute to minute. While they were gathering up their buckets and spades, Tristan had come running up, his springy hair shining in the sunlight.

Her brother had been shocked by her muttered explanation, turning to watch the stretcher winding its way slowly back to the waiting ambulance while the woman in the flowery dress was being helped up the beach too.

'Good grief, Dem, but what exactly happened? Give me details. Nobody was killed, I hope?'

Briefly, she'd told him about Mr Lister's terrible wound, and his sister going into labour, and then had rushed through an explanation of how she'd offered to find new accommodation for three evacuees.

'Three who?' Her brother had stared at her, bemused

by this baffling information, and then swung on his heel to study the faces of Eustace, Timothy and Janice in turn. 'You don't mean … this lot?'

'Yes,' Demelza had said faintly.

'Good grief.'

'I'm sorry, I didn't know what else to say. It's an emergency.'

Tristan had studied her face, and then nodded slowly. 'Very well, when you put it like that… Look, I know the placement officer. Jim used to play in the football league before the war. We'll go and speak to him, if he's even in the office today. It is Saturday, after all.'

'And if he can't find them anywhere to live?'

'Demmy, you can't bring them home with us. Dad would have fifty fits. You know he hates visitors.'

'But look at their faces,' she'd whispered.

'For goodness' sake.' Her brother had rolled his eyes. 'Well, I suppose they'll have to come home with us if there's no help for it. But only for a few days, mind. It wouldn't do forever.'

They had walked up into town together, and soon located the Placement Office in the same grand old Victorian building that housed the Fire Guard Service. They'd left the children to wait outside rather than trail damp, sandy footprints all the way up to the first-floor office, but Demelza had kept glancing out of the window to check they were still there, so she'd seen the women approach them and had bristled inwardly, wondering what was going on below.

On their way down from the first-floor office, they'd passed several women laughing and chatting as they

46

headed up to the second floor of the tall red-brick building. Women in the neat, dark uniforms of the Fire Guard with helmets to match, marked with their official title so people knew not to interfere with their business.

'I wonder where they're going,' Demelza had said, craning her neck to watch them go.

'Up to their rooms, I expect. The unit has sleeping quarters here,' her brother had explained.

'You mean they live here? On their own? But they're … they're all women.'

'Yes.' Her younger brother had laughed at her expression. 'It's an all-women unit. Didn't you know that?'

'I must have done. I just didn't think… I mean, it's all so strange, isn't it?'

'That's the war for you.'

Still a little stunned, she'd tried not to stare as they walked past the unit's ground floor offices. The doors were all open down there, and she could see cupboards of equipment, with women checking through them or poring over maps on the walls. It seemed to be a busy but friendly atmosphere, all the women talking and smiling. And the uniform was really very smart, she thought enviously.

There was a large, typed notice on the door. She glanced at it curiously.

RECRUITING FOR FIRE WATCHERS.
Are you fit, female and preferably unmarried?
Then your country needs you!
Speak to our recruiting officer Jean
and do your bit for England.

Demelza immediately imagined herself in that uniform and helmet, walking the streets with the other women of the Penzance Fire Guard, and felt heat in her cheeks. How marvellous that would be, she thought, daring to indulge the fantasy for a moment. To be free and independent, working for the war effort like so many other women her age. Yes, it would be dangerous. But how much more exciting it would be than farm work! And if the Fire Watchers were allowed to stay here during their shifts, to be ready for whenever the air-raid sirens went off and they were needed for patrol, it would mean not living at home anymore, at least for part of the week.

Outside, they'd found the children talking to the three strangers she'd seen out of the window. And then, quite out of the blue, the tall, fair-haired woman had introduced herself as Violet, Lily's aunt, while her forthright mother had insisted on taking the kids home with them instead.

There had been nothing more to say.

Her grand plan for taking the unfortunate children home with them had been wrenched out of her hands, and it was with a sinking heart that she said her goodbyes to Janice, Eustace and Timothy, and walked back towards the sea front with Tristan in the brisk April sunshine.

'That was useful,' Tristan said, glancing back at the women who'd swooped on their charges like long-lost relatives.

'I really would have liked to take them home,' she admitted, feeling oddly tearful. It was silly, perhaps. But having three children to care for would have been a welcome change to her dreary routine of housework and minor chores around the farm.

'I know.' Tristan put his arm about her shoulder and

gave her a quick squeeze of reassurance. 'But don't kid yourself, sis. Dad would have gone spare at the mere sight of them. He'd have called them urchins and ragamuffins, and probably made them sleep in the barn. It would have been like the time you brought that stray cat home with you, the one with all the fleas and the bellyful of kittens. Only far, far worse, because the cat couldn't understand the insults he was yelling at her, but those kids certainly would have done.' Much taller than Demelza, despite being several years younger, her brother peered down into her face. 'It's better this way. Don't you think?'

'I suppose.'

'That's the ticket.' Tristan straightened with a chuckle, glancing back over his shoulder. 'Cheeky little things, aren't they?'

'No cheekier than us at that age, I daresay.'

He raised his eyebrows. 'I was never cheeky. Not to Mum, not to anyone.'

She was surprised; Tristan barely ever mentioned their late mother. And when he did, it was usually in the softest way possible, with a catch in his voice. Their mother's unexpected death had affected them both powerfully. But she often thought it had hurt Tristan the most, being so young at the time that he had never fully understood what had happened or why.

Though to be fair, Demelza didn't know why either. And there was no point asking their father, for he couldn't bear to hear his late wife's name spoken, let alone answer any questions about her death.

'No, you weren't cheeky. Quite right.' Demelza looked at him thoughtfully. 'You were always the quiet one, in fact. You never got into trouble. Out of the two of us, I was the brat.'

'Not much has changed there, then.' Her brother grinned at her fulminating stare and began to whistle an old Cornish ditty under his breath. 'Now, didn't you say you had some shopping to do while we're in town?'

At Penzance Hospital, Lily gave Mrs Maynard's hand another encouraging squeeze, and then left her to the rather less friendly ministrations of the duty midwife. Emily Maynard had been examined, after rather a lengthy delay, and declared to be in the early stages of labour by the ageing midwife, whose name was Sue and who smelt suspiciously of gin.

Noting a few signs of disorder that would never have passed muster at the convalescent home – not with eagle-eyed Matron on duty – Lily decided to hang around a little longer.

It was early evening by the time Lily finally took herself off to discover how Jeremy Lister was doing, on his sister's behalf, and was told that he had undergone emergency surgery to remove the bullet and been wheeled to a recovery room, still under sedation. It was while she was talking to another nurse outside his room that a doctor arrived and stopped in the corridor.

'Oops, that's the head doctor,' the nurse muttered, and hurried away on some remembered errand.

The head doctor was a tall, distinguished-looking man in his mid-fifties, a stethoscope about his neck, his white coat somewhat crumpled but perfectly clean. His silvered hair sat sleekly across a domed forehead, his eyes a gentle blue, but with deeply crinkled edges as though he were permanently narrowing them at people, or possibly just smiling all the time. She hoped it was from smiling, though the way the other nurse had bolted at his arrival made that seem unlikely.

'You're the nurse who found Mr Lister on the beach, I take it?' the doctor asked, looking Lily up and down in surprise. 'You're much younger than I expected.'

'I was admitted for my basic training earlier than usual,' she explained. 'Because of the shortage of nurses.'

'Where did you do your training?'

'On the job' she admitted. 'I'm still too young to be admitted to a basic nursing course. But as soon as I'm old enough, I want to go to the Queen Elizabeth Hospital in Birmingham. A friend of mine went there for their three-month course,' she added, thinking of Eva Ryder, now happily married as Mrs Carmichael, 'and she said it was absolutely marvellous.'

'Ah yes, I know the place. Good reputation, sound practice.' Actually far from being frightening, he had a twinkle in his blue eyes that she liked; he reminded her of Doctor Edmund Lanyon recently retired from his post at the convalescent home where she worked, who'd always made the nurses feel part of the team rather than merely tolerating them. She couldn't stand stuffy doctors who thought they knew better than the nurses. 'Well, let me congratulate you, Nurse...' He paused meaningfully.

'Nurse Fisher, sir.'

'Let me congratulate you, Nurse Fisher, on a job well done. Abdominal wounds are the worst. Huge amounts of soft, vulnerable tissue, blood vessels galore, and when they tear...' He made a face. 'Well, without your presence of mind, that man would probably be dead right now. Instead of which, with a dash of luck, he should make a full recovery in time.'

These words sent a warm thrill of pleasure through her. She'd feared she might have made a terrible gaffe, as Mrs Maynard had accused her at the time, by moving the wounded man and exposing the wound so she could assess it. But apparently that had been the correct thing to do.

'I'm so glad,' she said. 'Well done.'

'Oh no, you must congratulate yourself. To the victor, the spoils. You were the one who compressed the wound and slowed down the rate of blood loss just enough to give the poor fellow a sporting chance of survival. I was just the chap who came in later to fish out the metal and sew him up again.' The smile in his eyes finally reached his mouth, and he held out a hand to shake hers. 'Excellent work.'

'Thank you,' she said shyly.

'I'm Jerrard, by the way. Doctor Jerrard. In charge of this...' He paused again, this time turning his head slightly to take in his surroundings, and his lips thinned, a look almost of disappointment in his face. 'Facility,' he finished. 'For my sins.'

Lily said nothing. But she could guess why he didn't think much of the hospital. It was both cramped and poorly lit, and somehow chaotic and rambling at the same time. She imagined it had not been built to be a hospital. Or else the architect had been rather eccentric.

'You're not Penzance-based,' he continued, frowning, 'or I'd have met you already. And that's not a Cornish accent, is it?'

'Well spotted.'

'So, where do you ply your trade, then? Not London, presumably.' When she stared at him blankly, Dr Jerrard pulled another wry face and said, 'Forgive me. Where do you work? Which hospital?'

'Symmonds Hall Convalescent Home for Wounded Servicemen.'

'In St. Ives? Old Edmund Lanyon's place? Well, no wonder you've such quick wits. The man's practically a legend in Cornwall. Is he still practising? I heard he'd had a heart attack.'

'Dr Lanyon has just retired,' she admitted, nodding. 'Or semi-retired. It's been quite hard to persuade him to take a back seat, actually.'

'I can imagine. Though I've heard good things of his grandson, too. Is he in charge there now?'

'Dr Lewis, yes. That's what we call him. So we don't get confused between the two Lanyons.'

'Of course. I'm sure he'll be as exacting as his grandfather.' Dr Jerrard made a humming noise under his breath, looked her up and down again, and then said, 'Any chance I could tempt you to jump ship?'

'I'm sorry?'

'I need nurses who know what they're doing. Nurses I can rely on in a pinch. Most of mine are either on their last legs, or barely skilled enough to know a bed pan from a...' He stopped, seeing her shocked expression, and apologised. 'Do forgive me. Of course, all nurses who haven't gone off to the front are worth their weight in gold, and I'm grateful for every one of them in this hospital. But I've not nearly enough of them to run this place safely.' His smile turned cajoling. 'So, if you ever fancy a change of scene from St. Ives, the offer stands.'

Lily laughed, sincerely flattered, and thanked him again. 'That's very kind of you. But if I ever fancy a change, it's likely to be retraining as a midwife.'

His eyebrows rose. 'A midwife?'

Lily felt flustered, never having intended to say such a thing. But midwifery had been on her mind more and more lately. In the midst of all this gloom, helping to bring forth new life seemed so worthwhile.

'Yes, well, it was very nice to meet you,' she said uneasily, and hurried back to Mrs Maynard, who was progressing nicely in her labour.

'Your brother's likely to make a full recovery, the doctor says,' Lily told her, and was rewarded with a tearful smile.

'Oh, thank you, thank you!' Emily Maynard flopped back against her pillows, running a hand over her damp forehead. 'Such good news. You're an angel.'

'Nonsense,' Lily said briskly, with a glance at Sue, who was reading a magazine in a corner of the labour room, barely paying any attention to her patient. 'Well, I'd best be off now. Or I'll miss the last bus home, and that would never do. Good luck with the baby.' She patted Emily's hand. 'You're doing brilliantly. Just remember to breathe.'

'Well, I can hardly forget to do that,' Emily replied, looking almost incredulous at this advice.

Lily tried not to smile. This was her first baby, after all. And she was going through labour as a widow, she reminded herself, which must be an awful experience for the poor woman.

'You'll see what I mean,' she said kindly. 'Deep, calm

breaths. That should see you through the worst of it.'

As she headed out of the hospital in the direction of the bus stop that would eventually take her back to her aunt's house in Porthcurno, Lily caught a glimpse of Dr Jerrard in the distance, standing outside a side entrance of the hospital on his own, smoking a cigarette. To her chagrin, he spotted her and raised a hand in farewell. Lily waved back, self-conscious and uncertain, and then hurried on back towards the town centre, her heels clacking on the pavement.

If you ever fancy a change of scene from St. Ives, the offer stands.

She was secretly pleased that a senior doctor had appreciated her talents so much he was willing to upset another doctor by nabbing her. As long as that was all it was, and no funny business. She knew what some doctors could be like, with hands everywhere and not afraid to use their position to seduce junior nurses. Matron had been keen to enforce that message from the first day she arrived in St. Ives.

But Lily got the feeling Dr Jerrard hadn't seen her in that light; he was merely desperate for better staff in Penzance. And having seen their resident midwife, she could understand why.

Unfortunately for him, Lily thought, she didn't fancy a 'change of scene'. She was very happy and comfortable working at the convalescent home. All of her friends were there, especially her best friend Mary Stannard, and the place was as cosy as a pair of old slippers to her now. Besides, there was Sister Rose's wedding to Dr Lewis coming up soon, and she wouldn't want to risk missing their special day.

Still, it had been a flattering offer, hadn't it?

CHAPTER SIX

Porthcurno, South Cornwall, late April 1942

Arriving late at Porthcurno's Eastern House for the third day running, Violet dashed through the door marked HOUSEKEEPER and threw off her hat and coat. 'Bloomin' kids,' she muttered as she straightened her uniform and checked her seams were straight.

Her mum's wonderful idea of rehousing the three London evacuees in their tiny cottage in the heart of Porthcurno village had not gone exactly to plan. For a start, Alice was not terribly keen on Janice, who in turn was a slippery article, never there for chores and always talking back in a rude way when reprimanded. Then there were the two boys, who kept Violet awake at night, making a racket or wrestling each other with thuds, bangs, and occasional shrieks.

'Hush now, Vi, they're just kids,' Mum had told her firmly when Violet tried to upbraid them. 'There's no harm in them.'

At which Alice had buried her head crossly in a book and Violet had been forced to bite her tongue for the umpteenth time, lest she spark a bitter row with her mum.

'*No harm in them*. Huh!' Violet settled her starched white cap on her blonde locks and made a grotesque face at herself in the mirror, sticking out her tongue, rolling her eyes and making a weird groaning noise like Frankenstein's monster. 'Oh yes, Mum, no harm at all.'

Luckily, there was nobody to see her pulling funny faces, hidden away as she was in the private office she'd been allotted along with the title of 'Housekeeper'. True, her 'office' wasn't much bigger than a broom cupboard but she could at least be alone there.

Violet still had to pinch herself some days, to be sure she hadn't dreamt her promotion from chief mopper-upper to Housekeeper and would soon wake up, still a lowly cleaner in a pinny. In her white cap and immaculate uniform, with its smart charcoal skirt and white blouse, and perfectly seamed nylons too, she certainly looked the part. But her wide blue eyes told a different story, always a bit panicked in case something appalling might happen for which she'd get the blame.

All of her life she'd got the blame when things went wrong. Why should now be any different, just because she'd landed a plum job and was the envy of the other cleaning staff? When she'd first agreed to take over the role, she'd been proud as Punch, being elevated to Housekeeper status, and at such an important facility too. Eastern House was one of the country's top-secret listening posts, with important visitors constantly coming and going, all hush-hush and often under the cover of darkness. Thankfully, the military side of the operation was looked after by army staff, so she didn't have to worry too much about the secret tunnels housing sensitive equipment that extended deep into the cliff, where the government personnel worked. Instead, she was in charge of making sure accommodation and public rooms were clean and in tip-top condition, that meals appeared on time and were nutritious, and all staff did what they were supposed to at the correct time. Which was complicated enough, she thought, without adding all the top-secret business to her plate.

Being Housekeeper was like being queen of all she surveyed, with this starched cap as her crown. Violet *ought* to have been riotously happy in her new job. Yet she wasn't. Quite the opposite, in fact. Because it had turned out she hated responsibility. She hated having to boss her former friends about. She hated knowing they were all moaning about her behind her back, just as she herself had moaned about the previous housekeeper.

And she was constantly on edge in case she forgot something vital or messed up, and England lost the war because of it. Which was ludicrous and silly, even she had to admit that. Nobody lost a war because a housekeeper forgot to change the flowers in the guest quarters. Not even if Mr Winston Churchill himself were to turn up on the doorstep, and personally complain about wilting peonies. Though it had been rumoured that he might indeed visit Eastern House soon, so that wasn't beyond the bounds of belief.

Someone knocked at the door in a peremptory manner.

'What on earth…?' Violet demanded, and then hurriedly corrected herself, trying to sound suitably posh and like a housekeeper. 'I mean, do come in.'

Mr Cotterill stuck his head around the door. He was the well-dressed gent who ran Eastern House with an easy smile that hid a will of iron. His dark hair was slightly silvered at his temple, which made him look older than he was, which couldn't be much more than his early thirties.

'Bad time?'

'Oh, hello, George,' she said in relief, turning away from the mirror. George being married to her friend Hazel, she found it hard at times to remember he was her boss. 'Nothing like that, no. I was just...' She paused and glanced at the wall clock. 'Blast, did I forget a senior staff meeting again?'

'I'm afraid so.'

'I'm sorry, I've been at sixes and sevens this week. It's them kids ... the evacuees. I was late getting them off to school this morning because they were playing up as usual, and I left this week's schedule at home.' She saw him frowning and added quickly, 'You was ever so kind to let us put the kids up at the cottage, by the way. Mum wants you to know how grateful she is. Poor little mites. They've had a rough go of it, and no mistake.'

'Yes, I'm sure.' George cleared his throat, looking awkward. 'But if you could remember to call me Mr Cotterill when we're at work? And I'll call you Miss Hopkins.'

'Sorry, I plain forgot what we agreed.' Violet could have kicked herself. '*Mr Cotterill*, of course. I'll remember next time, honest.'

'Thank you.' George Cotterill hesitated. 'Look, the fact is, I've had a complaint about the children.'

Violet's mouth compressed. 'A complaint?'

Her mind immediately leapt to old Arnold Newton, who ran the small shop in Porthcurno. His premises were only a three-minute walk from their cottage, and her mum had already had a few run-ins with the man, who claimed the evacuees had been nicking fruit and veg off the trestle table in front of his store.

But apparently it wasn't Arnold Newton this time.

'I'm afraid they've been running amok around the village, even sneaking past the guards to get onto the beach. You know the whole coast here has been mined. It would be too awful if one of them set off a mine and was maimed or killed. That's why the beach is off bounds to everyone except the military.'

'Oh, my gawd.' Violet shook her head in embarrassed despair. 'I'm so sorry, Ge— Mr Cotterill. I'll speak to them tonight.'

'See that you do.' He went out, but then popped his head in again, adding, 'And you did miss a senior staff meeting this morning. If you've lost this week's schedule, just ask my secretary for a replacement sheet. These staff meetings can be a bother, I know, but it's important to attend so we're all on the same page, yes?'

'Yes, Mr Cotterill,' she agreed, her heart sinking at the reproof in his voice.

After he'd gone, Violet sat behind her desk, determined not to feel overwhelmed by the daily meetings she had to remember or the heap of paperwork that awaited her attention. It was lonely work without the camaraderie of her mates in the cleaning crew, but she could do this job. She just needed to get more organised and keep her boss happy by following the rules.

'Yes, sir ... no, sir.' She dragged the first document towards her, picked up a pencil and furiously began to tick off a list of torn or missing linen to be replaced. 'Three bags full, sir.'

* * *

On a fine spring evening at the hill farm above Penzance, rooting through storage room clutter in search of some old material she could reuse for a patchwork quilt, Demelza came across an old chest that had belonged to her mother. Inside, she discovered a hoard of old letters, notes and recipes, plus a dusty, leather-bound journal with her mother's signature written in faded ink across the fly-leaf.

Opening this book gingerly, she flicked through a few handwritten pages, noting the various dates at the top of each new entry, and realised with a shock that it was her mother's private diary, and that she'd kept it for roughly the two to three years before she'd died.

Hearing her father below, stamping in from the fields with the dogs, she bundled the journal up with the scraps of material she'd found and took it hurriedly to her bedroom. There, she secreted the book under her pillow, determined to look at it as soon as she could be alone.

'Where's my supper?' her father demanded, looking round when she appeared. He was standing at the sink, boots off and his braces down, rinsing mud off his hands. 'Come on, girl. I'm starving here. My stomach thinks my throat's been cut.'

The two black-and-white collies muscled around her, whining and hoping for cooking scraps as usual. When they saw that she was empty-handed, they ran to their corner instead to watch proceedings.

'There's a pie warming in the range,' she said, bristling at his tone, 'and there's no need to speak to me like I'm a servant.'

Drying his hands on a tea towel, he turned to stare at her. 'I beg your pardon, Missy? Which of us has been out on the farm since before dawn, with only a pasty and a bottle of beer to stave off hunger? When I walk in of an evening, I expect to see my supper on the table, or at least ready to be served. Not *warming in the range.*'

Demelza glared at him, her cheeks flushed, her head fit to burst with all the furious words she wanted to yell at him. Her brother, who had followed their father in and was dragging off his own muddy boots in the kitchen doorway, shook his head silently at her.

She knew what that meant.

Dad was in a foul mood and looking for a fight.

'Well?' her father prompted, his eyes narrowed on her face. 'If you've something to say, spit it out. Don't stand there like an idiot.'

He was deliberately goading her, hoping for an excuse to raise his hand to her. Shaking away her fury, Demelza took a deep, unsteady breath and went to the range to check the pie. It was nearly done. She closed the door again, hoping she hadn't lost all the heat, thrust a few more sticks into the burner, and turned to finish preparing the veg.

'Dinner will be ready in fifteen minutes,' she told him. 'There's fresh tea in the pot.' When he didn't move, she poured out a mug for him and added a dash of milk, wishing he would leave her in peace. 'Aunt Sarah is sitting by the fire in the snug. She's had a bad day, poor thing. Lots of aches and pains. Why don't you join her and smoke a pipe while you wait?'

'Smoke a pipe *before* supper?' Her father's laughter was scathing. 'You've bats in your attic, girl.' But he took the mug and sloped off into the snug to see his sister, whistling to the dogs to follow him. 'Here, Pip. Here, Sam.'

Tristan finished washing his own hands and nodded to her. 'That was wise. Aunt Sarah will calm him down.'

'What's happened?'

'We lost a lamb today. Stillborn.' He sounded dejected. 'Cord was wound twice about its neck. Nothing we could have done.'

'Oh no, poor thing.' Demelza hugged herself. They always lost one or two during lambing season but her father could never resign himself to that. 'No wonder he's in one of his tempers. How's the ewe?'

'She'll survive.'

'Thank goodness for that, at least.'

Demelza put a few handfuls of chopped cabbage taken from their own cottage garden on to boil. She'd sown the seeds while there was still snow on the ground and feared they might rot in the cold, wet soil. But the vegetable had thrived, and now most nights there was cabbage for supper.

Tristan pulled out a chair and sat heavily at the kitchen table to gulp down a mug of weak tea. She knew he preferred it strong, but with rationing so tight, they never had enough tea leaves to make a proper brew these days.

'Tris,' she ventured as she stirred the gravy pan, 'what would you think of me signing up for the Fire Guard?'

When he said nothing, she turned to find him staring at her as though she'd sprouted two heads.

'What?' she asked defensively. 'They need new recruits for watching during air raids and putting out small fires. There was a notice on the door. Didn't you see it when we went in?'

'I saw it,' Tristan admitted. 'But that's beside the point. It's dangerous work.'

'I don't mind a bit of danger. We are at war, after all.'

He thought for a moment, and then shrugged. 'I know what you mean. It's not been easy watching my friends from school days enlisting and going off to do their bit. But what we do here is important too. We're feeding the nation. And until Dad agrees to take on some Land Girls, we're going to need you here on the farm.'

'But it might only be a few nights a week. I could do both, couldn't I?'

'That doesn't sound very practical, sis. You'd be exhausted, up half the night on fire watch, and then working here during the day. Farming's hard labour. You have to put your whole heart into it, or not at all.' Tris leant back in his chair, looking up at her with a worried frown in his eyes. 'Lord knows, I'm the last person to tie you down to the farm if you don't want to be here. But we talked about this, didn't we? We agreed it wouldn't work.'

'You mean, you said no. That's not the same as agreeing, Tristan.'

'All right. What about Father?'

She returned to the gravy, which was bubbling and thickening. 'What about him?'

'Demmy, please...'

'No, I can't waste any more of my life here, getting yelled at all the time, with never a "please" or "thank you", no matter how hard I try.' She took the gravy off the heat and turned to strain the steaming cabbage through the new colander they'd bought in town. 'This is what I want,' she added stubbornly, not looking at him.

'What is?'

She jerked in shock, realising her father was standing

in the kitchen doorway, his sister leaning on her stick by his side, and her hand shook, splashing hot cabbage water over her knuckles. With a cry of pain, she stared down at her pink, smarting hand and sucked in her breath, all of her nerve endings screaming.

'For God's sake, don't just stand there.' Tristan seized her hand and thrust it under the tap, running cold water over the scalded flesh. 'What do you think you're doing?' he asked under his breath. 'I told you, this isn't the best day to be going up against him. Just drop it, would you?'

'What are you two whispering about?' their father demanded.

'I ... I was clumsy, that's all.' Demelza wetted a dish cloth and wrapped it around her hurt hand. 'Go and sit at the table, Dad. You've got your wish. Supper's ready to serve.'

To her surprise, her father didn't pursue the matter but helped Aunt Sarah to her seat, and then went quietly to his place at the head of the kitchen table.

While she spooned out the vegetables, Tristan hovered about as though she were an invalid, even fetching the pie from the range so she wouldn't have to put her wrapped-up hand near the heat.

She saw his encouraging smile, and realised her brother was relieved because he thought she'd changed her mind about applying for war work.

But she hadn't.

She'd only postponed the awful moment when she'd be forced to tell her family she was leaving the farm, and why. She was determined to do it. All she needed was a little courage.

CHAPTER SEVEN

St. Ives, West Cornwall, early May 1942

The assembled townsfolk gasped in rapture at the sight of Sister Rose Gray entering the parish church in a gorgeous pale green wedding dress, the frock complementing her red hair perfectly, a spray of delicate white flowers clasped in her hands. Lily, squeezed into one of the front pews in the parish church at St. Ives, watched with breathless excitement as Rose shook out her dress and then began to walk down the aisle at a slow and majestic pace, on the arm of retired doctor Edmund Lanyon, in the absence of a father to give her away.

Rose and her sister had grown up in the orphanage next to the convalescent home, all owned by the wealthy Symmonds family. Last year, she and Eva Ryder, a fellow nurse and one of Lily's dearest friends, had discovered that Mr and Mrs Treverrick, the couple running the orphanage, had been starving and mistreating the children. After a covert investigation, they had brought the matter to the attention of old Lady Symmonds, who had been horrified and very grateful to them for exposing the truth. The Treverricks had been sacked on the spot, and the children were thankfully all recovered now. Though Lily knew only too well that some scars ran deeper than the skin.

Now Rose was giving up her beloved nursing to get married and run the orphanage instead, while Dr Lewis Lanyon, her husband-to-be, continued to serve the convalescent home as their senior doctor. His elderly grandfather, Dr Edmund Lanyon, giving Rose away, still popped onto the wards from time to time, of course. Since his heart attack at Christmas, he'd been warned not to work full-time. But everyone knew Dr Edmund was sweet on Matron, and so couldn't seem to stay away from the place.

Dr Lewis, waiting for his bride beside the altar, turned to watch her too, his face full of pride, his eyes shining with tears.

The groom cut an impressive figure in his sharp pin-striped suit and his short dark hair slicked back, his smart leather shoes polished to a high sheen, and a pristine white handkerchief peeking out of his top pocket. And if he was much taller than his diminutive bride, nobody there would have dared comment, for Rose was notoriously sensitive about her height and always had a sharp rebuke at hand for anyone foolish enough to joke about it.

It was clear to everyone that they only had eyes for each other. And not surprisingly, for they had waited months for this moment. Lily knew how much it had cost Rose to stay single and on the wards when every fibre of her being yearned to take her place beside Dr Lewis as his lawfully wedded wife. But with the war on, and the shortage of staff at the convalescent home, Rose had been determined to put duty first until a suitable replacement could be found for her position.

Luckily, three new nurses had started work at the home in recent weeks, two of them undergoing training on the job, but one – Mathilda Buckley – had been in nursing for ten years and was already a Sister. Mathilda had transferred from a hospital in Bristol to keep an eye on her elderly parents in St. Ives, and so Rose had finally been able to hand in her notice and agreed to have the banns read, secure in the knowledge that her place would be taken up by capable hands.

'Oh, look at them, bless their hearts,' Mary whispered beside her, and nudged Lily. 'And the dear little kiddies too…'

Rose had elected for five children from the orphanage to follow in her wake, three bridesmaids in pretty lace-trimmed frocks – Lily herself had helped cut up a pair of Lady Symmonds' lace curtains to make the frills – and two page boys in their Sunday best.

One of the boys was Jimmy, a high-spirited nine-year-old whose cruel ill-treatment at the hands of the Treverricks had spurred Rose on to investigate the orphanage. With his courage and cheeky demeanour, Jimmy had soon gained a place in the hearts of everyone at the convalescent home. Best of all, he was soon to be adopted by the happy couple, and Lily knew how much Rose was looking forward to calling Jimmy her son.

The priest smiled benignly at this vision of loveliness, and stepped forward, prayer book in hand. 'Dearly beloved, we are gathered here in the sight of God and in the face of this congregation…'

Mary heaved a sigh of deep satisfaction. 'About time too,' she said in Lily's ear, and was promptly shushed by Matron, seated right behind them.

Lily suppressed a grin, watching with approval as two of her favourite people in the world were joined in holy matrimony. She felt an odd twinge of pain though, knowing that she herself would never get married and thus never get to walk down the aisle in a lovely dress like Rose. Not after the things she'd suffered – being molested by her uncle – and the way she now always instinctively responded with horror and revulsion to being kissed. No man should have to put up with a wife who couldn't bear to be kissed. It wouldn't be fair to either of them.

But love wasn't everything, Lily told herself stoutly, and tried hard to believe it. Devoting her life to nursing and helping others instead of being a wife and mother wasn't so bad a trade-off, was it?

'What's that noise?' Mary hissed in her ear.

Lily stared at her friend, distracted, and then heard it too. An aeroplane in the distance. Several other people had clearly also heard the engine drone and were looking up as though they could see through the church roof and tower and identify the kind of plane that was approaching. The vicar, on the point of concluding the main part of the service, paused and flicked a glance towards the stained-glass windows.

Dr Lewis tensed and gazed down at Rose, who held tight to his arm.

'I pronounce that they be...' The vicar cleared his throat, his gaze on his restless flock, some of whom had actually left their seats and were peering out of the porched church door. 'Man and wife together,' he concluded, 'in the name of the Father, and of the Son, and of the Holy Ghost. Amen.'

Among the congregation, there was a rumble of approval and 'Amen's from those still seated.

'We may have to curtail the blessing somewhat,' the vicar said uneasily, 'and move straight to the vestry.'

But as Dr and Mrs Lanyon turned towards the vestry to sign the register and complete the official paperwork, a siren went off nearby and the church began to empty.

'I'm sorry, you'll have to sign later,' the vicar told the couple, his brow furrowed. 'We'd better shelter in the crypt until the air raid is over. All are welcome to join us,' he said, raising his voice to be heard and including a meaningful look at all the children from the orphanage who had turned out to see their new director married.

Rose turned to Lily and Mary. Blushing fiercely, the new bride had tears in her eyes, and not for joy.

'Damn and blast these Germans,' Rose exclaimed, much to the vicar's discomfort. 'Is nothing sacred?' There was fear in her eyes too as she surveyed the orphans, some of them as young as six years old. But she forced a tremulous smile to her lips. 'Come on, kiddies. Time to go underground again. Maybe there are some games we can play while we wait.'

Her new husband turned to help his elderly grandfather down the aisle, while the vicar checked for any stragglers.

'Don't worry, Rose,' Lily said as they all hurried along the arched passageway that led to the crypt entrance. 'It's probably just another of their disruptive fly-bys.' But a terrible bang shook the old church to its foundations and sent them all scurrying for the steps down into the crypt.

'Or not,' she said under her breath to Mary, her heart thumping fit to burst. 'Goodness, that was close.'

'Somewhere in the town, do you think?' Mary whispered.

'I hope not.' Lily pushed away her fear and kept smiling, if only for the sake of the children, who were looking scared now. If there was a direct hit on the church, they would all be buried alive under the rubble and not dug out for days. Maybe even weeks. It didn't bear thinking about. 'How about a sing-song, eh? Just like we do at the orphanage when there's an air raid.'

The vicar flicked a switch, illuminating the church crypt with a handful of dusty lamps around the walls. But the place was still damp and dirty, and smelt of old bones.

'Good idea, Lily.' Rose sat on an old tomb in the crypt, gathered a small girl up onto the flouncy knee of her green wedding dress, and began to sing in a husky voice, '*Row, row, row your boat, Gently down the stream... Merrily, merrily, merrily, merrily. Life is but a dream.*'

As all the other children gradually joined in, followed by the vicar and Dr Lewis, who was looking both fiercely proud of his new wife and apprehensive about the air raid, Lily raised her voice in song too. And as Lily sang, she watched her newly wedded friend with awe and admiration. When she first came to St. Ives, she'd thought Rose an awful bore and even a complete tyrant, ruling the wards with a heart of stone. But she knew better these days. To get married one minute, and the next be singing your heart out in a cold, damp crypt while enemy aircraft circled overhead, aiming to obliterate you in a rain of deadly fire. To have your perfect wedding ruined and still be able to smile and comfort others...

That took real courage, Lily thought, and hoped she might one day have a chance to show as much pluck and determination herself.

Thankfully, the air raid passed off without any serious damage to the town, and only a few minor injuries from flying debris. In the convalescent home during the week following the wedding, it felt strange not to see Sister Rose bustling about the wards as usual. But she knew that Rose – who had forgone a proper honeymoon for one night in a posh seaside hotel with her husband and was already back at work – could be found next door in the orphanage if she ever wanted to drop by for a cosy chinwag.

'Oh, Lily,' Mary called to her in passing from under a towering heap of fresh bed sheets bound for the upstairs linen closet, 'um … Matron was looking for you earlier.'

'Do you need a hand?' Lily asked, worried.

'No, but I'd kill for a cuppa.' Mary staggered up the stairs, her load teetering. 'See you at lunch?'

'Wouldn't miss it for the world.'

Matron was looking for her? She could guess what that was probably about. As she splashed her hands and face in the nurses' washroom and straightened her cap, Lily wondered what life would be like with three new nurses on the wards. It was wonderful to have a full complement of staff at last, instead of being constantly shorthanded. But she knew the two younger girls would need extra training, which would normally have been undertaken by Rose but might fall to her or Mary at this rate. No doubt that was why Matron wanted to see her.

Oh, she did miss Rose. It was tempting to nip next door

while the wards were quiet and see how she was getting on. But she expected her friend would be in an absolute whirl for the next few weeks at least as she settled down to running the orphanage as a married woman, and interrupting her just for a chat and a slice of cake would be unprofessional.

Rose and Dr Lewis planned to move into their quarters at the orphanage over the summer, but for now they were leaving the orphans in the care of Lady Symmonds and her companion, Sonya, each night, while Rose drove home every evening with the doctor to their house in St. Ives. Lily felt sure that the temporary arrangement had been made to ensure Dr Edmund, still recovering from his heart attack at Christmas, would not be left alone. But Rose had whispered to her after the wedding that they had a plan to ensure Dr Edmund would be well cared for after their permanent move to the orphanage.

Matron came out of her office as Lily passed it, a folded sheet of paper in her hand. 'Just the girl I need to see.' She waved her inside with an impatient look. 'I've had a letter about you from on high. Can you guess what it's about?'

Oh Lord, Lily thought, blushing. What could she have done this time?

'Not a clue, Matron.'

Matron winced at her uncouth speech. Or perhaps her accent. Lily was never quite sure what she had done to offend Matron, but she was always wincing whenever she opened her mouth.

'Hands behind your back and stand up straight, girl. And try to speak properly. You mean you *don't know*, Lily.'

'That's what I said, ain't it?'

Matron winced again. 'It's a letter from the District

Hospital Board, requesting your transfer to the hospital in Penzance. Why, I cannot imagine. But it appears a Dr Jerrard there has asked for you by name.'

'Gawd.'

For once, Matron didn't pull a face. 'Well, precisely what I thought. It's a very odd state of affairs. I've seen transfer requests before in my time, but never from a minor establishment like this to a larger hospital, only the other way around.' She peered at Lily intently. 'You're sure you don't have an explanation for this? Do you know Dr Jerrard?'

Embarrassed by her piercing stare, Lily admitted to her encounter with the doctor in Penzance, and what had happened there.

'But I don't know why he's writing to ask me to transfer, Matron,' she added hotly, 'because I told him straight, I weren't interested. I said all my friends were here, and St. Ives is where I wanted to stay.'

'I'm much gratified to hear it, Nurse Fisher. Unfortunately, it's not so much a request as an order.' Matron passed her the letter, which looked very official, and was short and to the point. 'There's nothing I can do. It's the war, you see. They can make you go anywhere they want. No questions asked.'

Lily read the letter twice, and then handed it back, suppressing the urge to swear. 'But it's not fair, Matron. This is … well, it's my home.'

Matron's face softened, and she came round the desk to give Lily a vague, patting hug. 'My dear girl…' Straightening up, she shook her head. 'Well, there's nothing to be done, I suppose. But at least there's an offer of free accommodation just a short walk from the hospital.'

Lily said nothing, thinking bitterly of all the friends she would be leaving behind. Damn that Dr Jerrard; if only she had never gone to the hospital with Mrs Maynard, none of this would be happening.

'Do you know anybody in Penzance?' Matron enquired. Lily shook her head.

'Well, you're a young girl and friendly enough. I'm sure you'll soon make new chums among the nurses in Penzance.'

Lily gave her an uncertain look but merely asked, 'That letter said within the week. Does it really have to be so soon?'

'Yes, but let's say Friday. That gives you a few days in which to train up those two new junior nurses in their duties.' Matron sighed. 'Such a shame. And when we've just lost Sister Rose too.'

Since Matron and Sister Rose had forever been at loggerheads, Lily found it hard to believe her fake look of wistfulness.

A bell rang down the corridor.

'Ah, time for my morning inspection of the wards,' Matron said, and checked her reflection in the mirror, patting her hair and pursing her lips, before pausing on her way out the door. 'Look, I'm sure you'll do very well in Penzance, Nurse Fisher. But if you take my advice, you'll keep things on a professional footing with the doctors there. Especially this Dr Jerrard.' She shook her head at Lily. 'Asking for a nurse by name, indeed.' Her thin, hand-drawn eyebrows soared. 'Quite, quite irregular.'

CHAPTER EIGHT

Home from work, Violet hooked her hat over the stand, kicked off her shoes, and traipsed into the cosy back room of their cottage in Porthcurno, calling out cheerily, 'Home, Mum!' before stopping dead.

Joe Postbridge was sitting in the armchair opposite her mother, his grey woollen cap on his lap, an awkward expression on his face. He came to his feet in a hurry as he realised who had come in, putting on his cap and then whipping it off again. 'Miss Hopkins.'

Not 'Violet', then?

It seemed they were back to polite formalities. But it had been a while, she supposed. No reason to assume he still cared for her, after all. She willed herself to smile and stay calm, but she'd forgotten how creamy his Cornish accent sounded. And that deep voice...

Joe was looking at the rug rather than at her, twisting his cap in his hands. 'How d'you do?'

'Very well, thank you,' she replied automatically. 'How do you do?'

He was standing stiffly and almost to attention, she noted, though his left leg – partly a metal replacement, after he'd been wounded in action in the Navy – was obviously giving him problems, for he winced as he shifted his weight off that foot.

'I'm all right, Miss Hopkins.' Slowly, he lifted his gaze to her face and stared at her intensely. 'Forgive the intrusion. I only stopped by to see how you was all getting on. But I don't want to hold you up. Not at supper time. I'd better see myself out.'

'Nonsense,' her mum said comfortably, already rising from her chair. 'Supper can wait a while. I'll freshen the pot, shall I?' She bore away the tea tray, and jerked her head significantly at Violet, indicating that she should stay and talk to Joe. 'Back in a jiffy.'

Violet had first met Joe Postbridge down on the beach at Penzance last summer. On that occasion, Lily and Alice had been with her, and they'd all been paddling barefoot. It had been a shock to be caught in such an undignified situation, but Joe hadn't seemed to mind, nor had his mother, a friendly, smiling woman whom Violet would have liked to get to know better.

But the blasted Jerries had ruined everything. One awful night last summer, a German bomber had flown along the coast, looking for the listening post at Porthcurno, but by some dreadful error, had bombed Joe's farm instead. His mother had died in the attack. Added to that, rumours about Violet had already been flying around Porthcurno at the time, thanks to a nasty lad from back home in Dagenham who'd been posted to Eastern House and bumped into Violet by accident. Patrick Dullaghan, a born mischief-maker, had started whispers that Violet was a traitor, all because her brother-in-law, Ernst, was half-German.

'How are you getting on at the farm?' she asked, striving to hide her hot cheeks by fussing unnecessarily with the sofa cushions. She wished her heart would stop thumping. They'd only shared a few kisses, after all; it was hardly the stuff of one of Alice's heady romance novels. 'I hear you've taken on some help.'

Joe had heard Patrick's rumours and, just for the briefest of periods, blamed her for his mother's death. Not that she held that against him. His father had died young, so he and his mother had been very close. Losing her so suddenly had hit Joe hard; Violet imagined this first winter without her had been very lonely indeed. Especially given that he was new to farming, having inherited the property last year when his uncle died.

'That's right,' Joe agreed, still on his feet, looking decidedly uncomfortable. 'I've three Land Girls just started this month. They're not bad.' His smile was grave. 'Hardworking lasses, stronger than I expected, and they've had some training.' He paused. 'To be honest, it's been good to have company again.'

She'd later learned that brave Ernst was working for the British government behind enemy lines. But since her brother-in-law's safety depended on secrecy, she could hardly explain any of that to Joe. Worst of all, Violet had not been able to inform Lily and Alice that their beloved father was not an enemy spy, but a hero, and still very much alive.

Having rearranged the cushions to her satisfaction,

Violet sat on the sofa and stared up at him glumly. Back in February, when Joe had shown up at the double wedding of Hazel and George, along with Eva and Flight Lieutenant Carmichael, she'd hoped he was ready to move past the dark times they'd been through together. He'd sat beside her at the wedding and chatted quite amiably. It had almost been like old times. But nothing had come of it. Joe had gone back to his lonely farm on the cliffs above Porthcurno and she'd been promoted to Housekeeper at Eastern House, and they had barely seen each other since.

'Well, that's nice,' she said, though her head was shrieking at the idea of Joe on his own with three young women. 'Where do they sleep?' She found herself stammering, her cheeks fiery with embarrassment. 'I … erm … I mean… You're not struggling for room, are you?'

'I've space enough for another ten Land Girls,' he said bluntly.

There was an awkward silence.

'Oh, do sit down, Joe,' she burst out, 'you've giving me a crick in my neck, looking up at you like this.'

He sank back into his armchair, not saying a word.

Avoiding his troubled gaze, Violet stared into the small fire in the grate instead, which had burnt down to glowing embers. But the weather wasn't cold enough to merit stoking the fire or putting on another log, she decided. They were in May now, and it was only the occasional damp evening that could be a bit chilly.

'So, why did you call round?' she asked, maybe a little too sharply. But she was uncertain and on edge, and she resented feeling like that in her own home. An Englishman's home was his castle, after all, so the same had to apply to an Englishwoman, she thought fiercely. Even when the castle was only a cottage, and the woman only a tenant. 'And don't tell me it was to ask after us. You've barely had the time of day for me in months.'

When Joe still said nothing, she risked a quick glance at him. He had such a lively, handsome face, and those eyes… Large, dark, liquid, with sweeping long lashes… The eyes of a romantic film idol. But she thought his cheeks looked almost hollow these days, as though he hadn't been eating properly without a woman in the house to care for him. Hurriedly, she banished the sympathy that came rushing with that thought. It was none of her concern if Joe Postbridge wasn't making time for a proper evening meal. He was a grown man; he could look after himself.

'I heard about the children…' His voice trailed off.

'Our evacuees? What did you hear, exactly?' She could hear herself speaking in that cold, clipped voice that she used when she was very angry, but couldn't seem to stop herself.

'That there'd been a few complaints. About the noise, and a bit of tomfoolery around the village.'

'That's none of your business.'

'No, but it's a small cottage,' he said awkwardly. 'Not much room for so many people. And you've Alice to think of too.'

Mum was deliberately taking her time in the kitchen, Violet thought. Trying to push the two of them together, no doubt. She listened with impatience to the whistle of the kettle and the clink of cups being rinsed and dried.

'We can manage our own affairs perfectly well.'

'I'm sure you can,' Joe said, frowning.

'And I'll thank you not to listen to gossip about us.'

'It was hard not to,' he said, glaring at her now. 'I've not even met these children, and I've had three separate people stop me to have a good moan about them.'

She thought she heard accusation in his voice and her insides twisted with embarrassment.

'Well, if that was all you came to say,' she said between her teeth, jumping to her feet like she couldn't sit still a moment longer, 'I should really go and help Mum with the supper. Goodnight, Mr Postbridge.'

'Now hang on a minute, Violet,' Joe said, also getting to his feet, his own face flushed. He picked up the stick he used when walking, as though planning to leave. 'You want me out of here, I see that. I'm sorry I've upset you by dropping by. But let me say my piece first, and then I'll go.'

His use of her Christian name flustered her. The snug back room suddenly felt warm and intimate, and the last thing she wanted was to be reminded of how this man had kissed her once. Though now it was all she could think about…

'Fine,' she said unsteadily, and sank back onto the sofa.

'Look,' he said, frowning now, 'I'm sorry if I raised my voice there. I hope I know better than to raise my voice to a woman. But I only came to say that you'd be welcome to bring the kids up to the farm of a weekend, so they can let off steam where they'll be in nobody's way.' He winced and perched awkwardly on the edge of the armchair with the leg outstretched, as though his false leg was causing him pain. 'Kids always have more energy than the rest of us. Better for them to play in the fields than charge up and down the stairs here and annoy your neighbours.'

81

'Oh,' Violet said, feeling awful for having snapped at him.

'Well, that's the offer.' He paused, and their eyes met properly for the first time. 'You don't need to come yourself, if you'd rather not. You can send the kids up on their own. I'll make sure they get a bite to eat and come home to you before dusk.'

'That's very kind of you, Mr Postbridge.'

'Joe,' he corrected her softly.

She smiled at last, but faintly, afraid she might cry. 'Joe.'

Her mother chose that inopportune moment to come bustling in with the replenished tea tray. 'Care for a fresh cuppa, Joe?' she asked cheerily, though her lightning-fast glance between their faces had shown she knew perfectly well she'd interrupted a scene of some kind. 'And why don't you stay for supper? I've a nice piece of mutton on the boil, and I was just about to put the potatoes on.' She hesitated. 'Unless you've another appointment elsewhere?'

Violet saw Joe wrestle with himself, and thought for a moment that he would take this opportunity to go home.

But he didn't.

'Violet?' he said, looking straight at her.

She took a deep breath. 'Yes, stay and have supper with us. Alice will be glad to see you again. She'll be up in her room, I expect, reading one of her library books. And you can meet the kids … when they finally turn up.'

'I'd like that very much, thank you,' Joe said.

The front door banged at that moment, and Violet stiffened at the noisy thump of feet along the hallway. The evacuees were back. She hoped to goodness they wouldn't embarrass her. Next thing, three breathless, dirty-faced urchins crowded through the doorway, staring at their visitor.

'Who's this, then?' Eustace demanded, knocking his dark wayward hair out of his eyes.

The boy's hair really did need cutting, Violet thought, pressingly aware of how unkempt they all were. Timothy's shirt had a tear in the sleeve, and the hem of Janice's school dress needed to be let down before she disgraced herself. And none of them looked clean. But it wasn't her fault they were in a mess; she was at work all day, and barely had time for herself in the evenings, let alone opportunities to mend torn clothing and insist on hot baths for her new charges.

Joe stood, smiling. 'I'm Joe, and I've come to invite you all to my farm at the weekend. If you like the sound of that.'

'A farm?' Timothy squeaked. 'What, with animals and all?'

'You could say that,' Joe said slowly, though Violet knew his farm was mostly arable. 'We've got some hens and pigs, and a few cows now.'

'Pigs smell,' Janice said, wrinkling her nose in disgust.

'You can run about all you like, and climb trees, and so on. It's a few miles from the village too, so there'll be nobody to hear you up there.'

'Sounds wizard,' Eustace said, and nudged his little brother. 'We can play Spitfire versus Messerschmitt.'

'I'll be the Jerries,' Timothy shouted, his eyes blazing with excitement, and he wheeled about the back room with his thin arms outspread, making a roaring noise like an aeroplane at top speed.

'Careful,' Violet's mum exclaimed as the boy nearly sent the tea tray flying. 'Oh my goodness, you kids will be the death of me.' She grabbed hold of Timothy and hustled him out of the room, gesturing for the other two to follow. 'Right, upstairs for a wash before supper, you lot. And how many times have I told you not to wear your school uniforms to play in?' Her mother bundled the children up the stairs. 'They'll be rags by summer.'

Once they were all gone, Violet sat back and watched Joe pour the tea and add milk to the cups.

'Thank you,' she said quietly. 'It looks like that's a yes. And I'm sorry about before ... the way I snapped at you. It wasn't very fair of me.'

'Don't give it another thought.' Joe handed her a cup of tea and sat with his own. 'Those kids are putting a brave face on, but we both know they can't have had it easy. Orphans, aren't they?'

Violet nodded, unable to speak because she felt a little emotional at the note in his voice. Which was silly. It was just the new job and the longer hours tiring her out, she decided, blinking away a tear. She needed to toughen up if she was going to help those kids upstairs. Her mother had persuaded her to house the three of them, bless their hearts, and now it was her responsibility to see things done right.

'I may not be a child anymore, but I know how it feels to have lost both parents.' Joe sipped his tea, staring at nothing. 'They need all the help they can get.'

He'd changed since his mother's death, Violet thought, and gulped at her own cup, the tea weak but steaming hot.

Her sister's girls too had changed after their mother

died, growing up so fast they were now almost unrecognisable from the fresh-faced children they'd been before the outbreak of war. Lily, in particular, seemed determined to prove herself independent and professional, to the point of appearing almost hard-hearted at times.

But how had Joe Postbridge changed?

Was he still the quiet, smiling soul she'd found so attractive down on the beach at Penzance, or had that man gone forever?

CHAPTER NINE

Treading carefully in clogs through the dirt of the farm-yard, Demelza called to the hens and scattered a few handfuls of seed for them, then stood watching as they ran to grub at it, pecking and greedily jostling together, feathers still damp from a recent shower of rain. She rested the battered old seed basket on her hip and stared down across the sloping fields towards the rooftops of Penzance, the jutting outline of St. Michael's Mount, and the hazy blue line where the sea met the sky. There was a large boat at anchor far out in the bay. Not a picturesque fishing vessel as she might once have expected to see there, but some kind of military craft in metallic grey. It looked brutal and inhuman beside the green cliffs and sparkling blue sea of the natural world. But better to have such visible protection, she told herself, than to leave Cornwall wide open to an invading force.

She'd once seen her mother standing like this, she realised, struck by a sudden memory of a young Demelza running about after the hens and giggling while her mother stood in a gingham apron, ginger curls tied back with a ribbon, staring out across Penzance.

'What are you looking at, Ma?' she'd asked, turning to stare that way too, as though expecting to see something miraculous.

'The world, Demmy,' her mother had said, and smiled at her. A sad smile, she now realised. 'The big wide world.'

The hens were clucking about her feet now, impatient for more. She threw a few more fistfuls of seed here and there among the grasses growing up in cracks between the old stone flags and left the hens to fight among themselves. Going back into the farmhouse, Demelza put away the seed basket and opened one of the drawers under the vast kitchen table.

Buried under wooden spoons and metal utensils was her mother's journal. She'd smuggled it downstairs that morning in a pile of dirty linen, intending to read a few entries over lunch as she was always too tired when she flopped into bed at night to open a book, let alone pore over the faded loops of her mother's handwriting. She uncovered the small lump of cheese she'd cut for herself when sorting out her father and Tristan's lunches, and nibbled on it frugally, along with a crust of bread. Cheese was tightly rationed now, and she didn't want to munch her way through it too quickly.

Some of the pages were covered in dense scrawl, but she flicked through to one of the shorter entries, dated late March. The year had to be 1930, she calculated, though her mother had not marked it as such. The year of her mother's death. She herself would have just turned twelve that spring. Tristan had been eight. She didn't know her mother's date of birth but guessed she must have been in her early thirties then, because she'd married Demelza's father at the age of twenty.

The faint barking of a dog made her tense. To be found reading this journal would provoke such a row … and her father might even snatch the book away and throw it on the fire, like as not. He hated even to hear her mother's name mentioned, let alone talk about why she'd died. But the dog's bark was still a long way off, and she knew her father would be enjoying a quick nap after his lunch by now, somewhere out in the fields, where he and Tristan had been checking the boundaries and mending fences.

She ought to be safe enough for now.

Demelza stood at the kitchen table and began to decipher her mother's handwriting, reading aloud.

Heavy snow today took us all by surprise, this late in the year. A sheep wandered off and Joshua was out all night looking for it. When he couldn't find it, he came back furious. Later, it was found dead, tangled in barbed wire.

We're desperate for money so I understand why these losses make him so angry and miserable. But why does he need to take it out on me every time something goes wrong on the farm? I've had to wear my frilled long-sleeved blouse two days running to hide a bruise on my wrist, so little Demelza wouldn't see it and ask questions.

I live in dread of someone finding out this isn't a happy marriage.

Demelza closed her eyes in horror. She almost did not want to read on. But some devil drove her to find out the worst.

She flicked through a few more pages, hoping to find something more cheerful to read.

I was late getting the children up for school today because I had that bad tummy again, and Joshua shouted at me.

I don't understand why he has to be so cruel. I realise now I should never have married him. But he was so different when we first met, the summer I was nineteen and he was twenty-three. He was my knight in shining armour. He couldn't do enough for me back in those days, and the way he stood up to Dad that day, I'll never forget it. 'I'm going to wed your daughter whether you like it or not, Mr Sowton.' I was so proud of him. All I wanted was to be a good wife to him and a mother to his children.

Now all he does is shout when his supper is late or I dare to speak back to him.

Where did all the love go? Was it my fault? I keep thinking that I must have done something to deserve this, that I'm a bad wife. But then I stop and tell myself he's just a bully, and the only wonder is I never saw it before now.

Demelza's hand shook as she turned another few pages, trying not to cry, though her eyes burned with unshed tears.

Joshua has finally done the worst thing possible, the thing I'd feared most. He took his belt to Tristan today, all of nine years old. Poor little boy, all he did was bring a bad report home from that mean, stuck-up teacher of his, Miss Perkins. Joshua started shouting about it, saying Tristan was making the family look bad and he needed to buck up his ideas, or else.

Tristan said Miss Perkins had it in for him, and next thing I knew Joshua was laying into him with the belt. I screamed at Joshua and tugged on his arm, and he stopped. But not before he'd caught me a shiner with the back of his hand. He said he was sorry and it was an accident. But I won't be able to go out now until the bruise has gone down, for there's no easy way to hide a black eye.

Luckily, Demelza wasn't there. She was at her friend Sally's house until gone six, and I asked little Tristan to promise not to tell her. As for my black eye, I told her I'd walked into a door, and she'd have to fetch the shopping this week, to save me going out in such a state and all the neighbours staring.

I could have told her the truth. But I feel so ashamed. And I know what a bright spark she is, and so brave. She might have told her father off about it and made him angry again.

I'm so unhappy. I've run out of hope. If I didn't have the children, I would have killed myself a long time ago.

Demelza couldn't contain her sobs, her tears running down her cheeks and splashing on the journal, smudging the long-faded ink. The sound of barking had grown louder. Hurriedly, she thrust the journal back into the utensil drawer and snatched up a tea towel, drying her eyes and cheeks. Before she'd finished, the back door was thrown open, and her father strolled in, the dogs at their heels.

'What's up with you?' her dad asked suspiciously, looking around the place as though expecting to find someone there with her. 'Why have you been crying?'

She didn't answer at first, hurrying to the sink to splash her face. Head down, she said indistinctly, 'I've been chopping an old onion I found, that's all. To make a … a stock. You know how they always make me cry.'

Her heart thumping loudly, she prayed he didn't ask to see the onion, or she'd have to tell another lie, about throwing it out because it was bad. But to her relief her father merely grunted and elbowed her aside to wash his own hands and face.

'You're back early,' she said, hoping to distract him.

'Pip got a thorn lodged in his paw. I've come home to see to him before it gets infected.' He dried his hands, looking round at the dog, who was limping about in a dejected manner. 'I left Tristan mending the fence up by Spinner's Field. It's a big job; he won't be back until dusk, at least.'

She made small talk while she cleared the table so he could examine Pip under the big kitchen light, and once the wound had been cleaned and patched, she waited until he'd taken the dog into the back room and then rescued her mother's journal from the drawer. With the book hidden under her cardigan, she ran lightly up the stairs to her bedroom. She thrust the journal under her pillow again and then sat on the bed, trying to compose herself. But all she could think of her was her mother's unhappiness and despair.

Her eyes swam with tears again, and she sniffed into a hanky, sucking in her sobbing breaths and trying not to make a noise in case he heard her and came to see what was going on.

If I didn't have the children, I would have killed myself a long time ago.

She so clearly remembered walking in to find her mother on the bathroom floor, cold and still, curled like she might have been sleeping. Dad had told them she'd taken too much of her medicine, and it had been an accident – but her own fault, for being so careless. She'd assumed at the time he was only saying something so mean because he was so sad about her death, just as she and Tris had been.

But now she wondered if her mother had deliberately taken too many of the pills prescribed for her sleeping problems, in order to escape the horror of her marriage…

Three days later, Demelza left Aunt Sarah sitting with a sickly lamb they'd been nursing back to health and hurried down the hill into Penzance. Her father and Tristan had driven to a neighbouring farm to collect bales of hay, as their own supplies had finally run out, and they would not be back for at least half an hour. But the more quickly she completed her top secret errand, the sooner she could return home unseen.

Standing in front of the red-brick building that housed the Fire Guard Service, she took a deep, steadying breath and stared up at the new poster that had appeared on the door. The poster showed a man and a woman both staring bravely up at the night sky, wearing the distinctive helmets and uniforms of the Fire Guard, and it said in bold capital letters above their heads: BRITAIN'S FIRE GUARD IS BRITAIN'S DEFENCE. Beneath, it showed a group of recruits watching a training presentation, beside the words: *The strength of Britain's defence depends on these three things: Training, Readiness, Courage.* She wasn't feeling particularly courageous. But she was determined not to go home without signing up as a volunteer.

A man was coming out just as Demelza entered the building, and they collided, his hands seizing hold of her as she stumbled.

'Steady there,' he said with a deep voice.

'Hey, watch where you're going,' she said at the same moment, instantly alarmed, and shaking off his hands. 'There's no need to grab hold of me like that.'

'Sorry, I'm sure, Miss,' he muttered, and stood aside to let her pass, for he was so well built, he was blocking the entire passageway. Her gaze flashed to his face, which looked vaguely familiar, but then he was gone, heading out into the sunlight. Turning to stare after him, she recognised the uniform he was wearing and realised where she'd seen him before. It was one of the ambulance men from that day on the beach. The huge one who'd reminded her of a bear.

She felt the urge to call after the man and ask how Mr Lister was since his gunshot injury, but stopped herself. It was none of her business, after all, and she didn't want the man to think she was chasing after him, or anything horrible like that. Men too easily got the wrong idea for the flimsiest of reasons.

A woman in a dark blue army-style uniform with shiny buttons and an arm band marked 'Fire Guard' was seated behind a desk in the main room, head down, dealing with paperwork. The sign on the desk in front of her said 'Fire Guard Sector Captain', which impressed Demelza immensely. The woman had startlingly short grey hair and large smiling eyes that looked up at Demelza quizzically as she approached the desk. She looked to be in her fifties.

'Hello,' the woman said, 'I'm Sector Captain Enys. Can I help you?'

Demelza's heart was thudding so hard, she felt sick. Dared she defy her father and apply for war work? And if she did, would he come down here and drag her home like a naughty schoolgirl?

She almost turned and fled, but then she thought of her mother's desperation, and how she'd taken her own life as a way out. She had no intention of hurting herself like that. There were far better ways of escaping her father's iron control. And if he did come down here, hoping to drag her home again, the law of the land would be on her side, she reminded herself. This was voluntary war work, but it was still important. Even Farmer Minear, with his reputation for always getting his own way, couldn't hope to fight the government.

'Yes,' she said, a little breathlessly. 'I'm Demelza Minear, and I want to join the Fire Guard Unit. To be a fire warden or watcher, or whatever it's called.'

The woman put down her pen. 'How old are you, Demelza?'

'Twenty-three.'

'Fit and healthy?'

'Yes.'

'Are you afraid of hard work?'

'I grew up on a farm.'

'That's a no, then.' The captain laughed, and then glanced at her left hand. 'Are you married?'

'No.'

'Planning to get married?'

'Not even remotely.' Demelza grimaced. 'I don't have a boyfriend and I don't want one, thank you.'

'I know exactly how you feel. I never married either. Some chaps can be absolute beasts, can't they?' The captain looked her up and down. 'Look, it's not an easy job. We work three- to four-day shifts, and you'll need to be on call during that time. That means you'll spend the night upstairs when there's no air raid, in case the siren goes off in the middle of the night.'

'Upstairs?'

'That's right. It's all girls together, mind. No men allowed in the bedrooms. We usually have plenty of room,' the captain added with a wry expression, 'but there was a direct hit to the nurses' home recently, and we agreed to let some of them bunk here until the hospital finds them suitable new accommodation. So you'll be sharing living quarters with some of the nurses too. As you can imagine, it gets quite lively here. Especially first thing in the morning when everyone's queuing for the bathroom.' She paused. 'We only have the one bathroom, I'm afraid, plus an additional WC out the back. Will you mind that?'

Demelza shook her head, almost unable to contain her excitement at the thought of living away from home for half the week.

'You can stay here the other nights if you've nowhere else to go. Or, if you're local, you can go home on your days off.'

Demelza almost said she'd like to stay full-time, but then recalled Tristan and felt guilty. She couldn't wholly abandon her brother.

'I'm local. I'll probably go home when I'm not on call.'

'Good, that will free up some bathroom time.' The captain grinned. 'In that case, Demelza, congratulations. You've passed the test.'

'I have?'

'It's not a very tough test, I admit. But we're desperate. The Germans have upped their bombing campaign all along the coast here in the past six months, and they've even started using incendiary bombs, which are the most awful things imaginable. We tend to work in pairs here, so I'll put you with someone more experienced for your first few months. Mags might be a good fit for you. She's often paired with our new recruits. I'll introduce you to her when you come for your first training day.'

'How exciting, thank you.' Demelza hoped that she and Mags would get on. 'Though I'm afraid I'm still not sure what kind of work I'll be doing.'

'In the first instance, your duties as a Fire Guard will be to put out any small fires that don't require attendance by the Fire Brigade, check that local premises pass regulations for fire drills and readiness, and investigate any buildings which may have been destabilised by bombing or fire damage.' She seemed to sense Demelza's apprehension. 'Don't worry though, you'll be fully trained before we let you loose with a ceiling pike.'

Demelza blinked. 'A what?'

'Never mind that now.' She held out a calloused hand with bitten-down nails. 'Welcome to the unit. I'm Jean and I run this place, for what it's worth, though when we're working, you'll have to call me Captain Enys.' They shook hands. 'If I haven't put you off, pull up a pew and we'll get started on the paperwork straightaway.'

CHAPTER TEN

Penzance, West Cornwall, May 1942

Lily couldn't believe it was already mid-May. Time had flown by so quickly since she'd met Dr Jerrard in April and then received that shocking letter of transfer to Penzance Hospital, forcing her to leave St. Ives. But now that she was finally here, she was determined to make the best of it. She woke up early on her very first morning in Penzance to a cheerful patch of sunlight on the wall of her dorm room and the unusual sound of traffic in the street below. A truck rumbling past the building had woken her, she realised, listening as it picked its way slowly through the town. Then she swung her legs out of bed, too restless to lie still any longer. The other two nurses in the dorm were still asleep, Josephine buried under her covers, Vera snoring gently. Grabbing her towel and washbag, Lily rushed along the corridor to the bathroom, only to find she was fourth in the queue. 'There's an outdoor convenience,' the girl at the head of the queue told her kindly, 'if you don't need a proper wash.'

'I need a wash,' Lily said reluctantly, and leant against the wall, trying to be patient.

The young woman immediately in front of her, wearing a very long, old-fashioned nightdress, turned and smiled in a hesitant way. 'It's Lily, isn't it?' she asked in a thick Cornish accent.

Lily was surprised. 'Have we met?'

The girl nodded. She was short and well-built, with ginger curls and a very direct way of making eye contact.

'You've probably just forgotten,' she said, and shook Lily's hand awkwardly, hampered by the large striped towel she was carrying. 'I'm Demelza. We met on the beach that day when you were helping Mr Lister. The poor gentleman who got shot?' She bit her lip. 'Did he ever recover? Do you know?'

'I believe he did, yes.'

'That's wonderful news, thank you. I think about that day all the time. In fact, it's the reason I'm here.'

Lily frowned. 'How's that?'

'I brought those three children to see the placement officer. He works out of an office on the first floor in this building. And that's when I saw that they were recruiting. Otherwise I might still be at home on the farm...' Demelza paused after this mysterious statement. 'Your aunt was walking past with your grandmother and sister. I believe they took the children home with them, when we couldn't find anywhere for them in Penzance.'

'Goodness me.' Lily was staring at her, amazed. 'Yes, they did. You could have knocked me down with a feather that night when I walked in to find the three of them sitting in our kitchen. So that was down to you.'

'Are they settling in all right?' The Cornish girl looked genuinely concerned.

'I don't actually live with my aunt anymore. I was only visiting at the time. But they looked happy enough, yes.'

'I'm glad. She seems like a good sort.'

'Aunty Violet? Oh, she's a marvel. And so good with kids. She helped look after me and my sister back when our mum died. Mum left the shelter in Dagenham in the middle of an air raid and went back home for something, we never knew what. Bomb landed right on the house. There was nothing left...'

Lily blinked, hearing an odd tremble in her voice. She'd pushed the memory of her mother's death away for so long, sometimes it felt like it hadn't happened. She probably just needed more sleep.

'I'm so sorry,' Demelza whispered.

'Well, we've all lost someone.' Hurriedly, Lily changed the subject. 'You're not a nurse, are you? So I guess that means you're a Fire Guard. My roommates told me the nurses' home was bombed a few weeks back and we've all been shoved in together here.'

'Jam-packed, isn't it? I only just arrived too. I'm a trainee with the Penzance Women's Fire Guard. That was the recruiting poster I saw that day.' Demelza smiled. 'The job just called to me, you know?'

'Well, rather you than me.' Lily was impressed. Being a Fire Guard was a seriously dangerous job; she certainly wouldn't want to do it. All members of the Fire Service, like the ambulance drivers and the ARP, went out into the streets when everyone else was diving into shelters. She glanced along the line of waiting girls. 'Is this the only bathroom?'

'I'm afraid so.' Demelza gave her a faint smile. 'Apparently, you have to take a bath at four in the morning to avoid the queues.'

'I'd rather queue, thanks. Unless I come off-shift in the middle of the night, which I suppose might happen. But good luck with your training. A Fire Guard? It sounds proper exciting, though dangerous too. You must be so brave.'

'I'm not brave at all,' Demelza admitted. 'But I'll do anything if it means living away from home.'

'Like that, is it?'

'I left a note for my dad, not telling him where I was going but saying I'd be back next weekend on a couple of days' leave. Then I just walked into town with my bag.' Demelza grimaced. 'He must have been hopping mad when he read it. I'm not looking forward to facing him when I finish this first shift.'

Lily nodded sympathetically, recalling how keen she'd been to get away from Porthcurno when she first applied to do her training at the convalescent home. Not that any of her family were hard to live with, exactly. She'd just wanted to feel more independent.

'Well, it can be lonely, the first few months away from home. I'm taking up a nursing position at Penzance Hospital so we'll probably see quite a lot of each other. If you need any advice or a shoulder to cry on, you know where I am.'

'Actually, I don't.'

Lily pointed down the corridor. 'Room Three. I'm sharing with Vera and Josephine.'

'Room Seven.' Demelza moved up to the head of the

queue as one girl left the steamy bathroom, toothbrush in hand, and another thankfully took her place. 'I'm in with Rosemary and another girl whose name I didn't catch. But I only moved in two days ago and I'm still not sure which end is up.'

'Me neither.' Lily grinned at her. She instinctively liked this Cornish girl, with her odd utterances and straightforward way of talking. 'I got dragged here from St. Ives against my will; staff shortages, I was told. I wasn't happy leaving all my old mates behind, I can tell you.'

She felt a twinge of sadness as she wondered what they would be doing at the convalescent home right now, and how dear Mary was getting along without her. St. Ives felt so far away.

'But Matron said I'd soon make new friends,' Lily added with a wink, 'and I can see she was right.'

As she hurried through winding streets towards the small hospital in Penzance, Lily spotted a dark-haired girl she recognised a little way ahead. It was Janice, one of the London evacuees that her aunt was looking after, walking into town on the opposite side of the road.

After a moment's confusion, she remembered that Janice had been enrolled at the secondary school in Penzance, being too old for the village school in Porthcurno. No doubt she and Alice, who worked with the younger children at the school, would have travelled in on the bus together that morning.

But Alice was nowhere in sight and, to Lily's surprise, Janice was not heading towards the school. Instead, she turned down a side-street and halted outside a tea shop, which had just opened for the day. While Lily too stopped in surprise, she watched Janice speak briefly to the woman who was opening the shop awning, and then go inside.

Curious, Lily crossed the road, slipped down the side-street and peered into the tea shop, where she saw Janice seated at the back with two other girls, who both looked considerably older than her. Lily hesitated, wondering if she ought to go in and ask Janice why she wasn't heading off to her lessons. But then she turned away, unwilling to interfere, and continued her journey to the hospital, chiding herself for having even considered it. It was none of her business if the girl wanted to skip school. She could recall a few times during her own school days when she'd fancied a break and had skipped lessons to spend time with friends instead. Why spoil Janice's fun?

But it might be worth discreetly mentioning what she'd seen in her next letter to Alice. Her sister had sharp eyes and was good at observing other people; she'd probably have an explanation to hand for the girl's odd behaviour.

At the hospital, Lily was taken on a quick guided tour by Sister Reynolds – a grim-faced woman in her forties – handed a uniform and shown to the nurses' washroom and cloakroom, and given a long recital of rules and regulations that must on no account be broken.

'Yes, Sister,' she replied meekly, nodding and listening intently, just as she had learned to do whenever Matron was bleating on about 'the proper way to behave'. She then washed her hands and scrambled into her new uniform before heading off for her first shift on the wards. Before she'd even got ten steps into Ward Three (one of the ladies' wards), the air-raid siren went off somewhere nearby in the town.

'Oh, here we go again,' one of the other nurses called out cheerily, and Lily found herself surrounded by women in nightdresses and dressing gowns, some walking with sticks, others being pushed in wheelchairs by nurses. Rolling up her sleeves, she caught the arm of an elderly lady who appeared to be struggling with her knitting.

'Shall I carry that for you?' Lily suggested, gathering up the trailing blue wool and wrapping it around the ball, which had two needles sticking out of it like chopsticks. Taking the lady's arm, she said conspiratorially, 'I'm new here. Just started today.'

'I know that, dear. I've never seen you before.' The lady smiled at her benignly. 'I'm Mrs Crawford. Trouble with my bowels.'

'I'm Nurse Fisher.' Lily stopped to open the ward door for the patient. 'I don't suppose you know where the shelter is?'

'Follow the signs, dearie. Follow the signs.'

Though in fact Lily didn't need to follow the signs – which she later realised were written in red lettering high on the walls of all the corridors – as it was simpler to follow the crowd of patients shuffling or wheeling that way.

'In my last hospital, some of the patients couldn't get down the steps into the shelter, as it was so deep underground. They had to lie under the beds instead, protected by nothing but blankets. And by the time we'd sorted them out, it was often too late to get to the shelters ourselves, so we'd have to lie under the beds with them.'

'Goodness,' Mrs Crawford said faintly.

'It was a home for wounded servicemen,' Lily explained. 'I loved working there. But I'm sure I'll love working here too.'

'You mean, you were lying under the bed with a ... a man?'

'That's right.'

'But that's shocking. Weren't you afraid?'

'Of the bombs?'

'Of the *men*,' Mrs Crawford whispered, staring at her.

They had reached the door marked 'Shelter', and Lily began helping her charge down the stairs.

'Well, most of them weren't really up to doing anything awkward. They were the most badly wounded, you understand. So, I think we were safe enough from wandering hands.'

'Telling the patients warm stories, Nurse Fisher?' a voice came from behind them, and Lily looked back in surprise to see Dr Jerrard at the top of the stairs, closing the door behind him.

'Of course not, Doctor,' she said primly, a little concerned not to get off on the wrong foot in her new job. 'I was just explaining to Mrs Crawford here how we used to manage air raids at my last place of work.'

'Patients under the beds?'

'That's right.'

'Yes, we got that circular too. Luckily though, we'd just invested in a couple of Morrison Shelters, the type that can be used indoors, and set them up in a side-room for those who can't manage the stairs. Much more civilised.' There was a bite in his voice, and she guessed he hadn't thought much of the government advice either. 'Most of the invalids are carried down the stairs by orderlies, of course, or on stretchers. I'll be damned if I'm going to leave people on the wards unless it's more dangerous to move them than not.'

The stairs were not very well lit once the door at the top was shut and Lily worried about the elderly lady missing her footing.

Mrs Crawford whimpered. 'Oh, I hate that noise.'

Lily knew she meant the terrible thump-thump of the anti-aircraft battery positioned on the coast; it was going off now to protect the town, shelling the enemy planes with shrapnel as they flew towards Penzance. They made an awful racket, but didn't seem to put the Germans off, Lily thought bitterly.

As they reached the bottom of the stairs, Mrs Crawford thanked Lily, wandering away to one of the benches with her knitting. By then, the strange tinny sound of the German planes could be heard overhead, even though they were well underground.

'Scared?' Dr Jerrard said quietly, right behind her.

'I'd be an idiot if I wasn't,' she replied, maybe a little too sharply, given that he was a doctor and she a lowly trainee. 'But I never let the patients see it. That wouldn't be very professional of me, would it?'

'No, indeed.' He leant against the rough, white-washed wall of the hospital cellar, glanced at his watch and then folded his arms with a look of weary resignation. 'Let's pray it's a short one. I've been up most of the night keeping a patient from dying on us, and was just about to perform an emergency operation. Appendicitis. If it's not whipped out soon, the poor chap probably won't make it.'

A thin wail sounded overhead and the whole building shook. Dust fell from the low ceiling. Several of the patients shrieked, and there was much low-level muttering, people staring upwards in consternation. Some of the other nurses were walking around the cellar, reassuring people and offering them water. She recognised Vera, one of the nurses who roomed with her at the Fire Guard Unit, and gave her a quick grin and thumbs-up. Vera winked in return. She was a big, friendly girl with masses of glossy black hair, tucked up neatly under her cap at the moment, and her cheeky smile more than made up for her alarming tendency to snore.

'That was close,' Lily said, a little breathless. Her hands were cold and clammy, and she linked them at her waist, hoping nobody would notice them trembling.

Dr Jerrard studied her thoughtfully. 'I'm guessing you didn't get many air raids in St. Ives.'

'Oh, we had a few close calls.' Lily willed herself to calm down. It was no worse than the start of the Blitz in London, when waves of enemy planes had seemed to come over every few hours, day and night.

But it was hard not to panic, trapped in this narrow, dim space with so many people. If the building were to take a direct hit… She remembered staring at the rubble of their house where her mother had lain buried, and her heart thumped sickly now, loud as the anti-aircraft guns.

'It weren't exactly a regular thing, though,' she added, and was shocked by how thin and high-pitched her voice sounded. *You're terrified*, she told herself contemptuously; *pull yourself together, girl!* 'The convalescent home ain't in St. Ives, you see. It's on the outskirts. Not such a big target for the Jerries, I suppose.'

'I'm sorry to have dragged you away from your safe haven, Nurse Fisher.' His voice softened. 'You must think me very high-handed, arranging your transfer without asking first.'

She considered telling a polite fib but then decided to be straight with him. That was one of the only good things about the war; it had taught her not to waste time being less than honest with people.

'I weren't best pleased, no,' she said bluntly.

He laughed under his breath. 'Then I apologise again. But we really do need quality nurses here. And all my instincts tell me you are an excellent nurse.'

'Thank you.' To her surprise, she couldn't help smiling at this praise, when she really ought to be giving him a piece of her mind for uprooting her from St. Ives and all of her friends. Still, maybe she had become a little too comfortable at the convalescent home and a change of scene was going to be good for her; more of a challenge, perhaps. 'I hope I live up to your expectations, Doctor.'

When the doctor said nothing, Lily looked round after a minute to see his head tilted back against the wall, and his eyes closed, almost as though he were taking a quick nap standing up. She didn't know how on earth anyone could be so relaxed, given that they might be about to die at any moment.

Another close thud rocked the hospital. More shrieks and moans. This time the lights flickered and went out. She heard Vera's cheerful voice reassuring some of the patients from the children's ward, hurriedly telling them a story to distract their young minds. Dust fell on her face like fine sand, and Lily brushed it away in the darkness, trying not to lose control while she listened to people lighting matches and rummaging for torches and candles. Once there was enough light to see by, she would go and help Vera with the kids too. For now though, she bent her head and closed her eyes like the doctor had, as tight as she could.

Only she was praying, not sleeping.

CHAPTER ELEVEN

The last time Violet had been up to Joe's farm above Porthcurno had been the night of the bombing and his mother's tragic death. Every moment of that terrible evening was engraved in her memory, and it was awful having to get out of his van now and smile as the three kids ran about in the sunshine, whooping wildly, tearing about and obviously having the time of their lives, while she tried not to blurt the thoughts jumbling about inside her head.

In particular, she averted her gaze from the hay barn, though she could see it had been rebuilt since the night the German high explosive had blown it apart, destroying the adjacent shelter where his mother had taken cover. She wanted so much to discuss that night and the dreadful things young Patrick Dullaghan had said about her, and why he'd lied in that malicious way.

But Joe wouldn't understand.

He'd only be reminded of the rumours that had caused him to blame his mother's death on Violet Hopkins, supposed German spy and the woman he'd been walking out with that summer. And she didn't think she could bear to see that look of betrayal on his face again. *Least said, soonest mended.* That's what her own mum would say, if she was here. Which she wasn't, as Mum had decided to stay home and try baking a no-eggs cake from a special recipe in one of her magazines. Violet wasn't sure it sounded very appetising; but if anyone could bake a tasty cake without using eggs, it would be her mum, whose café had been famous back in Dagenham.

'You've made changes' was all she said instead when he invited her to look around the farmyard. 'That's new.' She pointed to a large green tractor. 'Oh, and you've ploughed up the meadow. What a shame.'

'Dig for victory, and all that.' Joe looked unhappily towards the sloping meadow, which had once been so beautiful with its wild flowers and stretches of grass under shady trees. 'Crops are what's needed these days, not meadow land. We can't import much, with all the supply ships being bombed, so we have to grow what we can. Besides, these new government subsidies for arable farming aren't bad. You just have to prove you're using every available bit of land.' He nodded to the tractor. 'Which is how I was able to afford Bessie.'

Violet bit her lip, trying not to laugh. 'You named your tractor Bessie?'

'Tractors have got personalities,' he informed her severely. 'Every good farmer knows that. She's a Bessie, that one. Stubborn and temperamental, but she'll get the job done if you treat her right.'

There was such a note of affection in his voice, Violet

wasn't sure whether to be jealous of the tractor or amused. Changing the subject, she turned to call the children and realised with a start that they were nowhere in sight.

'Now where have those blessed kids gone?' Feeling a little panicked, she began calling to them. 'Timothy? Eustace? Where are you?'

'You worry too much,' Joe said easily, and began to make for the farmhouse with his characteristic limp. He was leaning on his stick, she noticed, but not heavily. 'That's why I invited the children up here, remember? So they could run about and let off steam instead of sitting indoors on a lovely summer's day. I'm sure they'll be fine, wherever they are.'

He led her inside and showed her around the downstairs of the farmhouse, and she dutifully admired the changes and improvements he'd made since she was last at the farm. After he'd taken her through to the kitchen to find drinks for the kids – if they ever reappeared, she thought gloomily, convinced that they must be up to no good – she heard the sound of feet in the hall, and three young women came trooping in, laughing and chatting.

They were wearing the dark green and brown uniform that proclaimed them as Land Girls, but even without that, Violet could have guessed from their fresh, glowing complexions and the copious mud with which their clothes and faces were flecked. Two were quite comfortably built with ample chests and hips, but the third was willowy-thin and looked like a puff of wind might blow her away. All three had pretty faces, and again Violet felt a ridiculous pang at the thought of Joe spending his days in their company.

They all stopped dead on seeing Violet.

'Oh, we didn't know you had company,' one of the well-built girls said, and tugged off her cap to reveal chestnut locks bound up in a hairnet. 'We were just coming in for lunch. Do you want us to come back later?'

Joe looked horrified and shook his head. 'Of course you must eat. Come in.' He filled the kettle and put it on the range while the Land Girls milled about, cutting thin slices of bread and buttering them, fetching pungent cheese from the larder, and measuring out tea leaves into a large pot. Joe looked at Violet apologetically. 'What do you think the children would like to drink when they come back? There's some old appleade somewhere. Or we have milk.' They had a few heifers on the farm, even though it was largely arable land, and some she-goats too, so she imagined they would never be short of milk, cheese or butter.

'Milk would be grand,' Violet told him shyly. 'They like milk.'

'And for you?'

'I'm fine with tea. Here, let me help.' She turned towards the range at the same time as him, and felt an odd shiver when they collided, both flinching, embarrassed. 'Sorry.'

'I'll do it. You take a seat.'

There were benches either side of the long kitchen table. After glancing anxiously out of the window but catching no glimpse of the three evacuees she was supposed to be caring for, Violet perched on one of the benches, watching Joe make a pot of tea. The Land Girls, having organised their lunch, pulled out the bench opposite and sat together to eat, looking at her curiously.

'I'm Selina,' the willowy-thin girl said, holding out her

hand. She had a plummy accent, which made Violet immediately wary, but her smile seemed genuine enough. 'And this is Pickles.' She laughed when the girl with the chestnut hair protested on a wordless groan, her mouth full of bread. 'I mean, Penny. We call her Pickles because she absolutely *loves* eating them. And that's Caroline on the end.' She nodded to the large, fair-haired girl who, with her pale skin and very pink cheeks, looked like an overgrown china doll. 'Judging by your accent, I'd guess Caro's from your neck of the woods.'

'London, you mean?' Politely, Violet shook hands with all three girls. 'I'm Violet, I live down in Porthcurno with my mother and sister. We're from Dagenham.'

'I'm from Ealing,' Caroline told her between bites of cheese, and then promptly dissolved into a fit of hiccups. 'Nice … hic … to meet … hic … you.'

They all laughed, and Joe, coming to the table with a large tea pot and five cups, shook his head.

'You girls… How's it been going out there today?'

'We've sown all of the five-acre field,' Selina said. She seemed to be their self-designated spokeswoman. 'And Pickles herded the cows over to Long Top for better grazing.'

'Oh, before I forget, that big heifer with the funny-looking ear—' Pickles began breathlessly, and Caroline interrupted her, still hiccupping.

'Daisy.'

'That's right, Daisy… She's limping again, Joe. You may need to get the vet out.'

'Right you are,' Joe said gravely, and nodded. 'Thank you, girls. You lot are working miracles for me out there. To be honest, I don't know how I ever rubbed along without you.'

He began pouring out the tea, adding, 'It's your free time now: Saturday afternoon to Monday morning, as agreed. So, have a good weekend, and I'll see you here, six a.m. Monday, ready for drilling the barley. Weather permitting.'

The young women grinned and continued eating their food while looking from Joe to Violet with obvious curiosity. No doubt they thought the two of them must be courting, Violet thought, and instantly felt her cheeks go hot with embarrassment. If only they knew the truth, which was that Joe still hadn't forgiven her for what had happened last summer, however much he was trying to give the opposite impression. The awful events of that night still lay between them like an invisible barrier, even if he wasn't aware of it himself.

And perhaps she hadn't entirely forgiven him either. It wasn't nice to be suspected of being a spy, after all, especially by a man you were fond of. A little more than fond, she admitted to herself. It still hurt to remember the way he'd turned away from her…

But Joe seemed oblivious to their stares. 'I'd better walk out to Long Top and take a look at Daisy's hoof after lunch.' When he glanced at Violet, she hoped to goodness he was equally oblivious to her flushed cheeks. 'Would you like to come with me, Violet? And the children too, of course.'

Taking her mug of tea with a murmur of thanks, Violet nodded. 'Sounds like a plan,' she agreed, forcing a cheerful smile to her lips. She was very much aware of the girls watching them, and she had no intention of washing her dirty linen in public. 'Though the way they took off, I'm not sure we'll ever see them bloomin' kids again.'

* * *

She was wrong, of course. As soon as they began the long walk up to where the cows were grazing, Violet heard shouts and laughter and turned to see the three children running towards them along the muddy track.

'Woah!' Joe called out, catching little Timothy as he tried to thunder past them. 'Where've you lot been, then?'

'Climbing trees,' Janice told him, flushed and with mud sprayed up her socks. There was a nasty graze on her knee, but she didn't seem to mind it. 'And counting butterflies.'

'Ah, we've plenty of butterflies down here in Cornwall,' Joe agreed, nodding with apparent approval.

'Look at the state of you all,' Violet exclaimed over the grass stains on Janice's pinafore dress and the hay stalks caught in Timothy's hair. 'And you, Eustace,' she added, turning to the older boy. 'You've not torn another shirt sleeve, have you?'

'I had to rescue Janice from up a tree,' Eustace said stoutly, hiding the offending arm behind his back. 'Not my fault. I was being a fireman. That kind of thing happens to firemen.'

'Quite right,' Joe said, and then caught Violet's glare. 'Um,' he added, rubbing his chin, 'how about we all walk up to Long Top together, and take a look at my cows?'

'Cows!' Timothy almost shrieked, his eyes wide. 'I love cows. Are they the black-and-white ones?'

'They're called Friesians, the black-and-white ones,' Joe said, laughing. 'Run ahead and you'll soon see them.'

The children ran up the steep track, having strictly promised not to alarm the cows by shouting too loud or invading their field, and Violet and Joe trudged more slowly on behind them. Violet felt unhappy, not so much

116

about the mess the kids had got into, but the way he'd looked at her when she was telling them off. He thought she was a nag, which wasn't true. She just wanted to do her duty and keep the children looking reasonable while they were in her care. But Joe had been so kind to invite them all to the farm today, and even to pick them up in his van and save them the walk up. She didn't want to spoil everything by taking offence where none was intended.

'Is your leg bad today?' she ventured after a while, not sure she ought to mention it at all, but aware of his constant wincing and rubbing at his thigh where she suspected the false leg met his own flesh.

A false leg must be a very uncomfortable thing to wear, day in, day out, she considered, and couldn't help wondering what he looked like without it. Which made her cheeks burn and her heart thump harder – embarrassingly, not just a result of the steep climb.

He had pulled a face at her question. 'Maybe a little.' He cleared his throat and pointed out the hardy wildflowers in the hedgerow. 'You can pick a few on your way back and take them home. There's nobody to see them up here. It's a waste.'

'Mum always had a vase of flowers on the sideboard before the war,' she admitted. 'Thank you.'

'The war's changed a lot of things. A lot of people, too.'

'When do you think it'll all be over?'

'I don't know. I doubt anybody knows.' Joe shrugged. 'When one side has run out of men to kill?'

'Oh, that's an awful thought.' Violet clapped a hand to her mouth. 'You don't mean it?'

'I'm afraid I do.'

Distant birdsong made him glance up and then fling an arm to the sky, exclaiming, 'Look, a lark. First of the season.'

They stood a moment, listening to the bird's dazzling song filtering from high above them in the May sunshine, full of joy and almost miraculous in its celebration of life, and Violet felt like weeping.

As she listened, she thought of that time long before the war, and the handsome, smiling young man she'd been so in love with. They'd both only just left school but they'd known what they wanted, and that was each other. Leonard had proposed to her and she'd accepted, and for a few glorious months everything had been perfect, with Violet planning the wedding and saving for a posh frock, the envy of all of her friends. Then he'd caught the flu, of all things, and quite unexpectedly sickened and died in the space of around ten days. She'd never been the same again.

To get out of the smog for a few hours, they'd once gone for a country walk in the spring, the year he died, and heard a lark singing up above. It had been the most beautiful thing she'd ever heard. And that was when Leonard had proposed to her. Listening to that lark.

Joe lowered his head and looked at her searchingly. 'Did I upset you just now, Violet?'

'Of course not,' she said automatically, but they both knew it was a lie.

'I'm sorry if I did. I certainly didn't mean to. It's just...' Joe ran a restless hand through his short dark hair. 'I listen to the wireless of an evening when the girls have gone up to bed, sitting there on my own in the dark, with the blackout curtains up and the wind whistling about the house, and sometimes it's hard not to…'

'Give up hope?' she whispered.

He nodded silently.

'That's what they'd like though, isn't it? For us to lose heart. The Germans, I mean.'

'I suppose so.' They began to walk again, but this time Joe kept close to her, his eyes intent on her face. 'You do your bit though. Working at Eastern House, that is. Everybody knows what they're doing for the war effort. Finding out what the Jerries are up to even before they know it themselves.'

'I can't talk about it, Joe. You know that.'

'Careless talk costs lives.' He nodded his understanding. 'But in general, you're happy in your work? You're Housekeeper now, aren't you? Your mother was telling me all about it the other day when I called at the cottage. You got a promotion.'

Damn Mum, she thought, but nodded. 'That's right.'

'And do you enjoy it?'

Goodness, she thought, this hill is so steep. They were nearly at the top though. She could see and hear the children up ahead, climbing on the five-bar gate into the cows' field. Her heart was racing like she'd been running, not walking at a sedate pace. She nodded and opened her mouth to say yes. And then closed it again. Somehow, without meaning to, her feet seemed to have thrown in the towel and stopped walking.

'Violet?'

Joe had stopped too, watching her in concern.

'Of course I enjoy it, it's very…' To her shock and dismay,

119

she realised she was crying. What on earth was wrong with her? 'Gawd, I don't know why I'm making such a first-class fool of myself. Sorry, so sorry.' Tears streamed down her cheeks and she hunted fruitlessly for the hanky she'd thought was up her dress sleeve. 'Oh, bloomin' 'eck.'

'Here.' He handed over a red-and-white chequered handkerchief. 'What is it, Vi? What's the matter?'

'Nothing.' Violet dried her eyes, not looking at him, too horribly embarrassed for words.

'You don't like being Housekeeper?'

'No, it's fine. Though to be honest ... nobody likes me now.' She rolled her eyes, her voice suddenly very high-pitched. 'It's all very well, being in charge. But the girls look at me like I'm ... like I'm bloody Hitler,' she finished in a rush.

'I'm sure they don't think that.'

'You say that, but you're not the one getting the filthy looks.' She bit hard on her lip. 'I hate it, Joe. I wish I was just plain Violet Hopkins again, cleaner and general dogsbody. I used to have a laugh with the other girls, you know? Hot cuppa and a ciggie at breaktimes, playing practical jokes on each other. It was good fun.' She blew her nose, trying to hide in the hanky, aware that she must look a fright with her nose and eyes streaming, and her cheeks hot with shame. 'Now I scuttle back into my office at tea breaks and sit there alone and watch the clock until home time. I'd give it up, but I don't want to let Mr Cotterill down.' She was sobbing again, she realised. 'He's relying on me ... to ... to keep the place ... running smoothly.'

'There now.' Joe put his arms about her and drew her

head onto his shoulder. 'I'm sure you're doing a grand job, Violet. It's this bloody war. It gets to all of us in the end.'

She sucked in a deep, shuddering breath and held it for as long as possible, trying to stop sobbing. *Get yourself together, woman*, she told herself, eyes shut tight.

The stupidest thing was, she didn't know what she was crying about. It was all true, what she'd told him. But none of it was worth weeping over like a grieving widow. He was right, she thought, standing rigid in the circle of his arms. It was the war. Her nerves were torn to shreds, that's what it was. She wasn't crying about losing her friends at work; she was crying for all the brave boys who had died, and the men, women and children blown to smithereens by German bombs, and the kids taken from their homes and sent to live with strangers, and the lovers who would never see each other again, and Joe's mum who had died alone and in the dark without being able to say goodbye to her son.

'I know,' she whispered unsteadily. 'I'm just being stupid.'

'Not stupid. Human.'

She gave a shaky laugh, pulling away. 'I'm sorry. You ask me here for a nice day out, and all I do is make your jacket soggy.'

Eustace, watching them from the gate into the cows' field, gave a piercing wolf-whistle. 'Ooh, young love,' he called down to them. 'Go on, give her a kiss, Mr Postbridge.'

The other two children chuckled.

'What did you say?' Joe straightened, frowning at the boy. 'That's quite enough cheek from you, my lad.'

Hurriedly, Violet dried her face, pushed his hanky into her sleeve, and started walking up the slope again.

'Let's see these cows, then,' she said firmly.

Typical of eagle-eyed Eustace to put two and two together about them, she thought, avoiding Joe's embarrassed glance. Not that this was even remotely 'young love'. More like a very brief former fling that ought to be left to die a natural death. He'd only put his arms about her to stop her impersonation of a bloomin' watering-pot. Not because he felt anything like affection for her.

But she felt better for her little bout of weepiness. It had steadied her nerves about her new job, in fact. Now she felt ready to face anything.

It was early evening by the time they got home to the cottage, Joe dropping them off before driving back up the hill with the gentle glow of the setting sun behind him.

'Mind you wash your hands and faces before supper,' Violet told the kids wearily as they clattered noisily up the cottage stairs. 'And Janice, wash those muddy socks in the sink, wring them out, and hang them to dry in front of the range.'

Taking off her hat and coat in the hall, she turned to find Alice standing in the doorway to the kitchen.

'Hello,' Violet said, surprised and a little alarmed by her niece's unusually solemn expression. 'What's up?'

Alice held up a letter she'd been reading. 'This is from Lily,' she said in a low voice. 'I think you'd better read it, Aunty Vi.'

CHAPTER TWELVE

Demelza's first day as a Fire Guard trainee had been a weary nightmarish succession of information sheets, instruction booklets, lists of rules, and absolute command-ments drummed into her ears. Then, just as she'd thought she was getting the hang of things, the air-raid siren had gone off and all hell had broken loose.

A shrill bell had begun to ring throughout the down-stairs of the building, drilling at her eardrums. Women had appeared from nowhere, running about and shouting to each other as she stood bewildered in the cloakroom, caught in the middle of trying on her new uniform, which was basically a dark blue boiler suit worn with an armband marked Fire Guard. They'd banged lockers and thrown off clothing, and dragged helmets over their neatly set hair, and barely looked in her direction, except for one, who'd stopped to yell, 'Get to a shelter, you idiot,' before dis-appearing after the others.

Brought back to earth with a bump, Demelza had pulled on her day clothes again and scurried out to find the building deserted. Luckily, she'd been able to follow people in the street to the nearest shelter, below an arcade of shops, and sat out the air raid there, listening to the thump of anti-aircraft guns and wondering where she was meant to have been. It later turned out she should have been in the cosy cellar below the unit itself, though the team she'd seen getting dressed had gone out during the raid and helped the ambulance service in rescuing several people from a burning building before making it safe and checking for any unexploded bombs in the area.

She'd tumbled into bed that night utterly exhausted and would have slept through even an air raid except that somebody shook her violently in the early hours and dragged her down to the cellar to wait out yet another bombardment.

'This is getting ridiculous,' her roommate Rosemary had muttered, flicking irritably through a women's magazine while they waited for the all-clear. 'That's five raids this week. And I heard it's even worse further along the coast. They must have everyone in Germany making bombs. You'd think they'd run out sooner or later.'

'I hope they do,' Demelza had told her fervently, though she'd known there was little chance of that. Sometimes it felt as though there was no end in sight...

Seated on an old mattress on the floor, Demelza had hugged her knees to her chest and laid her head across her arms, trying to sleep. But Rosemary had started talking boys and dresses with a friend nearby, and the chatter of girls had kept her awake for ages. After what felt like hours, her weariness had won out, allowing her a little sleep. But the young woman who had been sleeping next to them, still wearing a nurse's uniform as though she'd just come off shift when the raid started, had eventually shaken her and Rosemary back to consciousness with a gentle hand.

'Back to bed, sleepy-heads,' the nurse had told them, yawning herself. 'Didn't you hear the all-clear? Though it's almost dawn now. Barely worth trying to get any more kip.'

'I'm willing to try,' Rosemary had moaned.

They'd both staggered back to the room they shared with Ellie, who'd gone home for a few days, fallen thankfully into bed and dragged the covers over their heads.

Some time later, Demelza woke to a room flooded with light and the other two beds empty. A quick glance at the clock told her what she'd dreaded. She had somehow overslept, missed breakfast, and was now late for her first-ever work shift.

Barely stopping to splash cold water on her face, brush her teeth, and drag a comb through her hair, Demelza hurriedly dressed and ran down to the main room, where she found her team already assembled and discussing the day ahead. A spontaneous round of applause rang out as she pushed through the heavy double doors and she blushed, stammering her excuses under the derisive eye of the unit commander.

'You're new, so you'll get a pass this time,' Jean said sharply. 'But three lates and you're out. Is that clear?'

'Yes, Captain Enys.'

'I've been reading out the pairings for trainees. You'll be with Mags.' She nodded to the posh girl Rosemary had been chatting to in the cellar last night. 'You've missed the briefing, so if you have any questions, you'll have to address them to her.'

Demelza made her way over to Mags as the others dispersed. 'Sorry about being so late. It's not that I can't get up early, more that I'm used to being in bed by half past nine.'

Mags, who was a shapely girl with jet-black hair skilfully moulded about her face, shot her a look of acute dislike. 'Where's your uniform? You can't go out in civvies.'

'In my locker,' Demelza admitted. 'I'll go and change straight away. What's our first job?'

'Checking premises for safety regulations. And get a move on, would you? If we're quick and get all our calls done before lunch, we'll have time to drop into the Pally.'

Mags followed her into the cloakroom where Demelza hurriedly struggled into her boiler suit, rolled the Fire Guard armband up over her sleeve, and grabbed a helmet down from the top shelf.

'The Pally?' she queried. 'Do you mean the Palace Bar?' It was a café-bar down near the harbour that had opened just prior to the outbreak of war; she had never been in there, but had heard stories about the place. It was the kind of noisy late-night venue where soldiers went to drink.

'Of course.' Mags reapplied her lipstick in her locker mirror and then began filing her nails; as soon as she'd finished, she pulled on a pair of thick safety gloves, and looked pointedly across at Demelza. 'Don't forget your gloves. Or you'll have hands like a labourer's within a week.'

'Oh, my hands are already pretty bad. Sheep farmer's daughter.'

Mags gave her a dismissive smile. 'Well, you'll have to handle a lot worse than mud and sheep droppings in this line of work.' And with that, she flounced out, leaving Demelza to follow, still fumbling with her outsized gloves.

'These are enormous,' Demelza said, hurrying after her. 'How are we supposed to pick anything up with these on?' She tried flexing her fingers and could barely move the stiff material.

'They were made for men's hands, not ours,' Mags said simply. 'You'll get used to them.'

They collected a small leather toolkit each, strapped it to their belts, and stepped out into the sunshine. A brisk wind was blowing off the sea and traffic was passing slowly in the street. Demelza recognised a grain wholesaler who was friends with her father among the drivers, but didn't dare call attention to herself by waving.

By now, her dad would be on the warpath and itching to get her back home. Best not to get people talking about her before she was ready to explain to him what she was doing.

Looking bored already, Mags consulted her clipboard.

'Number fifteen Bay View Terrace. They've been reported for not having a fire bucket.' She set off down the street at a march. 'Come along, farmer's daughter. You're not herding sheep now. No dawdling. You only get two weeks to learn the ropes. If you're still struggling after that, you might get thrown out.'

Demelza bit her tongue and followed without comment. She'd met other girls like Mags. Cool and unfriendly, and usually boy mad. But that didn't matter. She hadn't joined the service to make friends; she'd joined to make a difference and to escape her father's reach. Miraculously, she'd managed one of those goals already. Now it was time to work on the other one.

Outside air raid time, it was soon clear that the life of a Fire Guard was a fairly dreary one that consisted mostly of chatting to shopkeepers and householders about the need to keep fire buckets or blankets handy and exits clear of obstacles. They finished their round in good time, which seemed to please Mags, who took off her helmet and patted her hair.

'The Pally it is, then,' she said airily, pausing to check her reflection in a shop window before heading down a windy side street towards the harbour. 'We can't drink on duty – more's the pity – but a drop of coffee will set me up for the rest of the day. And there's someone there I need to see. You can wait outside if you like.'

'No fear,' Demelza muttered. 'I'm coming in too.'

'Suit yourself.'

But as they crossed towards the Palace Bar, her eye was caught by someone she recognised coming towards them. A schoolgirl, by the look of her regulation grey skirt and stout shoes. It was the young girl from the beach, one of the evacuees she'd helped rehouse. Janice, wasn't it?

'Hello again,' she said as they all drew level with the door to the bar, and such a ludicrous look of guilt crossed over Janice's face that Demelza instantly knew she must be up to no good. That suspicion was compounded by the fact that the girl was wearing scarlet lipstick and had removed her blazer so that she was less easily identifiable as a schoolgirl. Her dark hair, ordinarily worn in braids, was loose and curled about her shoulders. 'Do you remember me?'

'Y-Yes,' the girl stammered.

'Where are you off to?' Demelza frowned. 'It can't be lunch break at the school already. It's too early.'

'I ... I just nipped out before lunch. Doctor's appointment. I've got permission to be out of school, honest.'

'Is that so?' Demelza didn't believe a word of it, but sensed Mags' impatience to be going. She turned to the other Fire Guard. 'Look, you go ahead. I'll catch up with you.'

'Fine,' Mags said flatly, and pushed through the door into the café-bar without looking back at them.

Demelza studied Janice's averted face, noting the embarrassment and unease there. 'Were you planning to go into the Palace Bar too?'

'No, of course not,' Janice exclaimed, her eyes wide with horror, 'what do you take me for?' She sank her teeth into her lip, coating them with scarlet. 'Told you, I got a bleedin' doctor's appointment, ain't I? Not that it's any of your business.'

'No, I suppose not. But if you're in some kind of trouble—'

'I ain't in no trouble.' But the girl's eyes told a different story as she cast a regretful glance towards the bar door, and then tried to move past Demelza. 'Look, I've got to go. I'll be late.'

'Wait, at least tell me how you're getting on in Porthcurno? How are they treating you there?'

Janice hesitated, shifting from one foot to the other. 'They're nice people. Very nice. Especially Gran Hopkins. Though that Alice ... she reads a lot.'

'Is that a bad thing?'

'I dunno.' Janice shrugged, sulky now. 'Can I go now?'

'Of course.'

Demelza watched the schoolgirl trail slowly up the road they'd just come down, stopping at the top to look back at her once more before disappearing around the corner, her face stormy. Demelza was more convinced than ever that Janice had intended to go into the Palace Bar. But why? The girl was only fourteen, wasn't she? Who on earth would she be meeting in a sophisticated place like this? It was all very odd.

A little uneasy herself, she went inside the bar and soon located Mags flirting with a group of off-duty soldiers at the bar. It wasn't at all the sort of place she would ordinarily have visited. Not even for a special occasion. But then her father wasn't a pub-goer, so neither she nor Tristan had ever spent much time in watering holes, let alone somewhere like the Palace Bar.

Feeling like a fish out of water, Demelza took off her tin helmet marked 'F.G.' and patted her sticky-feeling hair, wishing she'd had time to check her reflection in a mirror first. But she smiled at the soldiers as Mags introduced her in an offhand manner, and even replied to one of them who politely asked how she was getting along in the Fire Guard. Above all, she tried not to let her inexperience show. She wasn't a school kid like Janice; she had to get used to a different lifestyle now that she had left home, even if only for three or four nights a week.

She scoured the place as discreetly as she could. The café-bar was lit dimly by wall bulbs in red fabric shades above every booth, the warm red cast of the light matching the booth seating. There was a small dais at one end of the bar which no doubt was used by musicians in the evenings, as the Palace boasted 'Live Music' on the sign outside. But although there were several groups of people drinking and even eating in the booths, she saw nobody waiting on their own or watching the door with expectation.

Perhaps she'd been wrong about Janice's intentions, she decided. Or perhaps she'd been coming in here for some other reason than to meet someone.

'Who on earth was that girl you were talking to?' Mags asked as they stood waiting for their coffee, which took forever to arrive. But there was only one man serving, and he seemed rushed off his feet, his expression pre-occupied as he took orders, poured drinks, and wiped down the counter with a damp cloth.

'Oh, nobody in particular.' Ignoring the curious glances of the soldiers, Demelza pulled off her thick gloves and tucked them into her belt as Mags had done. 'Just a friend of a friend.'

But she thought it might be a good idea to have a quiet word with Lily Hopkins about it next time they bumped into each other. Just in case that girl needed rescuing from herself. Assuming their ends of shift ever collided again...

CHAPTER THIRTEEN

On her rounds, Lily was delighted to come across Mr Jeremy Lister again; he was sitting up in bed on Ward Three, studying a hardback book on fishing with fascinated interest.

'Well, I never…' She stopped beside the bed and checked his chart. His vitals looked excellent, so she guessed he must have been making a good recovery from his ordeal. 'How are you feeling today, Mr Lister?'

He stared over the book at her in obvious confusion. 'I … I'm not doing too badly. Sorry, but … have we met?'

Lily laughed. 'You could say that. I helped you the day you were shot. Though you probably don't remember. I'm not sure you were fully conscious.'

'Well, blow me.' Jeremy Lister put down his book and held out his hand, his incredulous gaze fixed on her face. 'You must be … Lily, is it?'

'Spot on,' she said cheerily, shaking his hand. 'Nurse Fisher when I'm on duty though. Or I'll catch it from Matron,' she added conspiratorially, and began to take his pulse. It was slightly elevated from the last reading, but the excitement of their meeting now had probably caused that minor fluctuation.

When she'd taken his temperature and marked it on the chart, he asked her, 'But what are you doing here, if you don't mind me asking? The doctor told me you worked in St. Ives and were only visiting that day.'

'That's right.' Lily tidied his pillows. 'But it seems their need was greater here in Penzance. So I was transferred.'

He lay back against his pillows, and she could see the strain about his eyes and mouth as he smiled up at her, the book forgotten on the bed. 'St. Ives's loss is our gain,' he said, but she saw how his hand dropped to his belly, where a thick bandage could be seen through the loosely buttoned striped pyjamas. 'I'm really very grateful to you, Nurse Fisher. Dr Jerrard told me after the operation that I probably wouldn't be alive if it wasn't for you.'

'Goodness, I wouldn't go that far. Anyone would have done the same.' She paused, smiling. 'How is your sister, by the way? Did she have a girl or a boy in the end?'

'A boy. Matthew.' He looked away. 'After her late husband.'

'Both healthy?'

'Perfectly so. Again, thanks to you in part. I'm sure Emily would never have realised she was about to give birth if you hadn't spotted the signs so promptly. So we're doubly grateful.'

'Don't mention it.' She grinned, a little self-conscious. 'Your sister wasn't my first unexpected labour. You could say I have a talent for that kind of thing.'

'Obviously.' Jeremy Lister studied her curiously. 'Is that a London accent?'

'Dagenham.'

'Righty-oh.' His mouth compressed. 'If you came here to escape the bombing, you must be disappointed.'

'I'm more worried I brought it with me.'

'Nonsense.' He gave her a nod as she moved onto the gentleman in the next bed along. 'Thank you again, Nurse Fisher. My sister said you were an angel, and she wasn't far wrong. I owe you my life.'

Lily felt quite flustered by Mr Lister's insistence that she was some kind of ministering angel, and didn't know how to respond. She loved helping people, but it was always as part of a team and that was how she preferred it. Someone like Dr Jerrard might enjoy a patient's open gratitude, and deserve it too, but she just felt awkward and embarrassed.

At the convalescent home, the nurses had always enjoyed plenty of laughs and jokes with the patients, and she still preferred that light touch to being thanked so earnestly. Not for the first time, she wondered how her friend Mary was getting on back in St. Ives, for she would now be one of the more senior nurses. Mary would be lording it over the new trainees, and maybe having a little harmless fun at their expense. She hoped a letter would soon arrive from her, so Lily could catch up with all the gossip.

A wave of homesickness swept over her as she finished her round in Ward Three, and it was only when someone repeatedly said her name that she came back to the present moment with a jerk.

It was Dr Jerrard, blocking her way out of the ward. 'Nurse Fisher? Lily? Ah, the brain has engaged. Welcome back.' He was with a grey-haired lady in a dark grey uniform with a starched white apron and a pleasant smile.

'I want to introduce you to Miss Riley. She's the senior regional midwife in West Cornwall and heads up our team here as well. You might as well know; I've been singing your praises to her. So don't let me down.'

A little baffled by this, Lily shook hands with Miss Riley. 'Hello, it's nice to meet you.'

'Nurse Fisher.' Miss Riley looked her up and down. 'You're rather younger than I expected.'

Lily looked at the doctor for guidance. 'Sorry?'

'I told her you had excellent instincts with pregnant women,' he explained. 'Miss Riley plans to run some training courses over the summer and is looking for nurses who might like to dip a toe, as it were, into the wonderful world of midwifery.'

'Oh.' Lily beamed at the woman, suddenly understanding. 'Yes, I'd be very interested. Thank you for suggesting me, Doctor.'

'My pleasure.' Dr Jerrard nodded and moved on down the ward to speak to one of the patients.

Taking out a notebook, the midwife took her outside into the corridor for a quiet chat. 'Can you describe what kind of experience you have with pregnant or labouring women, if any, Nurse Fisher?'

Miss Riley struck her as a down-to-earth type, and Lily quickly felt at ease with her as they fell to discussing Lily's experience in the field of obstetrics, which entailed having delivered Hazel Baxter's baby girl on her own during an air raid – whom Hazel had named Lily, as a touching thank you – and looking after Mrs Maynard in the first stages of her labour.

'But I'm very keen to learn more,' Lily concluded.

'I'm glad to hear it.' Miss Riley beamed. 'And I'll put you on my list. Once I've found a suitable venue for the midwifery lectures and workshops, I'll be back in touch.'

Lily was delighted. She loved nursing, of course, but there was something about midwifery that fascinated and excited her. While the war was on, she felt her growing skills as a nurse, especially one with experience of war wounds, would be put to better use looking after hospital patients than delivering babies. But there was no harm in looking into the subject before the war was over.

A terrible thought crossed her mind as she returned to her duties. What if the war never ended? Or if it ended with Britain losing? But she straightened her spine, thrust her chin firmly in the air, and pushed that awful suspicion away. *Poppycock* is what Matron would have said to such an idea. There would be time enough to worry about Germany invading if such a dreadful day ever came. For now, she had patients to see and her duties to perform as competently and calmly as possible.

Violet tied on her work apron and glared at herself in the mirror, feeling utterly and thoroughly fed up. First, Lily had sent Alice a letter from Penzance claiming she'd seen young Janice truanting from school, and of course Janice had flatly denied it when accused, bursting into floods of tears and running hot-cheeked up to bed before anyone could get any sense out of her.

Then, the most awful news had come to Eastern House. Her boss, George Cotterill, had missed a step and fallen downstairs over the weekend, breaking his leg. Obviously, her heart went out to the poor man, and to his wife Hazel too, still nursing her new baby girl. But she'd heard his replacement was to be Danny Bellows, one of his assistants, a man who disliked Violet intensely. As a lowly cleaner, she'd made the occasional flippant remark to Danny and paid no attention to his sharp replies, never thinking that one day he would be her immediate boss. Now she was Housekeeper, she would have to report to him almost daily. How Danny must be itching to give her a hard time.

'You'll just have to be proper careful and not give that evil so-and-so any excuse to send you packing,' her mother had said upon hearing the news.

'Of course I'll be careful,' Violet had insisted, but chewed on an already hard-bitten fingernail. 'Only Danny's so good at getting a rise out of me, I dunno how I'm going to manage to keep quiet. Not until George's leg is mended and he's back at work. Why, that could take six months at least.'

Her mother agreed unhappily that she was probably right.

'Well, I don't give much for my chances,' Violet had said gloomily. 'Danny's a beast when he wants to be. And he knows just how to goad me into being cheeky.'

'Then just say nothing.'

Violet had stared at her mother in dismay. 'Nothing?'

'Not a dicky bird.' Her mum had shrugged, going back to the cooking pans she was scouring. 'That'll fox him.'

'I can't stand there like a statue, Mum. What if he asks me a question?'

'Well, answer it. But use as few words as possible. And whatever you do, don't embellish.'

'Emb... What?'

'Don't do what you always do, love, and go off on one

of your tirades. Or make a joke at his expense. Just stick to yes sir, no sir, and...'

'Three bags full, sir,' Violet had muttered, remembering having said something very similar behind George Cotterill's back before.

'Laugh all you like. But it's good advice, Vi. He can't say you've been cheeky if you don't open your mouth.'

Violet had been thinking about it all morning. Say nothing to her new boss for six whole months? It didn't bear thinking about.

Heading down the corridor to the mess hall, she was horrified and thrown into confusion by the sight of Danny Bellows talking to another member of staff.

Hurriedly, she started backing up, but he spotted the movement and called after her, 'Just a minute, Hopkins. Don't disappear back to your cubby hole. I'd like a word with you.'

Cubby hole? Cheeky blighter, she thought grimly, but fixed a bright smile to her lips and stood waiting, hands thrust into the pockets of her housekeeper's starched white apron.

'Mr Bellows,' she said as he approached, and resisted the urge to give him an ironic curtsy.

Danny was a narrow stick of a man, hollow-chested and with trousers hanging off skinny hips. Violet thought he'd probably disappear if he stood sideways.

'You'll have heard, no doubt,' Danny said in a voice as slimy as ten-day-old dripping, 'about George Cotterill's accident.'

'Uh-huh.'

'I'll be taking over until he's back at work. Which could be quite a long time.'

She merely nodded this time, reminding herself not to

risk saying something rude. His thin brows snapped together at her silence. No doubt he'd expected her to launch into some offensive comment about his inability to do the job and how she hoped George would come back even with his leg in plaster, because she'd be happy to push him around in a wheelchair if it meant Danny went back to being George's assistant and general dogsbody. However, she merely thought all those wicked things to herself, staring back at him without saying a word.

'Well,' Danny continued, 'now that you're Housekeeper, I'll be expecting a report from you every morning.'

'A report?' she echoed blankly.

'I want to make sure you're doing the job properly.' His smile was horribly smug. 'For instance, I noticed as I came into work today that all the windows need a proper clean. No doubt that's a low priority job to you, but in my book first impressions matter. Especially when Ministry dignitaries could be descending on us at any moment.'

She made a protesting sound, wondering if he knew something she didn't, and he put a shushing finger to his lips.

'But we mustn't discuss that kind of thing, must we? Loose lips sink ships.' He was sneering at her now. 'And you're not exactly on the "Need to Know" list, are you?'

In an effort not to say anything rude, Violet pressed her lips together so hard that they began to lose all sensation.

'Anyway,' he went on, 'those filthy windows need some attention, especially along the front of the building. How many cleaning staff have you got under you?'

Violet held up both hands, one with all four fingers and thumb extended, the other with only the thumb showing.

'Six?' Danny frowned. 'Then why not simply say so?

What's with the dumb show?' When she stared back at him blankly, he demanded, 'Is something wrong with your voice, Hopkins? Do you have a sore throat?'

She nodded vigorously. What an excellent excuse for not speaking; if only she'd thought of it sooner.

'I see.' Danny took a step back from her, as though worried she might be contagious. 'Well, get it sorted. And none of your usual lip, understood? Remember,' he added nastily, 'I'm not wet like George Cotterill, and my wife isn't one of your pals. So if you step out of line—'

'I didn't know you was even married,' she blurted without thinking, and then blushed, seeing his hard stare.

'I'm not, as it happens. Too smart to put my head in that particular noose. But I see your sore throat is miraculously better now.' His sneer returned. 'Might I suggest you get on with your first daily report? I want to see a list of all the housekeeping work you've done in the past week. And no making anything up.' He leant closer, prodding her shoulder with a thick finger. 'Don't mess me about on this, Hopkins,' he said, punctuating every other word with a hard prod, his bad breath in her face, 'or I'll see to it that you get the sack and never work here again. And your mate George won't be able to save you.' He sniffed and stalked away, adjusting the lapels of his new jacket. 'There's a new sheriff in town.'

Her temper boiling, Violet stuck two fingers up at Danny's retreating back and even thrust her tongue out as well. Unfortunately, in the split-second that her hand jerked out and her tongue waggled, her new boss looked back and caught her.

Oh blimey, she thought, meeting his incensed glare. That's torn it. Violet Hopkins, you complete idiot…

CHAPTER FOURTEEN

'Go on,' Mags urged, handing Demelza the ceiling pike – a length of metal with a hooded tip. 'You saw how I did it in the other property. Now it's your turn. Give it a good poke.'

They were standing in a terraced house on Regent Terrace in Penzance. Its nearest neighbour had been all but demolished during the night in a high explosive bombing raid, leaving its first storey open to the sea breeze off the bay and with rubble strewn across the street. Now the owners of the two houses on either side were currently at a local shelter for the displaced, in just the clothes they stood in, waiting to be told if their homes were safe to return to.

Settling her helmet more securely on her head, Demelza peered up at the wobbly looking ceiling of the sitting room and then raised the metal pike in a tentative fashion, pushing gently at the boards overhead.

'Give it a bit of welly,' Mags said impatiently and, grabbing her hand, thrust upwards with the pike.

There was an ominous creak, the whole structure tilted

at an alarming angle, and then dust and debris began to rain down on them as the ceiling sagged to one side.

'Out, out, quick!' Mags dragged a stunned Demelza by the arm and they fled together through the front door, pursued by the most terrifying rumbling sounds, emerging into early morning sunlight coughing and spluttering.

Inside, thankfully, the rumbling had stopped. The house was still standing. But it was clearly not safe to live in.

Mags' helmet and shoulders were thick with dust. 'Phawg,' she said incoherently, wiping her mouth. Even her eyelashes were tipped with dust.

Looking down at herself, Demelza realised that she too was coated in debris. 'Oops.' She brushed flakes of white ceiling paint off her arm. 'I think they may need to redecorate.'

Both girls looked at each other in mortified silence, and then burst into choking, hysterical giggles.

'*Give it some welly*,' Demelza repeated, mimicking Mags' posh voice, and bit her lip as Mags doubled over, her hoarse bark of laughter echoing down the empty street.

'You two girls gone mad, or what?' an ARP warden called across to them, shaking his head as he wandered past with a ladder balanced over his shoulder and a bucket of sand in the other hand. He too looked like he'd been up all night.

'It's either laugh or cry, darling,' Mags threw after him, but her expression had sobered. 'I suppose we'd better report back to the unit. And let them know at the shelter that this one isn't fit to live in.'

'Probably better for that ceiling to have come down on our heads than on a kiddy,' Demelza said thoughtfully.

Mags nodded, taking out her pad and starting a new report card. 'So … Number Three hasn't sustained any obvious damage, but Number Seven will need extensive repairs before it can be habitable.' She chewed the end of her pencil before adding in her elegant scrawl, 'Possible structural damage to external walls.'

While Mags was completing the time and date sections of the report card, Demelza chalked 'UNSAFE: DO NOT ENTER' on the door. Sometimes they cordoned off bomb-damaged areas, but the long front gardens would probably mean passers-by were in no danger. Pushing the chalk back into the top pocket of her boiler suit, she rubbed her hands together to clean them. With a final glance at the jumbled, chaotic remains of Number Five, where a bathtub still lay half-covered by a forlorn mattress in the lawned garden below, they packed up their toolkits and walked back to the unit. A demolition crew would be sent in later to knock it down completely and shore up the houses on either side, unless they felt the place could be salvaged, which looked unlikely.

The bombing raid had seen three separate teams going out last night during the tail-end of the raid itself, which had been terrifying. Luckily, she and Mags had not been anywhere near the active bombing sites, directing the Fire Brigade instead to a cottage on the edge of town that was burning, and staying for several hours after the fire was doused to make sure everyone had got out and the smouldering building was secure.

'There … there wasn't anyone at home, was there?' Demelza asked, her chest tightening at the words. She knew Mags had spoken to the neighbours further down the street about what had happened. 'When the bomb fell, I mean?'

Mags shook her head. 'They were all in the Anderson shelter out back, thank goodness. But they'd left the dog behind. Not enough room for it in the shelter, apparently.' Her eyes were sad. 'Poor thing.'

It was too horrible; Demelza felt her eyes well up with tears, thinking about the unfortunate animal, and chastised herself, having heard that at least one person had been killed in last night's bombing raid over Penzance and the surrounding area. They had to focus on people, Jean had told them at the briefing yesterday, after some foolish soul had nearly got herself killed scrambling after a cat as a bomb wailed through the night sky.

It was the end of her four-day shift, which meant she had the choice now whether to go home for her three days off, or stay in the unit. Here, she would be constantly woken by traffic outside and shift-change bells, and people coming and going at all hours, and the almost nightly scramble for the cellar when enemy planes were sighted. At home, things would be a great deal quieter, and indeed she longed for the privacy of her bedroom, looking out over peaceful green fields dotted by grazing sheep. But if she went home, she would have to face her father. And she'd been dreading that more and more as the days wore on, a deep gnawing in her gut as she imagined how angry he must have been on getting the note she'd left for him and Tristan.

After they'd handed in their kit and reports, Demelza and Mags shuffled upstairs for a wash and sleep.

'See you Tuesday, then,' Mags said, and disappeared into her room, her face aloof once more. She'd said she would be staying in Penzance over their time off, insinuating that she had someone special to see this weekend. One of those soldiers from the Palace Bar, perhaps?

With weary, fumbling fingers, Demelza stripped off her dusty, dirty boiler suit and dumped it into the unit wash basket on the landing before heading for the bathroom, which mercifully appeared to be vacant. A long soak in the tub made her feel more human, but limp too and ready for bed.

She emerged from the bathroom half an hour later, yawning weakly and hoping she could get a few hours' kip before making the decision whether or not to chance returning home.

Someone called her name as she stumbled back to her room, wrapped in her dressing-gown. It was Lily, dressed in civvies.

'Hello,' Demelza replied, smothering another yawn behind her hand. 'How are things at the hospital?'

'Madly busy.' Lily looked troubled. 'Look, I've just had a message from my aunt. The school's been in touch with her. You remember Janice?'

Demelza nodded. 'Of course. Is something wrong?'

'Seems like Janice's been bunking off school. You know, truanting. Not just once or twice but most days.' Lily paused, her eyes narrowing on Demelza's face. 'What is it?'

'I'm sorry, I meant to tell you… I spotted her myself in town the other day, about to walk into the Palace Bar down near the harbour, and she told me some whopper about skipping school for a doctor's appointment.'

'A bar?' Lily looked forlorn. 'Why doesn't that surprise me?'

'Is she in a lot of trouble?'

'The teachers are saying she needs to be rehoused in Penzance. That it's too hard to get hold of Aunty Vi whenever Janice doesn't turn up to class. She's in danger of getting kicked out if she doesn't toe the line. And I was wondering…'

Demelza, her brain tired, blinked up at her. 'Wondering what?'

'If you would be able to take her?' Lily touched her arm reassuringly. 'I mean your family. You said they live in Penzance, didn't you?'

'Yes, but—'

'The government will pay them for taking her,' Lily said, misunderstanding the reason for her hesitancy. 'Your dad can apply to the placement officer and the money will be transferred to him.'

'Oh, Lily, I don't know. My father … he's a farmer, you know. And he's not keen on children. He wouldn't be able to look after her.'

'But you'll be there for part of the week, won't you? And don't you have an aunt who lives with you?'

Demelza nodded. 'My aunt Sarah. Though she's not very strong.'

'And a brother too?'

'Tristan,' she agreed reluctantly. 'But I don't know if Janice will like it any better than living in Porthcurno. Farms are noisy, muddy places. And she'd have to walk several miles into town every day. And back again in the evenings.'

'She strikes me as a strong, healthy girl. I'm sure she'll manage. And my aunt Violet says Janice doesn't want to live in Porthcurno anymore, because it's "dull as ditch-water", so I doubt she'll kick up a fuss about it.' Lily gave her a winning smile. 'You've just come off shift, haven't you? Will you mention it to your dad when you go home?'

Demelza couldn't find a valid reason to say no, and ended up nodding helplessly. But her heart sank.

'Ta.' Lily gave her a quick hug, beaming. 'I owe you one for this. It's not been easy for Aunty Vi, taking in three more kids. Anything I can do to lift a weight off her shoulders will be worth it.'

It was late afternoon by the time Demelza was trudging up the long road out of Penzance, her dirty clothes crammed into a bag slung over her shoulder. Lost in thought, she was just wondering what her dad would say when she walked in, when somebody beeped a car horn right behind her, and she nearly jumped out of her skin. Spinning round, she saw a familiar van pull up and stop beside her, and her brother lean out of the window.

'Need a lift?'

'You wicked beast, Tristan,' she said on a heavy breath, a hand to her heart. 'I could have died of fright when that horn sounded.'

'I'd have thought you'd be used to beeps and bangs and whistles, being in the Fire Guard,' he said, grinning.

'Ha ha, very funny.' She stuck her tongue out at her brother. 'How did you know I'd be on my way home?'

'I didn't. I've been to the wholesalers. Better hop in, then. Unless you want to walk?'

'Definitely not. My feet are killing me.' She climbed into the passenger side of the van and had to balance her feet on a bag of seed potatoes in the footwell. 'What's this?'

'Dad's decided to expand the cottage garden. Spuds and onions, if you please. We need more veg for the autumn, he says.'

He checked behind them and then drove off, whistling tunelessly under his breath. Demelza swallowed at the thought of seeing her father again. Her hands were suddenly cold and clammy; she wrung them together in her lap, wishing she'd stayed in the Fire Guard Station instead of coming home for the weekend.

'And what else does he say?' she asked, her voice shaking.

'That he's "considering" taking on a few Land Girls. Hence the need for more spuds, I expect.'

That surprised her, though it hadn't been what she meant. 'Oh, that's a change. I didn't think he wanted strangers staying on the farm.'

'No, he doesn't. But with you gone—'

'So it's my fault.'

Tristan pulled a face. 'Everything's your fault, didn't you know that? Well, if you didn't, he'll be sure to let you know the instant you walk in the door.'

'Don't joke about it, Tris. Can't you see I'm bloody terrified?'

He slowed to a crawl, staring at her sideways. Then stopped dead right in the middle of the road. 'What's this? You're not serious?' He studied her face. 'What do you think Dad's going to do? Give you a good hiding and lock you in the coal cellar?'

'Maybe.'

'Don't be daft, woman. He's not a Neanderthal. Anyway, even if he was that kind of brute, do you think for a minute that I'd let him treat my own sister that badly?' He took her hands and chafed them back into warmth, a frown in his eyes. 'For God's sake, Demmy.'

'Is he angry?'

Tristan hesitated. 'When he first read your note ... yes. He wanted to know where you'd gone. What kind of "war work" you'd signed up for. But I didn't tell him.' His smile was grim. 'I pretended I didn't have a clue where you were or why you'd suddenly up and left. But I told him to stop going on about nothing, and how we'd cope without you. Just like we coped without Mum.'

She stared at her brother in mute astonishment.

'What?' With a short laugh, Tristan released her hands and put the car back into gear as a milk truck lumbered up behind them on the hill. 'You didn't think he'd listen to reason?'

'I didn't know you'd stand up for me. I mean, I hoped ... but I know what Dad can be like when he gets in a temper.'

'Have a little faith.'

She found herself smiling. 'How's Aunt Sarah taken it? I hope he hasn't roped her into doing the cooking? Or feeding the chickens?'

'She's done both since you've been gone.'

Her jaw dropped. 'I don't believe it.'

'Well, I wasn't feeding the chickens. And you can be sure Dad wasn't either. So that only left poor Aunt Sarah.' He stuck his arm out of the window to signal a right turn and swung off down the farm track. 'It took her an hour the first time, mind. And then she forgot to start supper until it was nearly dark.'

'Oh dear.' Demelza bit her lip, guiltily aware that she'd left her invalided aunt in the lurch by volunteering. 'After having a stroke too...'

'To be honest, I think it's done her some good. She won't get better sitting around for hours every day, will she? Though it's true we've been eating dinner late without you. Very late some nights. Once, Dad almost gave up on her trying to boil a ham for us. Said he was going out for fish and chips. You should have heard Aunt Sarah yell ... I thought she was going to burst a blood vessel.' Tristan had a little chuckle at the memory. 'After that, I offered to prepare the vegetables for her. Not exactly my cup of tea. But it was either that or not eat until midnight.'

'Thank you,' she said, knowing how much it must have cost him to lose so much free time on coming home every night.

'Well, like you say,' he pointed out, 'there's a war on. We've all got to do our bit.'

They had come to a stop outside the farmhouse. The sun was setting and there was a soft glow about the old, ivy-clad walls. She heard the distant cries of sheep and a deep sense of familiarity washed over her. But she wasn't at peace. Her heart was thumping and she felt sick. She didn't move, taking deep breaths and trying to imagine this was just another burning building she had to enter, scared or not. Then she thought over what he'd said, and something in his tone struck her as odd.

'Tris,' she whispered, 'you're not thinking of leaving too, are you? Of enlisting, I mean?'

He was silent for a moment, his hands still clenched on the steering wheel. 'It's crossed my mind, yes.'

'Oh, Tris.'

'I won't, though. Not unless things get really bad. If it looks like we're losing the war, I mean.' He gave her a swift, reassuring glance. 'I know I'm needed here.'

'And if Dad does take on some Land Girls?'

He shrugged. 'I need to do something. I can't stay here forever. Not while so many are dying.'

'But I thought you didn't believe in war? I thought you hated the idea of fighting?'

'I do. But you know what Dad's like, always moaning on about Conscientious Objectors… "Bloody Conchies, those yellow cowards!" You think he's going to want a son who's a draft dodger? He wouldn't be able to hold his head up in public if they call up young farmers and I don't go.'

'I suppose you're right.'

His face had hardened. 'I'll just have to hope I get shot before I have to shoot anyone myself.'

She shuddered. 'Tris, don't!'

'Sorry,' he said simply, 'I know you don't want to hear that kind of thing. But we can't all be bloodthirsty types. And I'd rather be killed than be a killer.'

Demelza didn't know what to say to that.

Her brother got out of the van and came round to her side, opening the passenger door and reaching in for the sack of seed potatoes. 'Here, mind your feet, sis.' Dragging it out with a grunt, he gave her a quizzical look. 'Sleeping in the van tonight, are you?'

'Could you blame me if I did?'

But she climbed out reluctantly, swinging her bag of washing over her shoulder just as the front door to the farmhouse opened. Her father stood there, looking straight at her.

'Come home at last, have you?' he said as they walked across the yard, his voice rough.

Demelza stopped in the doorway, trembling slightly, and was shocked when her father dragged her close in a fierce embrace.

'It's good to have you back, child,' he said hoarsely before releasing her.

'I'm not home forever, Dad,' she said in a rush, worried that he'd misunderstood why she was there. 'I have to go back on Tuesday. For my next shift.'

'Shift?'

'I'm working for the Fire Guard,' she explained. 'Four nights on, three nights off, for the first six weeks.'

'I see.' His mouth had compressed, but he jerked his head in a sharp nod. 'Well, you're home for now.' He stood aside to let her and Tristan pass. 'Your aunt's in the kitchen, preparing supper. I expect she'll be glad of your help.' He paused, then added gruffly, 'Once you've had a chance to settle back in, that is.'

She made hurriedly for the stairs, catching Tristan's ironic gaze and trying not to grin in stunned relief. She had braced herself to face shouting and swearing from her father, and instead she'd got … almost a welcome home, by Dad's standards.

A sudden thought struck her. 'Oh,' Demelza said, and shocked herself by swinging around at the foot of the stairs, 'and there's an evacuee who might be coming to live with us.' She took a deep breath, determined to take advantage of his good mood. 'A schoolgirl called Janice.'

'I beg your pardon?'

'She's not had an easy start in life, Dad, and can be a bit of a handful at times. But I said we had plenty of room and would be happy to take her.' She met her father's incredulous gaze with her chin raised and a challenge in her eyes. 'We will, won't we?'

CHAPTER FIFTEEN

Porthcurno, South Cornwall, late May 1942

Violet, her hands plunged in cooling washing-up water, stopped and stared out of the kitchen window at the boys kicking a ball in the small backyard of the cottage. The repeated thunk-thunk-thunk of the ball hitting the wall as Eustace played had given way to shrieks and shouts now that Timothy had gone outside too, making the most of the fading light. It was good to see the boys enjoying themselves after several days of moping about the cottage and glaring at her occasionally like she was a bloomin' murderess, when in fact all she'd done was arrange for Janice to live with that friend of Lily's in Penzance. And Janice had been all the happier for it, as far as anyone could tell.

'Country life ain't for everyone,' she muttered to herself, and rinsed out the mug she'd been scrubbing, having failed to remove the tea stains.

'What's that, love?' Her mother came ambling into the

kitchen with the last two supper plates and stacked them on the kitchen counter. 'Here, you're running out of room on that draining board. At this rate, you'll be stacking mugs on the windowsill soon.' She snatched up a tea towel. 'I'll dry, shall I? Clear a bit of space...'

'Thanks, Mum.' Violet scrubbed the cutlery, not really seeing the knives and forks, her mind elsewhere. 'Do you think I was wrong to split them up?'

'Janice, you mean?' Her mother rubbed forcefully at a tea mug. 'Don't you fret. She weren't happy here, love. But them boys are. Look at them kicking that football like they're playing at Wembley, bless their hearts.' She peered into the mug. ''Ere, you haven't done a great job on this mug. It's as brown as a hen in there.'

'Who cares?' Violet pulled a face and started on the dirty plates, her shoulders slumped. 'Story of my life, that is. I never do a great job of anything ... except getting sacked.'

'And you think feeling sorry for yourself is going to help?'

'I'm facing facts, that's all.' She shook her head. 'I've made a right mess of everything.'

'Now buck up. You'll land on your feet, Vi. You always do.'

'Not this time.' Violet wiped away a tear with a wet, soapy hand. 'I got the sack, Mum. My first chance at a proper job, with good money behind it and my own office ... and I stuck two fingers up at Danny Bellows and he sacked me on the spot for it.'

Her mother was silent for a while, though she was breathing heavily, something she tended to do when brooding. 'I expect he deserved two fingers.' She paused. 'Maybe more than two.'

The boys were arguing about something now, their high-pitched voices raised in the dusk.

Violet leant forward and rapped on the window. 'Stop it, you two,' she called, and the noise abated.

'They need to come in and go to bed,' her mother said.

Violet didn't respond but went back to rinsing off the plates, her whole body bent over the sink. But she knew she couldn't keep quiet any longer.

'That's not the worst of it though, Mum,' she admitted at last. 'There's something I haven't told you.'

'More bad news?'

Violet bit her lip. 'Do you remember how Mr Cotterill let us have this place on a special rent because we were all working up at Eastern House?' When her mum nodded, watching her, she went on guiltily, 'Well, now that Lily's away nursing, and Alice has taken that job at the school, and I've been given the bloomin' heave-ho … none of us work at Eastern House anymore.'

'So what?'

'So Danny Bellows says we have to leave the cottage to make way for one of the officers' families instead.'

'Bloody hell.' Her mum stared. 'How long have we got?'

'A fortnight.'

'Only two bloomin' weeks?' Her mum sank down onto the stool, a wet plate forgotten in her hands, staring in dismay. 'But we've nowhere to go, Vi. And no money to pay for a new place.'

'I know, Mum.'

Her mother groaned. 'I should have taken on work to

help out. I've been trying to persuade Arnold at the shop to let me sell some of my cakes there, but he's a stubborn old so-and-so.'

'Cake money won't be enough to pay the rent on this place,' Violet pointed out, 'so there ain't no point worrying about that.'

'Well, you'll just have to go back to Eastern House. Talk to that Danny Bellows again. Apologise, if you must. But tell him he can't throw us out on the street. We've got them young boys to look after now. And what about Alice? She's sitting pretty with that posh job at the school, we can't have the poor girl living on the streets.'

'He won't change his mind. He was clear about that.'

She didn't describe how Danny had practically frog-marched her down to the main office to fetch her salary to date, sign her off the payroll, and inform the security guards to escort her to the gate out of Eastern House and never let her back in again. She wanted to wipe the whole episode from her memory. Not least because she knew she was to blame for everything.

'Talk to Mr Cotterill, then,' her mum insisted. 'He's a nice man, he'll sort us out. Or better yet, go and sweet-talk his wife. Hazel's a good friend of yours, isn't she? She'll make him tell that nasty Danny Bellows to give you back your job. Or at least let us stay in the cottage until you're fixed up with more work.'

'Can't.' Violet shook her head. 'George has gone away.'

'What do you mean, gone away?' Her mother's eyes widened in disbelief. '*With a broken leg?*'

'Hazel will have been driving the car. She knows how.' Violet swallowed hard. 'I went up to their quarters at

157

Eastern House, but apparently he's gone away to convalesce. Taken Hazel and the baby and gone to stay with her married sister for a few weeks, somewhere upcountry. They didn't even have an address where I could write to him.'

'But the boys ... this house ... we've been so happy here.' Her mother was crying now too, tears running down her lined cheeks. The sight made Violet's heart squeeze in guilt and unhappiness. 'What are we going to do?'

'I don't know, Mum.' Violet took the plate away before she could drop it, and set it gently on the draining rack instead. She had tried apologising to Danny several times, even pleading with the nasty man to let her keep her job, but it had done no good. The only option was to find herself new work that would keep their little family afloat. Eastern House was the biggest employer in the Porthcurno area, which meant she might have to look further afield. Where, though? 'But I'm the one who did this,' she added grimly. 'So I'm the one who has to fix it.'

Lily paused outside the arcade of shops on her way home from the hospital and wondered if she should go in and browse the clothing boutique in case anything new had come in since she last checked. Not that she was fashion-mad, like some of the other girls at work. But it would be nice to have something else to wear other than the rather worn, ill-fitting outfits she'd been relying on since leaving home. One of the nurses had asked her to an impromptu birthday party at the weekend and she'd declined, too bone-tired after a long shift to face loud music and drinking. But it was at the back of her head that, if she did ever go to a party, she had nothing very fashionable to wear.

Though, after receiving the latest letter from home, perhaps keeping her pay in her pocket a little longer would be a good idea. Her aunt had written a few days ago to tell her they were being evicted from the cottage in Porthcurno and couldn't get hold of George Cotterill to beg for help. She'd written back at once to suggest getting in touch with Eva, daughter to the colonel who'd once been in charge of Eastern House, sure that their old friend would speak for them. But Aunty Violet had replied yesterday, saying that since the colonel's redeployment to the southeast, Eva had gone back to London with her new husband, Flight Lieutenant Max Carmichael, and might not return for some time.

Besides, Lily thought, studying the well-tailored outfits in the shop window, it would be just as well to seem dowdy. She knew men always took an interest in her looks, and she simply didn't feel ready to deal with that again. Every time a man got too near, her nerves begin to jangle as she remembered how her horrid Uncle Stanley had dragged her into the barn on his farm, where they'd been staying when they first came down to Cornwall from London, and had touched and kissed her...

Lily jumped, heart thumping, abruptly dragged back to the present as a group of school children streamed past her, chattering in a lively fashion.

Catching a familiar face reflected in the shop window, Lily turned, calling after them impulsively, 'Janice?'

Janice looked back at her, surprised, and then excused herself from the others, who walked on without her. 'Hello again,' she said, coming up to Lily with a shy smile. 'Thank you for persuading Demelza to let me stay with her family out at the farm. It was very kind of you.'

'Nonsense.' But Lily smiled, glad she'd been of some use. She'd heard all about Janice's move from her aunt's letters, and also Demelza when she'd come back for her next shift, but then her aunt had been served the eviction notice and she hadn't heard anything more about it. 'How are you settling in?'

'Just grand. It's much nearer school, and I'll be able to come into town at weekends now too, and … and see my friends.'

Lily suspected she'd been going to say something else and then changed her mind. She recalled that Demelza had seen her trying to enter a bar in the town, and wondered what she was up to. But she knew there was no point pressing her for an explanation. The girl would only clam up.

'And what are they like? Demelza's family, I mean … are they being nice to you?'

'You mean, old Mr Minear calling me "Essex gel" every time he bloomin' sees me?' Janice's eyes flashed briefly, but she quickly returning to smiling. 'Oh, it's not so bad. I like her brother Tristan. Have you met him?'

Lily shook her head. 'Not yet.'

'Their aunt's a bit odd too. Speaks funny, with her mouth turned down, and walks with a stick.'

'Sounds like she's had a stroke.'

'I dunno what that means.' Janice shrugged, playing with her dark hair. 'But it's more fun than being cooped up in that tiny place in Porthcurno.'

'I'm sorry you weren't happy there.'

'Oh, don't get me wrong,' Janice said quickly. 'I was ever so grateful to have a roof over me head. And I love your aunt, she's a sweet lady. But there weren't no room to breathe, see? I had to bunk up with Alice, and the boys were on the floor in the front room. Not exactly comfy.' Her face lit up with joy. 'At the farm, they've given me a bedroom all to meself. It's proper la-di-da.'

Lily grinned, understanding perfectly. 'I shared with Alice for years. It wasn't much fun.'

'She's always reading books, that one.'

'I know.'

'And she snores something rotten.'

'Agreed.' Lily paused. 'Once I snuck over and popped a clothes peg on her nose. You should have heard her shriek. Woke the whole house.'

They both laughed, but at that moment, the air-raid siren went off. They stopped laughing and looked up into the pale blue sky in silence. There was a brisk wind coming off the sea that day, and the arcade awning above them flapped and snapped in the wind as they listened for the high-pitched whine of German engines.

'We ought to get to a shelter,' Lily said, taking command.

But she knew the nearest shelter had been closed after a direct hit to the building above it, and in her tired state, she suddenly wasn't sure which way to go.

'Quick, let's go this way,' Janice said, grabbing her hand and beginning to run.

Lily followed at the same harried pace, dashing through a shadowy alleyway and along an empty side-street, and then puffing up a steep hill, which she recognised as the road out of town. The wail of the siren had died by then and the silence was eerie.

'Wait, Janice.' Thoroughly confused, she slowed to a walk, asking in panting breaths, 'Where are we going?'

'Back to the farm, of course.'

It was hard to stay calm, having seen a few charred bodies brought into the hospital mortuary and plenty of walking wounded with horrific injuries, all in the past week alone. The Jerries seemed determined to bomb the hell out of Penzance, like all the towns along the Cornish coast. 'Hitler's softening us up for an invasion,' one of the hospital doctors had suggested only yesterday, and it was hard not to agree with that awful possibility. Already, Lily could hear the thin whine of engines far above them in the clouds, and looked up, catching the ominous glint of sunlight on metal wings.

'The farm? But we'll never get there in time,' Lily exclaimed, staring at the schoolgirl in consternation. She stopped and headed back towards the town, her feet aching. 'Come on, maybe it's not too late to find another shelter.'

A violent explosion somewhere ahead stopped her in her tracks. Her ears hurt from the impact, the sound seeming a thousand times louder outdoors than when heard deep inside a shelter. As she watched, slack-jawed, her hearing muffled, a thick plume of black smoke rose and billowed above the crumpled rubble of a building in the town centre.

''Ere, stop staring and start bleedin' running!' Janice insisted, and grabbed her hand again.

Behind them in the town, another explosion burnt the air black. Almost immediately, the far-off tinkle of bells from a fire engine could be heard, bravely on its way to the scene of devastation. Since their chances of finding a shelter in town were long past, Lily obediently took to her heels, and the two of them sprinted up the hill, red-faced and gasping for breath. Lily had naturally long legs, so rarely ever needed to walk quickly to keep up with others. Today, despite her long shift at the hospital, she was absolutely belting along, running faster than she'd ever done in her life, even at school sports day. And for good reason.

She had a vision of a German pilot high in the scudding clouds spotting their fleeing figures and steering their way to drop a bomb especially for them, incinerating them where they stood, and fear lent her wings. Her heart was thudding hard enough to burst by the time they flung themselves up a narrow, muddy track that led to a large, grey-walled farmhouse, smothered in ivy and with all its sea-facing windows reflecting the smoking town below.

'Here!' Janice gasped and flung open a set of double doors set into the ground, opening into what was clearly a large cellar. She sent Lily down the steps first and climbed in after. 'Follow the light,' she whispered unsteadily, and pushed her ahead in the flickering darkness. 'I'm right behind you. I need to close the doors.' And with that she reached up to drag the heavy double doors shut after them.

Panting, her feet throbbing with pain, Lily took a few shuffling steps into the dark and hoped not to bump into anything.

'Tris? Mr Minear?' Janice called out breathlessly. 'Hello, I can see the light. Who's in the shelter?' She paused. 'It's Janice, and I've brought a friend of Demelza's home with me. We got caught out when the siren went off so we had to make a run for it.'

Round a wooden screen, a lamp glowed, held aloft and swaying as it came towards them. Then a face emerged in its yellow light. It was a young man with a halo of bright ginger curls and a face like an angel, his smile warm and welcoming.

'Hello,' he said, and put out a calloused hand, which Lily shook, still dazed and breathing hard. 'How do you do? I'm Tristan.'

CHAPTER SIXTEEN

Horribly, the family on the top floor hadn't made it out of the house in time. Mr and Mrs Hunt, Mrs Hunt's widowed sister Melanie, and a two-year-old boy, name unknown. The neighbours weren't quite sure if the child had been Mrs Hunt's or her sister's. Mags had filled out the report sheet as best she could, her face pale and drawn, her hand shaking. Where the house had stood was a crater, filled with rubble and charred-looking objects Demelza knew were probably body parts.

She took a deep breath to steady herself, and then coughed and spluttered as dust and debris filled her lungs. She rubbed her face and realised she was crying too. She'd seen quite a few dead bodies now, though this was the first time she'd come to a bomb site and there'd been nothing left to identity. It was the fact that nobody had known the little boy's name, or even which woman had been his mother, that was haunting her. The consensus was only that they had moved in a few months back and hadn't been Cornish. 'Kept themselves to themselves,' one of the neighbours had said, averting her gaze from the remains of the building.

Even the Hunts' nearest neighbours on the floor below, the ones who'd been out at work when the siren went, had shrugged and been unable to help. Yes, they'd been new to the neighbourhood. But surely somebody here ought to have known that child's name and who his mother was? Surely a person couldn't die in this horrible fashion and there be nobody alive to tell us anything about him? Though there was precious little left to bury, so perhaps it didn't matter, she thought, looking about wretchedly. The bomb had disintegrated their bodies along with all of their belongings, so that the rubble looked oddly stark – heaps of stone, with the occasional garish flash of wallpaper.

But it ought to matter, Demelza thought, staring at the ruins. A person's life had to count for more than that. More than an anonymous grave or a coffin filled with stones so the mourners wouldn't realise there was nothing recovered but a few scraps of scorched flesh and a shoe strap.

'Demelza, pull yourself together.' Mags thrust a bucket and pump into her hand. 'There's a fire starting at the back next door. Follow that woman and put it out. Then we'll have to go on to the next site. Make sure it's safe.'

She obeyed without comment, following the neighbour, who was in her sixties and very chatty, out to the next door's backyard, where a fire had spread somehow to an outdoor toilet and shed.

'Can you hook this up to the tap?' she asked, passing the narrow tube through the kitchen window.

She was never sure how these small fires started, but they were often to be found in the aftermath of bombings, and it was one of their duties as Fire Watchers to put them out and report them to the Fire Service if they were too large to be handled with a hand pump or some sand.

'We kept flammables in the shed,' the neighbour was telling her, but Demelza wasn't really listening, working the pump handle as hard as she could. 'Do you think that's what caused the fire when the bomb fell?'

'Very likely,' she said, pausing to push back her helmet and wipe sweat from her forehead. The sun felt very hot today, but the scudding clouds had finally dispersed. 'Look, did you know the little boy's name? The one who…' She swallowed on a wave of sickness. 'The one next door?'

'No, I never even spoke to them. I think Mr Hunt had a gammy leg. That's all I know.' The woman paused. 'You all right, love?' She insisted on fetching a glass of water. 'You look a bit peaky. Perhaps you should take a breather. The fire's nearly out now.'

Demelza nodded, thanking her mechanically.

When the fire was finally out, she made her way back out to the front of the row of houses and found that the ambulance service had arrived in her absence. One of them was a woman who was carefully searching through the rubble with a bucket for human remains. The other was the fair-haired, bear-like man she remembered from the beach that day when Mr Lister was shot. The one who'd made her think of marauding Vikings, a thought which didn't quite match his ambulance uniform.

'You again,' he said in his deep voice, and she looked up into a rugged face and sky-blue eyes, blinking at him.

'Sorry?' She hadn't thought he'd recognised her.

'This makes three times we've met. I'd better introduce

myself.' He shook her hand. 'I'm Robert. What should I call you?'

Her head was still spinning. She dragged off her helmet. It was so hot, she felt like she was going to faint. 'Demelza,' she managed to croak.

'You don't look well, Demelza. Do you need to sit down?' Before she knew what was happening, he had scooped her off her feet and was carrying her up into the back of the ambulance, where it was quiet and dark. 'It's all right. You're not to blame. It takes us all like that sometimes.'

'What does?' she whispered.

'The shock,' he said bluntly, and pulled a flask out of a chest screwed to the wall of the ambulance. 'Here, sit on the stretcher there and get some of this down you.'

'What is it?' She sniffed at it dubiously, and then shook her head. 'Brandy? No thanks.'

'That's very commendable of you. But a quick swig won't do you any harm.' He crouched and held the flask to her lips. 'Go on, you'll thank me for it later.'

Feeling she had little to lose, Demelza took a hurried sip of the brandy, and then another, shuddering as the fiery liquid hit the back of her throat.

'Oh God...' She sagged forward and Robert caught her. 'Lie down.' He loosened the top button of the dark blouse she was wearing under the boiler suit, and she tried to push him away. 'Hush, I'm not going to molest you. You need air.' Once she was sitting with her eyes closed, he put away the brandy flask and stood over her. 'Feeling better yet?'

She was, she realised. The brandy had reached her tummy, and its warmth had started to revive her flagging spirits.

'A little,' she admitted reluctantly.

'Look, I've got to help my colleague. It's not a nice job and she needs a break. But you stay here until we're done. I'll tell Her Nibs out there you need a ten-minute break. That should keep her off your back while you recover.'

Her Nibs?

He meant Mags, she realised. 'Wait, why are you...?' Confused, she peered up at him, outlined against the bright sunshine. 'I mean, tell me to mind my own business, but you're very young for an ambulance driver. Why weren't you called up?'

Most younger men who hadn't enlisted in the armed forces had a physical problem of some kind that prevented them from being able to serve. Except for those whose professions were protected, like her brother and father. Though she knew if the war went on much longer, they too might be called up.

'I was,' he said easily.

'Sorry?' The pain in her head was slowly receding, she realised. She managed to sit up, staring at him. 'I don't understand.'

'I was called up. But I declined the draft and registered as a Conscientious Objector. Now if you'll excuse me...'

With that, Robert jumped down and went to join his colleague. A moment later, she heard his deep voice speaking to Mags, explaining that she was dizzy and needed a break. To Demelza's surprise, Mags did not immediately throw open the double doors of the ambulance and demand that she come out at once, calling her all the names under the sun. But the ambulance driver had such an air of authority about him, Mags had

169

probably been over-awed by his calm explanation and didn't dare interfere.

For a long while, Demelza stared at the empty doorway in dismay. She couldn't believe her ears and sat still, bewildered, wondering if those few sips of brandy had been enough to addle her brain. Because she knew her father's low opinion of Conscientious Objectors, how they were all lying cowards who deserved to be publicly flogged, and she point-blank refused to believe that about the man she'd just met. How could such a huge bear of a man, a blue-eyed Viking, a man who looked born to be a warrior, possibly be that most hated of creatures: a *conchie*?

Violet was wrapping her mum's best china in old newspaper, hoping to protect the cups and saucers Sheila had brought down from London with her against breakage, when there was a loud knock at the door.

Trying in vain to wipe newsprint off her hands, she hurried down the hall and unlatched the door. 'Yes?'

It was Joe Postbridge, leaning on his stick.

'Hello,' he said, and removed his cap with a bob of his head, just like an old-fashioned country gent saying good day to a lady. 'I heard about your troubles, and thought I'd better call by.' He glanced at her blackened hands. 'Have I come at a bad time?'

Her heart had sunk at the sight of him because the only place she'd been able to secure had been temporary lodgings in Penzance, just until Alice had taken her matriculation. After that, she had no idea where they'd be living. But she doubted it would be anywhere near Porthcurno, so there was a strong chance she might never see him again once they'd left the village, and that thought had lowered her spirits until they were almost in the gutter.

'Newsprint,' she explained briefly. 'You'd better come in, Joe. Hang up your cap and coat, and I'll put the kettle on.' She was trying to sound brusque and unfriendly, as though he meant nothing to her, because that seemed the best way to deal with things. But in truth she had never felt so heartbroken. 'So, what exactly did you hear, and what made you think I'd be glad to see you?'

Limping into the kitchen, Joe pulled up a chair to the table and sat. He watched while she washed her hands with coal tar soap, filled the tin kettle and set it on the range to boil, and then stood opposite him, her arms folded, chest heaving in her stained wrap-around apron.

'Are you not glad?' he asked mildly.

She opened her mouth to say no. And then shut it again. 'What I am,' she said, trying not to be rude, 'is busy.'

'Because you've lost your job and Danny Bellows has served you a notice of eviction from this place,' he said calmly, and added, with a glance at the cups she'd been wrapping, 'and you're packing up your china.' He glanced down the empty hall as the kettle began to hum on the hot plate, and frowned at the silence. 'Where's Alice?'

'Not back from work yet.'

'And your mother?'

'Gone to the shop. She spends more time round there these days than at home. She's soft on that old geezer, mark my words, though she won't admit it.' Violet's heart squeezed in distress, thinking of her mother's glum face since she'd heard they were being evicted. 'She'll have to learn to live with disappointment though, won't she?

Because we're leaving Porthcurno by the end of this week, come rain, come shine.'

His frown deepened. 'Where will you go?'

'We've been offered a room in Penzance. Above a shop.'

'One room? For all of you?'

'That's right.'

'Even the boys?'

Her mouth crumpled but she refused to let him see her cry. 'Only me, Mum and Alice. The boys are going to a new family. I don't know where yet. The placement officer will be in touch in the next few days. He'll drive them down there himself, he says, once he's found someone to take them in as an emergency case. So, I've to pack up their things as well. Not that there's much to pack.'

'And how are they taking it?'

'Oh, you know what young lads are like. Up in arms about it, saying they won't go. But I've told them it's the law. It's done and dusted, and no point arguing with the placement officer.'

'I see.'

Her arms tightened about her chest; that hadn't quite been the angry response she'd been hoping for.

She sniffed a few times, her vision swimming now, only just managing to stave off tears by clenching her jaw with steely determination. 'Best thing for them, of course, poor little blighters.' Her voice was croaky. 'Can't be bouncing about from pillar to post every few weeks. Kids need somewhere stable to live. A proper home.'

'Agreed,' Joe said, much to her outrage.

'Well,' she told him raggedly, a tear rolling down her cheek, 'you could at least be on my side for once, Joe

Postbridge.' She stamped her foot, her chest swollen with indignation and grief. 'If … if that's all you came to say, you can forget the bloody cuppa and get out of my kitchen.'

He stared at her, and then got up and walked back down the hall to where he'd left his cap.

'You get back here,' Violet choked, taking the bubbling kettle off the range before following him into the hall. 'I've changed my mind. I haven't finished with you after all. How can you say nothing when those evil so-and-so's are taking our little boys away from us? Haven't they suffered enough? And now they're to be stuck somewhere new, with God knows what kind of family?' She thumped herself repeatedly on the chest. 'At least *we* can understand them. *We're* their people. *We're* from the same place.'

'I know,' he said, cap in hand, not moving.

'So, what are you going to do about it?' she demanded furiously, tears streaming down her cheeks.

'I'm going to invite you and your mother, and Alice, and the boys,' he said quietly, 'to come and live with me up at the farm, rent free.' He paused, his dark gaze searching her face. 'Not to put you under an obligation to me,' he added awkwardly, 'but so you won't get split up. You can keep the money the government gives you for looking after those evacuees, so they won't go short of anything. And Alice can keep working at the school without having to squeeze in with you and her gran in one room above a shop, which I can't believe would be very comfortable for a young woman her age.'

Stunned, Violet rubbed her sleeve across her wet face. 'Oh.' Then she sank down onto the floor in the hall, which was uncomfortable as it had been laid with green, tile-effect linoleum to match the kitchen, and buried her face in her hands. 'Oh, Joe.'

He still didn't move, watching her. 'Is that a yes?'

'Yes.'

'Ah.' Joe dragged on his cap, sucked in a deep breath, and then blew it out in an exaggerated fashion. 'You're a hard woman to understand, Violet Hopkins. But I'm glad to be able to help you. And I promise, I won't expect anything in return.' He paused. 'Except your company, perhaps. It can get lonely up at the farm of an evening, even with those girls traipsing in and out. I'd be glad of a few more friendly souls up there, to play a hand of cards with or perhaps a game of chess.'

'I don't think I've ever played chess in my life.'

'Well,' Joe said, and held out his hand to help her up off the linoleum, 'high time you learned how, then.'

She couldn't quite believe his offer. But she was deeply grateful for it.

'Thank you,' Violet said belatedly. They were standing very close together, and she was suddenly aware of how empty the house was, their voices echoing in the hall. 'But we can't stay there for nothing. No,' she said, shaking her head, 'hear me out first. I can't pay rent, it's true, because I don't have a brass farthing to my name. But I know how to be a good housekeeper. So I'll help out at the farm in return for our bed and board,' she finished in a rush. 'How's that?'

'I won't allow you to skivvy for me, Violet.'

'Not skivvying, nothing like that. Just making sure everything runs smoothly. It's what I'm good at.'

'Well, all right. But wait until you see what I'm offering

you first before you get too excited.' He pulled a face. 'The Land Girls got most of the good rooms, I'm afraid. Though there's one large double bedroom going begging. I thought you and your mother could share that if Mrs Hopkins don't mind the idea. But you'll have to clear out the attic rooms for Alice and the boys.'

'Sounds like fun,' she said stoutly, though she hoped there wouldn't be too many spiders involved.

He smiled, and she realised he was still holding her hand. 'Proper rainbow after the rain, aren't you? Tears one minute, smiles the next.'

Violet blushed. 'Oh, do give over.'

CHAPTER SEVENTEEN

From a corner table at the back of the café, Lily jumped up and waved enthusiastically at the sight of her sister peering through the door. 'Over here,' she called, and saw several heads turn in mute disapproval.

Alice wasn't alone, she realised in surprise. They had agreed to meet up for tea and cakes, and to discuss what was going on with Aunty Vi and Gran, and the 'big move' as it was being called. But it seemed that Alice had brought friends with her.

With a shock, she recognised not only young Janice, but Demelza's brother, Tristan. When she'd met him the other day, she had not been looking her best, but thankfully the farmhouse cellar had been dark and dank, and as soon as the air raid was over, she'd hurriedly made her excuses and left. So it was unlikely he'd seen her blotchy cheeks and messed-up hair from dashing up the hill to avoid being bombed. All the same, she found herself instinctively glancing at the oval mirror on the wall to check she looked acceptable.

Get a grip, Lily told herself irritably.

She'd felt drawn to Tristan as soon as they'd met, and had annoyed herself by stealing constant glances at him in the dim glow of the lamplight, where no doubt he'd looked more handsome and intriguing than he really was. But she had no desire for a romantic entanglement. Her work had to come first. Only as he held out his hand again, and she shook it, Lily felt the most curious charge in her fingertips, and embarrassed herself by blushing and stammering something foolish.

'Nice to meet you in the daylight,' she told him, and then sucked in her breath. 'I mean, not in a cellar.' Blinking, she hurriedly transferred her smile to Janice. 'Hello again, I hope we can manage to have a conversation this time without the Jerries ruining everything.' Before the girl could reply, Lily turned to embrace her sister, adding, 'I'm glad I'm not at home to get roped into packing chests. Tomorrow's the big day, isn't it?'

'Yes.' Alice laughed. 'Joe's bringing the van round at nine and we'll all be moving to his farm. Can you imagine the chaos?'

'I can, actually.' Lily sat again with a smile. 'I didn't know you were planning a big get-together,' she added awkwardly, suppressing an urge to fiddle with her hair. 'I would have asked for a bigger table.'

'Tristan's only here because he came to walk me home from school,' Janice explained, 'and we bumped into Alice, and she said she was coming here, so...'

'So Janice decided to tag along,' Tristan added to that, looking a little uncomfortable, 'and since I'd promised to walk her home, I felt that I ought to come along too.' He drew out a chair next to Lily with a smile. 'I'm sure we can all squeeze in together.'

'Oh, Lily, I wish you could have been there to lend a hand this week,' Alice said, sitting close to the wall so that Janice could pull up a chair beside her. 'There was plenty of your stuff still lying around but you'll be glad to hear I packed it all for you. Your things are at the bottom of my bedroom chest, because I started with your side of the room.' Her sister frowned thoughtfully. 'At least, I think that's where I put them… Well, I expect they'll turn up at some point.'

'Thanks,' Lily said drily.

The smiling waitress came over, and after a quick glance at the limited menu, they ordered afternoon tea for four, which was quite an extravagance.

Lily tried not to keep glancing in Tristan's direction the whole time. But it was hard not to when his presence was so very male, and his handsome Cornish face practically glowed with health under that mop of ginger hair.

'Well, I call this pushing the boat out,' Alice said, gazing about the pretty little tea shop.

'Dead posh,' Janice agreed with a nod.

'And my treat,' Lily reminded them both. Eating out didn't involve a ration book, and she'd found stepping into a café or even a service restaurant occasionally had given her a chance to feel normal again, as though there wasn't a war on. It was even more lovely when she could share the experience. 'No, I insist; I hardly get a chance to spend my pay packet as it is, and this is your reward for giving me all the Porthcurno gossip.'

'I'll be paying for my own order,' Tristan told her at once, his serious gaze on her face.

'Of course,' Lily said primly.

'And I'm sorry to be disturbing your chat with Alice.'

'Not at all,' Lily said, shyly raising her eyes to his, and could have pinched herself in frustration when she realised she was blushing again. What on earth was wrong with her? She and men were incompatible; there was no point giving Demelza's brother the wrong impression. 'The more the merrier.'

They talked for the next half hour about the imminent move to Joe's farm, and how Alice would be housed in the attic along with Janice's two brothers. This space was apparently still very cluttered, so Alice would be sleeping on the sofa for now, letting the boys share the one attic room that had been cleared.

'Aunty Vi says she's planning to clear my room of old junk by next week,' Alice told her with a scowl, displeased by the prospect of sleeping on a sofa until then. 'Though I told her to leave anything exciting or unusual up there.' Her sister glanced about at their baffled expressions while munching on a buttered crumpet. 'Like a pier glass or a stuffed bird,' she explained, 'or a vase of ostrich feathers. You know, the kind of odd things you find in attics.'

Tristan nodded sombrely. 'Or a shrunken head.'

'Exactly,' Alice agreed.

Janice stared at them both in astonished silence, struggling to swallow her mouthful of fruitcake.

'Blimey, Alice,' Lily exclaimed, 'what on earth are you on about? There won't be anything like that in Joe's farmhouse, I'm sure.' She flashed Tristan a quick, puzzled smile, wishing she knew more about him. 'And as for you, please don't encourage her. My sister's got enough of a mad imagination already, thank you, without adding shrunken heads to it.'

He studied her curiously. 'You don't like shrunken heads? Personally, it's what I always hope to find when hunting through an attic.'

Alice clapped her hands in approval and Janice burst out into such noisy cackles of laughter that many heads turned towards them.

Lily felt like sinking through the tea shop floor in embarrassment. Yet at the same time she felt somehow lifted on a wave of delight. 'Oh, hush,' she choked, and buried her face in her napkin to hide her own laughter. 'What are you two like?'

She didn't know what to think of the way her heart was beating so fast and light, and how she could hardly look at Tristan without feeling utterly confused. But she recalled how she'd been quite smitten by a certain Private Daniel Orde last year, and it had all ended in a dreadful scene when he'd misread her signals – or read them only too well – and tried to kiss her. And she'd run from the young soldier like the devil was after her, when he'd meant no harm at all.

The last thing she wanted was to repeat past mistakes.

After checking that Janice was settling in well with Demelza's family, Lily paid her share of the bill and waited while Tristan paid his. Then they reluctantly went back out into the chilly spring afternoon and said their goodbyes. Tristan was walking Janice back to the farm, and Alice was hurrying to the bus stop to get home to Porthcurno.

'Good luck with the move,' Lily told her sister, and kissed her on the cheek. 'Once I get a few days' leave together, I'll hop on a bus myself and come see your dusty old attic room. Unless you're still sleeping on the sofa by then.'

'Better than being bombed,' Alice said with a shrug, and waved as she dashed down the street towards the bus stop.

Janice thanked Lily politely for the afternoon tea, and then it was time to shake hands with Tristan.

'It was nice to talk to you again,' Lily said with as much dignity and poise as she could muster, given how hard her heart was thumping. 'I'll give your regards to Demelza, shall I? I'm bound to see her sometime between shifts, either tonight or tomorrow.'

'Thank you.' His eyes met hers, and she felt an odd shock go through her, as though she'd been electrocuted. 'Next time my sister's home, why don't you come up to see us? Maybe have supper? I'm sure Demmy would love to show you around the farm.'

Her mouth was so dry she could hardly find the words to reply. 'Supper? Oh yes … I'll have to, erm … that's very kind.'

Lily stood watching with a fixed smile as they walked up the road, lifting her hand as Janice turned to give a final wave at the corner. Then she gave a little groan, feeling shaky and hollow inside, despite all the crumpet and cake she'd devoured, and began to trudge wearily back to her own digs, wishing she'd never met Dr Jerrard or agreed to come and live here in Penzance. Life had been so peaceful back in St. Ives, with no puzzling or disturbing entangle-ments. Everyone there had known not to flirt with Nurse

Fisher, because she didn't like it and always said no to a date. And that was how she'd liked it. No complications, no upsets. But now, for the first time in forever, she caught herself imagining a date with Tristan Minear, and clapped her hands to her hot cheeks.

'Oh no,' Lily whispered to herself, shaking her head frantically. 'No, no, no, no, no.'

'Wakey, wakey, Rip Van Winkle!'

Demelza stared up into Mags's face, dazed and still surfacing from a nightmare of sirens and screams. Behind the girl's head a bulb burned brightly in a low-hanging metal shade that was still swinging as though somebody had knocked it in passing, casting long shadows bouncing up and down the walls.

'Hmm?' She was slumped over the desk in the Fire Guard waiting room, she realised, and sat up slowly, her entire body aching. 'Goodness; I must have drifted off for a minute.' There was drool at the corner of her mouth; embarrassed, she wiped it away with the back of her hand. 'What ... what's happening?' She yawned extravagantly. 'Did I miss anything?'

'Oh, nothing much,' Mags said, fixing her with an ironic eye. 'Except maybe the air-raid siren going off, the anti-aircraft battery making its usual racket, then the Fire Guard bell sounding, and the other duty teams scrambling on alert all around you. But don't let any of that disturb your beauty sleep.'

'Oh no!' Demelza jumped up so fast, she knocked her chair flying, much to the chuckling amusement of one of the other girls, running past in her Auxiliary Fire Service uniform. 'I'm so sorry, Mags. You should have woken me sooner.'

'I was in the loo, if you must know.'

'Right.' She blinked hard, trying to wake up properly, her head still groggy. 'Well, give me a couple of minutes and I'll be with you. I just need to get my gear on.'

'Luckily, darling,' Mags pointed out with her trademark saccharine smile, 'you already did.'

Bewildered, Demelza looked down at herself, and only then realised she was indeed clad in her Fire Guard boiler suit and boots. In a flash, she recalled having gone out with Mags early in the shift to attend a small house fire on St. Michael's Street. They'd trudged back into the station at about two in the morning with soot on their faces and everything stinking of smoke. She must have crashed soon after scrubbing her face and fingernails in icy water, completely exhausted after four nightshifts in a row.

'Thank God,' she breathed, and grabbed up her helmet and toolkit from the desk. She clipped the kit to her belt and stooped for a bucket and fire pump. 'Where to?'

'Not too far.' Already kitted up, Mags collected her own bucket and pump on the way out. 'There's been a big one fallen on several residentials and Derrick's Factory round the back of Tower Street, near the school. All teams have been told to report there.'

Outside, the sky was still dark, though a pale glimmer in the east indicated that dawn couldn't be far off. They dashed along the quiet streets, glancing up instinctively from time to time to pinpoint the location of any German aircraft still in the vicinity. But the Jerries seemed to have dropped their high explosives on Penzance and then moved off along the coast in search of more targets, or perhaps further inland, because the skies above the town were empty and the anti-aircraft guns silent.

'It's quicker this way,' Demelza said abruptly, leading them off the main street and down a dark alleyway. Her local knowledge was about the only advantage she had over Mags, she thought grimly, and she was bloody well going to use it.

They emerged from the alley opposite the bombing site, where a huge fire was burning, its heat so powerful that Demelza flinched, staring up at it in horror. The loud cracklings and occasional crash of falling timbers inside the worst-hit building were quite terrifying. Several houses had been hit and two fire engines were already in attendance, the men pumping water onto the blaze as fast as they could.

As they ran across the street, an ambulance came racing around the corner and skidded to a violent halt behind one of the fire engines.

Demelza saw Robert jump out of the ambulance followed by a slender young woman who looked tiny beside him. He spoke to her briefly, gesturing towards the fiercest part of the blaze, and then pointed her away from it, towards one of the adjacent buildings, which had not yet caught fire.

'High explosives and a number of incendiaries,' one of the Fire Brigade was yelling at a Fire Guard team already on site. 'I'd guess they were aiming for the factory, but they've managed to take out most of the block too.'

Even Mags looked taken aback by the ferocity of the

blaze. But she tucked her helmet strap under her chin, and shouted, 'Come on,' to Demelza above the noise.

They ran across to where a small group, including the Fire Brigade, Fire Guard and several ambulance crews, were discussing strategies. 'We can't save this one,' the head fireman was telling everyone, a hoarse-voiced man in his fifties with silvery sideburns, 'or its close neighbours. But if we concentrate on wetting the surrounding buildings, we should be able to prevent the fire from spreading further.' He instructed his crews to turn their water hoses onto the untouched buildings on either side. Then he came towards the ambulance crews. 'We don't know if anyone was trapped inside, but we've seen no survivors, nor any sign of bodies yet. You may have to come back later.'

'What can we do to help?' Mags asked at his elbow.

The head fireman turned and looked them up and down, noting their uniforms and special armbands. 'Best you stay well clear, Miss. Like I told the others, this is a major fire. There's nothing here for the likes of you Fire Guards. Anyway, there's a good chance there'll be nothing left of these buildings but shells by morning. And some may collapse while we're trying to put the fire out. So we need to keep this area clear.'

Mags glared resentfully at him as the ambulance woman ran past with a stretcher, having spotted a possible casualty in one of the nearby houses. But she didn't argue.

'Shouldn't we check the fire hasn't spread to that building?' Demelza heard herself say, pointing to an early Victorian building that had been turned into flats decades before, and was horrified to see several heads turn to stare at her. 'M-maybe I'm wrong,' she stammered, 'but that one looks vulnerable to me, right on the end of the row there.'

'All right,' he said impatiently, waving them away, 'go and take a look if you must. But for God's sake, be careful.'

Gratefully, they ran along the row, keeping well back from the valiantly working fire fighters. Struggling to draw breath, Demelza felt her eyebrows singe in the heat and was glad once they were past the worst of it. But as they approached the darkened, empty Victorian building on the end, Mags gave a muffled exclamation and flung out her arm, staring at one of the houses on the edge of the fire.

'I say, there's someone still in there,' she shouted back at the fire crews, but the noise of the fire and the pumps was so great, nobody could hear her. 'On the top floor.'

Robert emerged from the smoke and burning debris, a huge figure with a rolled-up stretcher lodged under one arm.

'You've seen someone hurt?' he demanded.

'Not hurt,' Demelza told him urgently. 'Trapped by the fire.'

'Up there.' Mags pointed to the top floor, though there was nobody at the window now. 'I can't be sure, but it looked like a child.'

The house was already on fire on the ground floor, black smoke billowing out of its broken windows and wide-open entrance, the blast having blown the front door off its hinges. The firemen had been soaking it with water and the façade was dripping, steam rising into the pale dawn light. Robert hesitated, following the line of her arm. Then they all saw it. A small face at the window peering out from behind dark curtains, and a hand raised towards them in a wave.

'Good God,' the ambulance driver muttered, staring. He dropped the rolled-up stretcher and ran into the building, disappearing into the smoky interior.

'What on earth's he doing? He's not a fireman; he'll be killed.' Demelza grabbed Mags' arm in horror. 'Even if he can get up there in one piece, he won't get out alive. Look how quickly the fire's spreading.'

Mags said nothing but looked up intently at the top floor. But there was no further sign of the small face at the window.

'Over here,' Demelza yelled to the nearest firefighting team. 'A man's just gone inside to rescue someone. We need hoses.'

Three fire fighters detached from the others and moved quickly down the row, soaking the exterior with their hoses as the fire began to take hold. Moments ticked by and the open doorway of the house continued to pour out black smoke, licks of flame around the window frames hissing under the water pumps. Sick with apprehension, Demelza crept closer to the front door, willing the ambulance driver to reappear.

'Keep back, Miss,' one of the fire fighters yelled.

At that moment, a huge figure burst out of the doorway at a run, a small, limp shape wrapped in a blanket over his shoulder. It was Robert, and he came full pelt towards them, coughing and spluttering as he lowered the child into Mags' waiting arms. His face was blackened and scorched, and his sleeve was on fire. But he merely slammed it with his glove until the flames went out, and then knelt to check the child was still breathing.

'Is … is he still alive?' Demelza asked, full of dread, hovering behind them with a thumping heart.

'It's a she. About ten years old, I'd guess.' His voice hoarse from smoke inhalation, he staggered as he lifted her again and began to carry her towards the waiting ambulance. 'And yes, miraculously, she's alive.'

Demelza watched him go, a hand at her mouth, tears in her eyes; she had never seen anything so brave and heroic.

And yet he'd refused to go to war.

Why?

'Come on,' Mags said grimly, and dragged her away towards the Victorian flats. 'We've got a job to do, remember?'

CHAPTER EIGHTEEN

Porthcurno, South Cornwall, early June 1942

Violet lugged the last suitcase down the stairs, its thin sides bulging from all the items crammed into it, and was met at the bottom by a resentful-looking Joe.

'Didn't I tell you to let me help with the suitcases?' he demanded, and wrested it from her.

Deciding against a pointed reminder of his false leg, and how Joe would never have managed the stairs, his stick, *and* a heavy suitcase on his own, Violet gave him a wan smile instead. 'Sorry, I never thought to ask.'

She knew how sensitive he was about his war wound. Besides, they could probably have managed the suitcase together. It was just that she'd always done things for herself and it felt odd to be accepting help.

Joe dragged the case laboriously out to his van for his second run of the day, and then came back, wiping sweat from his brow. He took a quick swig from the bottle of ale Sheila had fetched him from the pub, and sat on the bottom stair with a gusty exhalation. She knew how he felt. It was another fine day, perfect for moving house, but the June warmth did make for thirsty work.

'Well, that's the last of them.' Violet wiped her hands on her floral apron, worn to protect her clothes against packing dust and dirt, and took a long last look around at the cottage where they'd been so happy. It felt so empty now, without all of their possessions littering up the place. 'I'm to leave the keys under the mat for the next tenants. So that's that. We can go once you're ready.'

Joe pushed his cap off his forehead and looked up at her quizzically. 'Aren't you forgetting something?' When she stared at him blankly, he gave a chuckle and said, 'Your mother? She went to the shop half an hour ago and hasn't come back yet.'

'I can guess what she's up to,' she said, shaking her head. 'That Arnold … he's a crochety old beggar. But she's had her eye on him from the start.'

Ushering him out of the front door, Violet locked up the cottage and slid the key under the outside mat.

'You turn the van, Joe. I'll fetch my mother.'

It was only a few minutes' walk to the shop, and Violet accomplished it swiftly, unwrapping her apron as she went and rolling it into a ball. Run out of the front room of his house, Arnold's was the only shop in Porthcurno, and it doubled as a Post Office. Through the back of the shop, you could see his sitting room, where old Arnold would wait in an armchair for the bell above the shop door to jangle, announcing a customer. Then he'd come through, stooped and flicking back unkempt white hair, eyes narrowed to see which of his regulars it was, with a smile for his favourites.

He knew everyone in the village by name, of course, for he'd been born in Porthcurno, as he told anyone who'd listen, and would 'likely die here as well'. After a period of daggers drawn between him and Mum, they'd become friends, of a sort. Though it struck Violet that friends didn't flirt quite as openly as those two. She disapproved, of course. She didn't think Arnold would suit her mother. For a start, he was nothing like her dad, bless his soul, who'd been a lovely, smiley man, always with a twinkle in his eye. And she felt her mum deserved better than a curmudgeonly old shopkeeper.

When she stalked in, the bell jangling fiercely overhead, her mum and Arnold were chatting, head-to-head, leaning over the counter.

Her mum jumped, straightening hastily as she looked round. 'Oh, it's you, Vi. I swear, you nearly gave me a heart attack, bursting in like that.'

'It's a shop, Mum. Did you expect me to knock?'

Arnold pulled a face at the intrusion and turned to put a large bottle of sweets back on the shelf behind the counter. 'Ready for the off, are you?' He had a slow way of talking, very measured and Cornish.

'Oh, is it that time already?' Sheila seemed downcast. 'Is everything packed in the van now?'

Violet nodded, eyeing the two of them suspiciously. What had they been whispering about when she walked in?

'Did you remember to scrub the front step? We don't want to give the next tenants a poor impression of us.'

'Yes, Mum.'

'And the back wall where Eustace must have kicked his blessed football umpteen times?'

'Yes, Mum.'

'What about the stairs, love? Did you sweep the stairs?'

Violet took a deep breath, trying to control her temper. 'Mum, the van's all packed, the cottage is empty, and Joe wants to get back to his farm. It was very kind of him to take the day to help us move in, but we mustn't keep him waiting any longer.'

'Yes, all right.' Sheila turned back to Arnold, her smile lopsided. 'Time to go. I'll miss our daily chats.'

'Don't forget your sweeties for the little lads.' He picked up a small paper bag from the counter and spun it with a practised gesture, the corners twisting to seal the bag. When she took out her purse, he waved it away. 'No, Sheila, it's on the house.'

Sheila?

'Well, that's very kind of you, Arnie.' Her mum smiled and patted her hair in a flustered way, and Violet looked away, rolling her eyes in disbelief. 'Though I'll be back once or twice a week, I daresay. Joe's farm ain't that far and the walk will do me good.'

'Until next time, then.' Arnold touched his forehead in a kind of old-fashioned salute, watching with an unreadable expression as Violet bundled her mother out of the shop.

'Mum, for goodness' sake ... at your age!'

'What?' Sheila looked bemused as they hurried back to the cottage together. ''Ere, I don't know what you're in such a flap about, Missy. So I've got a gentleman friend. I'm not exactly a spring chicken; I'm allowed.'

'As long as that's all he is,' Violet said, glancing back to see Arnold standing in the shop doorway, looking down the hill after them. 'A friend.'

'It's none of your business what he is,' her mum said airily. 'Though, to be honest, I haven't made my mind up about him. You can't be too careful at my age.'

'No, you certainly can't. Because one of you might have a bloomin' heart attack.'

'I beg your pardon?' Her mum glared at her, thrusting the paper bag of aniseed twists into her coat pocket. 'That's quite enough of your cheek, young lady.'

'He called you Sheila.'

'So what if he did? That is my name.'

'Oh, really? And there was me thinking your name is *Mrs Hopkins*.'

'Oh, well.' Her mum bit her lip.

Joe was waiting patiently in the van outside the cottage. They all squeezed into the front bench seat and drove away, with Sheila in the window seat, craning round to peer back at the village with tears in her eyes.

'I know we weren't there long,' her mum muttered, pulling out a hanky and blowing her nose. 'But I'm still going to miss it. The village too. Such nice people...'

'Mum, you said it yourself, we're only moving a mile or so up the road. Besides, the neighbours were always complaining about the boys. You won't miss *that*, I'm sure.' Violet shook her head and glanced at Joe, who was intent on the road, which, like most Cornish lanes, was narrow and bendy, with high hedgerows that hid oncoming vehicles until the last minute. 'Thank you,' she told him quietly. 'I've no idea how we would have coped without you these past few days.'

'My pleasure,' he said shortly.

He was a man of few words, Violet thought, and sat back, surprised to find she didn't mind that as much as she would once have done. She herself was a woman of many words, after all, as was her mother and even Alice, on the rare occasions when the girl could be persuaded to take her nose out of her book. He'd said plainly there were no strings attached to this invitation for them to live at the farm. It was an act of charity, nothing more. And she'd offered to act as housekeeper for him in return for bed and board, at least until such time as she could get another job and offer him rent. So there could be no question of feeling like she owed him something.

But it was at the back of her mind that she liked Joe … maybe *more* than liked him. And it seemed he might like her again too, after that awkward period following his mother's death. Now they would be living under the same roof… She dreaded the thought of making a fool of herself over him again, or of Joe making a pass at her only to regret it later, as he had done last summer. But it was pointless worrying about milk that hadn't even been spilt. They needed somewhere to live, and this was better than seeing the boys taken away.

All the same, she looked ahead with trepidation as the farm buildings loomed in the distance, and gripped her hands in her lap.

'Oh no,' she exclaimed.

Joe shot her a swift, worried glance, then looked back at the road. 'You all right?'

'Oh gawd, what did you forget, Vi?' her mum asked at

once, rightly interpreting her rueful expression. 'What have you left behind?'

Violet cast her eyes up to heaven. 'Only the boys' bloomin' football.'

'Nurse Fisher, there's a lady at Reception waiting to see you,' Matron said, making her disapproval clear by the way her heavy grey brows drew together and her lips pursed. 'A member of the general public,' she added, as if this was even more scandalising than being asked for by a patient or the relative of a patient, 'and she has a young person with her.'

'But I ... I'm still doing my rounds,' Lily said, unsure what this meant.

'It appears to be a matter of some urgency.' Matron glanced down at her watch. 'Your shift finishes at noon. It is now a quarter to twelve. I suppose, on this occasion, you could leave early.'

Perplexed, Lily handed her clipboard to the young trainee she'd been escorting about the wards. 'Nurse Mills, could you finish up for me? Just the way I showed you. Mark your findings on each bed chart and tick off the patient's name on the report sheet.' She hesitated, remembering the girl's earlier confusion. 'Make sure you put the tick next to the correct name.'

'Yes, Nurse Fisher,' she said, and headed off to see the final patients on their round with a new bounce in her step.

Matron and Lily glanced at each other.

'How she's coming along?' Matron asked, though warily. 'Any improvement?'

The girl's uncle was a trustee of the hospital and she'd only been taken on as a favour to him, since she had almost no experience of nursing and would not be able to apply for a registered training course for at least another year. But desperate times called for corner-cutting, as Matron herself had admitted when the girl turned up late for her first few shifts.

'She'll do all right,' Lily said with a shrug, perhaps more generously than Nurse Mills deserved.

Making her way to the hospital reception, she stopped along the way to talk to some of the patients and other nurses, pleased that she had made so many new friends in Penzance in only a few weeks. The hospital and her digs in the Fire Guard had become home to her, and although she still pined a little for her mates in St. Ives, letters from Mary full of gossip about the convalescent home and the orphanage under Rose's new management kept her spirits up.

She smiled at Dr Jerrard as he hurried into the children's ward, though he seemed preoccupied, as well he might. A young girl had been brought in last night, suffering from burns and smoke inhalation, not to mention shock, after foolishly concealing herself under her bed when the air-raid siren went off, so that she got left behind in the confusion when the family headed for the shelter. When a nearby building was hit, the girl had been trapped by a rapidly spreading fire on the lower floors. Thankfully, she'd been spotted at an upper window and an ambulance driver had bravely dived into the burning building to fetch her out.

It had nearly been an unspeakable tragedy, Dr Jerrard

had told the incoming day shift, adding that these new incendiary bombs seemed designed to spread fire as quickly as possible, and the hospital had ordered more bandages and medicaments in anticipation of an increase in burns cases. He'd had nothing but praise for the ambulance man, a Quaker whom Lily had met many times since starting work at the hospital; his name was Mr Robert Day, and it seemed he regularly dashed in 'where angels fear to tread' as the doctor had put it. She could well believe it, having seen a certain light in Robert Day's face that spoke of courage and determination, in stark contrast to some of the other ambulance drivers, who were becoming more tired and unenthusiastic the longer the war dragged on...

Lily rounded the corner and stopped dead at the sight of young Janice, her face pale and defiant, at the hospital reception desk. Standing beside the schoolgirl was a stern-looking woman with short hair under a plain black hat and with a silver crucifix about her neck, dressed in a grey tweed jacket and skirt. She was peering impatiently up at the wall clock as though unwilling to wait any longer.

'Janice,' Lily said, smiling at the girl, although she couldn't understand what on earth had brought her to the hospital. 'What a surprise. Are you hurt? Unwell?' When Janice shook her head in sullen silence, Lily folded her arms at her waist and looked at the woman accompanying her. 'Hello, I'm Nurse Fisher. I believe you asked to see me. How can I help you?'

'I'm Miss Rhodes,' the woman said coldly, not offering to shake hands. 'I'm the headmistress at the school here in Penzance. I'm afraid to say I'm here to hand Janice into your care since I've been unable to get hold of anyone at her current home placement. She claims your aunt is housing her brothers in Porthcurno.'

'That's right,' Lily said, baffled, 'but I don't understand. Shouldn't Janice be at school?' She checked the clock again. 'Is it a half day or something?'

The headmistress appeared to wince at her accent. 'I'm sorry to say that I have taken the difficult decision to suspend Janice from school for one week.'

'*What?*' Lily stared from her to Janice, who simply hung her head.

'I'm hoping a week at home will indicate to her the need for punctuality, regular attendance and, above all, proper behaviour on school grounds.'

'Hang on,' Lily said, feeling a flush creep into her cheeks. She was getting angry, she realised; something that rarely happened to her. But she'd suffered at the hands of a few mean teachers at school herself, and listening to Miss Rhodes wittering on about 'proper behaviour' was bringing it all back with a vengeance. 'You're going to suspend Janice because she was *late for school*?'

'If she had only been late for school a few times, Nurse Fisher, I would merely be sending a letter home with her, as usual. But my letters are either going astray or being ignored, since I've never received a reply to a single one of them.' Miss Rhodes' lips were pursed like she was sucking a lemon sherbet. 'No, this is far more serious. Janice, it seems, hasn't simply been late for school or truanting during the day. She's been working.'

Lily blinked. 'Come again?'

'She has taken paid employment in the town. A lunch-time job, Nurse Fisher, in...' Miss Rhodes shuddered. 'I can barely bring myself to repeat this, but she has been working during the school day in a disreputable establishment.'

'In a *what*?'

'A public bar, Nurse Fisher.'

'You've got to be kidding me.' Lily transferred her astonished gaze to Janice's averted face. 'You got a job in a bar? But you're only fourteen.'

'Believe me, I am not in the habit of "kidding" anyone. The place is called the Palace Bar,' Miss Rhodes went on, her voice dripping with distaste, 'and is situated near the harbour, if you wish to make your own enquiries. As soon as I discovered what she was up to, I informed the proprietor that she is under-age for working in an establishment that serves alcohol, and he told me she'd given her age as eighteen when applying for the job. Needless to say, he immediately terminated her employment.'

Lily felt a little sorry for Janice, whose eyes were swimming with tears. But she knew this was a really serious situation. If the headmistress refused to let her come back to school, Janice might never sit her matriculation exams, and that disaster could haunt her for the rest of her days.

'I spoke to Miss Fisher about it, one of our new assistants, who I believe is your sister. I thought perhaps she could shed some light on Janice's behaviour.'

'And could she?' she asked hopefully.

'I'm afraid not. Though she did suggest you were the best person to talk to, since Janice's current guardian is a farmer and may not be at home during the day.'

'Oh.'

Lily made a mental note to thank her sister for lumping her with this uncomfortable interview.

'So,' the headmistress continued in a grating tone, 'to be sure the wicked girl doesn't sneak off again, I am handing her directly into your care, Nurse Fisher.' Miss Rhodes' eyes snapped at her fiercely. 'As someone in a position of responsibility, I trust you will at least see her safely home.'

It seemed Lily had no choice in the matter. 'Of course.'

'I'm very glad to hear it.' Miss Rhodes handed over an official-looking buff-coloured envelope. 'Please make sure this reaches her placement family. It explains the terms of her suspension and the conditions Janice will be expected to meet if she ever wishes to attend my school again.'

With that dire warning, the headmistress turned and stalked out of the hospital, heels clicking on the tiled floor.

Lily watched her go and then spun to face Janice. 'Well, what have you been up to now, you silly little—' Lily bit her lip and stopped; to her surprise, the poor girl had started crying. 'Oh, come here.'

She drew Janice into a tight hug and let the girl sob her heart out onto her starched uniform.

'Janice, it sounds like you and me need a proper chat before I take you home. Over a nice mug of hot chocolate.' Lily looked down into her tear-stained face. 'What do you say to that?'

CHAPTER NINETEEN

'See you in a few days,' Demelza told her roommates, donning her coat and collecting her bag of dirty laundry before heading downstairs.

She felt guilty; both her roommates, like so many other women in the Auxiliary Fire Service, had been drafted in from other parts of Cornwall to augment numbers and didn't have anywhere local to go when off duty. While they had to stay at the Fire Guard, constantly bombarded by bells and whistles, she was able to go home, wash and dry her clothes, sleep in her own bed, and see her family for at least forty-eight hours, sometimes longer.

Once, she'd thought being away from home the most exciting thing possible, and had dreaded returning when off shift. Now though, Demelza suspected it was the only thing keeping her sane. She had no idea how the men away fighting managed it, but she guessed they must rely on each other for company and good spirits, just as the girls of the Fire Guard did.

'All for one and one for all,' they often chanted while

throwing on their uniforms and helmets and dashing out to an incendiary bombing or a collapsed building. This saying was a motto from a French novel called *The Three Musketeers*, her roommate Rosemary, who was a bit of a bookworm, had explained. But although Demelza wasn't a big reader, she had understood at once. 'You mean, we're stronger together,' she chimed in, and Rosemary had nodded enthusiastically. 'That's it, exactly.'

She had never thought of herself as being particularly courageous. There hadn't been much call for courage back on the farm, except when it came to dodging her father's fits of bad temper. But it was clear that the other Fire Guards were as brave as any soldier, ready to risk their lives to save others without a single word of uncertainty or self-pity. They might not be fully-fledged firefighters but they still fearlessly put themselves in harm's way, especially when assisting at fires or checking properties for bomb damage. She was so proud to be one of them, it brought tears to her eyes as she waved goodbye to Captain Enys and some of the others in the training room.

'Have a lovely break,' Jean replied, and then called her back. 'Hang on, Demmy. You live up the top of Alverton Road, don't you?'

'We're out that way, yes.'

'Well, you're in luck. My nephew's heading there soon. He's offered to take some equipment to the repair shop at Lansdowne. I'm sure if you ask nicely, he'll give you a lift home. Unless you prefer to walk?'

'No, I...' Demelza clammed up, suddenly tongue-tied as a familiar figure emerged from the back of the training room.

She was surprised to recognise Robert at first, but then remembered having bumped into him when she first came here to sign up.

'Your nephew, did you say?'

'My late sister's boy.' Jean turned. 'Robert, can you give Demelza a lift? She's going home to...' She hesitated. 'Where is it exactly?'

'Hill View Farm,' Demelza said breathlessly.

Robert nodded, eyeing her without expression. 'I know the place.' He stooped to kiss his diminutive, grey-haired aunt on the cheek. 'Speak to you again soon, Aunt Jean. Stay safe.' Turning to Demelza, he gestured to the door. 'Shall we?'

Traffic was surprisingly heavy, and even once they'd cleared the worst of it, avoiding absent-minded shoppers wandering straight into the road in front of his ambulance, they still managed to get behind a milk wagon slowly trundling up the steep hill out of town.

'I don't recall Penzance being this busy in June before,' Demelza commented, feeling she needed to make conversation as Robert had not said a word since leaving the Fire Guard Station. 'It's always crowded at the height of the summer season, of course. Even with the war on.' She twisted her hands in her lap, ludicrously shy. 'Maybe it's all the evacuees, come down from London. What do you think?'

'Possibly.' He changed to a lower gear as the heavy milk wagon slowed to a crawl. 'Though I only moved here last year, so I don't know what it was like before the war. I'm not Cornish-born myself, you see.'

That surprised her. 'But the captain is Cornish … your aunt, I mean.'

'Indeed she is. Same as my mother and maternal grandparents.' He paused. 'My mother died when I was quite young; I barely remember her. But my father was a Londoner. Though he's gone now too. Not in the war. He died back when I was twenty. Run over in the street.'

'How awful; I'm so sorry.'

'That was nearly ten years ago, but thank you.' He nodded, his expression almost desolate as he stared blindly at the back of the lumbering milk wagon. 'Anyway, that's why I came down to Cornwall after the outbreak of war. To look after my grandparents. I was worried how they'd cope with suddenly having to reach a public shelter during air raids.'

'Yes, that's always a problem for older people.'

'So I chose to live with them. Aunt Jean has moved in with us too, though it's a bit cramped. We try to organise our shifts so they don't coincide, but it's not always possible. If neither of us can be there, we've asked their closest neighbour to make sure they get to the shelter safely.' He made a face. 'They're quite frail, you see. Especially my grandfather. He refuses to admit it, but he needs a great deal of care.'

'So you all live together in Penzance?'

'That's right.'

Demelza stole a glance at his profile, burning with curiosity. She knew so little about Robert; there were dozens of questions buzzing about in her head, yet she dared not ask too many of them, for fear of betraying her interest.

'You said before that you're a Conscientious Objector,' she began hesitantly.

'I'd rather not talk about that right now, if you don't mind.'

'Oh, of course not.' She looked away, mortified by the flat tone of his refusal. 'I'm sorry.'

'No need to apologise. It's just not something I particularly want to discuss today.'

Demelza picked up her handbag and sack of dirty laundry, hot-cheeked with embarrassment. 'You … you can drop me off here,' she stammered, pointing to the grassy verge at the side of the road. 'It's not far to walk now.'

'Thank you, but I'll drop you at home, as agreed,' he said firmly. 'I'm not offended, if that's what you think. Maybe we can talk about my principles another time.' He flashed her a twisted smile. 'Besides, Aunt Jean will never let me hear the end of it if I allow you to get out halfway up this hill.'

She sat the rest of the way in silence, willing the milk wagon to pick up speed. But her brain was churning. If he was happy to talk about being a Conscientious Objector on another occasion, why didn't he want to discuss it today? Had something happened to upset him? He didn't seem upset. Yet he had practically snapped her head off when she mentioned it… It was foolish to be this fascinated by a man she had barely seen more than two or three times. But she couldn't help it. There was something mesmerising about him.

At the turn to Hill View Farm, Robert insisted on going all the way along the narrow, muddy track, despite the ambulance bobbing up and down at a snail's pace over the uneven ground.

'I'm taking you to your front door,' he said stubbornly.

Her anxiety mounting, she gripped the seat and stared straight ahead. Although surprisingly welcoming on her first visit home, her father had soon reverted to his surly ways, making it clear he still disapproved of her working in Penzance. It would only stir up an argument if he saw her arriving in an ambulance; he might assume she'd been hurt at work and insist that she give up the Fire Guard Service and come home full-time.

'Are you all right?' Robert asked, his brow furrowed as he studied her face and tense posture.

Briefly, she explained about her father's disposition, and how he was against her doing war work, as he'd claimed when she left the farm again after that first visit home. Though she couldn't decide if he was genuinely afraid for her safety or simply wanted his daughter back at the farm, doing her usual chores.

'I see,' was all he said, slowing to a halt in front of the house. It was hard to know what he was thinking.

Demelza opened the door. 'Thank you for the lift,' she said, and jumped down into the sunshine. 'I'll see you around.'

'Look,' he said quickly, leaning towards her before she could shut the ambulance door, 'how about we make it a date?'

'I'm sorry?'

'To talk about my reasons for being a Conscientious Objector. I can see that it matters to you.'

Demelza was stunned and didn't know what to say, staring up at him as though he'd grown two heads. Behind her, the farmhouse door opened and she glanced round to see Janice on the front step with Lily beside her, both staring at her and the ambulance in astonishment. What on earth was Lily doing here? she wondered hazily, and then recalled Tristan asking her to supper one evening when they were both off shift at the same time. Perhaps this was the night.

'Are you free on Monday, around lunchtime?' he carried on. 'That's before you go back on shift, isn't it? We could meet in Penzance for a drink. Maybe a bite to eat too.'

She blinked. He was serious. 'Yes, I suppose so.'

'The Feathers? At noon?'

She nodded mutely, so shocked she wasn't even able to smile, and slammed the passenger door shut. Robert swung the old ambulance around in the yard and, with a wave of his hand, drove back down the track towards the main road.

Demelza had her first-ever date on Monday.

CHAPTER TWENTY

In the shade of the farmhouse, Lily felt Janice shrink back in instinctive embarrassment. Demelza had turned from watching the ambulance and was heading straight for them; it was clear from her expression that her friend was puzzled to see Lily standing there.

'Hello,' Lily said with as much cheeriness as she could manage, given what she had to discuss. 'Hope you don't mind me intruding. But you see—'

'Tristan asked her to supper with us, remember?' Janice interrupted, and shook her head with a pleading expression behind Demelza's back, as if to beg Lily's silence.

A wave of sympathy swept over Lily, as she remembered all the pranks she and Alice had played at school, and the fear they'd always felt when their mum found out.

But how could she lie? The headmistress had entrusted her with an official letter. It wouldn't be right to conceal it from the family and it could lead to Janice's permanent expulsion. Besides, these weren't the girl's blood relations. They might give her a scold for skipping lessons, but they'd hardly tear a strip off her like a parent might. What difference would it make to them, after all?

Still, Tristan *had* invited her to supper, hadn't he? So maybe she could give Janice an hour or so of grace without raising suspicions. Though after supper, she'd have to hand over the letter to Mr Minear, as promised.

'That's right,' she said slowly, holding Janice's encouraging gaze. 'I've come to supper. But if you'd rather not—'

'No, you're very welcome.' Demelza had a strange light in her face. 'In fact, I've got so much to tell you...' She tailed off, frowning as her eyes fell on Janice again. 'You're home early. Is something wrong?'

'I wasn't feeling well,' Janice fibbed, 'and then I met Lily in town and we walked up here together.'

Clearly distracted, Demelza didn't question this odd coincidence. 'Well, better go and do your homework. I need to have a chat with Lily.' She dropped her bag and gas mask in the hall, and linked arms with Lily, whispering in her ear, 'Let's pop the kettle on. I want to pick your brains.'

'Sounds painful,' Lily quipped. But she didn't argue, watching Janice trail upstairs with her school bag; giving her some time alone to think was probably a good idea.

The girl had gradually opened up over the mug of hot chocolate Lily had bought her in the tea shop, explaining how she'd taken on a job because she needed money 'to get back to Barking with my brothers'. It seemed she was none too happy about life in the countryside and was missing her old haunts. Gently, Lily had pointed out how dangerous it would be to return to the nightly bombing blitz, and also that most of her schoolmates would have been shipped out as evacuees too, so there'd be nobody there to talk to. Janice's face had fallen as she realised the truth of that. But it was clear the girl was still unhappy and wished she could go home.

Demelza dragged Lily into the kitchen, which was still empty. Apparently, the farmer's sister was home, but in her room upstairs, from which she rarely ever stirred during the day. Lily had been dreading having to speak to Mr Minear on her own, but in the end she and Janice had found themselves alone until they'd heard the rattle of an old engine and gone outside just in time to see Demelza arriving. Lily had recognised her driver at once; Robert Day, the man who refused to enlist but had signed up to be an ambulance driver instead, being a Quaker and a pacifist.

'Why were you in an ambulance?' she asked Demelza, eyeing her curiously. 'You haven't been hurt, I hope?'

'Goodness, no, I just grabbed a lift home as he was coming up the hill anyway,' Demelza said in a breathless rush, filling the kettle and swinging it onto the range so fast that water slopped out, hissing on the rusty old metal plate. 'Oops.' She giggled, and clapped her hands to her cheeks, which looked as hot as the range. 'Oh Lord. I'm going to go mad if I don't tell you... Quick, is the kitchen door shut?'

Lily checked, intrigued now. 'Yes.'

'All right.' Demelza sat at the large pine table and hurriedly gestured her to sit too. 'Listen, if I tell you something private, you won't repeat it to anyone, will you? Because it's top secret and not for anyone else's ears.'

'Cross my heart and hope to die,' Lily agreed solemnly, crossing herself for good measure.

The kettle began to hum as Demelza hesitated, studying Lily's face as though still unsure she could trust her. In the distance, Lily could hear birdsong and sheep baa-ing, rural sounds that took her back to her first days in Cornwall, when she was still adjusting to life in the country after growing up on the outskirts of London. All those unfamiliar animals – cows, sheep, hens – smelling and making a racket; plus lush green fields and the restless blue sweep of the sea everywhere she looked.

Now she almost took it for granted.

Demelza bit her lip, then said hurriedly, 'Oh no, I can't. Sorry, but you'll think me the most awful idiot...'

''Ere, just spit it out, would you?' Lily laughed, shaking her head. 'What is it? Are you in love?'

Blushing scarlet, Demelza stared at her. 'Is it that obvious? I mean, I'm not in love. Not that; of course not. I barely know him. But oh, he is so different from all the other men I've met. And I think he must like me too, because he wants to take me for a drink.'

Lily smiled and squeezed her hand across the table. 'So, you've got a date. That's smashing.'

'Though he's too old for me. From what he said, he must be nearly thirty... Perhaps I should have said no.'

'Don't be silly.'

'But did you know that he's...' Demelza hesitated. 'Well, that he's a conchie? What will my father say if he finds out?'

Lily could guess only too well what Demelza's father would make of *that*. Plenty of other people she knew hated the 'conchies' (as they were known), seeing it as a betrayal of the men who'd bravely gone to war. But Lily didn't see it as such a dreadful thing. Not every man was keen to shoot people dead, after all. And besides, Robert was doing his bit here instead, and goodness knows where they'd have been without him some nights, huge strapping bloke that he was, dashing up and down stairs in burning buildings like nothing could touch him.

'Blimey, who cares what your dad has to say about it?' Lily was surprised that someone Demelza's age still worried about her father's opinion; she had to be at least twenty-two or twenty-three years old. But of course Lily had spent several years now without either parent and maybe she'd forgotten what it was like to be in that situation. 'All right, maybe he might have a go at you. But he can't stop you going. Your dad can go whistle.'

Demelza's eyes grew round. 'Yes, you're right. I … I'm not a child. It's none of his business.' But it sounded like she was trying to convince herself.

'That's the ticket.' Lily sipped her tea. She heard a dog barking out in the fields and saw her friend's head go up. 'Is that your dad coming back now?'

'Sounds like it.'

'Right.' It was time to reveal the true reason for her visit. 'Look, there's something I need to tell you. Probably best for you to know before your dad gets home.'

Briefly, while Demelza sat with a stunned expression on her face, Lily repeated what the headmistress had told her about Janice's absences from school.

'She gave me a letter for your dad,' she finished. 'It's a bit awkward, since I barely know him… I wondered if maybe you could give it to him instead and explain what's happened?'

'Me?'

Lily rummaged in her bag and slid the envelope across the table. 'There.'

'I'd rather not, sorry.' Demelza pushed it back, her eyes wide, shaking her head. 'I mean, if the headmistress asked *you* to hand it directly to him—'

'Please.' Lily slid it back.

The back door to the kitchen opened, and two sheep dogs ran in, barking excitedly at the sight of a stranger. But they were instantly silenced by a gruff word from the doorway.

Lily looked round, meeting the hard stare of Mr Minear, and stood. 'Hello,' she said, and wished again she could have persuaded Demelza to broach the subject of Janice's truanting.

She'd told Demelza not to mind what her dad said. But now, facing him, she didn't feel so brave herself. She'd only met Mr Minear once before, down in the farmhouse cellar where they'd all taken shelter during the air raid; he hadn't said anything, sleeping most of the time in an easy chair and occasionally smoking a pipe. His sister Sarah, a grim-faced woman with a walking stick and silver threads in her hair, had not been much friendlier; she'd been reading a book, barely lifting her eyes from its pages when Lily had politely introduced herself. Tristan had later explained in a whisper that his aunt had suffered a stroke at Christmas that had left her with difficulties walking and even talking, though their doctor had told them she might recover completely, given time.

Lily had happily spent that hour with the other young people instead, enjoying Tristan's dry wit and even playing a game of Snap with him and Janice. The newly manufactured wartime deck featured colourful parachutists, battleships firing at the enemy, and comical war scenes that amused them all to no end. But hadn't she always stood up to Matron at the convalescent home, when the old trout had been on the warpath over some misdemeanour or other? And stern Sister Rose too, before they became such good friends. And how about the countless times she'd risked her neck to stay on the ward with the incapacitated patients during bombing raids, even when the building shook and they all feared losing their lives?

'Mr Minear,' she began, straightening her spine and raising her chin, almost standing to attention, 'you maybe don't remember me. I'm Lily Fisher, the niece of the lady who's looking after Janice's brothers. I'm afraid I need to tell you—'

Demelza had stood too, scraping back her chair on the stone flags, and now cut short her confession. 'Janice has been truanting again, Father. She took a lunchtime job at the Palace Bar instead of going to lessons.'

Lily had to admit to being relieved by her interruption.

'I beg your pardon?' Mr Minear glared from her to Lily and back again. He leant his long, carved shepherd's crook against the wall by the back door, his face thunderous. 'What's that you say?' He came in, noisily thumping mud off his boots onto the mat. 'She's took work instead of doing her schooling?'

'That's about the sum of it, Father. The school's put her on suspension until it's sorted out,' Demelza went on bravely, though her voice shook a little. 'There's a letter for you.' And she held up the envelope.

'Where is she? I'll flay the girl alive,' he began heatedly, and then caught Lily's outraged expression. His mouth compressed. 'Well, she's not my child… Thank God for small mercies. But she can't stay here on the farm if they kick her out of school. I've my own work to see to. I'm too busy to be running around after some silly girl—'

'I'll look after her,' Demelza insisted.

'You're not here half the week,' her father pointed out in a grating voice, struggling out of his thick, padded jacket. 'Don't be daft.'

He really was quite an unpleasant man, Lily thought with distaste, watching him. It was hard not to contrast him with her own kind and soft-voiced father, Ernest Fisher, who had gone missing in action and she knew was probably dead.

The farmer turned back to Lily. 'What did she do it for, anyway? We feed her well enough, don't we? What did she need the money for?'

'She had some plan about taking herself and her brothers back to London.'

'Huh.' He grunted, looking unimpressed. 'Can't be in her right mind then, can she? Who'd want to be in that London? Half of it's been knocked flat by the Jerries.'

'I expect she's just homesick,' Lily said.

The dogs' ears pricked up and they both looked round as Tristan Minear shouldered his way through the half-open back door, wiping his muddied boots on the mat there.

'Hello,' Tristan said in surprise, staring across at Lily as he too leant his shepherd's crook on the wall behind the door. It was straighter and less fussily designed than his father's, just plain dark wood with a smooth crook. 'Have you come for supper at last?'

Momentarily struck dumb, she nodded and managed a half-smile for him.

'That tearaway city girl we took in,' his father threw at him hoarsely, 'she's gone and got herself throwed out of school.'

Tristan dragged a woolly hat off his head, his ginger curls bursting free. He had a smudge of dried dirt on his cheek and a few strands of sheep wool caught on his jacket, but Lily still thought him awfully handsome.

'Only suspended.' Lily forced herself to correct the farmer. 'For a week.'

Tristan shrugged. 'Is that what all the shouting was about? I thought a fox must have got in among the chickens, the way you were carrying on, Dad.' He put a hand briefly on his father's shoulder. 'We've a guest, remember?'

His father pulled a face but simmered down. 'I hope supper won't be late on the table because of this' was all he said and, after washing his hands in the sink, he sloped off with a cup of lukewarm tea.

Washing his own hands, Tristan gave Lily a long sideways look, a strange light in his eyes that she couldn't interpret. 'It's good to see you again. Maybe you'd like a quick walk before supper? There are still a few lambs in the top pasture.'

Her heart turned over. 'I'd love to see some lambs,' she said, and then added hurriedly, 'If Demelza doesn't need me to help with the cooking, that is.'

'No, go on, you enjoy yourselves,' Demelza insisted,

pulling on an apron and tying it comfortably about her middle. Her eyes twinkled as she gave her brother an approving look. 'Just mind you don't stay out too long. I'll be serving at six-thirty. You know what Father's like when he's made to wait for his supper.'

As Tristan pulled his coat back on and gallantly opened the back door for her, Lily had to remind herself that she and love were not compatible. *Don't you go falling in love with this one, Lily Fisher*, she told herself. *Don't you flippin' dare…*

CHAPTER TWENTY-ONE

Violet tied a pink chiffon scarf around her head to keep her hair from getting dusty, gathered her cleaning equipment, and nodded to Joe that she was ready.

'I'm going up, girls,' she called to the other two, and her nieces Alice and Lily appeared from downstairs, kitted out in blue overalls and headscarves. She grinned, recalling their first days at Eastern House, skivvying for a living. 'Just like old times, eh? Do you remember? All of us cleaning out the tunnels at Porthcurno ... and that time when there was a bug going round the soldiers, and they kept chucking up everywhere...'

'Good God,' Joe said, looking horrified.

'Hush, Aunty Vi,' Alice told her in mock reproof, wagging a finger like old Mr Frobisher used to do, their supervisor back at Eastern House. 'Careless talk costs lives.'

'Loose lips sink ships,' Lily added, and also wagged her finger, a mischievous smile on her lips.

Really, Violet thought, laughing at their silly antics, Lily was in the most brilliant mood this visit. Too often these days she seemed down in the dumps, as though the hardship of the war was really getting to her. But this time, there was a glow to the girl…

'Come on,' Joe said, and led the way carefully up the narrow, steep steps to the attic room they hadn't yet cleared. It was obvious from his slow, methodical gait that his leg was giving him trouble again. 'If we're to get this done before dark, we'd best make a start. There's no lighting up here yet, and there's plenty to do.'

One door was already open, displaying the room the boys had been using since their arrival at the farm, which looked like it needed a good tidy itself.

Joe threw the other door open and looked around at them, grimacing. 'Here we are, ladies. Bit of a mess, I'm afraid.'

The girls stopped dead in the doorway, staring in undisguised dismay at the vast array of clutter in the larger of the two attic rooms.

'Blimey,' Lily said, 'it's a regular junk shop up here.'

'Yes, sorry about that,' Joe agreed, clearly embarrassed. 'Mother had me store everything up here that she no longer wanted. She wouldn't let me throw anything out, however small.'

'Sounds like a right hoarder, your mum.' Alice stooped to pick up a dusty spray of ostrich feathers, examining them with rapt attention. ''Ere, these are nice. Do you mind if I keep them? They just need a bit of looking after…' Briskly, she shook the feathers clean, and everyone started coughing and waving their hands about as the air swirled with dust. 'Oops, sorry.'

'Let's open a window, shall we?' Violet said, still

coughing, and hurried to throw open the tiny arched window that overlooked the farmyard. No wonder it was so dark up here, she thought; there was a skylight on one of the sloping sections of roof as well, but it had been covered with a cloth.

When she turned, it was to see Joe pulling a large wooden chest out from an alcove.

'What's in there?' she asked. 'Old blankets? We could do with some more bedding.'

He was fiddling with the catch, which was rusty. 'I'm not sure. Mother asked me to bring this up here when my uncle died and left me the farm. She said it would just be cluttering up the place otherwise. I think she kept the family Bible in here, and a few old papers and other odds and ends. Account books, banking statements and so on.' The catch gave way at last and he threw the lid open, peering inside. 'Yes, there it is. Our family Bible.'

He brought it out reverently and handed it to Violet, who opened it. The first page showed his family tree, and for several minutes they knelt to study it.

'There's me,' he said, pointing to the beautifully inscribed entry for his name under his parents: Joseph Michael Postbridge. 'Mother even left a space for my wife and any children to be written in. She was so keen to have grand-children, forever going on about it. I always thought there'd be time...'

'It's a thing of beauty,' Violet agreed, hoping to distract him from his grief. 'And all these ... they're your ancestors?' There were many names, all written in different hands over the years. 'How far does this family tree go back?'

'At least four generations, by the look of it. Josiah

Postbridge – that was my great-grandfather – was born before Victoria came to the throne.'

'And who's this, then? Anastasia Emmeline Christiania,' Violet read the copperplate script haltingly, not even sure if she was pronouncing the names correctly. 'Blimey, just one of them names would be a mouthful. But all three at once?' She laughed. 'It can't have been much fun, filling out forms and what-have-you. Must have took her all of half an hour just to get her name down.'

'Anastasia … yes, she was one of my mother's favourites.' His smile was full of nostalgia. 'I remember her from when I was a little boy. Great-aunt Stacy, everyone called her. She never married. Ancient as the hills by the time I met her, and quite a dragon, if I'm honest. She lived out in India for a while and brought back a stool made from an elephant's foot. Left it to my mother in her will.'

'How gruesome,' Alice said with undisguised enthusiasm, who was lurking behind them, listening to this story. 'Is the elephant's foot stored up here, do you know?'

'Probably.'

Violet couldn't hide her surprise. 'Aunts with funny names and elephant footstools from India? I had no idea your family was posh.' It made her a little uneasy, in fact; she'd thought her and Joe would be a good fit. Now she wasn't so sure.

'Only on my mother's side,' he said, also looking uncomfortable about it, which reassured her. 'The usual thing, I suppose. Her family thought she married beneath herself.' He shrugged. 'At any rate, as far as I'm aware she was never in touch with any of them while I was growing up. Except for great-aunt Stacy, of course.'

Joe reached into the chest again and drew out a small, plain wooden box, studying it in surprise.

'Hello, what's this?' The box was locked. 'Damn. No sign of a key … but the lock looks simple enough. I expect a hairpin might do the job.'

'Alice, Lily, either of you girls got a hairpin on you?' Violet asked, glancing round at her nieces.

'Lucky for you I decided to pin my headscarf on,' Lily said, pulling out the pin and handing it over. She peered curiously down at the box. 'What's that?'

Violet caught a frown tugging Joe's brows together, and recalled what a private person he was.

Quickly, she said, 'Never you mind about that, love. You know, we'll get this job done quicker if we divide the room between us. Joe and I will clear this side. You and Alice can do the rest. Here, have a look whether there's anything worth saving in that old wardrobe. Go on, chop chop.'

When the girls had moved away, Alice grumbling under her breath, Joe set the box on a nearby table and inserted the hairpin delicately into the lock, feeling around for the mechanism inside. At last, it clicked, and he handed Violet the pin back with a word of thanks.

'Let's have a look,' he murmured, and opened the box.

Inside was a stack of neatly folded papers, some of them bound with faded red ribbon.

'Love letters?' Violet whispered, not wanting to alert the girls. This was obviously not something Joe had been expecting to find, judging by the look of consternation on his face.

'Unlikely, but…' He picked up a few, glancing through

them. 'Well, maybe you're right. They all seem to be addressed to my mother. By her maiden name.'

'Well, these letters must be from before she married your father,' Violet pointed out in a practical way, trying to be helpful. 'Girls do that, you know. Keep notes and mementoes, I mean. Maybe the letters are from him too.'

'I doubt it,' he said frankly. 'My father never wrote a personal letter in his life. Not that I know of, anyway.'

'Oh, come on.' She dared to nudge him with her elbow. 'Not even when he was courting your mother?'

Joe had pulled the red ribbon loose from one of the letters and opened it, glancing to the end to read the signature. His face became almost thunderous. 'This one's not from my father. I don't even recognise the man's name.'

Violet felt awful. 'Well, maybe this was someone who courted her before your father came along, only it didn't work out. Things like that happen.'

'She would have mentioned it to me.'

'Would she?' Violet wasn't so sure. 'Maybe it was only a quick fling. You know, a few weeks...'

'His name was Herbert,' he said in a tense voice, and opened another letter, which had been penned in the same handwriting. 'No surname.' He read for a moment, getting up to bring the letter closer to the window for better light. 'Good God. I don't believe it...'

'What is it?' she asked, seeing horror and disgust in his face.

'If this letter's right, it sounds as though he and my mother...' Joe swallowed, and then crumpled the letter in his fist, shaking his head angrily. 'I don't believe it. My mother would never have... No, it's simply not possible.'

Alice and Lily were glancing their way, curious at his tone.

'I know, let's you and me go downstairs and have a nice cup of tea,' Violet suggested diplomatically, scooping up the offending box of letters and leading him away. 'Girls, you carry on up here. I'll be back in an hour to check on your progress.' She raised her eyebrows at Alice, who was groaning. 'Don't you complain, Missy. It's very kind of Joe to let us have these rooms. So mind you do a good job, all right?' She bundled Joe out of the attic room, seeing his stunned expression. 'And don't break anything.'

'Yes, Aunty Vi,' the girls chorused, and then giggled.

Violet flashed them a quick grin through the doorway. Yes, she thought, taking a moment to enjoy the sight of her two nieces grinning and dusty in headscarves and overalls. It definitely felt like old times, all of them back together again and making mischief. She was glad Lily had found a new job and was enjoying herself in Penzance. But they'd all missed her lovely smile... If only her sister Betsy could have lived to see how well her girls turned out. Or if their dad, Ernst, had not taken on such a dangerous mission behind enemy lines that he might never come back from. Though neither Alice nor Lily knew anything about that of course; they thought their half-German father had been killed in action. And she couldn't tell them the truth, bound by the Official Secrets Act, however much she yearned to.

It was a crying shame, that was for sure.

Downstairs, her mum was in the kitchen, cheerfully busying herself by making a cake for tea, since they now had access to fresh eggs galore. Joe was standing blindly in the centre of the room as though in a daze, his hands clenched into fists by his side.

'Baking a cake, Mum? That's nice.' Awkwardly, Violet steered Joe towards the small front room instead where they often sat by the fire in the evenings. She could tell this was one conversation that he wouldn't want to have in front of her mother. 'We'll stay out of your way.'

'Want a brew, love?' her mum asked, peering after Joe curiously.

'That would be lovely, ta.'

Joe was standing by the window in the front room, staring out, when Violet went in and shut the door. She put the box of letters on a side table, and slowly unwound the pink chiffon scarf from about her hair.

'Joe?'

He didn't respond, his back still turned to her.

Poor man. It sounded from those letters like his mum had been a bit wild before she settled down with his dad, and while that didn't sound too dreadful to Violet, no doubt it felt different when it was your own mum. And most men preferred to think of their mums as saintly creatures who'd kept their legs closed except to have them. It must have come as a shock to discover that his mum had been 'no better than she ought to be,' as Sheila would say.

Violet went to him and put a hand gently on his shoulder. 'Joe, love? I'm sure there ain't nothing in there to upset yourself over.'

'You didn't see what was written in those letters.' His voice was tight, and he sounded furious.

'Then tell me.'

He struggled for a moment, then turned to look at her. To her astonishment his cheeks were dark red and there were tears in his eyes. 'I … I can't.' He dashed a hand across his eyes, swearing coarsely. 'I'm sorry. Pardon my bad language.'

'Gawd, I've heard worse than that in my time.' She tried to smile but her heart was squeezed in pain, seeing him so unhappy. What on earth had he seen to put him in such a state? 'How about you come and sit down with me on the sofa? Let's talk about this over a nice refreshing cuppa. Mum's putting the kettle on for us.' She attempted to inject a light note into the conversation. 'There'll be proper cake for tea too. With eggs and all.'

Joe nodded, but with obvious difficulty. 'She's a good woman, your mother. You're a good woman too, Violet. I'm glad I asked you all to join me here.'

'I'm not sure about that,' she said frankly, following him to the two-seater sofa. 'If you hadn't started cleaning out the attic, you'd never have found those.' She jerked her head towards the box of letters on the side table. 'Some things are best forgotten. I'm sure that's why your mum kept them locked them up all these years.'

'No, if she'd really wanted it forgotten, she could have burnt those letters. But she didn't. She left them for me to find after her death. That was deliberate.' Gathering some of the letters, Joe rustled through them slowly, choosing one and putting the others aside. 'You didn't know my mother; you only met her a few times. She was a very careful woman. She never did anything without planning it all out in advance.'

Violet watched him and bit her lip against saying something that might fret him further. She could see Joe had put his mum on a pedestal, but all the same, he was making an awful fuss over a few youthful indiscretions, wasn't he?

'But it was all so long ago,' she said eventually, trying not to be judgemental. He was right, after all; she'd never really known his mother. 'Does it really matter now?'

Joe closed his eyes as though she'd said something deeply wounding. 'Yes, it matters. It matters more than anything in the world.' When she stared at him in surprise, he showed her the date on the letter he was reading. 'See that? Barely three months before she married my father.'

'So? That happens sometimes. You break up with one person and meet someone else almost immediately.'

'You don't understand,' he ground out. 'This is from her, not him. She never sent this letter. Wrote it but never posted it.' He read aloud. '*You know I'm expecting and there's no doubt about it. It must be three months since that night in the woods.*'

Violet gasped. 'Oh my goodness.'

'*I hoped you would make an honest woman of me, Herbert. It never occurred to me that you wouldn't, or I would never have let you have your way with me. I feel like such a fool now. I was thrilled when I told you about the baby, and I still can't believe you fooled me so completely. All that time, I was in love with…*' Joe's deep voice faltered at last, '*a married man.*'

'Lord above,' Violet whispered, finally realising the awful truth. Joe hadn't been his dad's son, but another man's entirely. 'He done the dirty on her. Married, but pretended he wasn't.'

He stopped reading the letter and bent his head, his shoulders shaking. Tears ran down his cheeks.

'But she didn't post that letter, did she? I wonder if she ever told him.'

After a moment, he raised his head, and reached for the stack of letters again. 'There was one... I didn't understand it at first, but now...' He searched for a moment and then read out from a particularly crumpled-looking sheet of paper, '*I'm sorry if you feel that I deceived you. But I thought you understood the situation. You can't expect me to turn my life upside-down because of one little mistake. Please never contact me again.*'

'*One little mistake,*' Violet repeated, furious for his poor deserted mum. 'But she must have told your dad,' she added hurriedly, trying to make things right somehow, though it was impossible. 'I mean Postbridge, the man who brought you up. It must have been obvious she was expecting by the time he married her. So he knew what he was taking on.'

'What difference does that make?' Joe fumbled for his handkerchief and blew his nose, shaking as he tried to get a hold of himself.

'It means he *wanted* to be your dad. She didn't trick him into marriage.'

'Let's hope not.' He folded the letters and put them away again. 'But no wonder her side of the family never wanted anything to do with us. They must have known I was born on the wrong side of the blanket.'

'Snobs, all of 'em,' Violet said dismissively. 'Anyway, you're not illegitimate. Not technically. Postbridge gave you his name.'

'I suppose so,' he agreed grudgingly. He pushed his hanky into his pocket, seeming more composed. 'I'd like to read more of his letters to her some time. I want to find out more about this "Herbert" character. Her *married* seducer,' he added bitterly.

'He does sound like a proper scoundrel.'

Violet's mum came in at that moment, bearing a tea tray on which were some of her homemade biscuits as well as the teapot keeping warm under a knitted cosy, a small jug of milk, and two cups.

'Here you go,' she said cheerfully, shooting Joe a quick assessing glance. 'Tea's up.'

'Thanks, Mum,' Violet said, and smiled at her. But she felt more like crying.

Poor Joe. It surprised her how protective she felt towards him, even thinking a few hard things about his late mum, Joyce, who had never confessed while she was alive that he wasn't his father's flesh and blood. She'd known for a while that she wasn't just fond of Joe, of course, but in love with him. All the same, it surprised her to realise how deep her feelings ran…

The problem was, she had absolutely no idea how he felt about her. Not deep down. Though with the world tearing itself apart, and bombs falling more heavily than ever, did it really matter what was in anyone's heart these days? There wasn't much point in dwelling romantically on what could happen between them, not when there might not even be a future to look forward to.

Not if England lost the war.

CHAPTER TWENTY-TWO

The Feathers was doing a brisk trade on Friday lunch-time – mostly older gents propping up the bar, but a few soldiers and Navy men too, talking and laughing. Demelza looked shyly about the noisy, smoke-filled room, holding the door open behind her so she could escape if Robert wasn't there.

'Looking for me?'

She whirled to find Robert behind her, filling the doorway. 'Oh, hello,' she said awkwardly, and moved aside to let him pass.

He was still in his uniform, even off-duty, with his armband and cap badge pronouncing him a member of the Penzance Ambulance Service. Several people at the bar looked around at him on the threshold, and she thought she read disapproval in their eyes. Or was that only her imagination? Not that it would be entirely surprising if they did disapprove of him. After all, she felt the same way too, didn't she? For a split-second, Demelza wondered what on earth she was doing, agreeing to meet a conchie for a drink.

But one look in his eyes made her forget all that.

'Here, let's sit down.' He pulled off his cap, ran a hand through his fair hair – making her think again of that huge Viking from her beloved history book– and led her to an empty table near the window. 'This looks like a nice spot.'

It was bench seating against the wall. She sat and he pulled out a stool opposite. They were almost on eye level, she realised, and suspected he'd deliberately chosen a low stool to make himself look less vast and intimidating. The window was made up of old-fashioned, leaded, diamond-shaped panes, with a few panes of green and red coloured glass; it gave the place a cosy, intimate feel. Through the clear panes, she could see people and cars passing on the road. It was raining slightly, just a little drizzle that had wetted her coat on the way through town, but the pub was warm, a small fire burning in the grate, and she decided to shrug out of her coat.

'What would you like to drink?' he asked. 'I'm buying.'

'Thank you.' She had no idea what to order, not being a pub goer. 'Surprise me?'

He gave her a slow smile. 'Very well.'

While he was at the bar, she watched him covertly. There was so much about him that she admired. And yet so many questions she could not answer. More than ever, Demelza felt the lack of a mother figure in her life. Someone she could have confided in, or at least asked for advice. Though many of her friends from school had often complained bitterly about their own mothers' interfering ways and stern rules around going out on dates. Not that she was a schoolgirl anymore. But she'd never had a boyfriend and didn't know what to expect, and her spinster aunt Sarah was the last person she could turn to for advice about men. She wasn't even sure if this was a date, and if it was, whether that meant Robert was her boyfriend.

It was embarrassing to be so inexperienced at her age.

Robert came back, placing a half-pint glass in front of her. 'Try that, it's a Cornish Pale Ale. Brewed in St Austell.' He had a bottle of the same straw-coloured liquid, which he poured into a glass for himself. 'Cheers.'

'Cheers,' she repeated, and took a tentative sip. She had tried beers and ales several times before, as most of her acquaintances drank them, and hadn't enjoyed the taste. But she'd asked him to surprise her, so would have to make the best of a bad job. She controlled her urge to pull a face. 'Thank you.'

He grinned. 'Don't like it, do you?'

'Not much,' she admitted, and couldn't help smiling back at him. He was very personable. 'But I haven't drunk many alcoholic drinks, so I don't really know what I like.'

A man walked past their table, glanced at Robert with a cold eye, and then sat under the window with his drink. The blackout boards had been taken down for the day, but instead of looking out, he continued to glare at Robert from time to time, as though unhappy to find him in the pub.

'Do you know that man?' she asked in a low voice.

Robert did not turn around to see who she meant, for he'd already looked up as the man passed and was frowning into his drink now.

'Pay no attention.'

'He doesn't seem to like you.'

Robert shrugged. 'That's nothing to do with me.' He

downed some of his pint in an easy swallow. 'Folk don't like it when they see men like me around the place, that's all.'

'I don't understand.'

He flashed her a look. 'Don't tell fibs, Demelza.' When she flushed, he nodded. 'I've seen the same look on your face. Fit and healthy, but not joined up to fight?'

'Oh.'

'Yes, oh.'

She felt embarrassed. 'I'm sorry.'

'No need to be. It's only natural. You want an explanation for why I didn't enlist.'

'No, of course not. It's none of my business.' Again, he looked at her quizzically, and Demelza gave up. There didn't seem much point in pretending anymore. 'All right, I have wondered about it sometimes. Because I've seen you at work. Seen the things you do, and I know you're not a coward.' She hesitated, and then finished in a rush, 'So why choose to stay behind?'

Robert took another swallow of his ale before answering. 'Simple, really. I'm a Quaker, born and bred.' He put down his glass, staring into it. 'And, in case you didn't know, we're pacifists. We don't believe in violence.'

Demelza studied him, a feeling of relief flooding over her. She'd known there had to be a good reason. Though all the same, she wasn't sure what he meant about not believing in violence.

'I see.' She bit her lip. 'So, if someone came to attack you and your family...'

He nodded. 'Yes, I've thought about that myself, and I suppose I would have to fight back, in that instance, if negotiation or persuasion wouldn't work. But only if there was no other way to protect those I love.'

'So why isn't this the same thing? You'd be fighting to protect England and everyone in it.'

He met her gaze. 'It's the principle of the thing, chiefly. As a Quaker, I support a peaceful resolution to our conflict with Germany, not a violent one, and that means I can't take up arms. Not even to defend my country. Because that would betray everything I've ever believed in.' He finished his pale ale, a frown tugging his brows together. 'Though I do regret...'

'Yes?' she prompted him when he paused.

'When war first broke out,' he went on reluctantly, 'some of the Quakers I knew signed up straightaway to serve as stretcher bearers and orderlies at army field hospitals, or even as cooks with the Navy. Ideally, that's what I would have wanted to do myself. To be in the thick of it and serve the soldiers on the front line, whether that's in Europe or Africa, or wherever.' His mouth twisted. 'But my grandparents are so frail and elderly, I knew my primary duty had to lie with them.'

She studied him thoughtfully. 'So if your grandparents weren't around, or you felt sure they could be safe...'

'I would sign up for service abroad, yes. In a flash.' He glanced at her glass, which was largely untouched. 'Do you want another drink? Not ale this time.'

She smiled, hearing the teasing note in his voice. 'No, thank you,' she insisted, and took another sip, trying not to shudder. 'I'll get used to it.' She laughed under his ironic gaze. 'Honestly. Anyway, are Quakers allowed to drink?'

'There's no "allowed" entailed. We're not prisoners of

our beliefs. We choose them freely. But what about you?' he asked, pushing aside his empty glass and sitting back with folded arms.

'Me?'

'I've talked about my family. But I don't know much about yours.'

'They're farmers. That's all.'

'But you're doing your bit for the Fire Guard. Dangerous work. It's voluntary, though?'

'That's right.' She felt uncomfortable talking about herself.

'So, do you work on the land too?'

'When I'm home and I'm needed.' She paused, seeing the curiosity in his look. 'I suppose that makes me sound awful lazy. I'm not; I swear.'

'I didn't say a word.'

'It's just … me and Dad, we don't get on.'

He nodded slowly. 'And your mother? How does she feel about you being in the Fire Guard?'

'She doesn't feel anything about it. She's dead.'

'I'm sorry.'

Everyone said that, she thought. But she could tell from his face that he really meant it. The expected thing to say in response would be a polite 'thank you'. Instead, she shocked herself by saying, flatly and without emotion, 'She killed herself.'

His eyes widened. 'How awful.'

'I found her one day when I came home from school,' Demelza went on, almost brutally, unable to stop now that she'd started. 'Lying next to an empty bottle of pills. When folk ask what happened, Dad always tells them it was an accident.' When he said nothing, she went on breathlessly, 'But I reckon he only says that to save himself from the shame of having a wife who committed suicide. I mean, she must have hated him to do it. Don't you think?'

He considered this question with a sombre expression. 'Maybe,' he said at last. 'But we can't ever know the real truth of a person, can we? Or a marriage.'

'I can. My mother wrote things down, you see. To keep a record. So that somebody at least would know about it...' Her lower lip was trembling, and she couldn't seem to control it. 'After her death.'

'Ah' was all Robert said, but he reached across and laid his hand over hers. 'Listen, whatever drove her to suicide, I'm sure she loved you very much. Never doubt that.'

To her horror, Demelza's vision swam with tears. She'd been pushing aside all thoughts of her mother's journal in recent days, unable to cope with the things she had discovered. It had reached the point where she even wished she'd never found it, because then she wouldn't know about the torments her mother had undergone in her marriage. Now, Robert's quiet, sympathetic voice had reduced her to tears.

She fumbled for her old hanky and hid behind its threadbare folds. 'Sorry,' she said. 'I should probably go.'

To her dismay, he did not protest but stood at once, as though keen to draw this disastrous date to a close.

'If you wish,' he said.

What she wished, Demelza thought, watching him pull on his jacket, was that she could read his expression.

'Though I hope nothing I've said has upset you,' he added.

'Of course not.'

'Because I'm heading up to the hospital now,' he went on as she hurriedly gathered her things, 'and wondered if you'd like to come too.' When she stared round at him in baffled silence, he added, 'It's the little girl I brought out of the fire the other night. You remember? I just want to check how she's getting on before I go back on duty.'

She recalled the child he was talking about; she herself had watched him rescue the girl from the top floor of a burning building, showing total disregard for his own safety.

'Oh, yes.' Demelza cursed her silly heart for flaring with fresh hope at this perfectly ordinary invitation. She had tied herself in knots and even burst into tears on this first date, yet he was not washing his hands of her. 'Thank you.'

He liked her. And she definitely liked him, having finally dismissed her initial worries about his character. Yet what future could there be in this budding relationship? Robert was quite a bit older than her, or certainly came across that way. And he'd made it clear his priority was staying here to look after his grandparents, while she herself would like to move somewhere more exciting – like London – if the opportunity ever arose. Perhaps all they could hope was to snatch a few moments of happiness and friendship together, a brief respite from the bombs and the dark terrors of war.

At the hospital, they were shown to the children's ward by a pleasant, smiling nurse, where they found the little girl sitting up in bed. Her head was bandaged and she was very pale, but the nurse assured them the girl was recovering well from smoke inhalation and a bump on the head, received when she'd tried to escape on her own and had fallen down the stairs in thick black smoke before crawling back up to the relative safety of her family's top floor flat.

'She's a very brave little girl,' the nurse said in an indulgent voice. 'Aren't you, Adele?'

The little girl, who was thin and dark-haired, gave them a wan smile, whispering, 'Yes.' One of her arms was also lightly bandaged, the surrounding skin red and puffy-looking. Burns, Demelza guessed, and could only imagine how painful that must be. The girl was studying Robert thoughtfully, her head on one side. 'Are you the fireman who rescued me?'

'I'm an ambulance driver. But yes, I'm the one who carried you down the stairs.' Robert gave her a gentle smile. 'How are you feeling, Adele?'

'Much better, thank you,' she lisped in her husky voice.

'Have your family been to visit yet?'

Little Adele nodded. 'Mum and Ted came yesterday. Ted's my older brother. He brought me this as a present.' She held up a tatty ragdoll she'd been cradling. 'I'm calling her Eliza.'

'That's a nice name,' Demelza said.

'My other dolls are all burnt to ashes, my brother says,' Adele told them, and her eyes suddenly brimmed with tears. 'All my other toys and clothes too.' She clutched the ragdoll close. 'I … I only got Eliza now.'

Robert was frowning heavily. 'I'm so sorry.'

'Oh, but she's a very pretty doll,' Demelza said quickly, perching on the edge of the little girl's bed to give her a gentle hug. 'And I'm sure you'll get more.'

She knew how scarce everything had become though,

what with rationing and costs soaring, not to mention supply boats constantly being hit by the enemy. It was perfectly possible that, with all of their possessions lost in that bombing raid, this poor girl and her family would have next to nothing to their name for some years to come.

'Who are you two, then?' a sharp voice came from behind Robert. 'And what are you doing with my sister?'

Startled, Demelza released the girl and stood up straight. The tall and lanky young man who'd come scowling to Adele's bedside looked about sixteen years old, with a straight dark fringe of hair and hollow cheeks scarred with acne.

'You must be Ted,' she said as cheerily as she could manage, and thrust out her hand, though he ignored it. 'I'm Demelza, and this is Robert. We just came to see how your sister's doing.'

'Do-gooders, are you?' The boy was sneering. 'Well, our Adele don't need none of your charitable nonsense. Best be off with you.'

'Don't be rude to them, Ted. You know Mum wouldn't like it.' Adele wiped her tears away with the ragdoll, sniffing loudly. 'Anyway, that's the one who saved me,' she said in her hoarse, smoke-damaged voice, pointing at Robert.

'Oh yes?' Ted shot Robert a look of acute dislike. 'The *conchie*, is it?' He nodded when Robert said nothing. 'I paid a visit to the ambulance depot when I heard what happened, and your mate Bernard told me all about you.' Demelza recalled that Bernard was the name of the other ambulance driver she'd met down on the beach; it seemed even his fellow volunteers didn't think much of his choice not to enlist. 'Happen we should thank you for saving

239

Adele. But you shouldn't be here, when all's said and done. You should be doing your bit, like everyone else. So you can go now, a'right?'

'Ted, no.' Adele moaned, and hid her face behind the ragdoll.

Horrified by the lad's ingratitude, Demelza threw a quick, agonised glance at Robert, expecting him to be hurt or possibly even angered by his dismissal. But Robert's face was an expressionless mask.

'Goodbye, Adele,' he said, quite as friendly as when they'd first arrived, ignoring the young lad altogether. 'I'm glad you're on the mend. It was nice to meet you properly.'

Outside the hospital, they set off towards the town centre without a word, the afternoon already darkening with the threat of rain. Neither of them had brought an umbrella, so they would have to walk quickly to avoid getting soaked.

After a few minutes, her insides churning, Demelza looked up at his face. 'That boy shouldn't have spoken to you like that. Not after you saved his sister's life.'

But Robert merely shrugged. 'To him, I'm a monster. The man who refused to go to war. Of course he sent me away.' However calm his voice, she saw the hardening of his jaw as he stared across the roofs of Penzance and out to sea. 'And perhaps he's right. Perhaps I'm not fit to be in anyone's company.' Looking down, he met her troubled eyes. 'Including yours.'

CHAPTER TWENTY-THREE

Lily had agreed to walk young Janice home from school on days when she wasn't on shift at the hospital. Part of her liked to believe this was the act of a Good Samaritan, since agreeing to a strict curfew had been one of the conditions under which the headmistress had allowed the girl to return to school. In her heart, though, Lily knew the real draw for her was Demelza's handsome brother, Tristan. She would walk with Janice up the long, uneven, grassy drive and hope to catch a glimpse of the ginger-haired young man in the fields or around the farm itself, his slim figure only too evident in his tight-fitting blue work overalls.

Not that she had time for a flirtation, what with the hectic workload at the hospital and the bombs falling on Penzance and its surrounding areas more often now, even during the day. She was trying hard to keep calm and carry on, like everyone else in the country, but secretly she was scared when the enemy planes flew overhead, she had to admit it; scared half to death at times, even while sheltering deep in the hospital basement. There were tales of German pilots deliberately targeting hospitals, despite the red crosses painted on the roofs. And she had seen enough devastation to know how much damage just one bomb could do to a building, let alone to the people within it. A direct hit could obliterate a basement shelter, regardless of how safe you felt down there. But it made her heart glad to see Tristan smile, and to smile at him in return. Where was the harm in that?

One afternoon in June, she was escorting Janice up the hill when the girl, who had been walking more slowly than usual, stopped dead and burst into tears.

'Goodness, Janice, whatever's the matter?' Lily asked, hurriedly putting an arm about the schoolgirl's shoulders. Her nurse's instincts were on alert as she scanned Janice's face for signs of pain. 'Are you hurt?'

Janice shook her head. 'I can't go on,' she sobbed. 'I gotta tell somebody.'

'Well,' Lily reassured her, 'whatever it is, you can tell me.'

'You … you won't tell nobody else?'

'Cross my heart and hope to die,' Lily said automatically, and squeezed her hand. 'I hear all sorts at the hospital and never breathe a word to another living soul. You can trust me.'

Drying her eyes, Janice said unevenly, 'I can't get it out of my head. There's this boy at school … an older boy called Samuel.'

'Oh aye?' Lily thought she knew where this was going.

'We're not walking out together, it ain't nothing like that,' Janice said quickly. 'Samuel wanted to kiss me, only I don't like him much. So I told him no.' She gave a sob. 'He waited till the teacher sent me outside to bang chalk off the erasers, and then … he followed me out and kissed me anyway.'

'Oh God.' Lily was gripped by the horrid memory of her great-uncle Stanley slobbering over her in the barn at her great-aunt's farm. Through a constricted throat, she said, 'Go on, love,' giving her a supportive smile. 'Was that all he did?'

Her cheeks scarlet with shame, Janice nodded. 'I kicked him in the shins and ran back into class.'

'I hope it was a good, hard kick.' Lily gave her a reassuring smile. 'Did you tell the teacher what he done to you?'

The girl shook her head. 'I didn't dare. I knew he'd lie and pretend I asked him to kiss me. Then people would have said I was easy.'

Lily understood this fear only too well. Her great-aunt Margaret had made her suspicions plain after that incident in the barn. 'And did the boy say anything himself?'

'No, he kept his mouth shut. I think he was ashamed.'

'As well he should be, nasty little…' Lily stopped herself from using the worst word she knew. 'So, when did all this happen?'

'On my third day at the school.' Janice hung her head. 'I know it was weeks ago but sometimes I can't help remembering and…' She swallowed another muffled sob. 'Sorry.'

Lily enclosed the schoolgirl in her arms, understanding her pain only too well. 'It's all right. You don't need to explain, love. Something a bit like that happened to me once.'

'It did?' Janice whispered.

Briefly, Lily outlined what her great-uncle had done, though Stanley had gone a great deal further than Janice's young attacker.

'My Aunty Vi saved me from… Well, she stopped him.' Lily didn't want to go into too much detail and frighten the girl. 'I still think of it though, just like you. And I worry about it happening again. But it gets easier with time.' She hadn't realised that until now, she thought, surprised by the ring of truth in her voice.

'Really?'

'Of course.' Lily nodded, releasing her with a smile. 'So, you don't have to be afraid to make friends with boys. They aren't all like that bloomin' twerp.'

Janice laughed shakily. 'You're right, he is a twerp.'

'Is that the real reason you kept ducking out of school? To avoid Samuel?'

'Maybe. To be honest, I did think I'd be happier back in Barking. None of the boys there would ever have done something like that.' She paused. 'Though I've known 'em all my life. I s'pose that makes a difference.'

Lily thought about the situation for a moment, chewing on her lip. 'Do you want me to go and see the headmistress about this boy? I can tell Miss Rhodes what happened and make sure he keeps his distance in future.'

'Oh no, he's not spoken to me since.' Janice gave a satisfied smile. 'I expect he's worried I might kick him again.'

They continued walking and were soon at the farm. That was where Lily usually left her charge and either headed back to town or to the bus stop to visit Aunty Violet. But today she hesitated, seeing a familiar figure out in the sheep fields above the house. She shielded her eyes against the sunlight; sure enough, it was Tristan. He lifted a hand and waved to them both. Her heart beating faster than it ought to, Lily waved back.

How silly, she thought, and turned away.

'Well, thanks for walking me home,' Janice said shyly, and then skipped into the house with her school bag and gas mask bouncing on her shoulders, more cheerful since sharing that nasty incident. Perhaps she'd been worrying about it ever since, fearful that admitting what had happened would make her look like a flirt. Lily hoped she'd reassured her on that front, at least.

Although Janice had asked her not to involve the head-mistress, maybe she ought to mention the boy's attack to someone else instead. Demelza, perhaps. Yes, she'd do that as soon as she got the chance.

Looking back up at the sheep fields, she realised that Tristan was still waving. She narrowed her eyes, staring. No, not waving. He was *beckoning*. Blow me, she thought, astonished. Was he asking her to join him up there? She looked around but Janice had long since vanished and nobody else was about. So, it could only be her he was signalling to.

Lily struggled for a moment, and then gave in to temptation. She wasn't expected back at work until tomorrow afternoon and had nothing else planned for this afternoon. Plus, the June weather had turned lovely again after a few days of rain. A walk in the countryside might do her good, she told herself, heading for the rough, overgrown track that led uphill to where Tristan was working.

It was a warm day, but breezy. Her dress snapped and

fluttered about her knees as she walked, avoiding occasional clumps of stinging nettles and tall, damp grasses nodding vigorously. Reaching the top field, she went through the gate and turned to close it behind her, so no sheep could escape. Below, she could see right across Penzance and the wide bay where St. Michael's Mount rose above a narrow causeway near Marazion. The sea was a bright, sparkling blue to the horizon, but around the coastline was ruffled white with the wind.

Having grown up in the hustle and bustle of Dagenham, she couldn't remember ever having seen such a peaceful view. To her mind, even the impressive Atlantic coast at St. Ives could not compare with this, since it lacked the exotic, fairy-tale look of St. Michael's Mount.

'Enjoying the view?' Tristan asked from behind her.

'I'll say.' Lily turned, smiling shyly at the lad, aware of heat in her cheeks. She hoped he would assume any flush was down to the steep climb, though in truth, she was in pretty good shape after working so hard on the wards, and barely even out of breath. 'It's a marvel, it really is. You're so lucky to wake up to this every day of the week.'

He laughed, coming closer. 'I don't know about that.'

His old green jumper was slung about his shoulders and his shirt sleeves were rolled up to his elbows. His wellies and his trousers were both speckled with mud but she still thought he looked awful handsome.

'No, I'm serious,' she insisted, stammering a little. 'You should see where I grew up in Essex. It's chalk and cheese, honest to God.' She looked past him to where a mother sheep was grazing wearily as she nursed two identical baby lambs, their wool shining white in the sunshine, their legs still unsteady. 'Oh, how sweet!'

'Newborn lambs,' he told her, and then checked his watch. 'Well, born about five hours ago now. Our last lambing of the season, and long overdue too. It was a difficult birth. But twins often are.' He flicked back a few dangling curls of bright ginger hair. 'Dad sent me up to check on the ewe in case she was struggling. But she's on the mend, so no need to send for the vet.'

'Clever mummy sheep,' she said approvingly.

'Would you like to hold one of the lambs?' he asked, watching her delight as the newborns staggered away from their mother to gambol and play on the grass.

She gaped. 'Am I allowed?'

'I don't see why not. I've examined both of them at length, and so has Dad. I'm sure one more person man-handling them won't make any difference.' He caught one of the little lambs and took a moment to show her how to hold it, supporting its narrow body and outsized legs. 'Gently does it,' he said softly, transferring the lamb into her waiting arms.

'Oh, my goodness.' Lily was overwhelmed with joy, feeling the lithe woolly body against her chest. The animal jerked its gangly legs a few times, then lay still, seeming to accept her as a caregiver. 'He's gorgeous.' When he grinned, she shot him a quick worried glance. 'It is a *he*, isn't it?'

'It is, indeed. Well spotted, Nurse Fisher.'

She laughed. He was teasing her, but she didn't mind it. She'd handled a human baby soon after birth and they were wonderful too, so new and shiny. Little parcels of hope. But this newborn lamb was especially precious, a symbol of new beginnings.

The lamb bleated, its tiny mouth shaking, the high-pitched noise oddly loud so close to her ears.

'Oh dear, that doesn't sound good. You'd better take him back before he does something on my dress,' she said with a grimace, aware that the lamb was becoming restless. Tristan scooped him easily out of her arms and set the animal back on his cloven hooves. 'Bye bye, little lambkin.'

Once down, the lamb lurched and wobbled back to the safety of his mother's shaggy underbelly and began to suckle fiercely.

She smiled, watching him and his twin feeding again. 'That was just the loveliest thing, Tristan,' she said, beaming and folding her arms across her chest. 'Thank you.'

But Tristan did not reply. He was not looking at her, she realised, but had turned and was gazing along the coast.

'What is it?' she asked, frowning.

'Planes,' he said briefly, and pointed.

It was only then that she registered the faint drone she'd been hearing for several minutes now and recognised the sound for what it was.

'Germans?' she asked, a little breathlessly. 'Coming along the coast?'

He nodded without speaking. At that moment, the thin, familiar wail of the air-raid siren rose in the town below, a sound which instantly had her heart thumping in nervous response. All of her instincts told her to seek shelter. But how could she? They were out in the open air, almost at the top of a hill, barely a tree or hedgerow in sight. They could probably already be seen by the enemy pilots, even if they were still only dots from the sky.

Trying to stay calm, just as she would have done if on duty at the hospital, she mentally measured the distance between themselves and the old farmhouse further down the slope. It was a long way.

'We could probably make it back to the house if we run—' she began, but he interrupted her, shaking his head.

'No time.' Tristan grabbed her hand. 'Come on, I know a place where we should be safe. But you need to move quickly.'

They dashed across the field together, scattering startled sheep in all directions. Tired after a long shift at the hospital, and then the uphill trek out of Penzance, Lily stumbled several times over the rough, uneven grass. But she was stopped from falling by Tristan's supportive hand.

'Better hurry,' he said, though they had to slow as the ground grew boggier, his gaze intent on the sky behind them. 'They must have seen us by now.'

The German pilots were close, somewhere high overhead. The high-pitched whine of their engines was so loud it was setting her teeth on edge, like the sound of a dentist's drill. Her whole body was tensed for the eerie wail of a descending bomb, remembered from hundreds of night-time raids in Dagenham when they'd only just made it to the shelter in time, sleepy and still in their nightgowns. Back then, she'd still been a child. Now, though, she knew the bitter truth of what those bombs could do even when they didn't kill you. Panicked, she thought of the walking wounded who would arrive at the hospital after a near-miss in a bombing raid, with burns and shock and burst eardrums, and sometimes far worse. Injuries that would change their lives forever.

Lily was beginning to fear they would never get to safety in time when suddenly the pasture fell away in a natural cleft in the land.

'Watch your step,' he warned her, going first.

She scrambled after him down a steep and winding track between rocks to a small sheep enclosure with a kind of makeshift lean-to nestled to one side of the path.

It had no door, rather alarmingly, but a roof formed by thin branches woven together.

'In here, Lily.' Obediently, she ducked in after him, and Tristan stooped to set a dirty panel of corrugated iron across the open doorway, sealing them into the shady interior. 'If we stay put until the planes have gone past, we should be safe enough. I doubt they can see this place clearly from the air. And even if they could,' he added, wiping his hands on his trousers, 'I don't imagine they'd waste ammunition on it.'

She nodded. 'I hope Janice got down to the cellar in time.' She put a hand to her heart as she tried to slow her breathing. 'Your aunt too.'

'I'm sure they will have done.'

A thought struck her. 'What about your dad, though? Is he out somewhere on the farm?'

'Gone into town to buy supplies. I expect he'll find a public shelter until the raid's over, like everyone else.'

Silent by mutual consent, they stood listening as the enemy planes passed noisily over their hiding place and, to her great relief, moved on. Time passed crawlingly as they waited. Finally, in the distance, probably somewhere further along the coast, they heard a series of faint explosions.

'I'm sure that wasn't in Penzance,' he assured her quickly, his head still tilted up to listen. 'Wrong direction. Bombing the coast road, perhaps. Trying to make life difficult for us.' His mouth twisted. 'And succeeding, unfortunately.'

Lily hugged herself, shivering as she looked about herself. It was cool inside the shelter, the planks that formed the outer wall of the lean-to blocking the sunlight overhead. At her back was the rough stone wall of one of the crags that enclosed the sheep pen outside. She was standing on musty straw bedding in a dim yellowy-green light, filtered through the woven branches overhead.

'What ... what is this place?' She was whispering, she realised, which was silly. The bloomin' Germans could hardly hear them all the way down here. She cleared her throat and asked more boldly, 'A shepherd's hut, is it?'

'Not quite. My grandfather built it as a covered area to keep hurt sheep out of the rain in winter, especially them that couldn't be moved till the vet had been to see them. Though it makes a great hideout; I used to come down here as a boy sometimes to avoid my father.' He turned to look at her, and their eyes met. She felt a thrill move through her. 'I should take you back. The planes are long gone.'

The countryside was peaceful now the enemy aircraft had passed over; she could hear the distant baaing of sheep and, closer by, birdsong.

'They might come back.'

His gaze searched her expression. 'Lily, I shouldn't say this but...' His voice was hoarse, his face in shadow. 'The first time I saw you, I thought...' He stopped, swallowing.

Half-excited, half-afraid what he meant to say, she prompted him. 'Yes? What did you think?'

Tristan was also breathing fast; she could see his chest rise and fall under the thin shirt. 'I thought you were the most beautiful girl I'd ever seen.'

Heat bloomed in her face and she clapped both hands to her cheeks. 'Oh.'

'I still think it,' he continued doggedly, staring at her. 'I know I'm only a farmer's son, not anyone special. And maybe I oughtn't to be asking this. But would you like to walk out with me?'

She nodded, speechless, and couldn't seem to move, rooted to the spot as he came towards her.

'Lily Fisher,' he whispered, and took her in his arms. 'You're like a fairy-tale princess with your long fair hair.'

By rights, she ought to have laughed, never having felt less like a princess than right there, standing in straw, in a lean-to meant for sheep, after a long day's shift on the wards, her legs aching and her dress clinging to her warm back. But Tristan was so sincere, honesty shining out of his face under the halo of brash ginger curls. So instead, she bit back her laughter and stared up into his eyes, unspeakably flattered.

He kissed her on the mouth, and for an instant Lily tensed, her back stiffening, ready to pull away. Automatically, she expected to hate the sensation of being kissed, waiting for all those hard, bitter memories of her great-uncle's molesting hands to come flooding back and ruin everything for her. But Tristan's lips were gently persuasive, and after an initial flutter she felt nothing but sudden feverish desire and a longing to be close to him. Closer than was entirely sensible for a young nurse with a reputation to uphold, as she knew Matron would be only too quick to point out.

Oh, hang being sensible, Lily thought crossly. They were at war, weren't they? Bombs were falling even here in Cornwall. This could be her last day on earth.

'Tristan,' she said breathlessly, and closed her eyes.

For a long time, they stood kissing, and then Tristan lowered her carefully onto the straw and she did not resist. She felt swept away by his love-making in a way she had never thought could be possible, lost in a wonderful dream, her heart thudding wildly and his echoing it. But every dreamer has to wake up sometime. When he began to unbutton her dress, Lily came back to her senses and put her hands on his chest, pushing him away.

'No,' she murmured, and he drew back without protest, his gaze on her face. 'Not here, not yet. I'm not ready.'

Tristan brushed her cheek with the back of his hand, smiling. 'Whatever you say, Lily.' And he reached out a hand to help her up.

CHAPTER TWENTY-FOUR

Violet was scrubbing down the pine table in the farm kitchen when Joe came stalking in, a terrible look on his face.

'What is it?' she asked at once, straightening in alarm. 'Is somebody hurt? Or one of the animals?'

He shook his head. 'I've just been speaking to one of my neighbours, Gilbert, whose family's been farming in these parts forever. Gilbert knows practically everyone and everything in West Cornwall, so I mentioned *that man* to him.' He folded his arms but she could see he was quivering with rage. By *that man*, he meant his natural father, of course. 'Sure enough, Gilbert knew the name, and says he's still alive.'

'Oh, Joe.' Violet bit her lip, so sorry for him but not sure he would thank her for saying so. He was a man, after all, and men had their pride. 'Is his wife still alive?'

'No idea. But he lives in Penzance these days, Gilbert said. In one of them tall, Victorian terraced houses near the harbour. I couldn't ask what number, in case he got suspicious and wondered why I was asking. But I've a fair idea whereabouts he meant.'

'Will you go and visit him, then? Tell him who you are?'

Joe struggled for a moment, staring at the floor, and then shook his head. 'No, let the past stay past. No point raking him over the coals for it now. Mum's dead. Dad's dead. What would be the point?'

'He's your father, Joe. Your blood relative.' She paused, watching him sympathetically. 'And maybe there'll be other relatives to meet. You may have brothers and sisters. Cousins, uncles, aunts. Had you thought of that?'

'Aye, I've thought of it all.' He tore off his cap and ran a hand through his hair. 'I've done nothing but think of it ever since we found them letters. Why didn't my blasted mother burn them? Then I wouldn't know any of this. I'd be at peace.'

'Like my mum always says, if wishes were horses, then beggars would ride.' Violet went to him and put a hand on his arm. 'You can't unread what she wrote. You can't pretend it never happened. So why not go and meet this man? Find out who he is.'

'He's never made himself known to me,' Joe pointed out. 'He's known of my existence all my life. When Mum and I lived in Penzance, we were only a few streets away from him. All those years and not a word.'

'Maybe he promised your mother not to come. After all, she would have been horribly embarrassed to admit what happened all those years ago, wouldn't she?'

'Maybe.' His jaw worked silently as he thought. 'All the same, when Mum died, he didn't even come to the funeral to pay his respects.' He closed his eyes. 'And what about this place?'

'What do you mean?'

'Well, it shouldn't be mine, should it? My uncle left it

255

to me, thinking I was his flesh and blood. Only I wasn't. I was no relation of his at all.'

'Except by marriage.'

'That doesn't count,' he muttered.

'Now you listen to me, Joe Postbridge,' she said sternly, concerned by his unhappy mood. 'Your uncle left you this farm because he knew you. He could see you'd make a good farmer, and you have done. Who else was he to leave it to? And for all you know, he was in on the secret.'

Joe's eyes widened. 'You think my uncle knew?'

'Well it seems likely, doesn't it. If your father knew about it.'

He looked away, his face troubled. 'If that's true, it would mean I was the only one left in the dark.'

'Yes, for your own good,' she said, raising her brows at him. 'Look, your real father's alive and he's the only one who can give you answers. So go and meet him. Introduce yourself. Whatever you do, for gawd's sake, stop moping.'

His brows drew together and he glared back at her, but didn't argue. 'You've a sharp tongue on you, Violet,' he said, looking her up and down in her damp apron, her fair hair bound in a chiffon scarf to protect it from dirt. 'But an honest one too.' He drew out a chair and sat, staring at the gleaming wet kitchen table without seeing it. 'All right, I'll go and visit him. But on one condition. You have to come with me.'

'Me?' Violet, who had started scrubbing the table again, stopped and stared at him in astonishment. 'Why on earth do you want me with you?'

'If you're going to be my wife,' he said simply, 'you need to know all about me. I'll not have any secrets between us when we're married.'

She didn't know what to say or where to look. The wet scrubbing brush dripped cold water down her arm, right up to her blouse sleeve, which was rolled to her elbow.

'Your wife?' she repeated in a hollow voice. 'I … I don't understand.'

He stood again, his face sombre. 'Didn't I do it right? Well, if you say no, I've only myself to blame, as usual.' He tried to kneel down, and stopped, brows jerking together in frustration. 'I can't do it properly. Damn leg.'

Throwing aside the scrubbing brush, she caught his arm, shaking her head. 'You don't need to go down on one knee.' They were standing so close – head to head – and she could see directly into his eyes. The eyes that had caught her attention the very first time she'd seen them, so dark and intense, fringed with long secretive lashes. 'Are you asking me to marry you?'

He groaned. 'What else do you think I'm doing, woman?'

It was hard not to laugh. But the solemnity of the moment had her too much in awe. 'Oh, Joe.' She stood still as he leant forward and put his lips to hers. The oddest feeling swept over her, leaving her body trembling as he pulled back. 'Blimey.'

'So, will you?' he asked stubbornly, staring into her eyes. 'Marry me?'

Her hands were still wet and soapy. She wiped them on her apron, wishing her knees didn't feel quite so wobbly. 'Don't be daft. Of course I will,' she told him breathlessly. 'Though are you sure? Last year—'

He interrupted her with an abrupt gesture. 'Forget that, please. It was wrong of me to blame you for what happened that night.' He swallowed. 'My mother's death was down to the bloody Jerries and nobody else.' He put an arm round her waist, drawing her close again. 'I was angry and looking for someone to blame. I behaved like an idiot.'

'Maybe a bit,' she agreed, and let him kiss her again. Her head was in a whirl but somehow she managed not to make a fool of herself by fainting. 'You know, I would have come with you as a friend to meet your dad,' she added faintly, adjusting her chiffon head scarf, which had become slightly askew, and picking up the scrubbing brush again, 'so I hope that weren't the only reason you proposed.'

He laughed then, though his face was still grim. 'Now who's being daft?'

'Goodness, I wonder what Mum will say when I tell her.'

He gave her a funny look. 'Vi, would you mind very much if we held off on telling the others? I mean, just for now?'

Violet was surprised by this request, and a little thrown by it too. 'Why?' Her heart thumped uncomfortably. 'Do you think you might change your mind?'

'No, absolutely not,' he told her, and she believed him. 'It's just … I want the time to be right. Everything's so up in the air right now. Let me get my head around it all first before we tell anyone we're engaged. Is that all right?'

'I suppose so.' But she knew her cup of joy, which had been overflowing, was now feeling distinctly half-empty.

'Thank you,' he said sombrely, and cupped her cheek with his warm hand. 'I appreciate it.'

One of the Land Girls burst into the kitchen, and stopped dead, seeing them so close together. 'Oh, sorry,' she said, and began to retreat.

'No, it's all right, Penny, no need to disappear,' Joe said, his hand dropping away as he turned to the girl with a brusque smile. 'I have to talk to you lot about the planting schedule. Where are the others? Out in the barn? Wait, I'll come with you.'

He headed into the yard with the girl, pausing only to throw a look back at Violet that filled her with a strange, fierce emotion. For an awful moment there, she had feared his marriage proposal couldn't be serious, since he didn't want anyone else to know that they were engaged. But that one look had reassured her that Joe meant every word, and more, that he was as deeply in love with her as she was with him.

Violet returned to her work, scrubbing with more vigour than she'd ever done in her life. It was amazing to her that the grain didn't come clean off the pine table or the old brush bristles snap, she was putting so much elbow grease into it. But as soon as they'd gone and she could no longer hear Joe's deep voice rumbling in the yard, Violet dropped the scrubbing brush on the table and sank down into the chair he'd vacated, head in her wet hands.

'I'm going to be a married woman,' she whispered to herself, and gave a joyous sob. 'Oh Betsy,' she added, thinking of her dead sister, 'I wish you'd lived to see this. I'm going to be *Mrs Postbridge*.' She could hardly believe it herself, unable to stop grinning. 'I'm only bloomin' getting married!'

Demelza, having come home a day earlier than planned, wandered into the farmhouse kitchen to find Janice making herself a sneaky paste sandwich.

'Hello,' Demelza said, and threw her bag and gas mask

down on the table. 'They let me out early because of a bump on the head.'

Janice turned to stare at her, popping a few strands of hair into her mouth and chewing on them nervously. The girl looked a little red-eyed, as though she'd been crying, but Demelza decided not to ask any awkward questions.

'Had a bang on the head? How did that happen, then?'

With a grimace, Demelza washed her hands and face at the sink. It had been a long, tiring walk up from town, and all she could think about was going for a nap before supper.

'The stupidest thing... We were checking a building was still secure after that big raid the other night, and I shoved the ceiling pike up only to have the whole lot collapse on my head. Luckily, I was wearing my helmet. But it knocked me out for a minute. My partner, Mags, had to drag me out of there.' She put a hand to her temple, which was still throbbing with a headache. 'I was covered in dust from head to foot. It was embarrassing.'

'Blimey.' Janice looked alarmed. 'You're lucky to be alive!'

'I suppose I am,' Demelza agreed. 'Though it was more of a nuisance than anything else because Captain Jean told me to go off shift a day early. And I ... I had plans for tomorrow lunch-time.' She felt her cheeks flush under the girl's inquisitive stare. 'Maybe I'll walk into town anyway, rather than rearrange. I just hope Father hasn't got a long list of jobs lined up for me to do.' She paused, frowning. 'Talking of my father, where is he?'

Janice shrugged. 'Dunno,' she managed to say, busily chewing. 'Van's not here though. Gone into town, maybe?'

'And my brother?'

'I think Tris is still out with the sheep. At least, I saw

him up in the top field when I got home.' Janice paused, hurriedly swallowing her mouthful of paste sandwich. 'Lily walked me back today. But she never came in for a cuppa, and there was no sign of her when the siren went off.' She paused, thoughtful. 'Nor Tris.'

'I'm sure they both got to safety.' The all-clear had sounded nearly an hour ago now, so it was likely Lily would be back in the nurses' rooms above the Fire Guard Station by now. 'It's a shame I missed her. I like Lily, she's good fun.' Demelza yawned behind her hand. 'Sorry, I'm so tired. I'd better go for a lie-down.'

But as she headed for the stairs, she heard a noisy engine and the grate of gears, and guessed her father must be home. She knew he would expect a brew put on as soon as he walked through the door, and something made for him to eat, so she abandoned her plan for a nap and reluctantly went back into the kitchen.

Wiping her mouth with the back of her hand, Janice fled upstairs with a muttered, 'See you at supper,' as she passed.

Demelza couldn't blame her. She often had the same sinking feeling whenever her father appeared. He'd had a tough life, of course. But that was no excuse for making the people around him miserable too.

The door flew open and the dogs ran in, panting and making straight for their food bowls in hopes of something new there. Her father whirled into the house after them, dragging off his boots and struggling out of his coat. His restless gaze flashed to her at once. 'Ah, so there you are, Missy. Nice of you to drop by.'

Her nerves prickled at the barely contained fury in his voice. He was in a rare old temper, all right. It was all she could do not to copy Janice by fleeing upstairs. But she knew he would only stamp up the stairs after her, madder than ever and determined to have his say. What on earth had happened to put him in a rage though, and why was he glaring at her like she'd murdered somebody? Carefully, she refilled the kettle and put it on the hot plate to boil, racking her brains for an answer. Was there something she'd forgotten to do, perhaps?

'Hello, Dad.' Turning from the range, she gripped the back of a kitchen chair for support, smiling at him tentatively. 'The Fire Guard let me go home a day early this week.' When he made no comment, merely continued to glare, she added, 'I thought you'd be pleased to see me back. Many hands make light work, and all that.'

'That's as may be, but I've been talking to a few folk in town today. Scott, Mr Gregory, Old Tom… All that lot down at the market.' There was a dark flush in his face, she realised. 'And I didn't like what I heard.'

'Why, what's the matter?'

'There's been talk about you. You and some man you've been seeing.'

'A man?' Demelza met his gaze, horrified and suddenly aware what this was about. 'I … I don't know what you mean.'

'You've been walking out with a conchie, haven't you? An ambulance driver.' He shook his head, disgust plain on his face. 'A daughter of mine … taking up with a bloody coward? I told them it couldn't be true. Not my flesh and blood. Only you were seen in The Feathers with him, weren't you? Bold as brass, the two of you…' There was spittle on his lips as he came towards her, a menacing light in his eyes. 'What do you say to that?'

CHAPTER TWENTY-FIVE

Demelza took a few steps back, intimidated by her father's stare. Her first impulse was to deny everything. But that would feel too much like a betrayal of a man she'd started to respect and admire, and she owed it to her first real friendship with a man to stand up for him. 'His name's Robert Day. And yes, I did have a drink with him in The Feathers, it's true.' Demelza straightened her back and forced up her chin, though inwardly she was quaking. 'But he's *not* a coward.'

'He's a Conscientious Objector,' he sneered.

'Only because he's a Quaker.'

'What difference does that make? It's just an excuse so he doesn't have to lay his life on the line like the rest of our young men. You'll not see him again, do you understand?'

Breathing fast, Demelza shook her head. 'You can't tell me what to do,' she said in a defiant rush, not quite able to believe her nerve. 'I'm not under your control.'

'How dare you?' Her father raised his hand as though

to strike her. 'You'll not see that bloody coward again, is that clear? Or so help me, I'll give you what for.'

'Better go on and hit me,' she told him, refusing to shrink away, 'because I'm going to see Robert again if he asks. I don't care what you say or do. You're nothing but a bully.'

This shocked him, she could see it in his face. But he raised his hand higher, his face redder than ever. 'Don't you disrespect me, Demelza. I'm your father. If I have to take my belt to you, I will. This is my house, and while you live under my roof, you'll abide by my rules.'

'Fine,' she said flatly. 'Then I'll leave.'

She turned away, meaning to run upstairs and pack her few possessions, but he grabbed her wrist.

'G-Get off me,' she said on a gasp, stuttering in her rage as she struggled to get free. 'No wonder Mother killed herself, with a brute like you for a husband.'

His face paled, and at last he blinked. 'What?'

Demelza was discomfited by the change in him but there was no taking it back. 'I've read her journal. I know what you did to her. You treat them dogs better than you treated our mother.' She glared at him. 'I'm not taking advice from a bully and a wife-beater.'

'Don't you speak to me like that, girl,' her father thundered, and for a moment, she was afraid that he really would hit her, there was such violence in his face.

But she stood firm, determined not to let him see her fear. The yard door opened, bringing a flood of sunshine and windy air into the dim kitchen. When Demelza glanced that way, she was relieved to see her brother standing in the doorway.

'What's going on?' Tristan asked quickly, concern in his

264

voice. He was frowning as he came marching forward, almost as though to stand between them. 'Let her go, Father.'

Her father released her, but reluctantly. He turned to Tristan, no doubt hoping to anger him too. 'Your sister's been seeing a conchie. Walking out with him. What do you say to that?'

'I say it's none of our business, Father.' Tristan looked at her. 'You all right, Demmy?'

She nodded, though her heart was hammering fit to burst and she badly wanted to cry. Tristan nodded and walked calmly over to the range. He removed the kettle from the hot plate, as it was beginning to judder and whistle, setting it on the trivet instead.

'You're telling me you don't care what folk think of us, son?' their father demanded, his expression incredulous.

'I don't care what anyone thinks, only what's good for Demelza. And if she likes this man, that's all that matters to me.'

Their father began to bluster, but to her surprise Tristan ignored him. He went back to the door instead and spoke to someone outside in the yard, then came back with Lily in tow.

'We've got a guest for supper,' he told them both, presenting their visitor. 'I hope you'll make Miss Fisher welcome.'

Trying to gather her scattered thoughts, Demelza shot a harassed smile at Lily and knew at once that something wasn't right. The girl's dress was crumpled, and her long fair hair, usually dressed in smooth waves when she wasn't at work, was mussed up, and even had straw caught in it.

Her cheeks were flushed and her eyes shining. All in all, it looked like she'd been thoroughly kissed. In trepidation, Demelza glanced around at her father. But he was still fuming over Tristan's refusal to back him up and hadn't noticed the state Lily was in.

'I think that's a lovely idea,' she said hurriedly, and held out a hand to Lily. 'Come upstairs with me, I'll show you where to ... to wash before supper.'

Lily put a hand to her head and, horrified, pulled a piece of straw loose. 'Oh.' She exchanged an embarrassed look with Tristan as she allowed Demelza to drag her away. 'Yes, that's probably best. We were out with the sheep. I ... I'll be back soon.'

As they went upstairs, Demelza could hear her father's booming voice complaining about her to Tristan again, and her heart sank. It was time she left home for good, she decided, seeing no other way ahead. Her father would never let this drop. Even if she stopped being friends with Robert, there would be other things in the future that he didn't like, and yet more furious accusations to throw at her. What her father really wanted was for her to submit to his reign of terror. And that wasn't going to happen. She would never be free so long as she lived at home, that much was becoming clear. So she needed to leave.

Besides, today had been too much like history repeating itself. One day Tristan wouldn't be there to calm him down, and her father would hit her for real. Just as he'd so often lashed out at their mother when they were younger.

'Thank you,' Lily whispered as they slipped into Demelza's bedroom and closed the door securely on the voices from below.

'You're welcome.' Demelza returned her smile, though in truth she felt low enough to cry. 'See, there's a sink in the corner, and a mirror over it. You can borrow my hair-brush if you like.' Plucking another piece of straw from Lily's hair, she looked at it quizzically. 'Now I wonder how that got there…'

Lily bit her lip, her cheeks scarlet, staring at the rogue piece of straw, and then they both burst into uncontrollable giggles.

Tristan came up a short while later, knocking before entering Demelza's room. His gaze went straight to Lily, who was still tidying her hair, and his sister was moved by the emotion in his face. Whatever had happened between them, it was clear he was serious about the girl.

All the same, it was Demelza he spoke to first.

'Aunt Sarah's gone down to start supper,' he said quietly. 'I thought you should know.'

'Thanks.' Demelza got up at once and reached for the apron she'd thrown off earlier. 'I'd better go down and help her.'

Besides, no doubt he'd like to spend some time alone with Lily, she thought diplomatically, and made for the door.

'Wait a minute, Dem. I couldn't help overhearing what you and Dad were talking about when I came home.' Tristan closed the bedroom door behind him as though to ensure nobody could overheard what they were saying, and came further into the room. 'Is what you said true? Did … did our mother really kill herself?' His face was pale and drawn, as though steeling himself to hear a diffi-cult answer, but he'd spoken steadily enough.

Demelza's heart clenched in pain for him. Remembering her own despair when she first discovered the truth, she knew this wasn't how she would have liked to break the news to her younger brother, so bluntly and straight after a row. But it was pointless to lie, given what he'd overheard.

Reluctantly, she nodded, and saw his eyes close as though in instant denial. 'I'm pretty certain she did, yes,' she agreed softly.

'Why didn't you tell me?' The agony in his cry made her wince. 'I don't understand.'

Demelza gave him a fierce hug, wishing she could make everything better. But of course it was impossible.

'I'm sorry, Tris, I really am. But I only found out myself quite recently, and I didn't want to hurt you.'

Quickly, she went back to her bed and, lifting an edge of her mattress, produced the journal she'd hidden more securely there on her last visit home.

'Here,' she said, offering it to him, 'you can read it for yourself. That's our mother's journal. Dad told everyone what happened to her was an accident – that she took too much of her medicine by mistake – but since reading that, I'm sure he was just covering up the truth.'

Her brother took the book but didn't open it, staring down at the scuffed cover. 'Where did you find this?'

'In the old guest room. It was with some of her other things.'

He lowered his gaze to the floor, his ginger curls hiding his expression. 'But why did she do it? Does the journal say? Was it because of us?' He swallowed hard. 'Because of *me*? I know I was a difficult child, but—'

'What?' Demelza was horrified when she realised that

he was blaming himself for their mother's death. 'God, no. You mustn't think like that.' She gave him another hug. 'Honestly, it was nothing to do with us. She loved you, Tris. Read the journal; it's painful, but you'll understand everything afterwards. It was because of him.' Her voice was hoarse, and there was an ache in her chest that nothing seemed to ease. 'Father was cruel to her. Jealous, possessive. The only thing that kept her going was having us in her life.'

His head lifted and he searched her face, tears in his eyes. 'Then why did she leave us with him? If our mother loved us so much, why kill herself?'

It was a question that had tormented her too. But she knew he was looking for something stronger than her own doubts.

'I don't know; I suppose it just got too much for her.' Demelza touched his arm, still trying to reassure him. 'I don't think we should blame her when we don't know what it was like for her, being trapped here with him day after day.'

He gave a jerky nod, but she wasn't sure he understood.

'Look,' she said gently, 'I have to go and help Aunt Sarah make supper. She's still not well, and it's not fair to leave her to cope alone. Besides which, if I don't help, she'll call Janice instead, and that girl needs to focus on doing her homework.' She shot Lily a quick smile. 'Thank you for walking Janice home today, by the way.'

'Oh, it was no problem, Demelza.' Lily's blue eyes were wide with concern, watching the two of them. 'Look, I don't want to heap you with bad news but … before I forget, I ought to tell you something. Janice said a boy at the school made a nuisance of himself in her first week. Kissed her against her will. She gave him a kick and he's avoided her since. But it certainly explains why she was so keen to earn enough money to travel back home.'

'Oh no,' Demelza exclaimed, aghast. 'Does the school know?'

Lily shook her head. 'Janice doesn't want a fuss made. But maybe a discreet note to the headmistress…'

'I'll write one tomorrow. Poor girl. She should have told someone what happened.' Demelza felt guilty. 'We've clearly not been very good guardians if she didn't feel able to confide in any of us.'

'Well, she would have been bunking with my aunt Violet when it happened. So you shouldn't blame yourselves.' Lily gave her a reassuring smile. 'At least it's out in the open now and you can deal with it.' She paused. 'Look, do you need any help in the kitchen tonight? I can't claim to be a great cook but I'm happy to peel veg and lay the table.'

'I won't hear of it,' Demelza said firmly. 'You're our guest tonight. But talking of blame, while I'm gone, will you tell my brother that what happened to our mother wasn't his fault?' When Lily nodded vigorously, Demelza stood on tiptoe and whispered in her brother's ear, 'We'll talk about this later, yes?'

Then she left and hurried down to the kitchen. Her father was nowhere to be seen, but her aunt looked round sourly, mixing bowl cradled in the crook of her arm. Her stick was leaning against the table, so presumably she was feeling strong enough to walk without it tonight. Aunt Sarah had recovered well from the stroke she'd suffered at Christmas, no longer silent and bedridden, though some activities were still beyond her. It probably didn't help that she'd never been a very talkative woman, even before the stroke.

'There you are at last,' Aunt Sarah said with difficulty, her mouth still dragged down at one corner. 'Thought I'd make toad-in-the-hole. Though my brother says we've an extra mouth to feed.' She sounded unimpressed. 'We've barely enough sausages for two apiece now.'

'But we've some beef stock put by in the larder, Aunt. With a few extra vegetables and heaps of gravy, I'm sure we'll manage.' Demelza fetched the peeler and dragged the half-empty sack of potatoes to the table, adding curiously, 'Was that all my father said?'

'More or less.' Her aunt gave her an unfathomable look. 'He's gone out with his gun and the dogs now. Rabbiting, he claimed. Though it's an odd time to go shooting. And he didn't look happy.'

Demelza was tempted to tell her aunt about her father's condemnation of Robert, and maybe Janice's woes too, but decided against it. She was never quite sure whose side Sarah was on. Instead, she shrugged, saying casually, 'When does my father ever look happy?' and began to peel the spuds.

Once Demelza had gone, Lily rushed over to Tristan and they embraced, just as they'd done in the lean-to shelter among the rocks. It hadn't been her intention to let things go as far as they had, but the danger of the enemy plane overhead and her heightened emotions had left her flushed and uncertain, her only safety in his arms. Now, recalling his kisses, Lily closed her eyes, head cradled against his broad chest, listening to the deep, reassuring thud of his heart. Everything had changed, she thought dreamily, and yet nothing had. It was the strangest sensation.

'Do you think your sister knows?' she whispered, worried in case they might be overheard. 'I mean, about us?'

Tristan raised his brows. 'Given the amount of straw in your hair when you walked into the house, she'd be blind not to at least suspect.'

'Blimey, I wish you'd told me.' Lily felt embarrassed all over again, remembering how Demelza had plucked the pieces from her hair. 'I could have tidied myself up.'

'I didn't notice until then.' Tristan pulled back to smile down at her and ran a gentle finger down her cheek. 'Look, given everything else that's going on, what Demelza thinks is hardly important.'

'But if your father works it out—'

'Don't fret, he won't have noticed a thing. Too focused on my sister and her "conchie".' His voice turned hard and bitter. 'He's only ever been interested in appearances and what folk might say about us. Not what's in here.' He tapped himself on the chest.

She had spotted that his mother's journal was still clutched in one hand. 'I'm so sorry about your mother. That must be tough.'

He nodded. 'Thanks.' But she could see from Tristan's face how hurt and knocked off-balance he was feeling. 'It was … a shock, that's all. I always thought it strange, how she could have made such a mistake with her medication. But that's what my father told us, and I was too young at the time to question it.'

'Do you want to talk about what happened?' Lily knew from her experience as a nurse that people who'd suffered something traumatic often felt better after discussing it, even if only with a stranger.

Tristan tried to smile but failed miserably. 'Not yet,' he said at last, and kissed her instead. For a long while, there was a smothering silence between them. Finally, he lifted his head, leaving her in a breathless haze of desire. 'I'm sorry, by the way.'

'Sorry for what?'

'About what happened earlier.' His serious gaze met hers, and she could see contrition in his eyes. 'I nearly took advantage of you.'

'What?' She took a step back, almost offended. 'You didn't nearly take advantage of me at all. I'm not a prudish Victorian, you know.'

He looked surprised. 'I thought—'

'That I was "saving" myself for my wedding night?' she demanded.

'Something like that.'

She shook her head decidedly. 'There's a war on, ain't there? We've got to snatch whatever happiness we can get.' And she meant it too, relieved to have finally shaken off her fears about getting too close to a man. It was a liberating feeling. 'Only next time I'd rather not be propositioned in a sheep pen,' she added daringly, while he took her in his arms again. 'Maybe I am old-fashioned, but if we're going to be kissing and cuddling, I'd prefer to do it somewhere more comfortable. And preferably with no danger of getting bombed by the Jerries, either.'

And they both laughed at the absurdity of it all.

CHAPTER TWENTY-SIX

Joe pulled his van into a narrow side street near the harbour and parked outside an antique shop with both front windows blown out by a bomb; across the chipboard used to keep it secure, someone had written in big black lettering: OPEN FOR BUSINESS.

'That's close enough,' Joe muttered. 'We can walk from here.'

They had come to Penzance to visit his biological father – the man who'd seduced and then abandoned his mother. But it was clear that Joe was suffering from nerves by the way he forgot to put the handbrake on and the van began to glide downhill as he climbed out. Swearing under his breath, Joe darted back into the driver's seat to drag up the handbrake. The car stopped so abruptly he hit his head on the door frame and swore again, looking flustered.

Violet, who had already got out and was buttoning her coat against the sharp breeze off the sea, bit her lip to avoid laughing. Men, she had observed, never had much of a sense of humour when it came to their own mistakes.

'Will we get a chance to pop into any shops after our visit, do you think?' She settled her best hat on her head and arranged her shopping basket in the crook of one arm. 'It's not often we come into Penzance, so I promised Mum I'd see if there was anything tasty at the butcher's.'

'Of course,' he said – though she wasn't convinced he'd heard a word she'd said – and stuck out his elbow, offering her his arm.

It was just like they were married already, she thought, almost giddy with joy. Proudly, Violet took his arm and accompanied Joe along the road, wishing she could tell everyone they met that she was engaged to be married. So far though, she'd not even told Mum and Alice, though she hoped Joe would soon allow her to do so. Then she would be able to tell Lily, once she came to visit them again; she didn't want her own niece to hear such important family news from a letter or some chance encounter in the street. But it was burning her up from the inside out, not being able to shout from the rooftops that Joe Postbridge had proposed marriage and she had accepted him. It felt like a fairy tale.

They had not taken more than ten steps up the road when she stopped dead with a gasp. 'I don't believe it,' she said, and nodded ahead. 'It's Hazel Baxter ... I mean, Mrs Cotterill, as she is now. George's wife. Oh, and look, she's pushing a pram. She must have her new baby with her.'

Joe gave her a bewildered stare.

'Hazel?'

'You remember,' she said quickly, and tutted at his poor memory. 'George Cotterill, who used to run Eastern House.

He broke his leg, and then his bloomin' replacement gave me the heave-ho. That's why we had to leave the cottage.'

'Oh yes.'

She looked at him sympathetically. 'Your head's somewhere else, ain't it?' she said more gently. 'Listen, don't you worry. I've not seen her in a while, so I'd love to catch up on her news. Why don't you walk on ahead and see if you can find the house? I'll catch up.'

Looking relieved, Joe nodded and continued up the street alone, touching his cap as he passed Hazel, who glanced round at him in surprise.

Hurrying to meet her friend, Violet gave a big grin before embracing her. 'Don't mind Joe, he's shy,' she said with a wink. 'You look well though. What are you doing in Penzance? You could have knocked me down with a feather when I saw you. I thought you and George were still away, visiting your sister and brother-in-law upcountry.'

'We were,' Hazel admitted. 'We only got back last week. I meant to drop you a note but what with one thing and another—'

'Oh, never mind that. How's your sister?'

'As bossy as ever. But it was lovely to have a little holiday, especially with George still laid up with his broken leg.'

Hazel, always curvy, was looking rounder and softer-skinned than ever. Happier too, Violet thought, and felt a sudden urge to be that happy herself, to become a mother and hold a baby in her own arms...

'I'm in desperate need of new wool,' Hazel continued, oblivious to Violet's thoughts. 'I've run out and I'm halfway through knitting a lemon dress suit for baby Lily. So I had to come into town.'

'I still can't get over you naming the little 'un after my niece.'

'And why wouldn't I? Your lovely Lily helped me bring her into the world. Least I could do was name the baby after her.'

Lily had been trapped with Hazel during an air raid last Christmas, when Hazel had taken a bad fall and gone into premature labour. Thankfully, Lily's basic training as a nurse had covered some elements of childbirth, and she'd been able to calm Hazel down and help her give birth to a healthy baby. By all accounts though, it had been quite a frightening experience for both of them.

Peeking into the pram, Violet's heart melted at the sight of the fair-haired baby girl, fast asleep and well wrapped up against the wind, her tiny mittened fists resting on a thick fleece coverlet.

'Oh, my word, Hazel. What a pretty little girl. And a good head of hair already. You must be proud as Punch.'

'I'm over the moon about her,' Hazel agreed in her richly rolling Cornish accent, also bending to look in at her baby. With quick capable hands, she adjusted the woollen bonnet on the baby's head without waking her. 'And so is George, of course. He's been *marvellous*.'

Violet's former boss, George Cotterill, wasn't the baby's father, of course. But he hadn't hesitated to propose to the pregnant and recently widowed Hazel, who'd been his childhood sweetheart. After a misunderstanding years ago, Hazel had ended up marrying another local boy, Bertie Baxter. Their marriage had not been a happy one though, and it often made Violet angry to think how Bertie had abused his wife and knocked her about behind closed doors. After enlisting with a Cornish regiment, her husband had died on active service, leaving his widow to cope on her own with Charlie, their difficult teenage son. Thankfully, once George had started to court Hazel after a discreet interval, her son had finally stopped acting up.

'How's Charlie these days?' Violet asked, curious to know how the family had been getting on. It felt like forever since they'd all been working at Eastern House together.

'Charlie's fine, thank you. He's got work as an apprentice here in Penzance, in fact,' Hazel said proudly. 'I'll be meeting him for a bite to eat later.'

'That's good news. And what about George? I was so sorry to hear about his broken leg. I hope he's on the mend.'

'He got new crutches from the hospital a few days ago. Poor George … he's been having a difficult time trying to walk with them.' Hazel bit her lip, laughter bubbling underneath her voice. 'But he's determined to do it. Sitting about for weeks bored him rigid.' Then she touched Violet's arm, a warm sympathy in her face. 'Listen, I felt awful about what happened to you at Eastern House. Losing your job, and then the cottage too. That nasty little man…'

'Don't get me started.'

'George was so cross when he heard. You should have heard him swear; the air almost turned blue. But you know,' Hazel assured her, looking contrite, 'there wasn't much he could do about it.'

'It was my own silly fault,' Violet admitted. 'I lost my rag over something and nothing, and didn't have the sense to shut my big mouth when it mattered.' She brightened, pushing that past mistake aside. 'But like I told you in my letter, Joe's taken us in at his farm. Me, Mum, Alice, and even the evacuees we've been looking after.'

'And how's that working out for you all?' Hazel seemed concerned. 'Joe's not put you all to work on the land, has he? That's what happened when you first came to Cornwall, wasn't it? On your aunt and uncle's farm.'

'Oh no, he's got Land Girls there to help out on the farm. We don't need to do nothing, it's amazing. Though Mum and me, we can't bear to be idle. She's been cooking for everyone, and I … I've been cleaning the place up.'

Hazel had known her for a year now, and even shared her own cottage with Violet and the girls when they were left homeless last summer, so she easily picked up on Violet's hesitation.

Her eyes narrowed. 'Oh, yes?' She peered at Violet closely, who blushed. 'Come on, Vi, this is me you're talking to. What aren't you telling me? What's really going on at the farm?'

'Nothing … except…' Violet couldn't hide her joy. 'Joe's proposed to me,' she blurted in a rush. 'And I've said yes.'

'Oh, my Lord!'

She was so breathless, she could barely get the words out. 'I'm going to be Mrs Postbridge.'

'Violet…' Hazel grabbed her hands and drew her close for a tight, ecstatic hug. 'You absolute gem. I knew you and Joe would get there in the end. You were made for each other, I'm sure of it.' She pulled back to study Violet, her eyes full of happy tears. 'So, come on, when's the big day?'

'We haven't set a date yet.' She badly wanted to ask Hazel her advice about Joe's awful discovery but didn't have his permission to tell anyone else. 'There are … a few things to sort out first. But as soon as possible. To be honest, I've waited long enough as it is.'

Hazel laughed, nodding, still holding her hands. 'That's for certain. But he's come around at last. And that's what matters.'

'You won't tell anyone else, will you? Not even George,' Violet begged her. 'It's a secret.'

Hazel looked surprised. 'Of course I won't, if you'd rather I didn't. But why is it a secret?'

'It's a long story,' Violet told her cautiously. 'Joe's still getting his head around the idea, I suppose.'

'Ah, I see.' Hazel smiled. 'Men can be like that, you know. They don't take to marriage as readily as we do. He's probably still getting over the shock of having proposed.'

And they both had a good chuckle over that.

The two women parted with another warm hug and a promise to meet up soon for a cuppa at Hazel's place, which was within walking distance of Joe's farm. Violet walked on quickly, still smiling, and found Joe waiting for her outside a row of Victorian three-storey houses with small railed yards at the front.

'Sorry I was so long,' she said awkwardly, 'we got talking.'

'That's fine. You wanted to catch up with your friend.' He took her arm again, his face pale but determined. 'Ready?'

She nodded. Taking a deep breath, Joe knocked at the door of number twelve, which looked a little less well-kept than the other houses on the row. Paint was peeling on the red front door and window frames, the front step was scuffed with mud, and all the front windows were dirty.

It seemed to take ages before the door was finally opened by a grey-haired man in faded clothing, who stared out at them with evident surprise. So this was Herbert, Violet thought, studying him curiously.

'Yes? Can I help you?' He had a Cornish accent like Hazel, but unlike her, he sounded rather well-to-do, despite the rundown nature of the property. 'I'm not buying anything.'

'That's all right, Mr Davies,' Joe told him steadily, 'we're not selling.' He held out a hand. 'I'm Joe Postbridge. And this is my fiancé, Miss Violet Hopkins.'

'Postbridge?' The man's stare sharpened on Joe's face, and then his bushy grey eyebrows jerked together. He looked him up and down more carefully. 'Well, well...' After a momentary pause, he stepped aside, though Violet thought his manner was not exactly welcoming. 'In that case, Mr Postbridge, Miss Hopkins, you'd better come inside.'

Mr Herbert Davies took them down a dark hallway to a dingy room with blackout curtains still draped across the window, where he nodded at them to sit down and opened the curtains slightly to allow a little daylight in.

Violet, peering at the dirty floorboards with an expert eye, itched to fill a bucket with hot, soapy water and get scrubbing.

'So,' Mr Davies said, easing himself gingerly into a worn-looking high-backed armchair as though he had a back problem, 'you must be my son.'

Apprehensively, Violet glanced up at Joe, who had not sat but was standing stiffly in front of the fireplace, leaning on his stick as he studied his natural father.

'No need for me to introduce myself, I see,' Joe said, and she could hear the hurt in his voice.

'You're asking yourself why I was never in touch,' Mr Davies said, his gaze steady on Joe's face. 'Never came to see you.'

'Something like that.'

'You know that I was married when I met your mother?'

'And that you lied to her about it, yes.'

Mr Davies grimaced. 'I'm not proud of myself for what I did. Getting her in the family way, leaving her in the lurch … but when you're in love, sometimes you make mistakes. And I did love your mother. But I loved my wife too. And my other children.'

Joe said nothing, but his brows had knitted together and his lips were pursed, a bitter light in his eyes. Violet guessed he didn't believe a word this man was saying.

'Joyce wrote to me a while back. She said you'd been in the Navy and wounded in action. That you've got a false leg now. We hadn't been in touch since … well, since before you were born. But she wanted me to know about your war service.' He was staring directly at Joe's walking stick. 'Is that why you use a cane?'

'Yes.' Joe's face looked like it was carved out of stone. 'I did my duty.'

Mr Davies grunted under his breath. 'As did I,' he replied, a little testily, 'back in the first show. Not that I'd expect you to know about that. You wouldn't have been much more than a baby at the time, and I don't imagine your mother talked about me very often.'

'She never mentioned you at all,' Joe snapped.

'Like that, was it? Well, it's only to be expected. I suppose she just wanted to forget. Pretend it never happened. And war broke out not long after she'd had you, so … those were difficult days for all of us.' The old man winced and shifted in his seat. 'Long story short, I went out to France with the Duke of Cornwall's Light Infantry in the Great War.' He gave Joe a mock salute. 'Lance Corporal Herbert Joseph Davies, at your service.'

Violet's eyes widened at his middle name. *Joseph.* So Joyce had partly named her baby son after his real father. That would have been a risk, given the circumstances. But it showed she must still have had feelings for the man, even though he'd callously thrown her aside after learning she was pregnant. From Joe's arrested expression, she guessed he must be thinking the same thing. Poor man, Violet thought, her heart aching for him. This whole thing had been a dreadful shock, and would no doubt forever change the way he saw his late mother, whom he'd clearly worshipped while alive.

'I managed to get myself shot, of course, being a bloody fool and running along the top of the trenches for a lark,' Herbert continued, jerking a thumb towards his spine. 'German sniper cracked me in the back. Not that I remember much about it. I was bedbound for a year after they brought me home to Cornwall. Had to learn to walk again.'

Joe was very still, watching him.

'The wound still bothers me,' Herbert went on, nodding to Joe's walking stick. 'I have to walk with a stick too, when I leave the house.' His smile was grim. 'But I survived and that's the main thing. It's not easy, but you make do, don't you? I'm not blaming anyone or asking for pity. I did my duty to King and country, and that's all there is to it.'

Joe stared at him hard for another minute, and then seemed to relax his white-knuckled grip on the walking stick.

'I didn't know, sir. About your war wound, I mean.' He gave a harsh laugh. 'In fact, I didn't even know you existed until a few days ago, when I found a bunch of love letters from you to my mother. Before she was even wed. That's when I found out that the man I'd thought was my father wasn't, and you were instead. That was a shock, I can tell you.' His jaw worked. 'I only wish my mother had found the courage to tell me the truth to my face.'

'Now, you listen to me,' Herbert told him, clasping the worn arms of his chair and sitting up straight, his face stern now. 'Your mother had more courage than me. Joyce stood up to the nasty gossips around here and made the best of a bad situation, while I turned my back on her to save my marriage. And he was a good man too, your dad. Yes, don't stare. I call him your dad because that's what he was.'

Joe began to speak but the old man flung up a hand before he could get a word out.

'Postbridge was your *father* and don't you go thinking otherwise,' Mr Davies told him forcefully, though Violet was sure Joe would never have argued about that. 'My only contribution was the spark of life. And that don't take much skill or effort, let me tell you. But being a father, a family man, making the tough decisions... *That's* hard work.' He shook his head, glancing at his wedding photograph on the mantel as though remembering his own late wife and the children he'd brought up with her. 'So yes, that's why I never got in touch with you, not even after

284

your mother passed. I saw it in the newspapers. A crying shame, to lose her like that ... but what happened between me and your mum, none of that matters anymore. It's all ancient history and best forgotten. Your real father was Postbridge and he's dead. Mourn *him*, son; don't look to me for answers, for I've none to give you.'

Joe closed his eyes for a moment, and then said slowly, 'Thank you for your honesty. I've sorry to have come here and troubled you.'

Violet's heart plummeted, seeing the bleak look on his face.

'You ready to go, Vi?' Joe began limping to the door before she'd even got out of her chair. 'It's time I went home. I've neglected the farm long enough over this business.'

CHAPTER TWENTY-SEVEN

Lily arrived outside the Penzance Cinema on Saturday morning about fifteen minutes early, still messing with her hair and wondering if the new scarlet lipstick that had cost her so dear suited her colouring. She was nervous about her first proper date with Tristan, though excited too and eager to see him again. All she'd been able to think about in the days since that day at the farm was how easy and natural it had felt to kiss him. With Tristan, she had not experienced any of the breathless anxiety when Private Danny Orde tried to kiss her last year. Did that mean they were in love? Or simply that she was over the worst of her fears around intimacy? Perhaps only time would tell…

While she was waiting for Tristan, a stranger in a trench coat came up to her on the street, his gaze intent on her face. Lily glanced at the unknown man with an air of chilly disfavour, ready to send the chap off with a flea in her ear if he said the wrong thing or looked at her funny. As a young blonde nurse, she was accustomed to being approached by men she didn't know – sometimes with grins and a smooth patter, occasionally with leers and wolf-whistles – and had a variety of put-downs at her disposal that worked on all but the most persistent pests.

This man was not typical of such men though. For a start, he was unsmiling. His hands were shoved deep into the pockets of his trench coat while his face was hidden in shadow beneath the brim of his trilby hat. He was about Tristan's height but stocky with it, and his pointed chin was dark with stubble, though that wasn't unusual these days, with people struggling to get hold of everyday items like soap and razors.

'Miss Fisher?' the man asked, not looking at her but over his shoulder, his voice pitched so low she had to strain to hear him. 'Miss Lily Fisher?'

Lily was surprised that this stranger knew her name but tried not to show it, drawing herself up instinctively for extra authority. 'What's it to you?' she demanded.

'I have a message for you, Miss Fisher.'

That seemed unlikely, she thought, eyeing him with puzzlement. Unless Dr Jerrard had sent him. Sometimes the chief doctor asked for off-duty staff to come in again for an emergency. But there hadn't been an air raid for several days in Penzance, so there was little reason to assume the wards would be swamped today.

'A message? Do you mean from the hospital?'

'No,' he said, and turned swiftly as a passing car back-fired, staring down the street after it.

Uneasy, Lily also glanced around, in the hope of seeing someone she could ask to stand with her. There were a few others like herself who'd turned up too early and were now standing idly about, waiting for the picture house to open its doors. But they were mostly young kids or love-struck couples whispering together, and she knew none of them. It would feel awkward to ask a stranger for help, she decided, and looked back at the man.

'In that case—' she began briskly, but he interrupted her.

'No, don't draw attention to us,' the man said urgently, as though he'd guessed the way her thoughts were heading. 'Keep your eyes on me and smile. I'm here about your father.'

Lily froze, staring at him now. '*My dad*?'

'Hush, not so loud. It's not safe. Not out here on the street.' He nodded to a small alleyway near the cinema. 'Let's take a walk.'

'I'm not going down there with you,' she said indignantly, not bothering to keep her voice down, and several heads turned in their direction.

'For God's sake,' the man hissed, and grabbed her arm as she turned away. 'All right, have it your own bloody way.' He released her, frustration in his face. 'Ask me for a cigarette.'

'I don't smoke.'

'That doesn't matter. If anyone's watching us, they'll wonder why we're talking so long. So ask me for a cigarette and make it look good.' He forced a false smile to his lips. 'Unless you don't want to hear a message from your father?'

Shocked, Lily had to struggle to gather her thoughts. A message from her *father*?

Faintly, she heard herself ask, 'May I have a … a ciggie?' But her mind was reeling.

Did this stranger mean that her father, who'd gone

missing in action somewhere abroad, was alive? No, that was impossible. But perhaps as he'd lain dying Ernest had passed some final words onto his family through this man, presumably a fellow soldier. Perhaps it would be worth hearing what he had to say, at least. Though his clandestine manner was a little frightening.

'Of course,' he replied loudly, and produced a packet of cigarettes from which he tapped out two, lighting hers first and then his own. 'That's better,' he said in a soft, approving voice, and gave her that awful fake smile again, adding under his breath, 'Smoke it, then, you little numbskull.'

Her hands shaking, Lily obeyed, settling the ciggie between her lips and inhaling, which only led to a bout of coughing. The stranger somehow managed to glare at her while still smiling, which made her more nervous than ever.

'S-sorry,' she whispered, and tried to do better, blowing the acrid smoke straight out of her mouth instead of inhaling it.

'All right,' the man said in a thin thread of a voice, which she was sure nobody but herself could possibly hear, 'now listen to me.' He stood very close, his intent gaze meeting hers through the haze of cigarette smoke. 'Your father wants you to know he's still alive and not a German spy like people have been saying. No, don't react, you fool. Keep smiling and smoking. That's it… He's alive and thinking of you. He was recently informed of your mother's death and he's very sorry.' The man's smile faltered for the first time. 'And I'm sorry too,' he added, dipping his voice even lower. 'My condolences, Miss Fisher, to you and your sister.'

Her eyes widened. He knew about Alice too? Perhaps this wasn't some elaborate hoax, but the truth. Though how could her father still be alive? What a dreadful mistake on the part of the government to send her late mother that horrible telegram. But why had they never corrected that information if her father was no longer missing?

'T-Thank you,' she stammered, her eyes fixed on his face.

'Personally, I didn't want to carry this message for him. It's safer for your dad if folk think he's dead, see?'

She didn't see but nodded, staring.

'But it was tearing him apart, knowing you and your sister must think you're all alone in the world. And I owed him a favour, so I agreed to do it.' He glanced uneasily over his shoulder before adding hurriedly, 'But he can't come home yet, and he's sorry about that too. Not until the job's done and the war's over. So we need you to forget about him until then.'

'Forget about him?' She felt numb with shock. 'I can't do that.'

'You must,' he insisted. 'Like I said, it seems people have been talking about him in some quarters, and we can't have that.'

'What people?'

'That's not something that need concern you. But if anyone asks you or your sister, Ernest Fisher is dead, all right? He's dead and buried somewhere abroad, and that's all you know about it.' He dragged on his cigarette and steeped back, blowing a smoke ring into the sunny air. 'Do you understand?'

She stared, almost forgetting to breathe, her own ciggie quivering between her parted lips.

'Do you understand?' he repeated, almost menacing.

She nodded, her heart thumping hard.

'Right, message delivered. Tell nobody except your sister about this conversation. Or you could be putting your father's life in danger.' He dropped his cigarette, ground it out under his foot, and touched his hat brim. 'Miss Fisher.'

Then he walked away. Staring after him like an idiot, Lily plucked the disgusting cigarette, now stained with scarlet lipstick, from her mouth and threw it down too. A moment later, he turned the corner and was out of sight. Cars and vans were still passing along the street. The box office had opened up at last, and people were heading in ones and twos into the cinema. To her relief, none of them were paying much attention to her. No doubt those who'd looked their way earlier would have assumed the man had been a friend, or perhaps someone who'd stopped in hope of a brief flirtation and then given up.

She was stunned, her whole body trembling as she thought back over what the stranger had said. Her father was alive? She was overjoyed, if it was true. But he wasn't coming home yet... *Not until the job's done and the war's over.* What did that mean, exactly? What was his job? And why was it such a secret?

'What was all that about?' a voice asked from behind her, and Lily turned to find Tristan there, a frown on his face. 'Who was that man and why were you having a cigarette with him?'

'I ... I...' Her mind whirled. How could she tell him the truth? *Tell nobody except your sister about this conversation. Or you could be putting your father's life in danger.*

Holding out a hand to him, she said awkwardly, 'Tris,

please … I can't tell you what it was about. I know that must sound strange, but you need to trust me.'

'I want to. But when I saw you together just now, I thought…' There was a slight flush in his cheeks. 'Well, you were standing so close, it looked like you were about to kiss him.'

'No,' she exclaimed, horrified. 'It was nothing like that. We got chatting and he offered me a cigarette, that's all.'

'I see.' But Tristan was still frowning. 'What's his name, then? At least give me that.'

'I didn't ask his name,' Lily admitted, flustered, and saw the suspicion deepen on his face. Frustration seethed inside her; it had all been perfectly innocent yet she couldn't explain the encounter to him without breaking her promise not to talk about her father. Why couldn't Tristan simply trust her when she said it wasn't like that? Angry tears filled her eyes and she dashed one away impatiently. 'Look, I'm not in the mood to watch the film anymore. Would you mind if I just went home instead?'

He blinked but didn't protest, stiffly holding out an arm to her. 'If that's really what you want. But I'd better walk you back.'

'No, thanks,' she said, backing away, 'I can manage. You go inside. Watch the film. I … I'll see you another time.'

Hurrying away, she left him standing outside the cinema and stamped back towards the nurses' quarters, head down so nobody would see her crying.

She'd stupidly thought Tristan had real feelings for her, when it was no such thing. Not when he could suspect her of flirting with a stranger and not accept her denials. But she had more important things to think about than his jealousy. Her dad wasn't dead, but very much alive. Nor was Ernest Fisher a spy for the Germans, as those nasty troublemakers back in Dagenham had suggested because of his mixed heritage. As far as Lily was concerned, her dad was a war hero. She wanted to shout his courage to the rooftops. Yet somehow her lips had to stay sealed. She didn't know if she could bear it.

CHAPTER TWENTY-EIGHT

Penzance, West Cornwall, mid-June 1942

It was pitch black in the side street behind Derrick's Factory and the terraced row of sea-facing houses, many long since converted to cheery guesthouses. Demelza could hear the wailing sirens of the Fire Guard elsewhere in the town, and there was a glow overhead from multiple buildings on fire in Penzance. Here, though, it was relatively quiet, just a few people milling about in the confusion, some in their night clothes, others in uniform, directing them where to go.

Demelza was itching to be in the thick of the action, hoping none of her friends were in danger. It had been a long, exhausting night for the Fire Guard, the worst she could recall since starting this job; for hours, the night shift had been rushing about the town in darkness, mostly on foot, checking buildings for safety and putting out small fires wherever they found them. But then she and Mags had been directed here, to help evacuate the shop cellar being used as a shelter by the inhabitants of the terrace. There had been an unconfirmed sighting of an unexploded bomb somewhere in the vicinity of Derrick's Factory, which stood silent and in darkness further down the street. But now that job was almost done, Demelza desperately longed to know how her friends were faring on the other side of town, where the bombing had been heaviest in tonight's raid.

'Ill-met by moonlight, Fair Titania,' a voice said deeply, and Demelza turned, her heart beginning to beat fast at the sight of the dark silhouette behind her.

'Robert...' She adjusted her helmet, quite unnecessarily, and straightened her crumpled boiler suit, wishing Fire Guard uniforms were just slightly more flattering. 'What on earth... Shakespeare?'

'Well recognised.' He was laughing at her.

'I'm not a country bumpkin, you know,' she said, raising her eyebrows. 'I did go to school.'

Robert looked confused. 'I didn't mean to imply—'

'Oh, forget it. I'm just feeling jumpy. Nothing seems to be going my way at the moment.' Demelza forced a smile, wishing again that she wasn't so in awe of his intellect. He'd told her of a brief stint at a posh grammar school before his grandparents had moved to Cornwall, and it had left her feeling that he was out of her league. She knew that was ridiculous and that Robert didn't put himself above anyone. But it was hard to shake off that fear. 'I didn't know you were on duty tonight.'

'Neither did I. But it seems one of my compatriots has gone down with the flu, so here I am.' He gave her a mock salute. 'All yours, ma'am,' he added in a fake American drawl, looking for all the world as handsome as any actor from the pictures.

She had not seen Robert except in passing since their visit to little Adele and had feared he wasn't interested in seeing her again. Which would have made that bitter row with her father over 'the conchie' all the more humiliating. But his smile reassured her that it was still all on between them. And that thought made her heart leap.

'Well, I'm glad to see you, stranger,' she said daringly, allowing the tiniest hint of accusation to creep into her voice.

He understood at once and pulled a face. 'I'm sorry I haven't been in touch recently. But work has been hectic. I've taken up a position part-time at the local newspaper, you see, and with the ambulance shifts on top—'

'There's no need to apologise,' she interrupted him again, feeling awful now for having doubted him.

'No, I ought to have let you know. Not left you wondering.' His hand touched her shoulder. 'It's this bloody war. It's scrambled my brains, not to mention ruined my manners. I'm truly sorry, Demelza.'

She met his gaze and for a moment they stood, saying nothing, looking at each other with the flickering glow of fire lighting up the skies above Penzance. *I'm falling in love with him*, Demelza thought, and had to bite back the words, trying to say them with her eyes instead. Looking back at her, Robert smiled, and again she felt he had understood without her having to spell out her thoughts.

'Why are you here?' she asked awkwardly, aware of heat in her cheeks, 'and not at one of the other bomb sites? I heard it was pretty gruesome in the town centre tonight.'

'Yes, it was. But I'm not needed there right now. No more ... people to pick up.' That horrid pause told her everything she needed to know. There had been fatalities tonight. She looked away, swallowing as she realised he had edited 'bodies' to 'people' to spare her feelings.

How she hated this war…

'What about you?' he asked in his turn, glancing over his shoulder at the last of the evacuated residents from the underground shelter. 'This place seems untouched. What am I missing?'

'Unexploded bomb, apparently.'

Mags came hurrying up to them, her booted feet echoing in the narrow space between buildings, breathless.

'Dem, hang on, there's another shelter that hasn't been evacuated,' she said, with only a cursory glance at Robert. 'The night watchman just told me about it.' She flung out an arm, pointing along the side street into a pool of deep shadow. 'It's down that way, under the factory itself. Nobody seems to know if it's in use tonight, what with all the workers gone home for the day, but management might still have been inside. Somebody needs to check.' She paused, impatiently adjusting the helmet strap under her chin. 'I've got to escort the others to the emergency shelter. Could you take a quick peek in the factory?'

'Of course.' Demelza was pleased to have something useful to do. 'If I find anyone else down there, I'll send them your way.'

'Right you are.' Mags nodded and ran back the way she'd come.

Robert was frowning. 'Wait,' he said as she turned to study the factory buildings, 'you're not serious? You can't go into that factory on your own. You said there were reports of an unexploded bomb somewhere in the area.'

'It's my job,' she said stoutly, 'and besides, we haven't seen any sign of that bomb, so it could have been a mistake or even a false report. Kids do that sometimes for a laugh.' In truth though, she was concerned that nobody had yet spotted where this unexploded bomb was supposed to be. But she didn't want him to think she was afraid. Not when she'd seen him rushing into a burning building to rescue a child, with no regard for his own safety. 'It'll only take a jiffy.'

'Then let me go with you, at least.' He unhooked a torch from his belt. 'Come on.'

She was relieved by his offer but tried not to show it. 'I suppose that would be all right. Thank you.'

It felt odd to be walking down the street with him, shoulder to shoulder, but it also gave her a burst of pride. They were out here during a raid, making a difference to the war effort, often saving people's lives under fire, and that was important work. She hated the idea of being help-less in the face of Germany's attacks. If the enemy ever landed on these shores, she wouldn't run away; she'd be first with a pitchfork in her hand, or any weapon she could lay her hands on, that was for sure. While many men would have been horrified by her bloodthirsty instincts, she got the feeling that Robert understood and didn't judge her for it. Which was even odder, given that he was a pacifist.

When she rattled the factory door, she found it unlocked, which immediately made her heart thump. 'Looks like someone may have been in here when the air raid started.'

'Or they left in a hurry when the sirens went off and forgot to lock up.' He shone a torch inside but the factory floor was deserted, the rows of machines silent. 'We'd better check the shelter, all the same. I wonder where it is.' He ran the torch beam along the walls.

'There.' She pointed to the sign above a set of stairs.

'You stay here,' he said firmly and set off alone.

Infuriated by this chauvinist attitude, Demelza ignored his command and followed, soon catching up with him.

He stopped, shining the light into her face so that she blinked. 'What on earth… I told you to wait at the door.'

'And which of us is working as a Fire Guard?' she pointed out. 'You're an ambulance driver, Robert. I'm the expert here.'

His mouth compressed, but all he said was, 'It's too dangerous. You go back. Let me take the risk.'

'There may not even be an unexploded bomb,' she began, but at the moment her eye was caught by a glitter from above his head. Looking up, she realised part of the dark roof was gone, and she was staring up through a ragged hole at the night sky. Through the faint flush of orange from the fires raging elsewhere in Penzance, she saw a few pinpricks of stars. 'Oh God.'

He spun round, directing his torch beam upwards. Then, as swiftly as he'd turned, the light beam dropped to study the factory floor immediately below the hole in the roof.

'The bomb.' She gasped and started forward towards the shelter.

'Don't move,' he said urgently.

'But there may be somebody down there. If that bomb goes off—'

'I'll check the shelter,' he insisted. 'I want you to walk quietly back to the door and ask for the bomb disposal team to be called in.' When she glared at him, he added softly, 'Demelza, we need them to make the bomb safe. I'm not trying to claim superiority as a male. It's a fair division of labour.'

She couldn't argue with that; it made too much sense.

'Very well,' Demelza whispered, and began walking gingerly back towards the factory entrance.

She'd almost reached the door when there was a curious sensation of heat and light flaring all around her, like someone turning a barrage of lights on overhead, and then everything went black.

'Nurse Fisher,' one of the orderlies said, popping his head around the door of the children's ward, 'you're needed straightaway, Matron says. More wounded coming in.'

Incredulous, Lily looked up from tending a young boy who'd been injured during the air raid earlier. They'd been swamped that night, some of the injuries quite serious, and one elderly gentleman had sadly died while the doctor was operating on him.

'Blimey, more wounded?' She stared at the orderly with a growing sense of despair. 'I don't think we've a single bed free. Exactly how many bombs did the Germans drop on Penzance tonight?'

'There was an unexploded bomb at Derrick's Factory,' he explained. 'Apparently, it went off while there were still people in the building. One dead, by all accounts, and five wounded, two of them quite badly. Plus a few with shock and minor injuries. Dr Jerrard needs all hands on deck.'

'Battle stations, is it? Righty-o, I'll be with him in two minutes.' The boy whose cuts she'd been cleaning and bandaging was perched on a chair near the ward door, looking miserable; maybe all that talk of death and bombs had scared him, though he was at least fourteen years old and had come into the hospital alone. She pinned his sling into place with a reassuring smile. 'There, Toby, you're all done.'

'Thank you,' he said, still very pale.

'But promise me one thing,' she said more sternly, straightening. 'Next time, you need to stay in the shelter until you hear the all-clear. No more sneaking off to catch sight of enemy planes. It's too dangerous.'

Toby had crept out of the shelter when nobody was watching and headed for one of the old bomb sites where he and his mates often played, hoping to see one of the German planes in action, but had tripped in the dark and cut his forearm open on the rubble.

'I suppose so.' The boy's smile was wan. 'But do you think I can tell my friends I got shot at by one of the Messerschmitts?' He examined his bandaged arm dubiously. 'I … I can't tell anyone the truth. I'd be a laughing stock at school.'

'Honesty is the best policy,' she told him but gave Toby a wink. 'Cheer up. At least you can tell them everything you saw during the air raid. Just never do it again, all right?'

His face brightened, and he nodded. 'Yes, nurse.'

Leaving him to a young trainee, Lily washed her hands and hurried over to the emergency ward to help triage the new intake of wounded civilians. To her dismay, the orderly hadn't been kidding about the sheer numbers they were facing. She found a scene of carnage in the emergency ward, a number of people wandering about covered in dust and debris, mostly looking dazed and in need of a hot cuppa, but some with nasty gashes that would need tending.

'Bless me,' she muttered, and headed swiftly over to Dr

Jerrard, who was talking to Matron about bed availability for the more seriously injured.

'Ah, Lily,' the doctor said on seeing her, flashing his famous smile. 'Reporting for duty? Good stuff.' He ran a tired hand through dishevelled hair. 'No rest for the wicked, as you can see. Multiple casualties.'

'So I've been told. Where do you want me to start?'

'I need someone with steady hands in the operating theatre, but I've sent Becky home. She'd pulled a double shift and was shattered.' Becky was his usual theatre assistant, always there to mop his brow as needed and hand him the correct instruments when asked. 'Could you fill her shoes? I know it's not your area of expertise.'

'Of course,' she said without hesitation.

It was true that she had no training in theatre work. But she revelled in the thought of learning new skills. And at least her hospital work, gruelling and upsetting though it often was after an air raid, provided a distraction from her row with Tristan.

'Excellent. You'll need clean, gloved hands, a gauze mask and a fresh apron. Meet you in the operating theatre.'

Lily hurried away to get ready, excited but also a little apprehensive in case she made a mess of things. But as she stepped into theatre, masked up and eager to help, she stopped dead at the sight of the ginger-haired woman lying pale and still on the operating table. Her face was obscured by a large rubber mask, no doubt pumping anaesthesia into her body to keep her asleep, and a blood trail was smeared across one temple. But Lily would have known her anywhere.

It was Demelza.

CHAPTER TWENTY-NINE

'Oh no.' Lily rushed forward in horror but saw Dr Jerrard, in his own gown and mask, turn to stare at her. Somehow, she forced her thumping heart to calm down. 'I ... I know the patient. She's a friend. Demelza.'

'I'm sorry to hear that, but you need to put your feelings aside and behave professionally now,' Dr Jerrard told her, not unkindly but with cool control. His voice was oddly muffled by the gauze mask covering his mouth and nose. 'Can you manage that? Or should I call someone else to help me?'

'No, I'm fine.' She swallowed hard, trying not to stare at Demelza's badly bruised face, and nodded. 'I can cope.'

'Good show.'

'What ... what's wrong with her, Doctor? I mean, what are her injuries?'

'From a preliminary examination, some nasty cuts and bruises, and a few broken ribs. Plus, a severe blow to the head, though I hope that won't cause any complications beyond temporary concussion. Right now though, I'm primarily concerned by her struggle to breathe, which seems to be getting worse.' He placed a stethoscope on various points around her chest and listened for a moment. 'Unfortunately, our old X-ray machine packed up some months ago, and there's no time to send her elsewhere to be investigated. Not if we want her to live. But I'm fairly certain she has a pneumothorax.'

Lily stared. 'A what?'

'Air, or maybe blood, building in the chest cavity. I've seen it before in similar blast injuries. If she was thrown violently into the air by the force of the explosion, or part of a wall fell on her, one of her lungs may have been punctured, perhaps by a badly fractured rib. But however it happened, if I'm right – and I think I am – her lung is in imminent danger of collapse.'

'You mean, she won't be able to breathe?'

'That's precisely what I mean.' Dr Jerrard adjusted his mask and nodded to the tray of shiny steel instruments. 'I'll need to open her chest and insert a drain straightaway. That should clear out any trapped air or fluid and allow her lungs to continue working properly. But it's a delicate operation, and if I'm wrong or I make a mistake...' He glanced at Lily's colourless cheeks. 'You're sure you're all right to continue?'

Lily did feel a little queasy, but she nodded. 'Yes, Doctor.'

'I'm glad to hear it, Nurse Fisher.' He put out a hand. 'First, pass me the scalpel.' When she hesitated over the tray, he pointed to the exact instrument required and, shaking slightly, she placed it on his outstretched palm. 'Well done. Now, look away if you need to...'

But Lily didn't look away, and within a few moments

her pulse was steady again and she began to feel quite calm. It was only blood, after all. And women were perfectly used to seeing *that*, she thought firmly. She was determined to stay professional, passing the correct instrument each time the doctor asked for it, while also mentally willing Demelza to survive this dangerous operation, not only for her own sake but for her brother's too.

But inside she was fretting and distressed. Had Tristan been told yet that his sister was so seriously injured? Not that it was any of her business. Not anymore. Tristan had not been back in touch with her, and since Lily could never tell him the real reason she'd been so deep in conversation with that stranger outside the cinema, that was the end of their relationship. But oh, the pain he would suffer if his sister died…

Violet felt quite shaken. She'd stood from her armchair to take the note Alice was holding out, but now she sat again, the sheet she'd been darning trailing onto the floor, staring in horror at Lily's brief message.

'Blimey, Alice.' She breathed heavily, her heart thumping madly. 'When did Lily give you this?'

'Home time.' Absent-mindedly, Alice chewed the end of her plait, and Violet couldn't even rouse herself to chide her for it. 'She was waiting at the school gates for me and Janice. She gave me that for you, Aunty Vi, and then walked Janice home.' Her curious gaze searched Violet's face. 'I read the note on the bus. I know I shouldn't have, but … awful news, ain't it? Will you do it, though? Will you take Janice in again?'

Her mother came bustling into the room with a plate

of toasted crumpets and stopped dead at Violet's pale, wide-eyed expression. 'Oh my gawd, what is it, love? You're as white as a sheet. What's happened?'

Violet looked up from Lily's note, her insides churning with fear as she realised it could so easily have been Lily who'd been killed. Penzance wasn't safe anymore. It had been such a lovely, quiet seaside town when they first came to Cornwall, a place far away from the horrors of the Blitz. But everything had changed in recent months. From what the local gossips had been saying, the Germans seemed to be targeting it almost every other night at the moment, and now this awful news…

'There was an unexploded bomb,' Violet said shakily, trying not to start blubbing, 'One person killed, half a dozen wounded. Demelza Minear got caught in the blast.' At her mother's blank look, she added, 'You remember her, Mum. The farmer's daughter who offered to take Janice under her wing?'

'Oh yes, I remember. The heavy-set girl with the carrot-top.'

'Ginger, Mum.'

'That's what I said, ain't it?' But Sheila bit her lip, tutting at the news. 'Oh no, poor thing. Is she…'

'No, she's alive. Badly hurt but it looks like she'll pull through.' Violet took a deep breath, trying to stay calm for Alice's sake. 'Lily asks if we can take young Janice in again, what with Demelza in hospital and everything at sixes and sevens.' She glanced at Alice. 'Janice can share your bedroom and go with you on the bus. I know you're busy with your work at the school, but you'll look out for her, won't you?'

Alice looked concerned. 'Of course.' She accepted a thin, leathery-looking crumpet from her gran with a smile. 'Thanks.'

'I know she's a right tearaway,' Violet admitted, 'but Lily told me Janice's not been having an easy time of it at school.'

Alice didn't seem surprised by this. 'Yes, the headmistress called me into her office the other day. Apparently, Demelza wrote a letter to her about some boy pestering Janice. Miss Rhodes wanted to know what I knew about it, which was nothing. But the boy's been given a stern talking-to, she said.'

Violet's mother gave Alice a dubious look. 'Will that sort things out, do you think?'

'I expect so, Gran. Miss Rhodes is good at putting the wind up people. Sounds like he deserved it too.' Picking up a library book she'd been reading, Alice headed for the door, adding through a mouthful of crumpet, 'Unless you need me, Aunty Vi, I'll go to my room now. I'd like to finish reading this book before supper.'

'You go on up, love. We can manage.'

Once Alice had gone, Mum set the plate of crumpets on the low table between their armchairs and sat, shaking her head in dismay. 'Oh, Vi,' she said unhappily. 'What's to become of us? One poor so-and-so dead? All those others wounded. And in Cornwall too... I thought we'd be safer here.' She wrung her hands, looking pale. 'Sounds like Demelza was lucky not to lose her life. What else does Lily say?'

'Not much, I'm afraid. Looks like she wrote it in a hurry. I expect she's rushed off her feet at the hospital with all these air raids.' Violet passed her Lily's note. 'Here, I'm

307

going to find Joe.' She stood, carefully folding the sheet she'd been darning and putting it to one side so she could finish the work later. 'I'll need a lift into Penzance to collect Janice and her things.'

Her mum looked up from the note she'd been reading and pulled a face. 'Feels like we're using him as a taxi service.' She gave Violet a searching look. 'Now, Vi, be honest. You sure Joe don't mind all this backwards and forwards lark? I wouldn't want him to turn us out of his farm for being a blessed nuisance.'

Her mother was fishing for information about them again. Sheila wasn't stupid; she knew something was going on between Violet and Joe, and she wouldn't be satisfied until she'd winkled the truth out of her daughter.

Violet felt herself blush but said steadily enough, 'Don't be daft, Mum. Joe don't mind at all.'

'Hmm,' was all her mother said in return, quickly turning the subject to the other question she'd been badgering Violet about recently. 'And when are you going to start looking for work? You can't stay here all day every day, playing house for Joe.'

That was rather too close to the truth for comfort. It did sometimes feel like she was playing house, already in training to be Joe's wife. Violet opened her mouth, meaning to hint at her situation, and then shut it again. Until she had Joe's consent to tell her family about their engagement, she had to keep it quiet.

Besides, she did rather fancy the idea of a new challenge.

'I'll start looking soon,' she promised. 'You're right; I need to do an honest day's work again. There ain't enough going on here to keep me busy. Not with the Land Girls always on hand, and you and Alice helping out in the kitchen.'

Her mother reached for a recent newspaper and hunted for a pencil on the sideboard. 'I'll take a look in the local advertisements, shall I?'

'You do that, Mum. War work too. Circle anything that sounds promising.'

And with that, Violet whisked herself out of the room, worried she was going to give the game away if she kept chatting.

Heading outside, she found Joe in the yard, fiddling with a tractor engine. 'I'm sorry to disturb you—' she began awkwardly, but he interrupted her.

'You're not disturbing me, Violet.'

Joe withdrew his head from the engine cavity and came towards her, wiping oily hands on his overalls. There was a shy smile on his face that took her right back to the first time she'd met him, down on the beach at Penzance. How long ago that seemed now, she thought wistfully, and how much had happened since then to keep them apart. His mother's tragic death and all those rumours about her brother-in-law, Ernest... But she pushed that sadness aside and concentrated on what lay ahead instead: a happy marriage, if she could possibly manage it.

'Are you free to run me into Penzance tomorrow?' she asked, also smiling shyly, 'If it ain't too much trouble.'

'No trouble at all. Going shopping?'

'More an errand of mercy.' Briefly, she explained about young Janice, and what had happened to Demelza, and saw his face darken at the mention of her being caught in a bomb blast. His mother had been killed in an air raid too, just as her sister had been. There weren't many lives left untouched by this war, she thought unhappily. But her heart went out to him. 'She'll survive, Lily thinks. But the family will be at their wits' end.'

He nodded gravely.

'Best to take Janice off their hands, at least for a month or so. And I'm sure she'll enjoy being reunited with her brothers.'

'Well, I'll be happy to drive you there and back.'

'Thanks, Joe.'

'You're welcome,' he said softly.

The air was very still that June afternoon, and after a morning of mizzling rain, a thin sunshine was filling the yard. In the distance, she could hear the faint roar of the sea against the rocks. Although Penzance had been bombed regularly so far that year, there'd been no sightings of enemy planes in Porthcurno for some weeks now. She could hear birds tweeting in the trees and the distant laughter of the Land Girls as they worked in the fields behind the farm buildings. This remote part of Cornwall was a tiny slice of paradise, she thought, where the war couldn't find them. At least not today…

Violet and Joe looked into each other's eyes, unspeaking, sharing their secret with silent satisfaction. She wished they could stay like that forever.

At last, Joe shifted, breaking the spell. 'Vi, when are we going to tell your mother and Alice about … about us?'

'I've been wondering that myself. I thought maybe tonight, over supper.' She hesitated, seeing his face change. 'Is that too soon?'

'No,' he said, and she saw his momentary hesitation turn

to determination as he smiled. The sun seemed to strengthen, suddenly bright and hot on her back. 'No, that's perfect. Besides, I don't think I can keep it secret any longer.'

'It was your idea not to tell anyone.'

'I know,' he admitted, 'but only because I wasn't used to the idea yet.'

'You needed time.'

He pulled a face. 'Yes, and I'm sorry about that. I wasn't stalling, I just didn't know what to think. Everything seemed to be happening at once. And then finding out about my father…' He ran out of words and simply held out his hands to her. 'Forgive me?'

'There's nothing to forgive.' Violet took his hands, even though they were a little oily from the tractor. 'I love you, Joe.'

His eyes grew glassy. 'I love you too, Violet.' His voice was choked. 'I love you more than anything in the world.'

Since they were out of sight of the kitchen window, they dared to embrace, and she closed her eyes, joy welling up inside her. Whatever else happened, they would be together from now on. And one day, they would be man and wife. Unless the war intervened. Violet crossed her fingers behind his back and hoped fervently for the best. Because what else could she do?

At supper that night, as Joe and her family sat crowded together with the three Land Girls about the kitchen table, Violet waited until everyone had served themselves from the large, steaming pan of vegetable stew in the middle, and then banged her cup of tea with her fork. 'Can I have everyone's attention?' She blushed rosily as all eyes turned to her and the busy chat fell into silence. 'Erm, thank you. The thing is, I … I mean, we've got an announcement to make. Me and Joe, that is.'

'An announcement?' Alice echoed blankly, her eyes widening as she glanced from Violet to Joe. 'But what—'

'Hush,' Sheila said sharply, nudging her granddaughter. 'Let your Aunty Vi say her piece.'

'Yes, let your aunty do the talking,' Eustace repeated cheekily, and was also hushed sternly.

Penny – otherwise known as Pickles – stuck her tongue out at the boy while Eustace grinned at her across the table. The other two Land Girls giggled behind their hands, pink-cheeked, their hair tied up in headscarves.

Joe stood, his chair scraping noisily backwards. He looked at Violet, who nodded and also stood. 'As Violet said, we've something important to tell you.' The words came out huskily, and he stopped to clear his throat, frowning. 'We should probably have told you before. But I wanted to be sure. Not sure about … I mean, just sure it was the right time. And Violet didn't like to say nothing until Lily was here. But since we don't rightly know when she'll be visiting next—'

Violet made a small, exasperated sound under her breath, not meaning to interrupt her man but simply despairing that he would ever get to the bloomin' point. Joe took the hint, his gaze flashing to her face.

'Right, yes.' He had a quick swig of tea and noisily cleared his throat again. 'You see, what I'm trying to say is—'

'We're engaged to be married,' Violet blurted in a rush, and everyone gasped, all eyes shifting to her instead.

'Though we haven't set a date. And we don't have a ring yet. Because of the war, you know. But it's official. Joe and me, we're engaged.'

'Oh, my Lord,' her mum gushed, and clapped a hand to her mouth, her eyes already filling with tears of joy. 'Dearest Vi, my lovely girl...'

'Congratulations,' the Land Girls chorused, grinning at each other.

'I knew it,' Caro whispered, and Selina nudged her, shaking her head. 'What? I saw them talking the other day... It was obvious.'

'Blimey, do you hear that, Timmy? Joe's getting himself a ball and chain,' Eustace said, chuckling along with his brother as though this was a great joke. Violet longed to give the cheeky little blighters a piece of her mind, but to her relief both boys subsided into silence when her mum glared at them warningly.

'You're going to marry Joe?' Alice blinked, clearly shocked, and then jumped up to hug Violet. 'Congratulations ... though I'm amazed. I didn't see that one coming.'

'If you ever took your head out of a blessed book,' Sheila told her, 'you would have done. It's been obvious enough to the rest of us for ages.' She beamed her approval as Violet and Joe smiled at each other shyly. 'I suppose you won't want to be thinking about a new job then, Vi. Which is a pity, as I found a few good ones in the newspaper.'

'Oh aye?' Violet looked at her mum, suddenly suspicious. 'What did you have in mind?'

'They're looking for assistants at the undertakers in Penzance. For the washing and laying out of the dead. I thought it sounded right up your street.'

Selina choked on her food, and Caro gave her a few hearty thumps on the back, grinning.

Looking startled, Joe sat again rather heavily.

'Well, I'll certainly give it some thought,' Violet told her mum, also retaking her place at the table. She wasn't joking either; she was determined not to turn anything down if the hours and wages suited her needs. Besides, it was silly to be squeamish when death, or at least the threat of it, was becoming almost a part of daily life these days. 'The government says married women should do their bit too, as long as they don't have young children, so why not?'

Her mum looked impressed. 'That's the spirit, love. Maybe I'll join you. I could do with something to keep me busy.'

Alice nodded approvingly. 'Undertaking sounds like an interesting job. Better than factory work, that's for sure.' Now that the congratulations were over, she set to eating the vegetable stew again, shovelling it cheerfully into her mouth. 'This is very tasty,' she added between spoonfuls. 'Thanks, Gran. You're a good cook. Better than Aunty Vi, anyway.'

Violet threw her niece a dark look, suddenly wishing her at the bottom of the ocean, and then caught Joe's raised brows and burst out laughing.

'That's not fair; I'm a-a good cook,' she stammered. 'At least, I'm not *bad*. I don't burn things. Not often, at any rate.' She groaned in embarrassment, giving up the struggle to save her lost reputation. 'Alice, you little wretch, don't you go putting Joe off me five minutes after we've agreed to tie the knot.'

'That's all right, darling,' Joe said smoothly, and took

her hand across the table. 'As long as your mum's here, we'll survive.'

And everyone laughed, including Violet.

Darling.

She ought to have been offended by his joke. But her cheeks were glowing with pride instead. He was smiling and he'd called her *darling*. Violet's heart swelled in her chest and it was all she could not to weep openly with happiness. He'd been depressed for weeks now, and especially the past few days, and she'd feared he might never shake off that difficult encounter with his dad. But she could face the worst this war had to offer now, seeing the smile on his face.

CHAPTER THIRTY

Demelza swam slowly up from a heavy sleep that kept her eyelids glued together. Aware of strange aches and pains throughout her body, she listened in puzzlement to the soft murmur of voices somewhere nearby. She felt dazed, her head throbbing, her mouth dry, and could barely find the strength to open her eyes.

Where was she? What on earth had happened to her? She only had the vaguest memory of being alone with Robert in a dark, abandoned place – the factory with the unexploded bomb, she realised, gradually piecing the facts together – and heading for the door.

Then … nothing.

Robert.

Driven by a sudden fear, she forced her eyes open, and blinked, dazzled by the bright lights.

'Ohh,' she moaned, and hurriedly shut her eyes again. The throbbing in her head intensified, and she shifted, trying to find some ease for the pain, feeling a firm, well-starched pillow under her cheek. 'Where … where am I?'

Footsteps clicked across to her bed, and a cool hand touched her arm. 'It's all right, Demelza. You're safe.'

The voice was familiar. Demelza opened her eyes a crack, more cautiously this time, but the figure was standing in between her and the source of the bright light, which she realised now was a large window opposite her bed.

'Lily,' she croaked, recognising her friend's smiling face with immense relief. 'Everything hurts. What's happened?'

'You're in hospital, love.' Lily was checking her pulse now. 'And I'm glad to see you awake and talking. Last time you opened your eyes, you were right confused. We couldn't get much sense out of you at all.'

'I … I don't remember waking up before.'

'That's probably the sedatives.' Lily grinned, releasing her wrist. 'I won't lie, you've had us worried these past twenty-four hours. But your pulse is back to normal and you don't look quite as much like a stick of chalk anymore, thank goodness.' Pulling a fabric screen about the bed that softened the intrusive light, she gave Demelza a wink. 'I'd say you're definitely on the mend.'

'Derrick's Factory…' Demelza tried to sit up, wincing at the pain in her ribs, and Lily helped her at once. She was bandaged all around her middle, she noticed. 'There was a bomb.'

'Yes, love, it went off and you were caught in the blast. Blown straight out the door and into the street. You're lucky to be alive. You banged your head, broke a few ribs and punctured a lung. When you first came in, you were in a bad way, I can tell you. We thought we might lose you.'

Demelza stared up at her, shocked and speechless.

'Dr Jerrard operated on you and everything should be all right now,' Lily went on in a matter-of-fact way as though used to such horrors, which Demelza supposed she must be. 'But it's going to hurt for a while yet.'

'I need to thank the doctor.'

'He'll come to see you later today, I expect.'

Demelza closed her eyes, overcome by a wave of fatigue. 'Oh, my head hurts so bad. And my mouth...'

'Thirsty? Of course you are, the length of time you've been asleep.' Lily poured her a glass of water and brought it to her lips. 'Just a few sips now, love. Don't want to make yourself sick.' She removed the glass once Demelza had finished. 'Look, don't get me wrong, I know you had a job to do. But what on earth were you thinking, going into a building with an unexploded bomb?'

Demelza thought back. 'We ... we didn't know it was there at first,' she said haltingly, frowning as she tried to recall those muddled and misty last moments in the factory before the bomb went off. A horrible realisation struck her, and she sucked in a breath. 'Robert ... he was going down the steps to see if anyone was in the factory shelter. That was the last thing I remember.' An agony of fear streaked through her, almost unbearable. 'Did he make it?'

Lily studied her, a slight smile on her face. 'Yes, he made it.'

'Oh, thank goodness.'

'The building came down but he had the devil's own luck. He'd just gone inside the shelter when the bomb went off. The disposal team dug him out a few hours after you were brought in. There were a few other survivors too. I think they were only walking wounded though, nothing serious.'

'No deaths?'

Lily hesitated. 'The factory owner's secretary. Her name was Mrs Clemo, a widow with no children. A falling beam struck her head. She never regained consciousness. Poor woman...'

'How awful.' Demelza felt like crying. 'And Robert?' Her stomach churned with fear. 'How badly was he hurt?'

'A few nasty cuts and bruises, plus he broke his ankle and banged his spine. Dr Jerrard said he needs to stay in hospital until he's sure the damage to the spine is just bruising and nothing more serious.' Lily shook her head at Demelza's expression. 'Now, don't you go fretting yourself sick over him. The doctors 'ere are smashing, they'll see him right.'

Demelza nodded, and then stopped, wincing at the pain in her head. 'I know,' she whispered, fighting waves of nausea.

'You and Robert had a date, didn't you? I take it that worked out?'

'I'm not sure,' Demelza said, blushing under her friend's amused scrutiny. 'I think so.'

'I'd say it must have done. He's on the ward next door, but he's been asking to see you ever since you were brought in. But I didn't want to give permission until I could check with you.'

'Oh, yes, I'd like to see him.' Demelza bit her lip, which felt swollen and tender. Was her whole face bruised? But who cared, so long as Robert wasn't badly hurt. 'Though I must look a fright.' Her hand went to her hair, which felt matted and coarse. 'Do you have a comb?'

Lily nodded, smiling. 'Of course. I'll help you clean up when I've finished my rounds.'

'Um, can I walk to the lav first?' Demelza felt so stiff and sore, she was a little dubious at the idea of crossing the ward on her own two feet, even with Lily's support. But she really needed to go.

'Not quite yet,' Lily replied cheerfully, 'but don't worry, I'll be back very soon and help you with that too. No need to be embarrassed, it's all part of my job.' With a wink, she headed off to complete her other duties, and Demelza was comforted by her unconcerned air, glad at least that she had a friend here to look after her.

Her only worry was that Lily might be concealing the true extent of Robert's injuries from her, so as not to worry her. She didn't know much about nursing or medicine, but a damaged spine sounded very serious indeed. Demelza closed her eyes, her red-raw hands clamped together on top of the sheets. She had to see Robert soon or she would go mad with worry. Only once she'd seen his injuries for herself could she find any peace. He'd gone into that factory to help her out, so it would be her fault if he'd been badly hurt.

What if Robert never walked again?

Lily was so sorry for her stricken friend, who looked pale and bruised, and still very confused about what had happened. But she had grown to trust Dr Jerrard and knew him to be a safe pair of hands. If anyone would pull her through this awful experience, it would be him.

After she'd completed her round of the ward, she returned to Demelza's bedside and helped her with her ablutions first, then to clean herself up and comb her hair, promising that she would be allowed a proper bath as soon as the doctor sanctioned it. Although the tubes that had drained her chest cavity had been removed now, with all her bandaging still in place, Demelza was in no fit state to get into a bathtub. So, it had to be flannel washes with the screens round the bed for the time being, as she told her friend with an apologetic smile and a few jokes to lighten the difficult situation.

Hurrying out of the ward afterwards, a large vase of wilted flowers in her arms, Lily collided with a man in the corridor and recoiled with a startled cry.

'Blimey,' she exclaimed, nearly dropping the glass vase as she stumbled backwards. 'Watch it, would you?' To her surprise, the vase was plucked out of her hands, and she found herself facing Tristan. 'Oh, it's you.'

Much to her embarrassment, her cheeks bloomed with a sudden, irrepressible heat, as though reacting to his presence. All she could think about was the moment they'd last spoken, outside the cinema, when he'd more or less accused her of flirting with a complete stranger. That lack of trust still hurt her...

'Hello, Lily,' he said, and ran a hand through his ginger curls, his gaze moving up and down her, too restless to settle.

Tristan looked almost as embarrassed as she felt, Lily realised, feeling a stab of satisfaction at the thought. He had not been in touch since that day, no doubt having changed his mind about wishing to walk out with her. She had put him out of her mind, concentrating on work instead. But she couldn't deny a twinge of regret that he'd not asked her out again. For a brief spell, she had fancied herself quite happy to have a boyfriend at last.

'Erm, you've come to see your sister, I suppose? Demelza's in there.' She jerked her head back towards the ward she'd just left. 'She's woken up at last and is looking much better. I was just on my way to tell the doctor. Though it's not visiting hours yet, I'm afraid, and Matron would tear a strip off me if I was to let you in so early.' She was rambling, she realised, but couldn't seem to stop herself, stupidly nervous in his presence. 'You should probably come back at five.'

'Five o'clock?' He nodded but didn't move. 'Demelza's awake though, you said? She's going to make it?'

'You'd have to ask the doctor, but I think so … if her lung don't collapse again, that is. She gave her head a right bang too.'

'Yes, so your note said. Thank you for letting us know, by the way. It was very kind of you.'

'That's all right. Least I could do for … for a friend.'

His intense, brooding gaze was fixed on her face. 'I'm glad Demelza has you looking after her. I'm sure she couldn't have a better nurse.'

'Oh, well.' Her blush deepened and she longed for the ground to swallow her up. If only he would stop staring at her like that… 'For all she's on the mend, she'll be in hospital a while yet. It was touch and go when they brought her in. Best let her sleep for now, eh?' Belatedly, Lily realised he was still holding the vase of wilted flowers and took them from him with a shaky smile. 'Thanks, I have to throw these out, they're starting to pong something dreadful. Excuse me.'

322

Tristan stood aside to let her go, but as she began to walk unsteadily down the corridor, he called after her, 'Lily? Can we go somewhere private to talk?'

Lily half-turned her head with the flowers obscuring her face, tears a glittering sheen in her eyes, her lower lip beginning to wobble. 'I ... I'm too busy, sorry. Maybe another time.'

She strode away, fiercely glad he hadn't seen her crying, though annoyed with herself for being so emotional. It had been over between them before it had properly begun. No point crying over spilt milk, her gran would have said. All the same, she wished with every fibre of her being that she was free to tell him the truth about the man she'd met outside the cinema. But that would never happen, would it?

CHAPTER THIRTY-ONE

'Demmy?'

Slowly, Demelza pushed aside her chaotic, confused dreams and opened her eyes to see her brother standing beside her hospital bed. How long had she been asleep? The light from the window opposite was less intense now, and she guessed it must be late afternoon. Half the day, in other words. The realisation shocked and demoralised her. But she couldn't expect to be better immediately, she told herself. Recovery from something this serious would take time.

'Tris,' she whispered, her throat dry, and managed a wan smile. 'I ... I seem to have got myself blown up. Silly me.'

'Idiot,' he said, smiling, and bent over the bed to kiss her cheek. 'You look like you've been in a fight.'

'Is it really awful?' She hadn't been able to see much of a reflection in the tiny hand-mirror Lily had given her but had done her best to tidy her hair and clean her face.

'Good God, don't worry about your looks, sis. You nearly died, remember?' Her brother's warm eyes smiled at her. 'Cuts and bruises don't matter. They'll heal soon enough.'

'Help me to sit up, would you? My side hurts.' She grimaced at the tight bandages around her middle.

Carefully, Tristan eased her up the pillows. 'That better?'

'Much, thank you. It's good to see you.' But anxiety gnawed at her as she studied his face. 'You look funny though. What's up? Not another row with Dad?'

'No, nothing like that.' But his smile was crooked now. 'It's been a difficult few days, that's all.'

'I suppose Dad's been saying he told me so. He warned me I could get hurt if I joined the Fire Guard, do you remember? Now look at me.'

He shook his head, his gaze shifting away. 'Dad's barely said a word about it. But then, since I read Mother's journal, I've barely said a word to *him*.'

'He didn't come with you to visit me today?' She felt hurt, and wasn't sure she believed her brother's careful answers. Something was up with him. 'What's happened, Tris?' Fear spiked through her at an awful thought; were they all hiding from her that Robert was more badly hurt than Lily had claimed? 'Please tell me. Is it something awful?'

Tristan pulled a face. 'More stupid, really. I had a bust-up with Lily. You know we've been walking out?'

'I had guessed, yes,' she said, trying not to smile.

'Well, it's all over between us.'

'Oh no.' Her heart squeezed in pain for him. No wonder the poor boy was looking so knocked-about. Though she was surprised Lily hadn't mentioned it earlier. But maybe it hadn't mattered as much to her. Lily had always struck

Demelza as someone quite worldly-wise, while Tris was still a lad to her mind and deeply inexperienced. 'But why? What was the row about?'

He drew up a chair to the bed and sat, taking off his cap. Briefly, he described spotting Lily talking to another man outside the main picture house in Penzance, where they'd been meeting to watch a film together. A much older man with a sinister, shifty air, he said.

'Maybe there was a perfectly innocent explanation,' she said. 'Have you asked her about it?'

'Of course.' He looked away, a hurt expression on his face. 'I wanted to know straightaway who he was, but Lily was as shifty as him and refused to say a word about it.'

'Well, I still think you ought to have a proper talk with her. Maybe you'll bump into her one day when you're visiting me and you can ask her then...' Her voice trailed away when he said nothing in return. Perhaps the whole thing was a lost cause, she decided, and trying to help was pointless. Meanwhile, the throbbing in her head had intensified since she'd sat up, and she put a hand to her temple. 'I'm sorry, my head is banging like a drum.'

Contrite, Tristan stood. 'I shouldn't have kept you talking so long.'

'No, I'm glad you came. But what about young Janice? How's she coping with all this?'

'She's going back to live with her brothers in Porthcurno. We thought it was best, just until you're back on your feet.'

Demelza wasn't happy about that news. But it was a practical solution. She'd been fretting over how much extra housework her aunt Sarah would be saddled with now she wasn't there to help out a few days a week. And maybe it would do Janice good to be reunited with her younger brothers for a while. It was also something for her to focus on, stuck in this hospital bed; getting better so she could be there for Janice when the girl came back to them.

'That's probably a good idea,' she agreed reluctantly.

After all, it was unlikely she'd be able to return to work with the Fire Guard for a while after this. But at least spending time on the farm would give her a chance to consider what she really wanted from this life. With her days so hectic these past few months as spring had slid into early summer, she hadn't given much thought to herself. But meeting Robert had made her consider a different future than the one she'd previously envisaged…

'Give Janice my love,' she added sleepily, her eyes already half-closing again. 'Dad too.' Though the fact that her father hadn't come to visit stung her feelings. 'And Aunt Sarah.'

'I will,' Tris whispered, and drew the covers up to keep her warm. 'Get well soon, sis.'

Joe drove slowly past the row of terraced houses where his father lived, looking stalwartly forward, his chin jutting at an dangerous angle.

Violet risked a quick glance, but there was nobody in sight. 'I don't think he's home,' she said quietly, wanting to reassure him.

'I don't know who you mean,' Joe replied, and set his chin another stubborn inch higher. 'We're picking them up at the school gates, is that right?'

Sighing, Violet nodded. 'Do you know the way?'

'Of course I do. I was born in Penzance, remember?' He drove in silence, his eyes on the road, for the seaside town was far busier than the tiny village of Porthcurno and he was not the steadiest driver in the world. But after a moment he added, as though on an afterthought, 'I'm sorry, Vi. I shouldn't have snapped like that. It's just…'

He lapsed into brooding silence again.

'You don't want to think about him,' she suggested, watching his averted profile.

'That's it, exactly.' He gave a sharp nod. 'Least said, soonest mended.'

'Whatever you say, Joe dearest. We won't mention him again.' She pointed ahead. 'Ah, I can see the girls now. I told Alice to wait with Janice. And there's Lily with them.'

Violet was surprised by her own easy acceptance of Joe's funny mood swings. She'd always been a woman to speak her mind and not leave any dark corners unexplored. But something in her wanted to protect this man from his own demons, and she had an inkling she might do rather a good job of it, especially now she was to be his wife. She was suddenly struck by the realisation that they had more people to carry than seats to carry them.

'Maybe Alice can ride in the back with the bags,' Joe suggested as they pulled up near the school gates, clearly thinking the same as her.

'Won't that be dangerous?'

'There's a strap she can hang onto. And if I go slow round the corners, it should be all right.'

Joe jumped up and helped the girls put their bags into the back of the van. After hugging young Janice, Violet ushered her and Lily into the front, moving them along the bench seat, though it was really only big enough to take three. Four at a pinch.

'I'd love to go in the back,' Alice readily agreed when Joe suggested it. Her face glowed with good humour as she added, 'I'll pretend I'm a secret stowaway on a truck crossing the German border under cover of darkness.'

'Why on earth would you be a stowaway?' Janice called out of the front window.

'Because I'm escaping from the Nazis, of course,' Alice said, throwing the younger girl a withering look. While Violet watched, she slung her work bag and gas mask over her shoulder, and climbed into the back of the van, ignoring Joe's offer of a helping hand. She settled herself on top of the old sacks in the back and grabbed hold of the hanging strap for balance. 'You can close the door now,' she told them. 'I'm not afraid of the dark.'

'Well, you don't need to be,' Joe pointed out. 'There's a little window, see?'

But Alice pretended she hadn't heard him, pulling her knees up to her chest and going into 'stowaway' mode.

'Come on, love,' Violet whispered to Joe, trying not to laugh. 'Best do as she says and shut the door. Before she starts abusing you in German.'

He obeyed, though he looked surprised. 'Alice can speak German?'

'Oh yes, she learned it from her father,' Violet told him in a low voice, not wanting her niece to hear. 'Ernst taught both girls a smattering of German when they was only knee-high to a grasshopper – songs, nursery rhymes, and so on. Alice was quickest at picking up the foreign words though, and she done well in French too. I expect that's why they gave her the job at the school without any formal training. She was always the cleverest girl in her class.'

'I'm sure she was,' Joe agreed, waiting until she was in the front before closing her door and walking round to the other side.

She wondered if he was remembering the night his farm was bombed and how he'd overheard that little weasel Patrick Dullaghan accusing her of being in league with the Hun. Utter nonsense, based on nothing more than her brother-in-law's German roots, but people were often quick to assume the worst once gossip was doing the rounds.

Joe got in and started the engine, his tone distracted. 'I'd forgotten their father was German.'

'Only half-German,' Lily put in quickly, seated next to Janice between them.

'He was born in Germany though, wasn't he?' Joe persisted, and glanced across at Violet. 'I think you told me once his real name was Ernst, but he thought Ernest would help him fit in better.'

'That's right,' Violet admitted when Lily didn't respond, and then hurriedly changed the subject, seeing her niece's pinched face.

The girls had suffered dreadfully when those nasty rumours about their dad had started, and she doubted Lily wanted to be reminded of those days.

''Ere, you all right, Lily? I don't think they can be feeding you properly at that hospital. Are you getting your full rations?' Violet pursed her lips. 'You've lost weight and you're white as a sheet.'

Lily looked at her with wide eyes, stammering, 'Am … am I?' She rubbed at her cheeks as though to bring the colour back. 'Just tired, I suppose. It's been such a long week, I thought them bombs would never stop falling.' She laid her cheek on Violet's shoulder. 'To be honest, Aunty Vi, I can't wait to be home and forget all about work.'

It was clear that something serious was troubling her niece. And just as clear that she wasn't ready to talk about it yet.

'Poor pet, it sounds like those doctors have been running you ragged.'

'Mmm,' Lily murmured, her eyes already closed.

Violet felt so sorry for the girl. She wished she could wave a magic wand and make all of their troubles vanish in a flash. But she couldn't, of course. They simply had to endure whatever the bloody war threw at them and somehow keep going...

Violet slipped an arm about Lily's narrow waist and gave her niece a reassuring squeeze. 'Well, just wait until you hear our good news,' she whispered in her ear. 'This will cheer you up and no mistake. How do you fancy being a bridesmaid again?'

Demelza let herself drift away again on another tide of weariness, and when she next opened her eyes, disturbed by a strange creaking noise nearby, she found that the protective screens had been removed from around her bed and the ward was in semi-darkness. Someone was sitting beside her, she realised, sensing their presence rather than seeing them properly.

'Hello?' she said faintly, and turned her head to peer at the visitor. It looked like a man, his figure large and bulky.

'I'm sorry if I woke you, Demelza.' The deep, familiar voice made her heart leap with joy, and the warm hand that touched hers on the covers filled her with fluttering excitement. 'I only meant to sit here and watch you sleep.' His smile was ironic. 'This damn contraption makes more noise than I thought.'

It was Robert. And he was in a wheelchair, she realised.

'It doesn't matter,' she said, almost feverishly, and gripped his hand in return, her gaze searching his shadowy face. 'I'm just glad you're alive. And I'm so sorry about what happened at the factory. That bomb—'

'Hush, it's not important. Let's not talk about it.'

'But I have to know,' she persisted, desperation in her heart. 'Lily mentioned that a woman died.'

Robert nodded, his face suddenly sombre. 'Some of the management had been staying late for a stock take. They dived into the factory basement when the siren went off but Mr Derrick's secretary, Mrs Clemo, was killed when the ceiling collapsed.'

'I feel awful. If only we'd got them all out in time.'

'It wasn't your fault.'

'Oh, I wish I could believe that.' A shudder of guilt ran through her as she clasped his hand tightly, staring deep into his eyes. 'What about you, Robert? How badly hurt were you? I asked Lily but I'm not convinced she told me the truth.'

'The jury's still out on how serious it is. I don't have much sensation in my legs at the moment, I'm afraid. Hence this awful chair.'

Her eyes widened on his face. So she had been right to fear the worst. He might not walk again.

'I believe in you,' Demelza said with a tough smile, determined for his sake not to cry. 'You'll get better, Robert, and you'll walk again. I know you will.'

332

His fingers tightened around hers, and she saw a flash of something in his face. Then he too smiled in the same way.

'Of course I will,' he agreed heartily, but she could see how afraid Robert was that he'd be stuck in that wheelchair forever.

Yet, despite his fear, he was smiling for her sake, just as she was for his. What better sign did she need that they were made for each other? They were like two halves to the same coin, Demelza thought, thrilled by the way their fingers laced together so naturally and easily, as though they would never now be parted.

'As my grandmother is forever telling me,' Robert added, 'even in the darkest hour, all we need is a little faith.'

CHAPTER THIRTY-TWO

Lily lay on her back in the summer sunshine, eyes closed, enjoying the peace and solitude of an empty field bordering the cliff-path, about a mile or so beyond Porthcurno. By this time tomorrow, she thought, she'd be back at work on the wards. For now though, she had nothing to do but breathe in the fresh country air and let her mind wander. It was certainly a quiet spot for it, up above Joe's farm. She could hear birds singing, a few heifers mooing in the distance, and the steady rumble of a tractor engine closer at hand, accompanied by girlish laughter as the Land Girls mucked in together in a field out of sight.

From this spot, if she could be bothered to stand up, she might just be able to see the camouflaged roof of Eastern House, the secret government listening post the Jerries were always looking for, and the pretty sweep of the coastal path through wild flowers and long grasses towards the pale sands of the beach at Porthcurno. With a pang, she recalled those early days at Eastern House, soon after they'd journeyed down to Cornwall from

Dagenham. She and Aunty Vi and Alice had toiled in the busy corridors of Eastern House for months, keeping the place clean, mopping up after soldiers and staff alike, even working in the kitchen together under stern Mr Frobisher. It had been hard work, yes. But, after suffering far worse on her great-uncle's farm, it had seemed like heaven to them, and especially for her, perhaps.

As she let her mind drift, a familiar face loomed in her memory. Sun-tanned, handsome, with bright ginger curls that framed a smile. *Tristan.* Mentally, she cursed herself for a fool. How stupid she was to be pining after the Cornish lad when he'd made his suspicions so clear outside the cinema.

Yet still she hoped... When Tristan had bumped into her at the hospital, she'd seen his face change, and for a few wild seconds her heart had thumped, her face had burned with heat, and she hadn't known where to look. Anywhere but at him, of course. She still couldn't be sure what she'd seen in his face that day. Regret? Dismay? It was impossible to tell. Maybe he'd simply been embarrassed to see her and eager to get away.

'Oh, Tris...' She rolled over and buried her hot face in the sweet, cool grasses.

Until this weekend, she hadn't realised how much she'd missed this green and tranquil spot since moving to Penzance with its shopping streets and clustered rows of townhouses. Though even here in tiny Porthcurno the signs of war were unmistakeable, with an increased army presence drafted in to protect the listening post at Eastern House, and barbed-wire barriers everywhere, guards sometimes demanding identity papers simply to move about the village itself.

For months now, the government had been warning anyone living on this coast to prepare for the possibility of a German invasion, but invasion was such a terrifying thought, Lily tried not to dwell on it. The threat was inescapable though, and new posters reminding people to keep their gas masks to hand night and day had only served to frighten her more. She was a practical girl, or tried to be, but even she longed for this ever-increasing horror to end. For things to go back to those simple days before war was declared and the whole world had changed beyond recognition.

Everything had been so spoilt by this horrid war. She'd never seen Porthcurno Bay without the ugly blocks and other beach defences that littered the foreshore, but she imagined it must have been lovely before the outbreak of war, sand bleached almost white, dark rocks rising like jagged towers out of a sparkling, greeny-blue sea. Now, nobody played or bathed there, and fortified lookout posts all along the coast were a constant reminder of the potential German threat.

How was her father managing to survive beyond enemy lines? She didn't even know where he was or what he might be doing for their country. She would have to tell Alice soon but had been putting it off, afraid she might also be tempted to tell Aunt Violet and Gran. Talking about it to anyone else could jeopardise her father's life, or so the stranger had suggested. Yet how could she keep such a secret from her own flesh and blood? Her heart already felt like it would burst...

Sitting up, she hugged both knees tight against her chest, trying hard to remember her father's face. Ernest Fisher had joined up early in the war and none of them had seen him alive since. Her poor mum had even died thinking her husband had been lost in action.

'Where are you, Dad?' she whispered, and closed her eyes against a wave of intolerable sadness. 'Please stay safe and come home to us.'

Becoming aware of footsteps and laughter, Lily hurriedly dried her eyes and turned with a smile to find her aunt and sister trudging uphill to where she was sitting. Gran was following slowly, with flushed cheeks and a basket over her arm.

'What's all this?' she called out, hiding her distress as best she could. 'Poor Gran, you look all out of puff.'

'Just a bit steep, that's all,' Gran wheezed, but it was clear she was relieved to lower herself gingerly to the grass at Lily's side.

'We've brought a picnic,' Alice explained, taking the basket from their grandmother and beginning to root through its contents. 'Mmm. Slice of cold pie, sandwich, jar of pickles.'

'Hands off, you bloomin' tea-leaf!' Gran exclaimed, dragging the basket back towards herself. She had a tendency to use Cockney rhyming slang when deeply moved, as her own mother had been born in East London.

'I'm not a thief,' Alice complained, looking hurt. 'I only wanted to see what we had.' But she winked at Lily as she sank cross-legged beside her. 'I could murder a few pickles though, couldn't you?'

'I hadn't really thought about eating yet,' Lily admitted.

Alice raised her brows. 'Well, I'll have your share if you're not *that* hungry.'

'Oh no, you won't, Missy.' Aunty Violet had been spreading out the blanket she'd brought and knelt on it now to distribute the picnic fare. 'We came here to cheer our Lily up, not feed you extra rations. It's a family picnic, just for us.' She winked at Lily. 'We've left the boys with Janice, since Joe's out on the farm. And the Land Girls will soon be headed into Porthcurno for their afternoon off.'

Lily put her hands to her cheeks; they'd grown warm under the knowing looks her family was giving her. She hadn't realised her low mood was so visible to everyone and it felt awkward to be the centre of attention for once. 'Cheer me up?' she repeated, stammering slightly. 'I ... I don't know what you mean. I'm not unhappy.'

Gran leant across to pat her hand. 'We ain't blind, pet. Something's not been right with you for ages.' Her kind eyes smiled at Lily with understanding and indulgence. 'Come on, you can tell us what's wrong. We're your own flesh and blood; we wouldn't never judge you, I swear.' Her voice softened. 'Ain't nothing stronger than family.'

Alice nodded, already munching on a thin-looking bread-and-butter sandwich. 'Is it Tristan? Janice told me you and him had a falling-out.'

'Oh, did she, now?' Lily felt cross all of a sudden. Her hands clenched into fists and she hid them in her lap, looking away. 'Well, you can tell her to keep her bleedin' nose out of my business.'

It was awful, feeling like she couldn't have any secrets from her family. They meant well, but what had happened between her and Tris was too humiliating. It was still an open wound and they were simply rubbing salt in it.

Gran was shocked. 'No bad language, please!'

'We're not prying, love,' Aunty Violet told her, picking her words with obvious care. 'We just care about you. Since your mum passed, you know I've tried to take her place as best I could.' She hesitated. 'And as you've no other family left—'

Lily felt her heart twist in pain, interrupting her with an anguished cry of, 'Like my dad, you mean?'

Aunty Violet looked back at her unhappily. 'I can see I've upset you, Lily, though I can't for the life of me work out why. But there's no need to raise your voice to me, love.'

'Or to get your knickers in a twist,' her sister muttered. 'All over a boy too.'

'Yes, I split up with Tristan,' Lily exclaimed, 'but that's not what's really upsetting me. This face,' she said, jabbing an angry finger at herself, 'this isn't over a boy, Alice. It's about our dad.' She gulped in a breath, her vision swimming with the tears she'd been suppressing for days. 'We've been lied to. He … he isn't dead.'

Alice stared at her, no longer chewing. '*What?*'

'Dad wasn't lost in action. It was a lie. Only it's all top secret and if we're not careful, he could be captured and … and executed.'

Her aunt sat up straight, panic in her face. 'Hush, you don't know what you're saying.'

'Yes, I do,' Lily insisted, hot tears running down her cheeks now, her voice croaky. 'A man in Penzance came and found me the other day. He gave me a message from Dad, to say he was still alive and thinking of us. Only the man said I wasn't to tell anyone but you, Alice.' She rubbed a fist across her wet eyes. 'But how can I tell you, and not

Aunty Vi and Gran too? You're still only seventeen. I can't ask you to lie to your own family, it wouldn't be fair.'

Alice's face had gone pale. 'Dad … Dad's really alive?'

Lily nodded vehemently.

'Oh my gawd.' Gran looked round at Violet and then sucked in a breath, her eyes sharp and clever. 'You don't look surprised,' she pointed out. 'You knew about this, didn't you?'

Violet hesitated and then gave a tentative nod. 'I knew, yes.'

Lily couldn't believe her ears. Her heart began thudding violently. 'What? All this time, you knew our dad was still alive … yet you let us think he was dead?' Outrage swelled in her voice. 'Hang on, how exactly did you know about him? Who on earth could have told you?' Fresh tears blurred her vision. 'And what gave you the right to hide it from us? We're his daughters, for God's sake.'

'Oh, Lord.' Her aunt started crying too, twisting a hanky between her fingers. 'I wanted to tell you. But Colonel Ryder made me swear not to. He said… Well, he never said exactly, but he made it obvious that if I ever blabbed, I could be arrested and shot.'

'Shot?' Gran's eyes were huge as saucers.

'For treason,' Violet said miserably.

'I think he must have been exaggerating to frighten you,' Alice said in a small voice, and Violet rounded on her, shaking her head violently.

'No, it's all true. Because of those papers we signed when we started at Eastern House. Don't you remember? We all had to sign the Official Secrets Act. And when the colonel told me about Ernst, he said it was part of that, and I mustn't tell anyone,' she finished, weeping into her hanky. 'Not even you, Lily, or you, Alice. Please don't be angry. I wanted to tell you both. And you too, Mum.' Aunty Violet was sobbing now. 'Only I … I didn't bloody dare.'

'Oh, for goodness' sake,' her mother exclaimed, and pulled Violet into a fierce hug. 'You silly thing. Nobody's angry with you.' She threw a warning look at Lily. 'Are we?'

Lily, who couldn't believe that her aunt had known about her father all this time and never said a word, was indeed feeling angry. But she also knew it wasn't her aunt's fault. Not if telling them would have broken the Official Secrets Act and might even be considered treasonous. That threat alone would be enough to keep most people's mouths shut.

'No, of course not,' Lily said with difficulty, 'but I still don't understand. Why did the colonel tell you and not us?'

'Don't you remember that awful business over the rumours that I was a German spy?' Haltingly, in a tearful voice, her aunt reminded them all of how she'd been summoned to a private interview with Colonel Ryder last summer, the man in charge of Eastern House at the time. 'It was all nonsense, but I was terrified at the time; I thought the colonel was going to clap me in irons. Joe's farm had just been bombed and his poor mum killed, and that vile boy from Dagenham was putting it about that we were all in the pay of the Jerries because your dad was half-German.'

'Patrick Dullaghan. Yes, I remember that nasty little bas…' Alice's voice trailed away at Gran's shocked glance. 'But what did the colonel say about our dad, Aunty Vi?'

'Much the same as your sister just said. That your dad isn't missing or dead but working for the British government.

Only he swore me to secrecy too.' Violet held out a hand to Lily, her eyes pleading. 'Say you believe me, love. I didn't want to leave either of you girls thinking your dad was dead. But I didn't know what else to do for the best; I swear it.'

Lily felt her anger ebb. She could perfectly imagine how hard it must have been for Aunty Violet to keep quiet all this time.

'It's all right,' she said, and gave her aunt's hand a reassuring squeeze. 'At least we're all on the same page now.'

Gran produced a bottle of beer from her basket and took a generous swig from it before passing the bottle to Violet. She wiped her lips with the back of her hand before hiccupping loudly. 'Blimey, this Cornish beer is strong. But, Lily, who was this man that gave you the message? How did he know your dad?' Gran's eyes widened in horror. 'Oh my... What if he was only *pretending* to come from your dad? Maybe he was working for the Germans, trying to find something out about Ernst.'

Lily shook her head. 'I don't think so, Gran. He didn't give his name or say how he knew Dad, but he wasn't digging for information. He already knew who I was ... and about you lot too.'

'Sounds like he was British Intelligence,' Alice chipped in.

'He seemed like an all right sort,' Lily said, nodding. 'And he even said Dad had heard about Mum and was sorry he couldn't be there for me and Alice. But he'd come home when he could.' Her voice faltered and she blinked, battling tears again. 'When the war's over.'

Frowning, Alice said nothing, but sucked on the end of her blonde plait with more than usual intensity.

'This man ... he didn't say nothing else, love?' Gran

asked Lily, rummaging in the basket. 'Seems like a lot of trouble to go to for not much of a message.'

'I think Dad just wanted us to know he was still alive. Isn't that enough?' But Lily took a deep breath, carefully thinking back to her strange encounter. 'Hang on though,' she added, recalling their hurried and stilted conversation. 'There was something else. He said people had been asking about Dad.'

'What does that mean?' Violet looked worried.

Lily shrugged. 'I've no idea. Only the stranger insisted I had to tell anyone who came asking that Ernest Fisher is dead and buried somewhere abroad.' Automatically, she accepted the wafer-thin slice of cold ham and jelly pie that Gran was holding out to her, not hungry but being polite. 'He said that if I didn't, Dad's life could be in danger.'

'Blimey.' Alice jumped up, her face burning with colour. 'I know what that means. Our dad's a British spy.' To Lily's surprise, she seemed more excited than upset by this realisation. 'Isn't that just the most amazing thing ever?' Her eyes widened. 'I wonder how you get to be a spy?'

'Hush, girl,' Gran hissed, laying a stubby finger across her lips. 'Careless talk costs lives, remember?'

'Gran, for goodness's sake, nobody can hear us up here on the cliffs.' Alice waved a hand at the rolling patchwork of green fields before them and the sparkling sea stretching to the horizon at their backs. 'Unless you think that that blackbird there is a German agent, listening to every bloomin' word we say?'

'He might be.' Gran eyed the strutting blackbird with suspicion. 'I don't trust nobody these days.' At that moment, the bird flew off with a loud caw, and she grunted. 'See, he's probably off to tell the Fuhrer all about your dad.'

Lily couldn't help smiling, but her younger sister didn't react, already lost in thought again. 'Alice,' she said gently, 'I'm really sorry I haven't got more information for you. But at least Dad's not gone forever. When the war's over, he'll come home to us, I'm sure of it.'

'And if we lose the war?' Alice asked simply, staring out to sea as though searching the misty horizon for their absent father.

There was a short silence. Gran took another swig of beer and passed the bottle to Violet, who also knocked some back. Lily didn't know what to say and looked help-lessly at her aunt.

'One day at a time, eh?' Aunty Vi said with forced cheeriness. 'We still have plenty of things to be thankful for, and Lily's message from your dad is one of them. It's good news on a dark day; a reason to hope for a better future.'

'That's right,' Gran agreed, nodding wisely.

'Now let's eat up and finish this picnic,' Violet urged them. 'Before that cheeky blackbird comes back to steal our sarnies.'

Alice came back to sit down beside her aunt, but she kept her blonde head lowered and it was obvious to Lily that she was stewing inside. It was always hard to know what Alice was thinking, but it was clear the shocking news about their dad had affected her deeply. Her sister was young though; she would recover soon enough, Lily was sure of it, too distracted by her work at the school to dwell on personal worries. Though even that work no longer seemed enough to hold Alice's restless attention these days.

A gusty sea breeze mussed their hair and fluttered their blouses, bringing a whiff of salt with it. Lily bit into her pie slice, barely registering the fact that it was all jelly and soggy pastry, with very little meat. *A better future.* She'd been hoping for that too until Tristan came along and filled her head with nothing but romance, like so many of the other young women she worked alongside. It was time she put all that girlish nonsense aside and focused on her work and the war effort instead. That was what really counted.

All the same, her heart ached. She'd been in love with Tristan, she was sure of it. And part of her still was, even after things had gone wrong between them. Which meant she was probably a fool. Still, at least now she knew how brave her father was, risking his life every day to work secretly against the enemy. His courage and daring gave Lily something to measure herself against, even if she couldn't speak of it openly. Besides, Aunty Violet was right; even a little good news went a long way in times like these, when the war seemed to be dragging on forever with no end in sight, and the best people to rely on were family and neighbours, not silly young men whose feelings could be switched on and off like an electric light.

'Come on, who remembers this old tune from down the pub?' Gran asked cheerily, and at once began to sing, 'Knees Up, Mother Brown', in her husky, trembling voice.

One by one, they all joined her in the song, louder and louder, until the sound of their laughing voices filled the quiet Cornish air...

CHAPTER THIRTY-THREE

It was on a sunny afternoon, almost a week after the bomb blast, that Demelza woke from a nap to see both her brother and father standing over her hospital bedside, both men shuffling their feet and looking uncertain. Tris was carrying a bunch of wildflowers wrapped in brown paper, which he held out to her.

'Feeling better, big sis?'

'Not too bad today.' She yawned and eased herself up on the pillows, her side still sore under the tight bandaging. 'Flowers, Tris? For me?' She smiled, pulling the ragged bunch to her nose for a sniff, the bluebells, ox-eye daisy, even a pungent leaf of wild garlic, reminding her of home. 'Thank you. I'll get a nurse to put them in a vase for me later.'

She was surprised to see her father with him. He'd only come to see her once before, and that had been very early on, while she was still drifting in and out of consciousness, sedated by the doctors on account of her broken ribs.

'It's good to see you,' her father said, pulling up a chair

to her bedside. 'Tris has been keeping me informed, so I knew how you were. That you weren't at death's door. No point coming to see you until you were properly awake, after all.'

'I'm sure,' she said, a little tartly.

'So,' he said, studying her, 'you were the only one of the Fire Guard stupid enough to walk into a building where there was an unexploded bomb.'

Demelza flushed angrily. 'Actually, I wasn't alone that night. I was with an ambulance driver.'

'Not that bloody conchie again?' Her father glared at her. 'I thought I told you to knock that nonsense on the head?'

'Dad, for God's sake,' Tristan said, shifting uncomfortably.

'No, I told her how it would be if she went off to play at being a fireman. And look at her now. Half-blown to bits.' Her father shook his head at her. 'It's not a game, you know. It's not women's work, running about town in your little helmet, putting out fires and checking for incendiary bombs. You're lucky to be alive, girl.'

Demelza knotted her fingers together and swallowed her retort. Goodness, she thought, her father was harder work than ever. But she knew from experience that arguing with him would only inflame the situation and make his behaviour ten times worse.

She forced herself to smile at Tristan instead, recalling what he'd told her about his fight with Lily. She'd asked him about it last time he'd visited as well, hoping the two of them might have made up by then, but apparently he hadn't seen her to sort it out.

'Tris,' she said with an effort, 'have you made up with Lily yet? She was asking after you the other day.'

This wasn't quite true. Lily hadn't mentioned Tristan at all, though Demelza had, several times, hoping to spark some interest. But Lily had not taken the bait, continuing with her work and brushing off Demelza's remarks as though she hadn't even heard them. Which was telling in itself.

'What's this?' Their father glared up at his son. 'Is she talking about that blonde piece again? The young nurse you brought up to the farm?'

'None of your business,' Tristan said.

'You're my son. That makes it my business.' Her father was raising his voice now, and heads had turned in the ward to stare in their direction. This didn't faze him though; he seemed to enjoy the way people flinched when he grew loud and aggressive, using his voice as a weapon whenever possible. 'I've told you, boy,' he boomed, 'it's too soon for you to be thinking of courting. You're barely old enough to shave, let alone walk out with a girl.' He was almost snarling now. 'Besides, there's the farm to think of. I'm not getting any younger and them sheep won't shear themselves.'

'Hush, Dad.' Demelza cringed at the noise he was making.

'Don't you hush me, girl.' Her father punctuated his remarks with a jabbing finger. 'I'll say what I like to my own son, thank you very much.'

'Maybe so,' Tris said urgently, 'but this can wait, can't it? You're disturbing the other patients.' He ran a hand through his ginger curls, a flush in his cheeks. 'All we're saying is, please keep your voice down.'

'And I'm telling you—'

But whatever her father had intended to say was interrupted by a stern-faced woman in a spotless uniform who appeared magically beside the bed. It said 'Matron' on her badge. She drew a screen briskly between the bed and the rest of the ward, demanding, 'Now then, what's all this noise about?'

Demelza's father began to say something about her minding her own business, but the woman threw him such a stony glare that he lapsed instantly into silence.

'This is a hospital,' Matron continued in an icy tone, addressing both him and Tristan. 'There are sick people here who need their rest. If you two gentlemen wish to start a brawl, pray do so outside these grounds. And certainly *never* on one of my wards.'

'Sorry, Matron,' Tristan said at once, whipping off his cap and inclining his head. 'It won't happen again.'

Everyone looked at their father, who did not apologise but began to say in a blustering voice, 'Funnily enough, Matron, we were talking about one of your nurses—'

Again, Matron interrupted him, clapping her hands loudly and making a shooing gesture as though he were a child caught in a naughty prank. 'Out you go,' she instructed him in a strident voice, almost tipping him out of the bedside chair when he refused to move. 'Visiting time is over for you.'

'But I've only just got here.'

'I'm in charge of this ward and you will leave when I tell you. Or you will never be permitted back inside this hospital. Which would be a pity if you were ever taken sick, don't you agree?'

At that moment, a burly man appeared at her elbow, a bunch of keys on his belt. This man nodded to Demelza's father and then jerked a large thumb towards the ward door.

'Matron said *out*,' he repeated in a gruff voice.

'You'd best go, Dad,' Tristan said, not without a smidge of satisfaction. 'I'll meet you outside in five minutes.'

Their father was escorted to the ward door, but not before they both heard him shout back, 'Her name's Lily. Blonde nurse. You want to watch her, Matron. Trying it on with my son, she was. All right, keep your hands off me,' he added angrily as the burly man shoved him through the double doors to the ward. 'No need to push. I'm going, aren't I?'

After the doors had banged behind him, there was an awkward silence on the ward.

'I take it you're his son.' Matron looked Tristan up and down, her face cold and forbidding. 'Is what he said true? Are you having a relationship with one of my nurses?'

Demelza tried desperately to catch Tristan's eye. Poor Lily could probably be dismissed for having a boyfriend. Or would be if this woman had anything to do with it. But she needn't have worried.

Tristan looked Matron straight in the eye. 'Absolutely not. I don't even know who he's talking about.' He replaced his cap with a sharp nod. 'I'm very sorry about the disturbance though. I think he's been drinking.'

'Hmm' was all Matron said, and after another stare at both of them from narrowed eyes, she whisked away again on her rounds.

Demelza flopped back exhausted on her pillows. Her

bandages felt tighter than ever. 'Oh my goodness. What on earth's wrong with Dad? He must be going mad.'

'I wasn't joking about him having been on the drink. We stopped into the pub on the way here.'

'Oh.' She was astonished.

Her father had been raised a Methodist and disapproved of drinking. It wasn't unknown for him to enter a pub, as he often met other farmers there, but never in the middle of the day.

Tristan nodded grimly. 'I know.'

'What on earth can have made him do that? What's wrong?' She sat up when he said nothing, staring at him in dismay. 'Come on, what aren't you telling me?'

'I've decided to enlist.'

'Oh, Tris, no.'

'I've got to.' There was a stubborn look on his face. 'I can't stay on that dead-end farm anymore, not when all my mates have joined up. I look like a coward. So I'm off to do my bit soon.' But his face was pale as he dug his hands into his pockets. 'I told Dad yesterday. He hit the roof, of course.'

'I can imagine.'

'I said he ought to apply for Land Girls to help with the farm, and he went on and on about how he'd never live it down, having women working there.' He pulled a face. 'He said we should come and visit you because you'd talk me out of going.' His mouth twisted in a kind of smile. 'You won't though, will you?'

'If your mind's made up,' she said faintly, and gave a helpless shrug. 'What is there to say except good luck.'

'Thank you.'

Demelza wanted to be optimistic for her brother. And she suspected she would probably do the same in his shoes. But she also knew from the war lists how many young men went out to serve in the war who never came back.

She shivered despite the warmth in the sunny, south-facing ward. 'Does Lily know?'

Her brother's face closed at the mention of that name again. 'What's it to do with her?'

'Tris, come on. I know how you feel about her.'

'I told you last time, that's all over and done with. We finished it, all right?' Tristan dragged his hands out of his pockets and folded his arms, staring at the ground. 'Though perhaps when you next see Lily, could you please tell her...' He paused, his expression torn. 'Tell her I'm sorry about ... well, about everything.' His voice was husky and she could swear there were tears in his eyes, just as there'd been the last time he'd spoke of Lily. 'And you can tell her—'

'Yes? Tell me what?'

Demelza jumped at the unexpected question, one hand flying instinctively to her mouth. 'Oh my,' she whispered.

Lily had appeared at the bedside and was staring at Tristan with wide, intense eyes. He started forward with a gasp as though meaning to take Lily in his arms, and then checked himself abruptly, his colour ebbing and flowing again, his lips moving silently. It was the most romantic thing Demelza had ever seen. Then Lily broke the spell, blinking and shaking her head as though waking from a dream.

'I'm so sorry, but it's your dad... You've to come quickly.' Her gaze shifted to Demelza in the bed, and she bit her lip, thin brows tugging together in quick concern. 'Oh, Dem...'

Tristan didn't move. 'My dad?' he repeated.

Lily took another step towards him, nodding. 'He was found on the street outside. Brought in on a stretcher. The doctors are working on him now,' but...' Her cheeks were almost as white as her apron, but it was clear she'd recovered from her initial reaction on seeing him. 'Matron sent me to find you. She says it's urgent; you've to come straight-away.'

Demelza was horrified. Had her father been run over in the street? Or attacked by somebody? That burly man who'd thrown him out, perhaps?

Her brother looked confused too. 'I don't understand.'

'Oh, Tris.' Lily put a hand on his sleeve, her whole face quivering with sympathy. 'Your dad... He's had a heart attack.'

CHAPTER THIRTY-FOUR

Sunday afternoon was Violet's favourite time of the week. She loved having everyone at home and no work to go to, with the Land Girls nowhere in sight and even Joe staying indoors for once. It felt like family time, she thought, like the old days back in Dagenham, when they'd gather about the wireless in the snug living room for supper and a sing-song. She especially enjoyed having the three evacuees in the room, chatting away together while she and Joe sat close together on the old-fashioned settle. She could almost pretend they were *her* kids. Hers and Joe's, she thought fondly, glancing sideways at him. Hopefully, he would set a firm date for the wedding soon. The delay was making her nervous...

'It's no bloomin' good. I can't do it.' Seated at the corner table with his brother, Timmy dragged on his short dark hair. 'I told yer, I ain't no good at sums.'

'That's 'cos you're always doing them handstands,' Eustace mocked him. 'Every time you stand on your hands, a bit of your brain runs out your ears, see?'

Timmy glared at him, outraged. 'It does not.'

'Bleedin' does. Makes a right mess of the carpet, an' all.' The boy chuckled as though he'd said something side-splitting.

'Mind your language, Eustace,' Violet said automatically, barely looking up from the women's magazine she was flicking through, hunting for affordable recipes that would suit a summer wedding.

The little boy was pulling on his ear peevishly. 'You're a liar, you are.'

'And you're rubbish at algebra.'

'You do the sums for me, then. I don't understand 'em.'

'They're your sums, dummy. Not mine.' Eustace waved his book in the air. 'Look, I got me own sums to do, all right?'

'But Gran said you *had* to help me.'

'She's not our gran, stupid. She's Mrs Hopkins, innit? We ain't got no gran. Our gran's dead and buried, long since. Anyway, you smell.' Eustace blew a raspberry at his little brother. 'And you're a twerp.'

'That's quite enough,' Joe warned him. 'Any more name-calling and you'll be in hot water, my boy.'

'You tell him, Uncle Joe.' Timothy's lip quivered as he began to cry. 'I don't smell and I ain't no tw-tw-twerp,' he stuttered at his brother, rubbing a fist into his eye. 'You're a twerp. And you can't do sums, neither. Useless Eustace, that's you.'

'You're both a right pair of idiots.' Janice rolled her eyes and gave up on the book she'd been reading. She pulled up a chair and sat between her two brothers instead. 'C'mon, what sums are you stuck on, Timothy? Show us your book.'

Surprised, Violet glanced across at the three kids as they began to work on sums, dark heads bent together over their books.

With a wink, she whispered to Joe, 'It was a good idea to have Janice back to live with us. I've never known those two to do school work at home before. She's a good sister to them boys, whatever that nasty headmistress has to say about her.'

Joe nodded, but only absent-mindedly. He was fiddling with a toy plane that belonged to Eustace; the wing had snapped while the boys were playing outside, and he'd been attempting to glue it back together for nearly half an hour.

'This wing won't set,' he said in gloomy tones, and pushed the toy plane aside. 'I need stronger glue.' He rubbed his ear thoughtfully. 'Maybe Arnold might have some, down at the village shop.'

'Oh, if you're going that way, take my mother with you.' Violet returned to her magazine, studying a knitting pattern for a baby suit before moving hurriedly on. It was a little early to be thinking about baby clothes before they were even wed, she chided herself, though she couldn't repress a grin. 'She's always moping about the house these days, looking for something to do. But seeing Arnold should cheer her up to no end.'

The lounge door opened and Alice came in with her arms full of lace fragments for tatting. 'Gran asked me to bring this lot down to you,' she said. 'They were in one of them dusty old boxes in the attic.'

Joe grunted. 'My mother loved tatting.'

Violet smiled. She and her mother loved tatting too, when they had time for it, as it was a fiddly business. 'Ta, love.' Inspiration struck her about a use for some of that lace, but she pushed it aside for now. 'Pop it on the armchair, I'll sort it out later.'

'Won't you be too busy at work?' Joe asked under his breath.

He was pulling her leg, of course. She was starting her new job tomorrow, but it was only three half-days a week; there would be plenty of time left over for domestic chores. She knew Joe disliked the idea of her continuing to work when he was happy to support her, especially once they were wed. Or maybe it was because her work entailed preparing dead bodies for burial and dealing with grieving relatives, and he felt uneasy about that. But she had no such qualms. She'd applied for the part-time job as undertaker's assistant to keep herself active and involved in the war effort, and also to help fund the wedding. Her mum had applied for a position there too but they'd only offered her a Saturday job, sweeping out the premises, and Sheila had decided not to bother. 'Not worth it for a few pennies,' she'd grumbled, and turned her mind back to persuading old Arnold to let her sell homemade cakes and biscuits in his shop.

'I'll manage,' Violet told her beloved, and repressed the urge to stick out her tongue at him. She would be a respectable married woman soon, and ought to start practising now. Or so she kept telling herself.

'I think I might go out for a good long walk since it's not raining.' Alice had wandered over to the window and was standing there, looking out over the sunny fields. There'd been a few showers over the past few days but with the sky cloudless and blue today, it felt like a dry spell might be starting. 'Would you mind, Aunty Vi?'

''Course not, sweetheart.' Violet closed her magazine. 'Only make sure to take your boots off before you come back in. Last time you trod mud all through the house and Gran hit the roof, remember?'

'Yes, sorry. I'll be careful.' Alice gave them a smile and left the room, that faraway look in her eyes again.

Joe had turned to watch her go, and now said to Violet in a low voice, 'Something's happened, hasn't it? With Alice and Lily, I mean.' She hesitated, unsure how much she dared confide in him, and he took her hand. 'Look, tell me to mind my own business, but—'

'Not in front of the kids,' she whispered.

They got up and slipped quietly out of the room. To her relief, the children seemed oblivious to anything but the sums they were working on, not even looking up.

The kitchen was empty for once, with her mum busy upstairs, so Violet closed the door and faced Joe, her heart thumping. She had never told him the truth about her brother-in-law, Ernst. If they were to be man and wife though, surely she couldn't keep such a huge secret from him? Especially now that Alice, Lily and her mum all knew too. Besides, Joe had lived his whole life not knowing that his mother had lied about who his father was. She could only imagine what it might do to him if he ever found out his own wife had been withholding secret information from him too … but to break the terms of the Official Secrets Act by disclosing a state secret was monumental and terrifying.

'You're right.' She gripped the back of a kitchen chair, biting her lip as she stared at him. 'There is something I need to tell you. Only it won't be easy, Joe. So, bear with me, would you?'

By telling her mum and nieces what Colonel Ryder had said, she at least had been keeping it in the family. The two girls had deserved to know the truth about their father, and since Lily had discovered it anyway, letting Alice in on the secret had seemed only fair.

He was frowning, leaning against the range. 'You can tell me anything, Violet. You know that.'

'Not this,' she muttered. 'Or rather, I ... I'm not supposed to.' She wrestled with her conscience, feeling almost faint at the magnitude of what she was doing. Breaking the law was one thing. But England was at war and this could be seen as treason. 'I signed a piece of paper, you see. To swear that I'd never...'

He came towards her, concern in his face. 'Are you talking about your time at Eastern House?'

'In a way, yes.'

'Then I guess you mean the Official Secrets Act. That's the piece of paper you signed, isn't it?'

Surprised by his quickness, she nodded. 'How did you know?'

'You aren't alone, Vi,' he told her. 'Other folk in the village had to sign it if they knew anything that could compromise the listening post. So, you needn't worry that I won't understand.'

'Oh,' she said, wishing it was as simple as that.

'Careless talk costs lives, yes. But people still talk. My mother heard a few whispers herself and passed them on to me.' Joe pulled a face. 'Not strictly within the law, I know. But what goes on at Eastern House has been an open secret since the soldiers arrived; you can't hide a major operation like that in a tiny village.' He shrugged. 'So long as we're careful who we talk to, and make sure we can't be overheard, there shouldn't be a problem.'

He waited, watching her.

Violet tightened her grip on the chair back until her hands hurt. 'This isn't about the listening post.'

Joe's brows tugged together. 'What, then?'

'It's about Ernst Fisher. Alice and Lily's dad, the one who went missing in action?' Her mouth was dry. 'He … he ain't dead.'

'Well, surely that's good news,' he began, and then saw her petrified expression. 'Isn't it?'

'Yes, but you mustn't tell anyone else.' Her voice dropped to a hoarse whisper, her heart thumping violently as she forced herself to go on. It was hard for her lips even to form the words. 'It … it's a secret. *Top secret*, you might say.'

Joe's face changed. He glanced over his shoulder, as though afraid agents of the government were about to burst in and drag them both off to jail, but the door was shut and the farmhouse was quiet.

'Better not say another word,' he urged her, and came to take her in his arms. 'Do you hear me? Not another word, Vi.'

'But—'

'I don't need to know, so you don't need to say.' Tenderly, he brushed a stray lock of hair out of her eyes. 'Agreed?'

Violet stared into his face, relieved but puzzled. Her heart began to slow again, her breathing easier now.

'Agreed,' she repeated, and even managed a wobbly

smile. 'It's just, I've been thinking you ought to be told ever since you proposed. I don't like the idea of keeping secrets from my own husband ... especially after what happened with your mother,' she added awkwardly. 'But I didn't want to betray my country either.'

Joe nodded. 'Quite right too.' To her surprise, he didn't seem offended by her mention of his mother but smiled back at her, his whole face softening with it. 'Talking of getting wed, I haven't set a date yet and you've been more than patient. But it's time, isn't it? And I want you to be happy.' He hesitated. 'You know, I've never really said I was sorry about that thing with my mother. The way I behaved last summer ... I'm amazed you forgave me.'

'You were mad with grief. There was never anything to apologise for.'

'I treated you badly, Vi. And for no good reason,' he said. 'I listened to gossip instead of using my head. And I'm sorry for it.'

He kissed her lightly on the lips while she stood staring.

'How about late July for the wedding?' he continued. 'That would give us time to get the banns read, and for you and your mum to sort out the bridesmaids' dresses and make a wedding cake.' Joe grinned at her astonished expression. 'Don't think I haven't noticed you reading women's magazines, looking at all them dress designs and recipes. I may be a man, but I'm not daft.'

Violet was delighted. She'd never seen him show much sensitivity to her feelings before and had simply assumed he was the kind of man – rather like her own dear departed dad – who kept everything wrapped up inside. But it seemed the revelations about his mum had brought all those deeply buried emotions to the surface, and she loved the transformation, especially when it came with such a wonderful smile.

'Oh, Joe.' She flung her arms about his neck, happier than she could ever remember being, even before the war. 'A July wedding would be perfect. Thank you, my darling.' Her heart was thudding again, but this time for joy. 'You're an absolute diamond.'

CHAPTER THIRTY-FIVE

'You need to take it easy for a while, old chap,' Dr Jerrard told Mr Minear, passing the clipboard to Lily with a brisk nod. 'Nurse Fisher will look after you, I'm sure. But no more getting out of bed, you hear? It's not safe for you to be moving about unassisted, not so soon after a heart attack. If you need something, just call out, and someone will be with you shortly.'

Lily suppressed a grin at the doctor's stern tone, pretending to study the clipboard. Tristan's father had already tried twice to escape his hospital bed, despite being told he was on medication for a previously undiagnosed heart condition and needed rest and relaxation.

Farmer Minear grunted, 'I hear you, doctor,' but he sounded unimpressed. His gnarled finger jabbed accusingly in Lily's direction, taking her by surprise. 'I don't want this one waiting on me though. Any other nurse will do fine. But not her.'

'Not our excellent Nurse Fisher?' Dr Jerrard swung on his heel to study Lily with a mocking smile. 'But why ever not?'

Lily glanced anxiously at the man in the bed. The last thing she wanted was gossip about her and Tristan running rife in the hospital. To her relief though, Mr Minear merely muttered something about not liking 'blondes', which made Dr Jerrard laugh even louder.

'Can't say I blame you. Personally, I prefer redheads. But I won't hear a word against Nurse Fisher. She's one of our best.'

And, with a wink at Lily, the doctor went on his way, hands in the pockets of his long white coat, whistling cheerfully under his breath as he looked ahead to the next patient. Lily hooked the clipboard back on the end of Mr Minear's bed, her eyes carefully downcast, and then turned to follow the doctor.

'Oh no, you don't.' Mr Minear winced, putting a hand to his chest as though it pained him still. 'I know all about you and my son.'

'Is that so?' She whirled round to face him, her temper rising. 'And what exactly do you know, Mr Minear?'

He looked taken aback by her directness but blustered on. 'Don't raise your voice to me, girl.'

'I haven't raised my voice. Not yet.'

'Oh, threats, is it?' His eyes narrowed on her face. 'Well, I hope you're proud of yourself. Sending a boy to his death.'

Lily stared at him, confused. 'Sending… What on earth are you talking about?'

'As if you didn't know.' His tone was scathing. 'You're nothing but a hussy. And now he's off to the front because of you.'

Her mouth was dry. *Sending a boy to his death… Now*

he's off to the front... Tristan wouldn't have been crazy enough to enlist, would he?

'I'm not a hussy,' she managed to say, her head spinning. 'And I'll have to call Matron if you keep speaking to me like this.'

The threat of Matron reduced his voice to a mumble. 'No need to be like that,' he complained, and sank his unshaven chin onto his chest. 'Bloody women...'

Lily's eyes flashed, but she turned her back on him again and would have walked away if she hadn't met Tristan heading for the bed and been thrown into speechless confusion at the sight of him. Demelza was at his side, supported by her brother's arm and fully dressed for once, walking very carefully in her outdoor shoes, for she'd been discharged that morning. Robert, the ambulance driver, was with them as well, seated in a wheelchair being pushed by a trainee nurse.

Beaming at her, Demelza said, 'They're sending me home, did you hear? I'm not allowed to do any strenuous exercise for six weeks, and I have to spend several hours a day resting, which is a bore. But otherwise I should make a full recovery.'

'Yes, Dr Jerrard told me.' Lily smiled. 'It's wonderful.'

They embraced, and Demelza whispered in her ear, 'You look flushed. Has my dad been bullying you again?'

'Oh, nothing I can't handle.'

'Well, Tris has got some news that will soon distract him. Hang on a minute and you can hear it for yourself.'

Puzzled, Lily glanced at Tristan and caught him looking at her intently. *Sending a boy to his death... Now he's off to the front...* It couldn't be true, could it?

'Lily,' he said huskily and pulled off his cap, a clear indication that he wanted to speak to her.

She felt her cheeks flood with heat and hurriedly muttered something about needing to speak to the doctor. 'If … if you'll excuse me,' she told them, and fled up the ward to where Dr Jerrard was chatting with another patient.

It was pathetic, she thought crossly, not being able to handle seeing Tristan for more than a few minutes at a time. Every time she laid eyes on him, her tummy twisted itself in knots and she felt like a lovesick schoolgirl. Now, guilt mingled with fear at the possibility that he really had joined up and might end up getting killed – for she couldn't imagine a young farmer would know much about warfare – and then his blood would be on her hands.

It wasn't her bleedin' fault if he'd enlisted, she told herself, pretending to listen to the doctor discussing the treatment of an elderly patient with a hernia. And there was one silver lining to his having enlisted. If she never saw or spoke to Tristan Minear again, this nagging ache in her heart would lessen over time and eventually she would forget him.

Only problem was, she didn't believe a word of it.

With a sinking heart, Demelza watched Lily hurry away and Tristan's downcast expression. She wished she could explain to her friend that Tris was an idiot and simply needed a good talking-to. But that could never happen if Lily always darted away or was struck dumb by the sight of him.

'Hello, Dad,' she said, gripping her brother's arm once

again for support. 'I hope you're feeling better. You gave us quite a scare the other day.'

'I see you're out of bed at last,' was his only response, looking her up and down critically.

'Tris is taking me home,' she agreed, disappointed by his tone. She'd hoped his heart attack might have softened him, made him realise life was too short to be forever arguing with people. 'The doctor says I can complete my recovery at home.'

'I expect they need your bed for someone who's actually sick,' her dad growled, as surly as ever. 'Where's Sarah? I thought your aunt was coming to visit me today.' He stiffened, suddenly spotting Robert in the wheelchair, and his eyes grew hostile. 'Who's this?'

'Aunt Sarah didn't fancy the trip out,' Tristan told him, his own manner cold and withdrawn, for they'd argued bitterly over him enlisting. 'And this is Robert Day.'

Her father's lip curled back in scorn. 'Not the bloody conchie?' He leant forward in bed to glare at Robert in his wheelchair. 'You've some brass neck to turn up here after what you did, landing my daughter in the hospital.'

'Dad, for God's sake,' Demelza hissed, and turned to apologise to Robert. 'I'm sorry,' she began, her cheeks aflame, but he shook his head.

'No, let your father have his say.' Robert folded his arms across his broad chest, looking up at the older man expectantly. He looked massive in the tiny wheelchair, and she pitied the trainee nurse who'd been pushing the chair, for it must be quite a weight. 'Come on then, Mr Minear, let's hear it. You seem to know all about this without having been there yourself. How am I to blame for that bomb going off?'

Her father bared his teeth. 'Think you're so bloody clever, don't you? Sat there in that wheelchair, knowing I can't touch you. But just wait until we're both fit and well,' he ground out, 'and then you'll be sorry.'

'That wasn't much of an explanation,' Robert drawled. 'I'm still in the dark here. What am I supposed to have done *to land Demelza in the hospital*, as you put it?'

Her father rubbed at his chest again, wincing. 'Don't give me that. You know...'

'I don't, actually.'

'Tell him, Tris,' their father spat. 'Put him straight.'

But Tristan shook his head. 'I'm not getting involved, Dad.'

'But she's walking out with a yellow-bellied coward – a conchie. Call yourself her brother? What kind of man are you? You may have enlisted but you're not fit to go to war.'

At these cruel insults, Tris paled, but refused to be drawn. 'I told you, it's Demmy's business who she chooses to see. Not yours, and certainly not mine. She's a grown woman and if Robert is her choice, that's good enough for me.'

'But he nearly got her killed—' their father exploded.

'I'd have been in there alone if Rob hadn't agreed to come with me,' Demelza interrupted hotly. 'And he was the one who told me to get out. I'm probably only alive because of him.'

'Give over, of course you'd defend him,' her father insisted, his fierce gaze shifting to Robert, still watching silently from his wheelchair. 'I don't believe a word of it. You've been egging her on for weeks, conchie. Flattering her, filling her head with nonsense. All that guff about the Fire Guard... And look what's happened. She could have been blown to bits that night. Gone forever. My daughter. My only daughter.'

His voice cracked, and Demelza sucked in her breath, shaken to see tears in his eyes. Her father blinked them away angrily, but they kept coming, trickling down his lined, weather-beaten cheeks.

'I lost her mother. I won't lose her.' His voice was trembling. 'You hear me? I won't lose her. Not to the bloody Hun and not to you neither.'

There was an awkward silence. Heads had turned further along the ward, including the doctor's. No doubt Lily was listening too, or had at least caught some of it. Demelza didn't know where to look, but she was clinging onto Tris's arm for dear life, her nails digging into his jacket. Tris cleared his throat, staring at the ground.

'Wheel me back to my ward, would you, please?' Robert said politely to the nurse behind him. 'I think Mr Minear may need to speak to his children alone.' He saw Demelza's expression and said gently, 'Come and see me before you leave. I'm not going anywhere.'

She nodded, relieved that he wasn't angry. 'I will,' she promised, and sat next to her father's bed.

Her father had buried his face in his hands, but hearing the scrape of chair legs, looked up sharply.

'You're still here, then,' he said gruffly, as though he didn't care about her at all, but this time she knew better and wasn't fooled.

'And here I'll stay, Father,' Demelza said, folding her hands in her lap, 'until you stop this nonsense over Robert and start behaving like a reasonable person.'

Her father stared at her in disbelief, and then turned to

Tristan. 'Did you hear that, son? This one thinks she's in charge.'

'Maybe she should be,' Tris told him calmly. 'Though I have to tell you something important. I've applied for Land Girls to be allocated to us.'

'What?' He looked appalled.

'Father, you're in no fit state to look after the place on your own,' Tristan pointed out, 'and I'll be off on my basic training next week. It's a six-month course, and then I could be posted anywhere in the world. You'll need Land Girls to help you with the sheep or the farm will go under.'

Their father opened his mouth and then shut it again. Demelza expected Tristan to show some relief at this apparent capitulation, but his attention was elsewhere. Lily had just walked stiffly past them on her way out of the ward, her face averted, blonde hair rigorously pinned up under her white, starched cap.

'I'm glad you've seen sense, Father,' Tristan said, but with a distracted air. 'Look, I need to do something. Will you be all right on your own for a while, Demelza?'

She smiled at her brother. 'You go. Tell her you're sorry for being an idiot.'

Tris half-grinned at that, but then his smile faded as he headed out of the ward after Lily.

'Where's he going?' her father demanded petulantly. 'Not after that fussy blonde piece again?'

'You mind your own business, Father,' Demelza told him, and sat up straight, deadly serious again. 'Now, tell me more about my mother and how she died. And I want the truth this time.'

*　*　*

There was an ornate metal bench outside the hospital where Lily often took her lunch. She sat, checked her hair pins were still in place, and tucked her skirt neatly underneath her. Someone visiting a patient walked past and recognised her, and she smiled automatically, exchanging a few words. But her heart was pounding and she felt wobbly inside.

She had to grow up, she told herself. It was over between her and Tristan Minear. No more to say. Besides, she had bigger problems to think about now. Like her dad and where he was, and if she and Alice would ever see him again. Plus her career as a nurse, and what she ought to do about it.

Taking a deep breath, Lily drew a crumpled letter out of her pocket, unfolded it and re-read its contents. It was a note from Miss Riley, the senior midwife she'd met, letting her know she'd secured a venue for her series of lectures on midwifery, which were to be held at the parish hall in Marazion, a village on the other side of the bay, near St. Michael's Mount.

Was this what she wanted though? To retrain as a midwife?

Since coming to Penzance, she'd found real joy working as a hospital nurse, dealing with mundane ailments as well as coping with emergencies, even when victims of bombings and house fires had been brought in, some of them sadly beyond even Dr Jerrard's skill. She loved the challenge of a busy hospital, encountering new people and new situations every day. Though she also remembered how wonderful and fulfilling it had been to help Hazel bring her baby girl into the world, single-handedly and with the constant threat of German bombers overhead.

Perhaps this was a decision to be made in the future. She could attend the lectures now and decide later on whether to change careers.

'Lily?'

She knew that voice. Jumping up in a panic, she shoved the letter back into her uniform pocket as she spun to face Tristan.

CHAPTER THIRTY-SIX

'Yes?' Lily smoothed down her skirt and adjusted her belt, taking courage from her uniform. 'I'm on a break,' she added loftily. 'I need to get back to work in a minute. So, if you have something to say, you'd better do it quickly.'

'All right.' Tristan took off his cap and twisted it between his hands. 'I want to say … I'm sorry.'

She stared, taken aback. 'For what?'

'For being a first-class idiot.' He grimaced. 'That's what Demmy said I should say. That I've been an idiot. And she's right.' He took another step towards her. 'I saw you with that bloke and I thought … she's met someone better.'

'No,' Lily said impulsively.

'I know that now. I leapt to conclusions, didn't I? And I was rude to you too.'

'Yes,' she agreed, surprised but thankful that he knew what he'd done and was apologising for it.

'I just thought why would someone like y-you,' he stammered, 'someone beautiful and clever and absolutely perfect, want *me*?' He looked down at himself, a flush in

373

his cheeks. 'I'm nobody. Just a farmer's son.' His hands gripped his cap convulsively. 'Though I'm going to be somebody one day, Lily. That's why I joined up. To make a difference. To do something important for once instead of being stuck in this place all my life.'

Lily clasped her hands together at her waist, embarrassed and flattered at the same time, but also horrified by the low opinion he had of himself.

'Blimey, where to start?' She swallowed. 'I don't think I'm beautiful. But thank you. And I'm definitely not clever. My sister Alice, she's the clever one. As for perfect.' Lily rolled her eyes. 'A thousand times no.'

'I think you're perfect,' he insisted stubbornly.

'And I think you're somebody, Tristan Minear,' she said, taking an impulsive step towards him. They were only a few feet apart now. She could see little flecks in his eyes that caught the light and each springing curl on his head. 'And beautiful too.'

'Me? Beautiful?' He looked incredulous. 'I'm a ginger. Gingers are never beautiful.'

'That's nonsense' – Lily gave a vigorous nod when he started to protest – 'because you are. And clever too. Look how you managed to help that ewe and her twin lambs. They might have died if you hadn't known what to do.'

'That's not cleverness. That's just experience.' Tristan looked at her steadily. 'Look, I'm sorry for the way I behaved and the rotten things I said. I didn't mean them. I was a jealous fool. But will you forgive me, at least?'

She took a deep breath, touched by the sincerity in his face, and then nodded with relief. 'Yes, I forgive you.'

'Thank you.' He held out his hand and, shyly, she took

it. He took a deep breath. 'And will you marry me, Lily Fisher?'

'Will I *what*?' She stared at him, her mouth open.

'I'm in love with you. And I want you to be my wife.'

She couldn't quite believe what was happening. Tristan Minear was proposing to her... Once, she might have been utterly bowled over to receive a proposal from such a handsome young man. But it was entirely the wrong time and place, and she felt flustered rather than pleased.

'I thought you said we were going to be friends. Not married.' Pulling her hand from his, Lily took a step back. 'First, you accused me of flirting with that man at the cinema—'

'I never said that.'

'You implied it.' Lily gave him a stern look, and he lowered his gaze to the ground in shame. 'Then you wait ages to apologise, and five seconds later, ask me to marry you.' She shook her head at him in disbelief. 'I don't understand. We'd barely been courting five minutes before it was all over. Why bother proposing now?'

'Because I'm in love with you,' he repeated doggedly.

'But you've enlisted.'

'We could marry quickly, in a few days, before I leave for my basic training. I know others who've done that.' He saw her shocked expression and added hurriedly, 'Then, if the worst happened, you'd be looked after by the state, see? As a war widow.'

'Tris, we're both too young. I'm not ready to be a married woman and housewife, let alone a widow.' She took his hand and squeezed it gently. 'Maybe if we hadn't fallen out ... but honestly, it's better this way. It's given me time to realise I've got too many things to do before I settle down. After all, if we wed, I'd have to give up my job. And I love being a nurse.' As she said it, she knew it to be the truth, not just a convenient excuse. She really did love her work. Though she was excited to find out if midwifery would suit her better than hospital nursing. That was an adventure that lay just ahead… 'I love it more than anything else in the world.'

'Oh, Lily,' he murmured.

'Friends is good though,' she said softly, releasing his hand. 'Let's stay friends until the war's over. Then we'll meet up again and see how we both feel. How about that?'

Tristan ran a hand through his ginger curls, clearly unsure what to say. But he nodded. 'Can I write to you at least?'

'I'll be cross if you don't,' Lily told him, and returned his smile, feeling a weight lifting off her heart.

Demelza looked at her father lying in his hospital bed, and knew that she still loved him, despite everything. She'd been brought up to 'honour thy parents,' even though it was the last thing her father deserved. But some things were more important than manners, she thought, forcing herself to be resolute. Like the truth about why her mother had taken her own life, for instance.

'I've been re-reading that journal my mother kept,' she began, 'and I've got questions for you. No, I'm not going to accuse you again of mistreating her. But there are some things I need to know.' Demelza fixed him with a determined eye. 'It's important to me.'

'Oh, I see.' His large hands clenched into fists on top of the bedsheets. 'Go on, then. Ask your damn questions, girl.'

She hesitated, hearing that tone in his voice, and for a moment tears pricked her eyes as she remembered the anguished words she'd read in those pages. Screams and howls of pain scribbled in ink. Only she didn't want to cry. Not this time. Crying muddled everything and made it harder to get at the truth.

'Why do you think Mother took her own life?' It was hard to keep the note of accusation out of her voice, despite what she'd told him. Because who else was to blame, if not him? But she badly needed to know what her father thought about it. And the truth this time, not his usual lies and evasions. 'In her journal, she wrote about being unhappy. Not just in her marriage, but over other things too.'

'Aye, well, your mother was a sick woman. She had demons in her head.'

'Demons?' She looked at him sceptically.

'That's what *she* called them. The doctor gave her something for her nerves, but it only made her worse.' He glanced up and she saw remorse in his eyes. 'I didn't know how serious it was at the time. I thought she was bluffing, trying to get my attention. Then one day, she took all the pills in her bottle and … well, you know the rest. *You* found her.'

'Yes.' Her voice was husky.

'I'm sorry for that. I should have been there that day, not out in the fields. You were only a little girl too, barely so high.' He held up a wavering hand at hip level.

'Sweet little thing, you were.' He swallowed, his voice barely audible now. 'It must have been hard on you, Demelza, to see your own mother like that. Having to run for help, yet knowing nothing could help her ... except the angels.'

She was crying after all, she realised with a shock, and dashed a hand impatiently across wet cheeks.

'You told me and Tris it was an accident.'

'I had no choice over that. Taking your own life ... it's against the law. I had to say it was a mistake. And so did the doctor.'

'But you *lied* to us.'

He looked at her helplessly. 'How could I have told you young 'uns the truth? That your mother wanted to die and leave you all alone?'

She had to accept that he was probably right. When she'd first read her mother's journal, that was what she'd felt. The terrible sting of abandonment. It would have been so much worse as a young child; she could see how not knowing had been better, in some ways.

'I suppose so,' Demelza muttered.

He gave an agonised groan, showing his feelings at last. 'All right, maybe it was my fault, what she did,' he admitted, astonishing her. 'Maybe I wasn't loving enough. But I was taught as a boy not to go in for that sort of thing. Men have to be strong, my father told me. Not always kissing and cuddling ... that's a woman's thing.'

She tried to understand. 'You never told Mother you loved her?'

'Not in so many words, no. I ... I didn't know how.' His face began to crumble. 'Any more than I knew how to

378

bring up two children on me own once she was gone. That's why I asked your aunt Sarah for help. But that don't mean I didn't want you.' A tear rolled down his cheek, his lip trembling. 'Nor can I lose you now.'

She was horrified to see her father cry, but persisted. 'What do you mean? You haven't lost us.'

'Your brother's going off to war, isn't he? And you'll be getting married soon, I daresay. Probably to that fool of a conchie who won't fight for you.'

She groaned, looking away. 'Father.'

'But what if the Jerries come invading, Demelza? Who'll keep you safe, then? That man who stayed home while others went to fight?' His voice was shaking. 'He won't lift a finger to save you.'

'That's where you're wrong.'

'I hope so, for your sake.' He reached out a trembling hand to her, and then let it drop when she didn't move. 'That's why I didn't want you anywhere near the Fire Guard. Too dangerous by half. I've spent every night sick with worry, wondering where you were, if you were hurt or in danger...' He was crying again. 'I already lost your mother. When I think I might lose you too, my flesh and blood, it's more than I can bear.'

She jumped up, gripping his hand. 'Don't be daft,' she told him, blinking away her own tears. 'I'll be more careful in future, I promise. And though it's true I have thought about leaving Cornwall, that was before I met Robert.'

'Huh,' her father grunted, but his eyes were hopeful. 'Promise me you won't marry him.'

'I can't promise that. Besides, he hasn't asked me.'

379

'But if he did?'

'That's none of your business.' But she took pity on his misery. 'Look, you know I can't stay at the farm forever. As soon as I'm fit enough, I'll be returning to the Fire Guard.' He began to protest, but she shook her head. 'That's just the way I am. Can't keep still, I suppose. The fidgets, you used to call it. And maybe that's why I like Robert so much. Because he's the same. Two restless souls together.' She looked down at his hand in hers, once so strong and capable, it was now strangely frail. 'You know, I wish you'd sat us down once we were old enough to understand and told us about Mother. It was a shock to find out the way we did.'

'I was afraid you'd hate me for it,' he croaked, rubbing at his damp cheeks. 'Once you knew she'd taken her own life.'

Demelza bit her lip, saying nothing. She did blame him for her mother's suicide, and with good cause. But what could she say that wouldn't drive a wedge between them forever? He was still her father.

'I know it was partly my fault,' he said, nodding at her silence. 'I didn't treat her right. I wasn't a good husband. And I haven't been a good father either.' He made a rough sound under his breath. 'When I got that bad pain in my chest, I thought, this is the end … and I knew I'd made a right mess of it.' He winced at the memory and lay back against the pillows.

'Hush now, you don't want to have another attack.' She interlaced her fingers with his.

'No, you need to hear this.' Clearing his throat, he looked up at her. 'I'm sorry for the things I've done. And I want to be a better father to you, Demelza. To you both.' His voice choked up with emotion. 'In whatever time I've got left.'

'Oh, Dad,' she said, and buried her face against his chest.

As they were heading back inside the hospital, Tristan stopped and glanced up at the rooftops, an odd look on his face.

'What is it?' Lily followed his stare but could see nothing but soft white clouds in the blue skies above Penzance.

'I thought I heard a plane.'

As he spoke, the air-raid siren went off as though to prove him right, its eerie shriek echoing about the walls and roofs of the hospital buildings, louder and louder.

'Oh no, not again.' Lily grimaced, sick and tired of these remorseless attacks on the Cornish coast. When would it ever end? 'I'd better help with the evacuation of the wards. It takes forever to get them all down to the cellar. Though we have a couple of Morrison Shelters too, set up in a side room for the least mobile patients.'

Tristan touched her arm. 'I'll help,' he said.

'Thanks, though you might want to start with your dad. He'll need a hand, for sure.' She saw his expression and frowned. 'What's the matter?'

'I've been avoiding him lately.' He pulled a face. 'Do you remember my mother's journal? My father didn't come off well in it. In fact,' he added, and blanched, 'it looks like Demelza was right. My mother may have taken her own life because she was so unhappy.'

'That's awful,' she exclaimed, horrified. 'I'm so sorry.'

'I'm not sure I can face him, to be honest.' He ran a

hand over his face. 'But he's still my dad. So I can't avoid it, can I?'

'Dads can be complicated,' she agreed, and wished again that she could tell him about her own father.

But her eyes had narrowed on a couple of tiny silverish dots visible against the blue expanse of the sky.

'Oh, here they come again,' Lily said bitterly. 'I swear they only do it to wear us down, dropping their bombs, day in, day out.' She raised her voice over the wail of the siren. 'Only we won't be worn down, see? We'll never stop fighting. Not if they bomb us every day for a thousand bloomin' years.' She shook her fist at the approaching aircraft. 'So take that, Mr Jerry. And you can stick it where the sun don't shine!'

Tris laughed at that. 'My little spitfire,' he said admiringly. 'Those Germans don't stand a chance.'

'Not against the likes of us,' Lily agreed with a grim smile, and together they hurried back into the hospital to help with the evacuation.

EPILOGUE

From her vantage point in one of the end pews, Demelza thought Violet looked simply breath-taking in a pale blue dress with intricate lace collar and cuffs, rosebuds wreathed through her long fair hair, and a floaty lace veil she'd thrown back to reveal a face glowing with happiness. Joe was looking particularly handsome too, in that way most men do on their wedding day, she thought. An old-fashioned watch-chain hung from Joe's waistcoat pocket, and he wore a smart brown pinstripe jacket over his plain white shirt, his thick dark hair combed back, deep-set eyes softened by love and good humour.

Violet had told her beforehand that the Sunday-best waistcoat and the watch and chain had all belonged to his late father, Mr Postbridge Senior, and that he treasured these as his favourite possessions. His pride in wearing them on his wedding day was clear to see.

Having signed the register, bride and groom were now

walking back down the aisle together, hand in hand, to the majestic swell of music from the organist at the back of the church.

'Oh, Robert,' Demelza said on a sigh, hands clasped as she watched Violet and Joe sweep past, the groom on their side smiling down at them. 'What a vision she is.'

'And so tall,' Robert replied out of the corner of his mouth.

'Hush.'

Behind them came the three bridesmaids: young, dark-haired Janice, bearing a pretty basket of flowers, followed by Lily and Alice, both fair, willowy, and almost as tall as their aunt now. Their dresses all daintily trimmed with lace, they made a lovely trio.

Alice did look a teensy bit distracted, as though she'd rather be reading a book or maybe practising her German grammar, something she'd been doing nearly every day since term broke up and she no longer had to focus on her teaching work. But she was still young, and anything to do with family occasions was probably boring to her.

'I wish Tristan was here to see this.' Demelza sighed, thinking of her brother who was still away, undergoing his six-month basic training. 'Lily looks so pretty as a bridesmaid.'

Robert took her hand. 'You miss him, don't you?'

'Of course,' she said simply. 'He's my brother.'

The three Land Girls who worked with Joe at the farm, and whom they'd met several times now, came past, laughing and chatting. Selina, the poshest among them, looked like she was dressed for a debutante ball. Pickles was munching on something, as always, and Caro was complaining about the heat, but gave Demelza a cheery wave as they passed.

'Don't Vi look gorgeous?' Caro gushed. 'And Joe too.' She gave a low whistle. 'I never knew he was such a dreamboat. A dreamboat … in a waistcoat.'

And all three Land Girls burst into riotous giggles.

Demelza and Robert followed them and the newly-weds outside into the late July sunshine. Demelza had never been to Porthcurno Village before, but it was truly a special place. She could see why Lily was so fond of it and took every opportunity to come home on the bus.

Looking ahead, she could see sunlight sparkling on a blue expanse of sea just visible through the dark branches of the churchyard yew trees. Earlier, walking through the village from the bus stop, she and Robert had paused to admire the white edifice of Eastern House, heavily camouflaged and guarded, with barbed-wire checkpoints into the compound. A soldier had even stopped them in the street to ask their business and check their identity papers.

Things were rather more relaxed at the parish church, however, which was quite a hike from the village itself. Here, local kids ran shrieking between the gravestones and patches of neatly cut grass, playing tag while their mothers clustered eagerly at the gate, having watched Violet go into church and then waited throughout the long service just for a glimpse of her coming out. There was nothing better to lift the spirits than a wedding, one of the women had told Demelza when she asked why they were there.

'It makes my heart glad to see young people get wed,' the stout Cornishwoman had admitted, tears in her eyes as they watched Violet arrive at the church in a hired pony and trap, its leather harness and mane decorated with white flowers. 'Oh, isn't the bride a picture? Beautiful.'

Demelza had agreed wholeheartedly.

Now she and Robert tucked in behind Lily and Alice beside the church door, nodding to the vicar as he too emerged.

'Lovely service, Reverend Clewson,' Joe said, clearing his throat. He sounded quite emotional. 'Thank you very much, sir. You done us proud.'

Violet's mother, Mrs Hopkins, came out of the church last, arm in arm with a white-haired gentleman Demelza had never seen before.

Catching her curious glance, Violet's mother jerked her head at the man and whispered piercingly, 'This 'ere is Arnie.' The old gentleman muttered something in her ear, and Mrs Hopkins corrected herself, saying, 'Mr Arnold Newton, I meant to say. Runs the village shop. He's my new beau.'

'Mum, please,' Violet was heard to utter with a groan.

Lily and Alice shot a glance at each other and giggled silently, their shoulders shaking. Among those gathered outside the church was a smart-looking couple who, according to Lily's whispered information before the ceremony began, had motored down from London especially for Violet's wedding. Apparently, they would be attending the wedding reception and staying overnight at Eastern House before heading back to the big city tomorrow.

The woman was tall and impressive, with fair hair cut into a stylish bob and scarlet lipstick to die for. Her immaculate white suit with navy blue piping looked very expensive, and Demelza eyed it with admiration. It wouldn't last five minutes on their farm, of course; yet she yearned to own something as beautiful as that one day, and to be brave enough to wear it out in public.

The man walked with an ornate cane and was strikingly handsome. He'd brought his own camera too, a large Box Brownie, which hung about his neck by a strap. With his cane leaning against one leg, he was peering down into the viewfinder and taking candid photographs of the wedding party, the shutter click audible as he snapped shot after shot, rolling the film on after each one with a practised air.

Their names, Demelza had been told, were Eva and Flight Lieutenant Max Carmichael. Eva's father was Colonel Ryder, who used to be in charge of the troops at Eastern House but had now been redeployed to a garrison near London. She was assistant to a politician these days, after a brief stint helping out at Eastern House here in Porthcurno, which was where Violet's family knew her from. Her husband Max, it seemed, had left active service after a bombing incident had damaged his spine, but was now a flight instructor for the RAF.

Lily had whispered in her ear as they waited for Violet to be ready to enter the church, 'Eva and Max live partly in London and partly in Hampshire, where they've got a cottage near the airfield. Eva says they're *rapturously* happy together.' She had given an envious sigh. 'Ain't her outfit glorious?'

Beside them stood a smiling, dark-haired woman with a baby in her arms, chatting merrily to Eva. That was Hazel, whom Demelza had met in company with Violet and Lily once on a shopping trip to Penzance, and beside her was

George Cotterill, her husband and Violet's old boss at Eastern House. Lily had explained it all in detail the day they met up on the street, laughing with embarrassment as she admitted that Hazel's baby bore her name as she'd helped bring the little mite into the world. Hazel also had a teenage son called Charlie, who'd been sweet on Lily once; but he'd begun an apprenticeship in Plymouth and rarely came home these days.

Hearing about all these families split up by the war had made Demelza think of her own brother, so far away. She knew that Tristan was writing to Lily nearly every week, as he'd said so in his latest letter to her and their father. But, in a private note meant only for Demelza's eyes, Tris had admitted he wasn't sure how Lily felt about him. Her letters to him were always short and pithy, about work and her hopes for the future, never about her feelings. But Tristan had written in bold capital letters – and underlined it twice – that he was DETERMINED not to give up trying.

Violet and Joe stood outside the church in the sunshine, posing for photographs. A few rose petals were tossed above the bashful, smiling pair, spiralling gently down on the summer breeze.

'Lovely,' Mrs Hopkins said with a sigh, watching the petals fall.

'Three cheers for the happy couple. Hip, hip, hooray!' Robert cried, and everybody joined in the cheering and shouts of best wishes and good luck.

''Ere you go, Missus, have a few more of them "loverly" petals,' came a strident young voice.

Eustace, aided and abetted by his brother Timmy, had seized huge fistfuls of rose petals and now chucked them high into the air over the bride and groom. 'And good luck to yer both!' he added with a wink.

The cheers soon turned to laughter as Violet twisted about, grimacing and trying in vain not to spoil her carefully arranged hairdo.

'Oh, blow it,' she exclaimed, giving up with a good-natured grin while a sea of fragrant pink, white and red petals rained down on her and Joe. 'You bloomin' little rascals.'

'Hold still for a moment if you can, Mr and Mrs Postbridge,' the photographer called out, fiddling with his camera.

Violet turned her head to look at Joe, smiling into her new husband's eyes. 'Mr and Mrs Postbridge,' she mouthed, and he grinned in return.

Amid the noisy chaos, Robert pulled Demelza away from the wedding party and back inside the shady church porch.

'Robert, what on earth are you doing?' Demelza whispered, peering up at him from under the brim of her hat.

'Finally snatching a moment alone with my best beloved,' he replied, and bent his head to kiss her.

On tiptoe, Demelza clung to his broad shoulders, eyes closed, deliriously happy. 'Oh, Robert.'

Everything did seem to be working out for them, she thought. Maybe getting blown up had been a blessing in disguise. Not only had Robert's badly bruised spine healed after plenty of bed rest, but last week Dr Jerrard had confirmed there was no permanent damage and he could return to work whenever he wanted.

And she and Father had grown close at last. There was no more shouting and bullying at home, and Father had even started talking occasionally about his life with her mother, though only when his sister had gone to bed and it was just the two of them, sitting up to listen to the late bulletin on the wireless. Those were the moments she prized the most, when her father opened his heart and she listened without judgement, nodding and holding his hand.

'I'm rather jealous of Joe Postbridge at the moment, you know,' Robert said, smiling down at her. 'Demelza, will you marry me?'

It wasn't the first time he'd asked her and she felt sure it wouldn't be the last. 'I thought Quakers didn't swear oaths?'

'We can affirm. And commit to one another for life.' Robert flicked her cheek with a gentle finger. 'I take it that's another no?'

'It's a not yet. It's a wait and see.' Her smile was tearful with joy. 'I do love you, dearest Robert. But I can't leave my father and move in with you. Not with his weak heart. And we can't live together at the farm either.' She rolled her eyes at the thought. 'You know how Father feels about you.'

'Perhaps I can bring him around.'

She chuckled, shaking her head. 'Good luck with that. Anyway, I thought you wanted to work on the battlefield one day?'

'I do, yes,' he agreed soberly. 'Would you mind that very much, if we were married?'

'I want you to do whatever you think is right, Robert. Of course I wouldn't mind. You must follow your heart.' She smiled. 'As I follow mine.'

There was a wave of loud cheering from outside the church door, and then a roar of laughter followed by applause.

'Come on, we're missing all the fun.' Grinning, Demelza dragged Robert out of the porch to see what was going on.

As she emerged, she caught a glimpse of an odd little man in a trench coat and trilby – despite the summer heat – watching the wedding party from the back of the church-yard. Shielding her eyes against the sun, she squinted at him in surprise, and the man turned and vanished behind the yew trees. How very strange, she thought, but before she could mention it to Robert, somebody had seized her with a squeal of laughter.

'Did you see that, Demmy?' Lily was giggling, waving a bunch of fragrant flowers tied up with glossy white ribbons. 'Violet threw her wedding posy … and guess who caught it?'

'Always the bridesmaid, never the bride, that's you, Lily,' Alice chimed in, giving her older sister a nudge. 'But maybe that's about to change, eh?'

Demelza grinned over Lily's shoulder at Alice. 'Nice catch.' She added teasingly, 'I'll let Tris know in my next letter, shall I?'

'Better not. I don't believe in those old superstitions,' Lily said hurriedly. 'Though I love these ribbons,' she added, changing the subject. 'They're such pretty flowers too, aren't they? I'll put them in water when we get back to the farm.' Lily glanced from Demelza to Robert, and a sly smile crept over her face. 'Unless you'd rather take them, Demmy? You and Robert have been going steady for a while now. Isn't it time you tied the knot?'

'Alice, call the vicar back; I'm ready and willing,' Robert joked, slipping his arm about Demelza's waist and smiling down into her face.

'Maybe one day we'll be wed.' Demelza turned to look at Violet and Joe, happily posing for their wedding photographs with Mrs Hopkins between them. 'Maybe soon. Or maybe when this horrid war is over and we can all breathe freely again.'

'Feels like I've been holding my breath for the past two bloomin' years,' Alice said.

'Agreed.' Lily nodded, sniffing wistfully at the fragrant bouquet she'd caught. 'Oh, I swear, once this war's over, I'm going to—'

'Now the bridesmaids, please,' the photographer called out.

Go back to where it all began – don't
miss the first book in the glorious
Cornish Girls series...

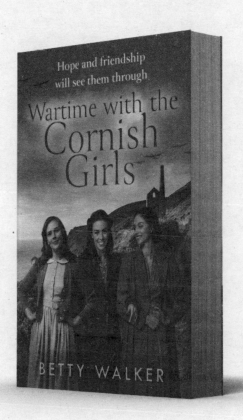

Available now in paperback, eBook
and audiobook.

And then follow up with some festive fun for the Cornish Girls…

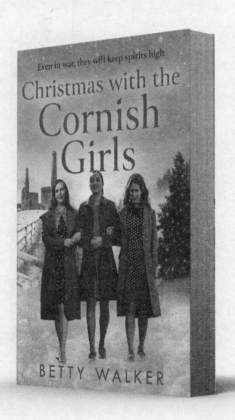

Available now in paperback, eBook and audiobook.